HARRY HERON: SAVAGE FUGITIVE

Book Four
of the
Harry Heron Adventure Series

Patrick G. Cox

Editing | Interior Book Design: Janet Angelo | www.indiegopublishing.com
Cover Design: DeeDee Book Covers | www.deedeebookcovers.com

Publisher's Cataloging-In-Publication Data
Names: Cox, Patrick G., 1946-
Title: Harry Heron : savage fugitive / Patrick G. Cox.
Other Titles: Savage fugitive
Description: [Florida] : [IndieGo Publishing LLC], [2018] | Series: Harry Heron adventure series ; book 4
Identifiers: ISBN 9781946824226 (paperback) | ISBN 9781946824233 (hardback) | ISBN 9781946824240 (ebook)
Subjects: LCSH: Europe, Northern--Armed Forces--Officers--Fiction. | Space warfare--Fiction. | Time travel--Fiction. | LCGFT: Action and adventure fiction. | Science fiction.
Classification: LCC PR9369.4.C748 H37 2018 (print) | LCC PR9369.4.C748 (ebook) | DDC 823.92--dc23

PUBLISHING
Our Brilliance . Your Success
WWW.INDIEGOPUBLISHING.CO.UK
WWW.INDIEGOPUBLISHING.COM
WWW.GETINDIEGO.COM

The Harry Heron Adventure Series

OTHER BOOKS by PATRICK G. COX

www.harryheron.com
www.patrickgcox.com

Chapters

HARRY HERON:
SAVAGE FUGITIVE

Chapter 1

Opposition

Harry clasped his hands behind his back and stood with his feet apart, adopting the pose so familiar aboard the 74 gun HMS *Spartan* when he last stood on that ship's deck in 1804. His mind went back to the strange incident amidst a sea fight with the French during the Napoleonic Wars that shot him into the twenty-third century along with his boyhood friend Ferghal O'Connor and Danny Gunn, who served as the ship's "powder monkey" running to and fro with cartridges to load the guns. He let his mind wander as he contemplated the nearest planet. There was so much to learn and so much to adjust to. Perhaps Ferghal was right. Maybe he did strive too hard to understand everything. He smiled briefly as he thought of his father's parting words when he and Ferghal set out for London, and, as Harry had hoped, a position as a midshipman in His Majesty's Navy. His father had reminded him that the true achievement lay in accepting responsibility to those under you, in taking care of their welfare, and in seeking to do one's duty to the best of your ability.

Everything had seemed so simple then. How different it had all become.

His smile faded as he wondered what anguish his parents had known when news finally reached them of his supposed death. He knew how much it had agonized them to attend a funeral with no body to bury, commemorating their son's life with a headstone in the grassy hillside of County Down, Ireland, and a plaque for himself and Ferghal in the ancient parish church.

Oh, Papa, how I wish I could see you, and Mama, and James and Mabel just once more. He glanced out at the vastness of space then took in the flickering lights of the control panels in the observatory. *I think you would find this century astonishing and unsettling, but interesting in the extreme.*

But his father was not here, and Harry must make his career in an entirely new era and in a fleet serving a confederation of nations that included France as an ally, not an enemy. That alone would have been unheard of in the nineteenth century. Having completed Fleet College with honours, Harry was now Junior Navigation Officer aboard a ship he and his fellows on the HMS *Spartan* would have considered the product of some madman's imagination had it been mentioned in *Spartan's* gunroom. His friend Kit Tanner would not believe him if Harry could return to tell of his adventures in space.

At least his sweetheart, Mary Hopkins, understood these things. He thought of their last holocall, and his mood lifted again. He adored music and worshipped her, a classical and very talented musician. But, as he ruefully admitted, he had not a musical bone in his body. The holocalls were expensive, but he looked forward to each one, an opportunity to hear her voice, see her face and hear her funny anecdotes about her latest concerts and interactions with fans and other musicians.

The ship's gentle voice in his ears brought him back to reality.

"You asked me to alert you to your next watch period, Harry. You are on duty in ten minutes."

"Thank you, Daring." With a sigh, Harry prepared to make his way down to the Navigation Centre. He grinned at a sudden thought. What would Kit or his father have made of his being able to communicate with the ship's AI through nothing but his thoughts? How would he have been able to explain the implanted link in his brain?

That gave him a chuckle and drove out the remains of his blue mood as he made his way out of the Observatory Dome, shutting down the displays as he went.

The Navigation Centre on the NECS *Daring* featured two tiers of consoles. The lower tier was a bank of helm and pitch controllers, and the upper tier featured chart displays and consoles for inputting the data required for navigation.

The entire forward hemisphere of the vast compartment was a display that gave a 180-degree view of whatever lay ahead of the ship as it travelled through space. Other screens allowed views on the quarter and astern, and the forward view could be altered to permit a wider view of the periphery around the ship. The light was kept low to avoid interference with the displays.

Considerable thought had been given to the relationships between the position of the Navigation Officer, the helm and the attitude controllers' stations. It doubled, as on most Destroyer Class vessels, as an alternative Command Centre, though there was a secondary Emergency Navigation Centre further aft. As Junior Navigator, Sub-Lieutenant Harry Heron occupied a seat at the large circular star chart display on the starboard side, leaving the central seat for the Executive Officer, and the seat on the port side of the display for the Navigation Officer.

Below and forward of the "Star Tank"—as the 3D display was called by the TechRates—a Master Warrant Officer occupied the central seat with the helm controls. To his left a Rate manned the controls for attitude, and to his right, a Rate manned the engineering relays. The holographic display of everything ahead and abeam showed the receding mining platform, the swarm of flashing lights indicating the drones transferring the contents of their hoppers to the platform.

Harry had been on this commission six months, and during that time had developed a good relationship with most of his fellow officers as well as the TechRates. The same could not be said of his relationship with Lieutenant Clarke, the ship's senior lieutenant and Navigation Officer, and Harry's immediate supervisor. No matter how hard Harry tried, it seemed the Lieutenant found fault with him, usually over something trivial. The constant criticism was a major reason Harry delighted in the occasions when he had the Navigation Centre to himself as duty Navigator.

Today was not such a day. Lieutenant Clarke was hovering and in a foul mood, nothing unusual, but today he had been relentlessly petty, browbeating Harry and micromanaging his every move.

Two decks above and further forward sat the Command Centre, which, unlike the Navigation Centre, gave the appearance of being completely open to space with its 360-degree display of everything around the ship. The cluster of seats and consoles around the Captain's chair at the centre put the Captain in the middle of the communication links to every department in the ship, and in touch, via the hypercommunications systems, with other ships and Fleet headquarters.

Captain Aisha Maia studied her latest exercise brief. Using her comlink, she ordered, "Commence evasive manoeuvres. Mr. Clarke, you have the con. The enemy for this exercise is the asteroid Delta Lima Golf Six-Five-Five-Niner."

"Yes, Captain." Lieutenant Aral Clarke activated the display of his beloved Manual of Evasive Manoeuvres in Combat, which he followed to the letter despite the technological advances that made it obsolete. With painfully slow two-finger typing, he input **LaGrange Pattern Seven://system DLG865 Alpha. Target/evasion://DLG 6559** using a keyboard he had rigged up, a relic of twenty-first century technology that he insisted on using.

Harry checked the manoeuvre courses and patterns. No allowance had been input for the mining platform. He considered the best way to broach the subject with his temperamental boss and decided to ease into it with the utmost politeness, as was his norm.

"Sir, there is an automated mining unit operating within the area that pattern will pass through at transit point four. I suggest a variation. We should set a course that keeps us clear of that area by at least point zero one of an astronomical unit."

"Rubbish! I disagree. These predetermined manoeuvres are calculated to allow for things like that. Besides, these mining types know they are supposed to keep clear." The Lieutenant punched in the command. "Helm, actuate."

Harry offered no rebuttal, and through his neural link to the ship, he watched the streams of code as the ship's manoeuvring functions commenced. As he expected, at the third dropout from the microtransits, alarms blared.

"Collision imminent!" ordered the Executive Commander through the comlink. "Close all airtight doors. All hands don survival gear—now!"

Harry stared at the looming automated mining platform, its robotic units spread around it like a school of fish. Using his link to the AI, he thought-spoke to the ship. *"Daring, emergency evasion! Now, full power to the port thrusters, full braking thrust. On my mark—now!"*

The ship twisted and lurched then turned away from the danger not a moment too soon while the Coxswain and his assistants stared helplessly at their unresponsive controls, not sure what had just happened.

The Lieutenant knew. "What the hell did you do, Heron? How dare you interfere when I have the con?" His face was beet red.

"My apologies, sir." Harry thought quickly. It was useless to attempt to reason with the Lieutenant. "The ship merely read my thoughts. I had no control over it. You must not have seen the mining drone that we avoided by less than two metres."

Clarke opened his mouth to speak and was cut off by the icy tones of the Captain's voice on the comlink.

"Mr Clarke, report to me in the Command Centre immediately." She paused. "Well done to whoever took that emergency evasive action."

Captain Maia looked up as her Executive Commander joined her in her Day Cabin. She had just had an unpleasant conversation with Lieutenant Clarke about the near miss he had caused. "Perfect timing, Anders." She waved a hand toward the display, which now revealed only the swirling greys of hyperspace. "I'm still getting used to Mr. Heron's ability. I think he just saved us yet again from Lieutenant Clarke's dogged insistence on doing things by the manual, as if modern technology hadn't been invented for a reason." She let out a frustrated exhale.

Anders lowered his voice. "Yes, I am well aware of Mr. Clarke's disposition. Mr. Heron tries his best to comply with his demands, though most of them are unreasonable and unnecessary."

"Keep an eye on it" said Captain Maia. "Mr. Clarke has a reputation, and he's not as good a navigator as he thinks he is, as proved by today's nerve-wracking mishap. A couple of other incidents in his record make me think he's a problem just waiting to happen, but for some reason—I wish I knew what—Fleet can't or won't replace him." She leaned closer. "There's a suggestion he has someone higher up keeping his back. That's the only explanation that makes sense, if you ask me."

"I'll have a word with him privately," said the Executive Commander.

Commander Anders Nielsen entered the Navigation Centre. "Mr. Heron, lay in a course for these coordinates. We have a lost sheep to find—a passenger liner."

Harry quickly input the coordinates to the interface using the touchpad.

As the Commander watched Harry, a frown creased his face.

"Why are you using the manual interface, Mr. Heron?"

"I am instructed to do so, sir."

"I see. But can't you do it faster if you simply use your link to the ship's AI?"

"Indeed I can, sir." Harry spoke without looking up, his eyes focused on entering the commands.

"Then stop messing about and do it," ordered the Commander. He glared across the centre at Lieutenant Clarke, who had looked up sharply when he heard the Commander's raised voice, a look Harry caught when he also glanced up in surprise.

Harry linked directly to the ship's consciousness. "Daring, set the course to these coordinates. Transfer course and movement command to helm and engine room, simultaneous link to Diamond and Hecate, please. Simultaneous entry to transit."

"Done, Harry," the ship responded, her voice distinctly female. "Does this mean you will be communicating your wishes to me in this manner in future?"

"I hope so. It was very frustrating having to work through the interface and at the same time listen to you waiting for me to complete the input."

"Was I impatient?"

"A bit."

Harry was suddenly aware that the Commander was speaking to him again. "My apologies, sir. I was checking my input."

The Commander frowned. "I said well done."

"Thank you, sir." Harry glanced at the Lieutenant, absorbed in his console. His glance took in the Coxswain's position, currently occupied by Chief Master Warrant Officer Abram Winstanley, and the helm console where two TechRates were immersed in their tasks. No one seemed to be paying the slightest attention to what was passing between him and the Commander. Yet he could tell from the studious concentration of the Lieutenant's posture, which almost, but not quite, mirrored the Master Warrant Officer's stiff back, that the exchange between him and the Commander had not gone unnoticed. Harry wondered how the Lieutenant would respond, but he dismissed the thought. He'd just have to deal with it if and when another confrontation arose.

He recalled a recent conversation with the Coxswain. Chief Master Warrant Winstanley had been very tactful. He had told Harry that his temper and obvious contempt for Lieutenant Clarke had been noticed. "I'm sure you know how to avoid the problem, sir," said the Chief Master Warrant.

Harry had nodded his understanding. Winstanley, the ship's Coxswain, her senior non-commissioned officer, was also responsible for discipline. That he had made it a point to speak to him was sufficient for Harry to take his warning seriously.

The Commander took his seat. "Swain, give us the rundown to transit, please."

"Yes, sir," said Abram Winstanley, acknowledging the command. "Transit in twenty seconds, sir. Fifteen, twelve, ten, eight, six, three, two, one—entering transit, sir. Drives at three quarter power. *Diamond* and *Hecate* in company."

"Good. Well done, all. Our orders are to assist in rounding up convoy HX4. They've lost the liner *Durham Castle*. Takes us off our main task, but that damned ship's packed with refugees. Mr. Heron, I will need that special skill of yours in the Ops Control once we close the last reported position." He stood up. "Mr. Clarke, join me in the cubby, please."

"Yes, sir." Lieutenant Clarke stood up and looked at Harry. Unnecessarily he said, "Take over, Mr. Heron, but call me if there are any problems."

"Aye, aye, sir," Harry responded automatically, his attention focused on running a course check. He missed the pained expression that crossed Aral Clarke's face. Harry had caught the deliberate inference that he was only nominally in charge because the Lieutenant had deigned to "grant" him permission, which implied that the Lieutenant didn't trust him to manage in a crisis, though Harry was the one who had gotten them out of the most recent near disaster that Clarke had caused. It was so ridiculous that Harry couldn't suppress a rueful smile. His thoughts went to his and Ferghal's voyage in the freightliner *Twee Jonge Gezellen* some twelve months earlier. *I wonder how the Lieutenant would have handled that adventure. Probably would have failed miserably.*

Allowing a brief grin to cross his face, Harry remembered his near perfect destruction of the freighter's control consoles and interfaces. His efforts had been extremely effective in preventing the criminal crew of the prize from retaking and controlling the ship, but it had left him, Ferghal and their crew with a ship that only he and Ferghal could communicate with in transit to Earth, with no certainty they would succeed in their endeavour to deliver her. As the Lieutenant originally in command had died at the hands of the wanted man Captain Heemstra, Harry, as senior Midshipman, had been left in command. Their reward had been early promotion to the rank of Sub-Lieutenant.

Consortium Brigadier Gillian Newton stepped from the shuttle and saluted the waiting guard and the Colonel.

"Welcome to Planet Lycania, Brigadier."

"Thank you, Colonel Rees." After they shook hands, she fell into step beside him. "I understand the native population are rather primitive—these creatures the scientists have named Canids because of their canine appearance."

"Shades of opinion on that. They wear some impressive clothing in terms of protection from the harsh environment on this planet, but their weapons are very primitive, and no one has been able to communicate with them or examine them properly."

"That was in my briefing—something about the research team having captured a few of them, and they held one long enough to discover these inhabitants are apparently monotreme marsupials. Then they escaped—from locked cages, no less."

"Did they break out?"

"Not that we could discover. They simply opened the locks and walked past the guards, who saw absolutely nothing." Colonel Rees shrugged in response to Brigadier Newton's surprised glance, then he continued. "We couldn't find out how, but now the natives avoid us, and that's fine by me. We haven't the forces to take on an entire population, despite what Johnstone's xenoarchaeological team are demanding."

"Very well, Colonel Rees. I'll address the troops after I've read myself into command, and then I will want a tour of all our facilities."

After they parted, Brigadier Newton pondered this situation. She'd seen the briefings and the demands, but with a garrison of just two thousand to guard the mining operations, Lycania was the source for vital rare metals essential to nanotechnology systems, plus it was a major source of elements used in fuel cell production as well as for the agriculture stations and satellites. She already had enough to keep twice that number of troops busy. And then there was the signal monitoring and decryption unit. Her commanders had been specific about it. That took top priority.

"Mr. Clarke." The Commander wasn't smiling. "I don't normally expect to intervene in the running of a division unless it involves a disciplinary matter. Your instructions to Sub-Lieutenant Heron are ridiculous. Why do you object to his using his internal link to the ship's AI? Do you know how valuable that is to us?" He held up a hand to stop the Lieutenant's protest. "If I have another such complaint from you about him, I will investigate it and take a closer look at how you are managing him."

Clarke reddened and shifted uncomfortably in his seat. "I feel very strongly that I should correct him and make him work the same as everyone else, sir. He's far too young for his rank, and that episode with the freightliner he and O'Connor supposedly recaptured is overplayed, in my opinion. It's made him overconfident. Besides, I can't monitor what he's doing if he uses his AI link, sir. About his old-fashioned way of speaking—well, that is just pretentiousness on his part, an attempt to be different." The Lieutenant let out a nervous bark of laughter that was very nearly a snort.

Frowning, the Commander studied the Lieutenant. "Mr. Clarke, the Grand Admiral promoted Sub-Lieutenants Heron and O'Connor after they pulled off something that neither you nor I nor the Captain could have done. If the Commander-in-Chief thinks they're old enough to be Sub-Lieutenants, it's not up to you to question that. As for your needing to monitor everything he does, why do you feel this compulsion? Is he incompetent at navigation? Not that I can see. As for Mr. Heron's speech, I don't have a problem with it and neither does the Captain. He is respectful and polite, albeit quaint at times, and his mannerisms do not negatively affect the efficient running of this ship, but your refusal to let him use his AI link does."

He paused until he had regained the Lieutenant's reluctant eye contact. "Am I clear?"

Lieutenant Clarke considered protesting, but he read the Commander's expression correctly, for once.

"Yes, sir."

"Good. If you can't work with him in your division, I'll move him to another, but I don't want to have to do that. He's far too good at navigation to be wasted somewhere else."

"Yes, sir," said the Lieutenant, and his face and bearing were respectful and compliant, but he was seething inside. As soon as he was out of the Commander's office and striding down the corridor, his fury was on full display to anyone who may have passed by and glanced at him.

Lieutenant Clarke resented this dressing down even though he knew that he was well outside his authority in the way he micromanaged Harry. Worse, he knew that Harry was more competent in navigation than he would ever be. Mathematics and the complex calculations required for navigating in space did not come easily to him, and he hated the way his subordinate seemed so at ease with these skills.

He thoroughly resented having his control over Harry questioned, even by a senior officer.

I'll say yes, sir, to your face, Commander, but in the Nav Centre, I'm in charge. We'll see how far Heron pushes the boundaries, and I'll decide where those boundaries are.

Clarke wasted no time unleashing his pent-up rage. He strode into the Navigation Centre like a pudgy peacock, and almost collided with ComOp Maddie Hodges who sidestepped him and shot a warning glance at Harry that trouble was coming.

"Mr. Heron." Lieutenant Clarke loomed over Harry's shoulder. "In my office, immediately." He sounded peevish, an annoying tendency accentuated by his nasal voice. Harry followed him into the small office at the rear of the Navigation Centre. Clarke shut the door and launched in. "I'm not going to tell you again. You're to use the interface with the AI when you're on watch, not your own special link. It's unsettling to the TechRates when you don't use the console and things just magically appear on their screens—or you tell them you've done something, but you haven't entered any commands."

"It isn't quite as easy as that, sir. The AI doesn't allow me time to input the commands in the normal way, sir. It reads my intention and simply does it."

"Don't give me excuses." The Lieutenant flushed angrily. "You have my instructions—now stick to them." His receding hair was a mousey brown, and his features betrayed a tendency toward flabbiness. The reddening of his face accentuated the otherwise pasty pallor that was his normal appearance. "That's an order."

"Aye, aye, sir."

Lieutenant Clarke grunted in annoyance and shifted in his seat. "Must you speak like that? 'Aye, aye, sir'," he mimicked in a mocking voice. "Isn't 'yes, sir' good enough for you? Get over yourself, man! I think it's a pose to sound posh, as if you were educated at the best schools in England, which you were not, according to your records, and you'd better change your ways as long as you're under my command, or you and I are going to fall out."

Harry knew exactly how to respond. "Aye, aye, sir." He gave the Lieutenant a level gaze and waited for what was surely to come now that he'd said it twice.

"You'd better learn some discipline, Mr. Heron. You don't speak to me like that and get away with it." Clarked smirked, sure of his superiority, at least in rank. "I'm reporting your insubordination to the Commander. I'm sure he'll be interested to hear about it. He and I just had a conversation on this very topic. I've tried working with you, Heron, but you either won't or can't work with me. Stick to the procedures and stay within the rules."

He adopted what he considered a conciliatory tone. "I know it can't be easy —this technology must be very confusing to you— but it's for your own good. You don't want a bad report from me on this deployment, especially one that says you're unable to follow orders. It will affect your promotion chances later. I'd much rather work with you, Harry, than fight you."

There was a loud snap as the stylus in Harry's hand broke. It sounded like a gunshot and caused the Lieutenant to startle.

Aral Clarke glared at the ruined instrument and then at Harry's face filled with contempt for him. He was about to say something when Harry stood up and cut across him, his voice taut with anger.

"I shall do my best to comply with your direction, sir, and you had better place me on report for the willful destruction of Fleet property." The ruined stylus landed with enough force in the waste bin to capsize it as he added, "Sir!"

"You can count on it." The Lieutenant felt a glow of satisfaction at having provoked Harry into an action he could use to take this upstart down. "You had better learn to think before you speak, and to show some respect to your superiors."

"Yes, sir." Harry's face was stony. His friends would have recognised the look and known that any further goading would result in someone suffering an injury.

The Lieutenant's link chirped not a minute too soon. To Harry's relief he heard the voice of the Commander demanding the Lieutenant's immediate presence in his office. Aral Clarke stood up and made a clumsy attempt to defuse things. "I have to run. As you heard, the Commander needs me." He frowned at Harry's rigid glare. "I'll consider your disrespect later. For now, consider yourself on warning. You're dismissed."

"Thank you, sir. I have some work to do on the chart updates, sir. May I carry on?"

"Yes—yes, of course." Clarke cast about for a comment to add that would sound commanding and managerial. "Remember, everything must be done through the interface, not through your link to the ship's AI."

Harry dropped into the seat at the chart console with more force than needed.

For several seconds he sat completely still, his eyes shut as he steadied his temper.

He exhaled to release some tension, and reminded himself that he could only do his best at this task and every task, and not worry about the rest.

Setting to work, he carried out the updates using the maddeningly slow method Clarke had demanded he use, which took longer than necessary. Around him, several of the watch noticed this and his disgruntled demeanour. They had become used to Harry's quick work, and wondered what had passed between him and the Lieutenant. Their wondering was dispelled when the Lieutenant scurried into the Navigation Centre. It was obvious he was not happy.

Pausing to glower at each station in turn, his eye fell on Harry.

"Good, so you do know how to do it properly, Mr. Heron. I'm glad to see that you are making an effort to avoid unsettling the rest of the team."

Abram Winstanley exchanged glances with his partner at the helm position. "Idiot," he muttered under his breath. "The lad has twice his ability in his little finger."

"Something to report, Master Warrant?" the Lieutenant asked.

"No, sir, just doing a helm check."

"Carry on then." The Lieutenant frowned. He had a feeling that the Master Warrant was not being straight with him, but he couldn't push it without losing his dignity. He took his seat and mirrored Harry's screen so he could oversee what Harry was doing. Of course the work was perfect. There wasn't a single damn thing he could find wrong with Harry's calculations.

He would never admit it, even to himself, but Harry frightened him. He was far too competent, and very efficient. To Aral Clark, Harry was a threat that had to be suppressed.

Abram Winstanley eased into a chair in the Master Warrant Officers' Mess Lounge. It boasted a casual arrangement of comfortable armchairs and gave the appearance of having external views, though these were in fact display screens. Various trophies and ornamental features gave it a less institutional feel, a home away from home for the senior Warrant Officers on board. He accepted a glass from the android steward.

"Thanks, Delta Fifteen. I need this." He sipped and nodded to his companion, another long-serving Master Warrant. "Tell you what, Sid, Mister bloody Clarke is a bloody idiot. He's riding Sub-Lieutenant Heron hard, and he thinks he's smart."

"Ah, yes, good old Clarke, always a problem. You wouldn't know, of course, who tipped the Commander off that he was having a go at Heron straight after he'd been chewed out by said Commander just a few minutes earlier, now would you, Swain?"

"Someone 'accidentally' left the comlink from the cuddy open to the Commander. I've had a word with ComOp Hodges—she was the Duty ComOp." He winked and took a drink. "I'll put a week's credit on the table says Heron saves the Loot's bacon before we finish this deployment—in spite of the grief he's getting."

"Bloody hell. So the Exec must have heard everything. I was in the anteroom. I'm glad I wasn't the one on the mat!" Sid grinned. "No taker on that wager either. I'd have to be an idiot not to know which of them really has what it takes—and it isn't the Loot. My money is on how soon Clarke screws up again—probably not long, and it'll be worse next time. That near miss with the mining platform—a few of us wondered if we needed to change underwear after that bit of fun. You'll have to take Heron aside, though, and caution him that if he loses his temper and gives Mr. Clarke what he deserves, he'll be in a court martial hearing quicker than he can say 'aye, aye, sir.'"

"Already done. He's a good lad, is Mr. Heron. I just hope it isn't something critical when the Loot does screw up. I want to live long enough to rob the pension fund blind."

Chapter 2

Called to Task

Harry stepped into the Commander's office wondering if this was the result of yet another complaint against him from Lieutenant Clarke. "You sent for me, sir?"

"I did." Commander Anders Nielsen indicated a chair. "Sit down, Harry. I have a task for you."

"Thank you, sir." Harry took a seat and waited. He felt nervous just being in the Commander's presence, but did his best not to let it show. His experience over the last few months on this deployment with Lieutenant Clark had made him cautious, and he had not yet got to know the Commander well enough to judge his mood.

"Anything you want to say before we begin?"

The question took Harry by surprise. He looked up and found the piercing eyes of the Commander fixed on his. He shook his head. "Not that I can think of, sir." A part of him wanted to protest that Mr. Clarke was still goading him, but the warning from Mr. Winstanley, coupled with his experiences in the Gunroom in the Royal Navy of 1801, had taught him that such bullying was to be expected, so he remained silent.

The Commander held eye contact, an unusual thing when talking to Harry, he realised. It had taken some time and a little research to understand that, to the Sub-Lieutenant, it was a matter of respect and courtesy not to do this. Prompting him again, the Commander was more specific this time. "Any problems with your present work?"

Harry's face went blank, and he went into auto-response mode to keep his cool. "No, sir, I do not believe so." He hesitated. The Commander seemed to expect more. "I enjoy the navigation and working with the others in the team for the betterment of the Fleet." It was a classic textbook answer that kept Harry in safe territory.

The Commander was tempted to challenge that, but he decided not to. "I'm glad to hear that, Harry. Now, moving on to why I called you here today. You are aware we have a science officer aboard. We were supposed to deliver him to the Fleet research ship *Endurance* at Pangaea. But this detour to find the *Durham Castle* on top of our main objective to gather intel on the Consortium's deployments means he will be with us a while longer. He has a project to pursue and needs someone to assist him. I am going to assign you to that work—in addition to your present duties."

"Aye, aye, sir." Harry felt relief. At least he would be out from under Lieutenant Clarke's thumb for some of the time. "I believe I have encountered the scientist, Mr. Schulte-Lubeck." He knew the very tall German by sight, as the man was hard to miss. He seemed to fill any space he was in, and his deep, booming voice did the same. "What does the task entail?"

"Rasmus is a specialist in explosive materials, and I understand you have some knowledge in that field. His project involves solid fuel propellants for missiles and for some of our surface weapons. I am assigning you to assist him with setting up a laboratory and the necessary analysis systems for his work so that he doesn't lose any time on his research while we swan about looking for the *Durham Castle.*"

"Very good, sir." Harry was beginning to feel more at ease and allowed himself a brief grin. "Though I fear my expertise in explosives is limited to the powder charges we used on *Bellerophon* and *Spartan* some four hundred years ago. My knowledge of the most recent charges is limited."

The Commander smiled in response. "Then this is an opportunity for you to learn more. Though it wouldn't surprise me if Rasmus doesn't pick your brain about the stuff you're familiar with."

Harry entered the laboratory allocated to Mr Schulte-Lubeck and took in his surroundings. There were several working surfaces and a number of curious instruments. It also held a rather robust chamber, the purpose of which he could not imagine. About the size of a small cupboard, it squatted in the middle of the compartment with a complex cone-shaped chimney atop it. He spotted the tall and rather spare figure of the scientist rising from his workbench, and advanced to meet him.

"Mr. Schulte-Lubeck?" Harry began. "Sub-Lieutenant Heron, sir. I am assigned to assist you, though I am not sure what you would need from me."

"Ah, yes." Rasmus smiled a welcome. "I am looking forward to working with you—your ability to speak directly to the computer will be most helpful—and I want to discuss with you some aspects of the manufacture of the coarse black powder your guns used."

"I shall be happy to offer what little knowledge I have on that subject, sir." Harry returned the smile with a small inclination of his head. "Though I confess I am mystified by your interest in such a poor explosive when compared to those available to us now."

Rasmus grinned. "You may be surprised—the method of manufacture and the source of some of the ingredients is of great interest." He waved a hand to indicate the compartment. "Welcome to our laboratory—and you must call me Rasmus. We do not need to be formal here."

Harry returned the grin. Instinctively he liked this strange giant of a man who never seemed to be still. "Very good, sir ... I mean, Rasmus. What would you have me do first?"

"Your Commander says you have some special ability with the AI network. I need these references available on the terminal on demand. Can you arrange them so that I can access them immediately?" He handed Harry a tablet with a seemingly endless list of reference material.

Harry nodded. "I can try, sir—Rasmus. It should be possible. I can ask the ship to respond to a voice request to produce any or all of these documents for you." He frowned as he skim-read the list. "I'm afraid I do not understand how to read or speak German."

Rasmus thought a moment. "Then how will you get the AI to do this?"

Harry smiled. "I shall just let her read this list through my eyes, and *Daring* will know what you want."

"Daring? Do you mean the ship?"

"Yes, the ship." Harry realised this could be difficult to explain, as few people knew that the ship had a personality. "She has artificial intelligence, as you know, but it seems to me that she has become a living entity as well." Harry paused, not sure how to explain this next bit. Then he took the plunge. "I have come to know the ship well—and I have felt on occasion that she is alive."

"She?" Rasmus cleared his throat and looked flustered. "I see." He frowned. "I wonder if she would speak directly with me."

"I don't see why not." Harry smiled. "I shall ask." He linked to the ship. "*Daring, have you been following this conversation?*" He had only recently discovered that the Fleet ships followed a modified form of the Laws of Robotics established by someone called Isaac Asimov in the twentieth century. In a recent discussion with the ship, Harry had pointed out that he needed privacy occasionally, which was why he asked this question now.

"*No, Harry. That would be rude, as you have told me before. What do you require of me?*"

"*I need you to make the references on this tablet available to my companion, Mr. Schulte-Lubeck. He speaks German. Is there a way you can respond to his requests by vocal command?*"

"*Yes, but it will require the use of a vocal interface used for normal voice commands.*" The ship paused. "*I have activated the vocal interface used for the environment and view screen commands. Please request your friend to speak to me so that I may adjust to his vocal frequencies.*"

"*I shall do so.*" Harry turned to Rasmus. "*Daring* says she needs you to speak to her. Then, to communicate with you, she will use the view screen or the interface that is normally used for environmental control. Please address her as *Daring*, and she will respond to you."

"I see." Rasmus nodded. "Will she speak German?"

"I expect so, sir. After all, she is a Fleet ship and programmed to provide information in all Confederate languages." Harry focussed on the display and let the list scroll rapidly. He could feel the ship reading it through his eyes. "I believe she has all the items you requested."

"Already? Well, let me try it." Rasmus felt a little silly as he said, "Good afternoon *Daring*, alles okay?"

"Ja danke, Herr Schulte-Lübeck, mir geht es gut. Ich habe die gesuchten Veröffentlichungen gefunden. Was soll ich als nächtes tun?"

Rasmus blinked. "Dankeschön!" To Harry he said, "It works perfectly."

"Good morning, James," Niamh LeStrange greeted her brother as the holographic image steadied. "I've a letter from Harry—he seems to be enjoying his new deployment on the *Daring*."

"So it seems." James Heron smiled. As ever Harry was editing the letters he sent to Niamh, making sure they were always upbeat and contained nothing to worry her. His own letter from Harry had seemed reticent about some aspects, but the Admiral had been able to read between the lines based on his knowledge of Harry and the people he was serving with. "I believe they're on escort duty now."

Niamh frowned. "Is that so? Well, I hope it's not into enemy space."

"It's on a regular convoy route." He stalled the objection he could see coming. "So it should be pretty routine. There have been no reports of any attacks in that area." He smiled. "I'm sure you'll get a full account from Harry—with paintings—when he gets back to their regular patrol base."

"Yes, I suppose so, but I have a feeling he doesn't always tell me everything." She grinned. "It's really rather funny the way he still thinks 'ladies' should be shielded from the gory details of some of his adventures."

James laughed. "Yes, but perhaps he knows your reaction to some of it all too well."

She nodded. "Probably." She changed the subject. "Now, the main reason I called is to ask if you intend to be at Danny's graduation ceremony from Fleet College. I hear he's been posted to the *Vengeance*. He's thrilled, although he really wanted to get a posting to *Daring* so that he could be on the same ship as Harry and Ferghal."

"Yes, I know. I had to 'do the Admiral' on him when he bombarded me with appeals to pull strings." He grinned. "Poor lad, I think I'm in the dog box there, but he'll be fine on *Vengeance*. Ben Curran is her Captain, and he knows Danny and will keep an eye on him."

"Well, at least it's a starship and not one of your smaller ships." She smiled. "And he'll get over it."

The Admiral reflected that his sister, like most civilians, equated a ship's size with safety. He suppressed a smile as he answered, "Yes, of course. He's still technically a bit young to be sent aloft, but then Harry is technically well below the legal age for his rank. And all of them are at least four hundred years too old to be in the service at all."

"Yes!" She laughed. "But they are the most sprightly and youngest quadruple centenarians I've ever seen. Guessing how they will respond to anything is always a challenge. I hear Ferghal has taken up unarmed combat as a sport."

"So I heard." The Admiral grinned. "But I hear he still has trouble striking a balance between sport and battle. A few people are reluctant to get on a mat with him." His smile widened in pride. "And Harry is fencing—took the trophy in the last Fleet competition—though his style is death or glory, I understand."

"So I saw," said Niamh with a sigh. "I was at the semi-finals, and he scared the life out of me when he disarmed his opponent. It really looked as if he would run through the poor fellow with his sword." She paused, a frown creasing her brow. "He's our only family, you know, and I hope you're keeping an eye on him. I would never forgive you or the Fleet if we were to lose them. He may be our twelve times great uncle, but he, Ferghal and Danny are like sons to me, and I'll wager you feel the same way."

"Midshipman Gunn reporting, sir." Danny stood to attention as he reported his arrival to the Officer of the Watch on the NECS *Vengeance*. He couldn't help recalling his arrival aboard the *Vanguard* with Harry and Ferghal when they were transported through time from a sea battle with the French in 1804 to the year 2204. He had been a terrified boy, his only experience being a powder monkey in the Royal Navy. Now, he was a newly commissioned Midshipman, but in some ways he felt just as frightened—he was merely better at hiding it now. He wished Harry or Ferghal were here to welcome him.

"Take a seat, Mr. Gunn." The Lieutenant smiled a welcome. "I'm Lieutenant Erikson, Weapons Department. I gather you are familiar with our sister ship, the *Vanguard*."

"Yes, sir," Danny replied. "We—that is Sub-Lieutenants Heron and O'Connor an' me—found ourselves on her four years ago." He blushed as he recalled. "It was pretty terrifying—but Mr. Heron saw us right."

"Rear Admiral Heron? I believe he is a relative. Is that true?"

"No, sir, Mister, I mean Sub-Lieutenant Heron." Danny reddened with embarrassment. It felt like he was already fumbling things. "He stood up for us and got us out of Johnstone's lab on Pangaea. The Admiral's sort of like our father now, but back then, he was the Captain, and we didn't know he would be on our side. We thought we'd been caught by the French when we landed on the *Vanguard* out of the middle of nowhere surrounded by all those men in strange suits." Danny cringed inwardly. He was talking too much in his nervousness, a habit he had yet to restrain.

The Lieutenant suppressed a smile. "I'm sure that was quite an experience, Mr. Gunn, but you've successfully passed out of Fleet College and you're a Midshipman now, and all that is behind you. You'll be working in Weapons most of the time, but you'll also be on a roster as the Captain's go-for. You'll have your quarters in the Gunroom, and your duties are in this chip." He consulted his screen. "I see you're a musician. I hope you'll join the ship's orchestra and perhaps one or more of the other music groups."

Danny's nervousness receded and his face brightened. "Oh, yes, sir. I have my instruments with me." He grinned impishly. "Aunt Niamh insisted—it was her condition on my joining the Fleet."

"What instruments do you play, Mr. Gunn?"

"The flute, keyboard and the Irish harp, sir, and I'm right good at it if I don't say so myself." Danny grinned again. Maybe this wouldn't be so bad after all.

Ferghal studied the circuit board, one reportedly replaced at the ship's last maintenance overhaul, and now showing fault signals. It seemed in order, but he had a nagging feeling that something was not right. The feeling was confirmed when the ship identified it as the source of a problem. He studied the schematic again, traced the circuit, and identified each component. There—he found it. One of the processors was in the wrong place. Running another check, he made a discovery.

The board had been modified, yet there was no record of the modification in the maintenance log. Isolating the unit, he slipped it out and installed a new one in its place. He used his neural link to the ship's AI to determine that all was now functioning correctly. Satisfied that it was, he logged the exchange and the fault.

As an afterthought, he told the ship, "Daring, *please inform me if there is any further modification or anomaly in this circuitry or any other.*"

"*As you wish, Ferghal.*"

Ferghal packed his tools and closed the panel, then sealed it and added a tell-tale to alert him to any further tampering. He made his way to Engineering Control in search of his Lieutenant.

"Good, you've finished." Lieutenant George was brisk. "The system reports normal function is restored. What was the problem?"

"This, sir." Ferghal unpacked the board and held it out for the Lieutenant's inspection. "The C858 processor had been replaced with a different component. I've changed it back again. But there's no record of its replacement in the maintenance logs or of any access to that unit."

The Lieutenant studied the board. "Damn, that's almost impossible to spot—how'd you do it?"

Ferghal hesitated. Like Harry, he had been trained from an early age to be observant and to notice things that were out of place. He had difficulty understanding why his colleagues and companions couldn't do the same thing. He considered the best way to explain. "It didn't look right when I checked the board against the schematic, so I went through it component by component, and that"—he indicated the rogue processor—"is not correct. When I checked with the ship, she confirmed it."

The Lieutenant nodded. "Okay. At least we've found this one. I better inform the Lieutenant Commander. He won't be happy about what you've turned up, but it will move you to the top of his star list." He smiled when Ferghal flashed a grin.

Consortium Brigadier Newton surveyed the alien city through her binoculars. "These cities are unoccupied? The locals—these Rottweilers, as they're called, interesting term—don't live in them? What do the scientists say?"

"The Rotties don't live in them, ma'am. Fact is no one has been able to figure out where they live, other than it seems to be in burrows somewhere. They have been seen entering and leaving what we thought were mines." The Major indicated the vehicle scanner currently showing nothing but interference. "That's all we get when we try to scan them. The tech geeks think it is some alien technology hidden in the cities, and they're trying to access it. Trouble is, as soon as they go into one, the Rotties arrive and chase them out."

"That explains why I have Dr. Ramswiki demanding we mount a seizure operation on one, the largest she can find, of course." She paused. "I don't like not being able to scan them. I think we'll have to support the doctor and see what they can find."

Chapter 3

Clarke Does It Again

———————————————

Captain Aisha Maia of the NECS *Daring* studied her latest orders with a feeling of frustation. Another set of searches to be undertaken for the missing ship separated from her convoy in an area where the Consortium had recently tightened its grip. At least *Daring* would have *Diamond* and a heavy cruiser in support. They'd probably need it.

Captain Maia gestured to her Executive Commander to take a seat. "Anders, we've a fix on *Durham Castle*. Fleet finally got the data from the convoy as to when and where she dropped out of transit. She hasn't shown up anywhere else, so she may have a drive problem, or something else has failed. According to the convoy Commodore, she reported having trouble with her nav system."

"Good. Now perhaps we can rescue her and get back to our routine," said the Commander. "Any update on Consortium activity?"

"Not since this morning's situation report. But then, who knows? With their current tactics aimed at cutting off food and raw materials, they may be holding back on direct action."

"As I read it, the report suggests they're regrouping for something."

"I picked up on that too. How's the situation on navigation?"

The Commander had to hand it to the Captain. She didn't miss much even if she appeared to keep her distance. "I'm watching it. I moved Heron to assist our scientist, and they seemed to get on like a house on fire. Mr. Clarke isn't happy, of course, because Heron isn't under his thumb all day every day, and he knows he can't push the Warrants the way he did Heron. The real problem is he feels threatened by anyone more able than he is. And he's so rigid on procedure that he refuses to do anything outside of the manuals. That's having a negative impact on everyone around him, particularly when we exercise emergency procedures, like that incident with the mining platform. His rigid adherence to the Manual of Evasive Manoeuvres in Combat is worrying as well. It hampers our manoeuvring."

"I won't have him endanger the ship," said the Captain. "If he's unable to use initiative and encourage his people to do so, then he's a danger to the ship and all of us. Can we move him to a less critical department?" Hesitating, she added, "A pity Heron is so junior. He's a far better navigator."

"It might be possible to move Lieutenant Clarke, but I suspect it would simply move the problem to a new area. Plus, none of the others have the Pilotage Course in their portfolios. Leave it with me, and I'll see what I can do."

"Okay, but Clarke worries me, and how he managed to get a pass in the Pilotage Course beats me. Plus, he has a history of poor command relations with his divisions on other ships." The Captain paused as she considered how to handle the situation. "I'll have a word with him. If that doesn't work, I'll have him transferred."

The three Fleet ships dropped out, bracketing the crippled liner. The Senior Captain aboard *Hecate* contacted Captain Reynard. "*Durham Castle*, our assessment team is on the way. We will remain in system but will be mobile in defensive patrols. Once the assessment is made, we will determine our next actions."

"Glad to see you, Captain. We're ready to receive your team."

"Good. They will be with you in the next few minutes."

At his station in Navigation Control, Harry held position and kept the *Daring* moving in a pattern that would make targeting her difficult. His link chirped.

"Heron," he responded.

"Hand over the con to Lieutenant Clarke. I want you to go to the *Durham Castle* with Lieutenant Lee and Sub-Lieutenant O'Connor. Their navigation system is down, and it will need that special trick of yours to get it back up." The Executive Commander's voice was terse. "Shuttle bay is on stand-by. You have ten minutes to get your kit together and get there. Be prepared for a few days away."

"Aye, aye, sir!" Harry's heart raced. To the Lieutenant, he said, "Sir, I have programmed the next three transits in this pattern." He pointed to his display. "The navigation system is set to repeat the pattern randomly for the last four jumps unless you wish to change it. May I hand over the con, sir?"

"I have the con." Lieutenant Clarke sounded annoyed. "You're relieved, Mr. Heron." He seemed about to make a further comment then thought better of it.

Harry found Ferghal and Lieutenant Lee waiting with several more TechRates and a Warrant Officer.

"Good, you're here." Lieutenant Lee greeted him. "Board, Warrant." To Harry, he said, "We may have to stay with the *Durham Castle*. Her nav system seems to have blown out an entire node and is refusing to respond to any of the usual rerouting routines. If we can't repair it, you and Ferghal may have to act as bridges and make the damned ship respond. You up for it?"

"I have a choice, sir?" Harry was a little surprised to be asked. He caught Ferghal's grin and nodded. "Of course, sir—we shall, as Master Warrant Berry is wont to say—give it a whirl."

In the Navigation Centre, Lieutenant Clarke checked Harry's programmed jumps. Convinced they were wrong, he grunted in disapproval, but he was unable to figure out how to confirm his 'hunch', so he said, "Helm, cancel the Sub-Lieutenant Heron's program. I'll enter a proper set." He cleared his throat loudly and shifted in his seat as he glanced around, hoping someone noticed that he was the one in charge here, but all heads were bent to their tasks.

After the minimalist fittings and decor of the *Daring* and her sister ships, the *Durham Castle* had something of a fading opulence about her. The officer waiting in the docking bay greeted them with relief.

"Thank God you're here. We're stuffed with refugees, and they're getting very twitchy. This way, please." He led the way. "Our people have opened the faulty node, but we don't have the spares to replace it, repair it or even jury-rig it." His scowl betrayed how he felt about that. "Being economical with our resources, according to our owners."

Lieutenant Lee grimaced. "Sounds like the sort of false economy our bureaucrats are always trying to impose. He shook his head and gave a weary sigh. "Just how the hell we're supposed to keep a ship going with no spare parts, I'm damned if I know."

Passengers gathered in almost every open space to watch the newcomers. Many seemed to be nervous or, at the very least, concerned about the ship and its safety.

"This ship is full of women and children," Harry remarked to Ferghal. "It will be no easy matter to transfer them to our ships if we cannot correct this problem. I have tried the link to the ship's AI, and though it works, it is almost as if the ship has become ill. I sense that it is confused, or possibly afraid."

"Aye, you're right," said Ferghal. "It seems frightened, almost like a child that has lost its way. I'll see if any other parts of the system are damaged or failing."

Harry nodded. "I shall see what I can discover while you effect the repair."

At the service duct in which the failed node was situated, it took the leading TechRate a matter of minutes to open the casing and expose the damaged boards. While this work commenced, Harry sensed that the ship was watching their activities with an almost paranoid anxiety. He decided to soothe the ship as if it were a startled horse.

"*Be easy, Durham Castle. We are here to repair you and restore your navigational programming.*"

"*I have had some other defects for a while, but no one repairs them. They keep trying to make my engineering functions perform other tasks, but those could fail at any time, and I can't self-repair anymore. If they are not repaired, I could fail in transit, and that would kill my passengers, which is forbidden by the laws I must obey.*" The terrified AI launched into a flood of information that intrigued Harry.

He took a different approach. "*If you identify the defects for us, we may be able to do it, but we do not have much time. Now, I have a new set of star charts for you, and my friends are replacing your damaged processors and circuitry. The charts are the latest and fully up to date, which will improve your systems. May I upload the star charts for you?"*

"Yes, but please replace the processors in my helm and hyper-pod control cortex—otherwise, they will fail as soon as we enter transit."

Lieutenant Clarke consulted his beloved Manual of Evasive Manoeuvres in Combat, and entered his changes to Harry's course and waypoints for their evasive holding pattern. He practically pounded the interface as he input commands. Satisfied, he sent his changes to the helm. "Warrant, amended course—commence series."

"Yes, sir." The Warrant spoke without looking up, and when he finally glanced at his screen, he felt an immediate sense of alarm. "Sir, this will take us within close range of a cluster of impact asteroids. The ship is flagging a collision danger."

"Ignore it. We'll be well clear."

"Yes, sir." The Warrant Officer entered his commands, and the ship began the series. Dropping out a few seconds later, there was a sudden lurch followed by the clamour of alarms.

"Proximity alarm," growled the Warrant. "Initiating evasive action."

"Lieutenant Clarke!" The Captain's voice had an angry edge. "What the hell are you playing at? That nearly put us in the middle of a cluster of asteroids. Make sure it doesn't happen again!"

"Yes, ma'am." Lieutenant Clarke actually sounded shaken for once. He entered a new series of commands and relayed them to the helm. "Amended manoeuvres. Enter these and commence pattern." The Lieutenant reverted the course instructions to Harry's original pattern.

"Aye, aye, sir," said the Warrant, hiding his grin, relishing the fact that it rankled the Lieutenant to hear him use Harry's old-fashioned reply.

Lieutenant Lee confronted the *Durham Castle*'s Captain. "Captain, this board is fitted with processors and components which don't match the spec for this function. Was this repaired or replaced recently?"

"Yes. We'd had a problem, and the company sent a repair team, but the supervisor admitted they weren't given the correct components. They did the best they could with what they had."

"You're lucky this didn't go in transit," said Lieutenant Lee, as he watched Ferghal checking other parts. "I'm surprised it even worked to get you this far." He gestured at the damaged components already replaced. "It's done a hell of a lot of damage to other parts of the system. This could have given your ship a major case of paranoia. These AI systems can go like that."

"Sir," Harry said, to get the Lieutenant's attention. "The ship is afraid we intend to wipe out its entire personality and impose a new one. I've done what I can to reassure it, but it says there are other faults. Ferghal knows where those are."

"Damn," said the Lieutenant. "Okay, Mr. Heron, do what you can to deal with that. Ferghal, where are these other problems?"

Ferghal told him.

"Right, Tzurek, Jakobs, get cracking. Use the schematic and get those nodes open. Find the defects and let Warrant Mecklin and Sub-Lieutenant O'Connor check them and do the necessary."

When the Lieutenant and Captain were left standing alone, the Captain said, "What did that young Sub-Lieutenant mean about the ship saying it has other faults? How does he know?"

"Ah. He's got a bit of a special ability, very useful, actually. He can talk to the AI directly. Something to do with an implant neural link." Seeing the Captain's skeptical expression, he added, "Trust me. It works. When the ability to reroute around damaged components is blocked, by the failure of certain critical units, as an example, the AI goes into a form of shock and can't deal with the problem." He nodded toward Harry. "I may have to leave these officers with you for the run home to ensure the network doesn't go haywire."

Captain Reynard wasn't convinced. "How can such young officers help if that happens?"

"You'll find they are somewhat unusual—that's why they were sent." He looked up as Harry approached. "Yes, Mr. Heron?"

"The charts are loaded, sir, and the ship is calculating the course. I have established a link with *Daring* so that she can work with *Durham Castle*."

"Well done. As soon as Mr. O'Connor has finished his checks and replaced all the duff components he's found, I want to run a full check of all systems. Then we'll see how we go from there." The Lieutenant's link chirped in his ear. "Yes, Ferghal?"

"We've repaired everything we can, sir," Ferghal reported. "There are still a couple of systems we can't fix, but they aren't essential, or they can be run through another unit."

"Great stuff," said the Lieutenant. "Right, Mr. Heron, do your thing and monitor the ship's reactions. Mr. O'Connor, commence a full system check, please."

With the checks complete and the *Durham Castle* reassured by the link to *Daring* and to himself, Harry reported to the Lieutenant.

"Well done," said Lieutenant Lee. "You're to stay aboard her and make sure nothing else goes wrong between here and Pangaea." The Lieutenant grinned. "Lucky devils—I'm sure you and O'Connor are eager to get back to that planet." He noted Harry and Ferghal's wary expressions of dread. During their past two deployments to Pangaea, they'd had nothing but misery. "Enjoy yourselves," the Lieutenant added with a smirk.

"We'll be sure to do that, sir. We'll even make sure to have an extra bit of fun for you, sir!" Ferghal's infectious grin and forced exuberance got the round of laughter he was looking for.

In the Wardroom, Lieutenant Clarke sat in morose isolation. He'd never been popular, and was certainly not one of the Fleet's brighter stars. In fact, if it were not for a well placed relative in Fleet Appointments, he'd certainly not have this current posting with the opportunity it gave, according to the relative, to prove himself. His gaze swept the Wardroom, taking in several other officers studiously avoiding his company. Damn them!

A little more luxurious than the Senior Warrants' Mess, the Wardroom boasted several models of earlier ships named *Daring* and a large painting of a fine-looking steam-driven ship plowing through the water at full speed. The comfortably furnished lounge opened onto a formally arranged dining space as well as the short corridor that served the individual cabins for its occupants.

Still a little shaken by the close call with the asteroids, which even he admitted was his fault, he gulped his drink and almost choked.

"Damn them all," he muttered.

"You wish for another drink, Lieutenant?" The android steward startled him.

"No. No, I don't. Push off." Damned androids, they gave him the creeps. Sinking back into his anger, he nursed his resentment. He'd struggled to get this far in the service, and he wanted to make a success of it despite everyone being against him. Apart from anything else, if he failed, he knew that Delle, his demanding wife, would ditch him in a trice. He frowned at the thought. Damn! He loved her and let her walk all over him, yet she treated him like a child. He was convinced the only reason she stayed with him was because she liked the status that his rank and position gave her, and she was impatient for his promotion. She never missed an opportunity to press him about it.

Chapter 4

Ambushed

The return to the *Daring* after the idleness of their time on the *Durham Castle* came with mixed feelings. It was good to be back at work, but for Harry, it meant dealing with Lieutenant Clarke again. It also meant not being able to put through holocalls to Mary on a daily basis. Coms were restricted on patrol to avoid betraying the ship's position, and personal calls were completely barred.

Daring and *Diamond* dropped out in the system designated on their charts as LG-61 near a large unnamed planet with a dozen or more moons swirling around it. A small yellow star appeared on their screens with a number of planets in their orbits, some perilously close to one another.

"Scan shows no other vessels in this system," reported the TechRate on the scanner station.

"Good," Captain Aisha Maia acknowledged. "Maintain scan—active, alternating, passive. Consortium ships are known to be active in this area. Navigation, bring us to an orbit matching the outer moon. I want to do a deep scan of the planet and the moons."

"Aye, aye, ma'am," Harry responded, and the ship's heading changed.

Harry watched the navigation readouts as the ship slowed and closed on the coordinates for orbit. Checking the information logged on this system, he found plenty to interest him. A youthful system in cosmic terms, it had a rather violent collection of inner planets evidently still in the accretion phase. Four ice giants prowled in the outer regions, their orbits at least stable, each having a cluster of moons of varying sizes. On the boundary between the inner and outer sections, a solitary gas giant sailed majestically around the star sweeping up debris. It was resplendent with a series of spectacular rings and a host of moons, some larger than many of the inner planets.

Deep in the hull, in the Engineering Control Centre, monitoring the power generation plant, Ferghal listened to the flow of commands. With luck, they would have a bit of time now to carry out some maintenance. One of the hyperpods was showing signs of potential instability, a dangerous situation should it fail in transit while under power. He had reported this to his superior, and they had discussed what actions would be necessary when the opportunity arose. This looked like the chance—they would be in system and not using the pods for at least a week. Ferghal began to assemble his task list.

The friendship between Harry and Rasmus grew, their conversations ranging widely following on from their discussions of the manufacturing process for gunpowder in the eighteenth century. Rasmus wondered aloud where the saltpeter came from.

Harry thought of the best way to explain. "It is—I mean was—distilled from the urine of beasts and extracted from the dirt of cowsheds, stables and even the floors of the homes of the poorest in our society—a difficult process involving a great stink and much skimming of the crystals which grow in the vats."

Rasmus was baffled. "How was this collected? Was this the only source you had?"

"I'm afraid I don't know all of the sources, Rasmus." Harry laughed. "I was a user, not a manufacturer. But I believe that some was obtained from natural sources such as the waste of sea birds, from deposits in caves and in mines where such nitrates are found naturally. In the latter years of the war, I believe these sources had largely replaced the urine extraction method."

Rasmus laughed. "Were there any accidents in the manufacture?"

"Many, sir." Harry grimaced. "The manufactories are—were—dangerous places, and accidents resulting in fire or destruction were frequent. Though, it had become safer with the introduction of new mechanisms for mixing and grinding, and with greater regulation."

"Still exploring explosives, are you?" Ferghal joined them, adding to Rasmus, "Some will tell you that I am the destructive one, but Harry is far more dangerous. He thinks of mischief others would not consider or expect of him, and then he carries it through to the great detriment of those it is directed against."

"It is knowledge such as this that sets you two apart," Rasmus told him. "I have watched you with your models and your work with metals—there are not many people who can work raw steel or iron the way you do."

"It isn't difficult," protested Ferghal. "It requires only heat and tools—anyone can do it."

"Not quite," Rasmus told him. "How do you know when the metal is hot enough? How do you make the small items I have seen you make?"

Ferghal had, with the permission of the Engineer commander, set up a small forge, the furnace powered by electricity, in a workshop. He was currently building a scale model of HMS *Spartan*, and this required the forging of all the metal parts he needed. It went without saying that this was a major source of fascination for many of the crew—especially as the detail that Ferghal was building into the model included the creation of every item he could recall seeing in the real ship.

"Aye, well, it is just the look of it tells you. Then you must aim the hammer carefully, using it to shape the metal and bend it to your pattern."

"My point exactly, you know the appearance you need. Most of us wouldn't recognise it at all—and where are your patterns? In your head, I suppose." Rasmus had a sudden thought, and leaned back, his arms folded. "If necessary, could you make a gun—one that could use the powder Harry describes?"

"I suppose I could," said Ferghal. "It would be tricky, for it would require a mould and ingots or ore, and the smelting of iron, no easy business. If I were to do something of that nature now, I should probably attempt to use whatever was already available—anything to secure an easier life!" He chuckled.

The blaring sound of the general alarm interrupted them.

Rasmus found himself alone as Harry, Ferghal and several others in the Wardroom went from relaxed enjoyment to alert response and departure. It took seconds for the Wardroom to empty—yet not one of the officers broke into a run. Rasmus finished his drink and retreated to his laboratory.

Taking his place in Navigation, Harry reported himself ready. "Closed up for manoeuvring, sir," he said, activating his console.

"Very good, Mr. Heron. Wait for my orders. We respond only to orders from the Command Centre, remember—no independent actions." Aral Clarke's voice sounded tense.

Out of his view, the Chief Master Warrant rolled his eyes, and ComOp Maddie Hodges shook her head then focussed on her comlink monitors. Lieutenant Clarke was not one of her favourite officers. She'd served under a few she considered prats, but he made them look good by comparison.

Harry thought Clarke's instruction stupid and unnecessary. Of course he would wait for orders. The Captain was in command and must direct the ship.

He began to carry out the plot checks he would need for any evasive manoeuvres the Command Centre ordered.

"Navigation, give me an intercept course to the enemy position. Evasive plotting, please—I don't want to be a sitting target if they can predict it."

Lieutenant Clarke's nerves were stretched to the breaking point. "Give me a course, Mr. Heron—quickly." Before he had finished speaking, the helm instructions filled the displays.

Consulting his options list in the ship's databank, Harry connected to the AI. "*Daring, give me an optimum to intercept target, please.*"

The ship responded with a stream of coordinates and headings that adhered to standard Fleet La Grange manoeuvres.

"*Not the La Grange,*" Harry told the ship. "*Those are too predictable. Run in a counter pattern, please.*"

There was a moment of streaming data and a solution. The ship queried, "*Shall I transmit to helm?*"

"*Do it and link them to Targeting. Our enemy knows our LaGrange Manual as well as we do—that's why I don't want to use those manoeuvres. A counter pattern may surprise them.*"

"Course laid in, sir," Harry reported. He tried to keep the excitement out of his voice, conscious that mere seconds had elapsed.

"Took your time," the Lieutenant snapped. "Warrant, activate. Let's move, people."

The ship entered the first of the series of micro transits that Harry had calculated, dropping out of the final jump slightly behind and beneath the larger of the two enemy ships.

The Lieutenant noticed the variation immediately. "What are you doing? Revert to standard manoeuvres now! Otherwise, you'll throw Targeting off completely."

Harry corrected the courses, but he did so reluctantly. He could've predicted the result. Immediately the enemy was all over them, matching them move for move.

The ship shuddered as several plasma bolts struck her.

"Navigation, what are you playing at?" the Captain demanded. "Keep him guessing. Weapons will track the target—just keep it unpredictable."

"We're using standard manoeuvres, Captain," said Lieutenant Clarke.

"Damn the bloody standard manoeuvres," she replied. "The Cons are all over us! Give me something unpredictable." When Clarke hesitated, the Captain said, "Now!"

"Shall I?" Harry asked. Not waiting for an answer, he said, "*Daring, we need to run manoeuvres that defy La Grange—activate them quickly.*" The ship shuddered again, and he felt it suffer damage to a part of its neural system. Another lurch and he was thrown half out of his seat, catching his knee on the console and sending pain lancing up his thigh.

"You heard the Captain," snapped the Lieutenant. "Give us something that gets them off our backs!"

"Aye, aye, sir." Harry wanted to laugh at the irony, but he stifled it. He sent to the helm the manoeuvre that his instruction to *Daring* had produced. The change threw the enemy off. Dropping out slightly ahead and above the enemy, she sent fire at the other ship. Harry sent the next manoeuvre to the helm as the enemy recovered, which brought them to a new position directly alongside. Both ships snapped off a series of plasma blasts and scored damaging hits. Harry's next set of manoeuvres took them apart and clear of each other, the enemy's navigation station having guessed a different intention in *Daring*'s manoeuvre.

The next series of courses saw the ships close again, and this time the enemy succeeded in scoring the most damaging hits before Harry was able to break off and leap the *Daring* away. His next manoeuvre brought the two ships closer than he had intended, and the enemy ship sheered away—a move that threw her targeting system off, which allowed *Daring* to get in the heavier punch.

The ship shuddered, and an alarm displayed on Ferghal's console. He ran his checks, isolated the damaged controls and rerouted the commands as the *Daring* assisted him. He was aware of a sense of pain in the system. *"Easy,* Daring, *hold together for us, and we'll get through this."*

"I am taking damage to my neural net," the ship explained. *"The attacker is well handled, and her weapons are penetrating my shielding."*

Ferghal switched to another part of the system and adjusted several settings. *"Is that better?"*

"It helps, but I've taken damage to my hyperpods, and I have hull breaches in several place."

"Diamond joining," the links reported. "Enemy breaking off. Enemy ships have entered transit."

"Take us back to the planetary orbit, Navigation." The Captain sounded pleased.

"Don't any of you get big headed," Lieutenant Clarke said as soon as the Captain's order was acted on. "You were slow to respond there, Mr. Heron. You shouldn't have waited until the Captain demanded action. And your deviation from standard manoeuvres threw targeting off completely. You'll have to do a lot better next time."

Harry opened his mouth to respond, struggling to contain his anger at his superior's refusal to acknowledge that following the standard manoeuvres had resulted in near disaster. His voice taut, he said, "Very good, sir."

The Captain's voice on the link broke the tension. "Well done, Navigation. When you deviated from the standard manoeuvres, it foxed the enemy targeting completely. Good thinking to run a counter set and link helm to targeting."

Harry felt the hatred of the Lieutenant's glare. He concentrated on an assessment of what he thought of as *Daring*'s injuries, which might affect navigation, and felt it justified his act of disobedience.

The Master Warrant on the helm glanced at his assistant and shook his head knowingly. A few minutes later the stand down alert sounded, and the crew began the task of checking damage and carrying out repairs.

"We have some hull damage, but not enough to prevent transit, sir." Commander Nielsen accepted the seat the Captain offered. "Two sub-compartments are open to space, and we have one hyperpod non-operational. All weapons systems are operational, and we have no loss of manoeuvring ability. We have five dead and twenty-two injured. Whoever decided to abandon the usual engagement course variations did us a favour. The Consortium had us dead to rights and could've knocked us out if we'd followed standard manoeuvres."

"You're right, Anders." The Captain nodded. "It wasn't Lieutenant Clarke, but I doubt he'll admit it, or be prepared to do it again the next time. It's not his style."

"I'd like to relieve him of the role he's in, but we have no one else at that rank with the Nav ticket besides Heron. I've had a formal complaint from Mr. Clarke regarding Heron's objection to the standard manoeuvres. He claims it throws off our targeting. Weapons says that's rubbish, and I agree."

"I'll ask Command to replace Lieutenant Clarke as soon as possible. Heron's deviation saved us, and I agree with you."

"In the meantime, I'll deal with this complaint. I think I'll move Heron to the Emergency Helm in Action Stations as soon as I can get someone trained to assist in the Nav Control. It will keep things under control until we get a replacement."

"Hmm ... okay, but I'll have a serious talk with Lieutenant Clarke. He'd better get used to the idea of abandoning that damned manual."

Chapter 5

Close Call

The Fleet ship *Vengeance*, her consort *Victorious*, and their escorting frigates dropped out of transit on target, catching a Consortium convoy and its escorts by surprise. Captain Curran smiled in satisfaction. The intel reports had been spot on, and his squadron was in the perfect position to do some real damage to the enemy for a change.

In hyperpace, two cruisers and their three landing ship platforms, or LSPs, continued toward their destination. The squadron would catch up once this little task was complete. Curran was enjoying his independence as Captain of the *Vengeance*. Soon enough, Admiral Hartmann would be joining the ship when her command conference at HQ was completed.

He checked his deployments and activated his link. "Strike squadrons launch. Target the cruisers on their flanks as we engage." He watched his display as the strike craft erupted from the fins on either side of the ship. In the distance, *Victorious*'s squadrons were also deploying as they closed the targets. He activated his link again. "Signal the escorts. Target the convoy. We'll deal with the cruisers."

Midshipman Danny Gunn concentrated on his targeting plot. The ranges closed rapidly. Compensating for trajectory and speed, he kept his weapons locked to his target, his finger hovering on the firing command. Judging the moment, he touched the interface.

The five heavy plasma projectors erupted in a cone of fire enveloping the smaller cruiser in an incandescent halo. He maintained fire until the other ship accelerated into transit, a spreading cloud of debris suggesting serious damage. He switched to a new target.

"Cease fire," said the Lieutenant Commander in charge of Secondary Weapons Control. "We're disengaging. Remain on alert. They've retreated, but our intel says they have some big ships in the offing." He studied his scan display. "Good work. Three of their cruisers will need major repair, and the convoy lost six of the supply ships. That will give them a headache for a change."

The ten targeting stations acknowledged his order, and Danny adjusted his scan to increase its view. Next to him, his friend Midshipman Andy Kelly grinned. "Good shooting there, hotshot. I reckon your last target will need some serious repairs."

Danny grinned broadly, thrilled by the compliment. "Thanks, but yours didn't get off light either."

"Concentrate, you guys," Lieutenant Ramsingh interjected. "Stay alert. They could be back at any moment."

Captain Ben Curran listened to the damage reports coming in from his heads of department. His Command Chair occupied the centre point of the spherical display of their surroundings, an exact replica of that provided in the Admiral's Battle Command Centre. As each department and division reported its state and condition, he felt justifiably proud of his command. With their weapons still fully functional, shield generators at 98 percent, engineering undamaged, hull integrity good, all damage to the outer hull contained and leaks already being sealed or isolated, the ship was ready for battle again.

He was worried about the intelligence assessment, though; it mentioned three enemy starships operating in this sector against his two. His destroyer and frigate escorts were down in number as well—two detached to make their own way to the nearest repair facility, leaving eight of these small and handy ships as the eyes and ears for the starships and the two cruisers.

He keyed his link. "Patch me to *Victorious*."

"Gamal," Ben greeted the second ship's Captain. "The intel report suggests we could find ourselves meeting up with a superior force soon. I'm pretty sure our last targets were waiting for a fleet. I suggest that we should push on. The forces at Calistos need our support. Any delay could leave them cut off."

"I agree. Even if we do encounter a larger force, we still have superior firepower, and your ship has the particle beam projector. That thing was bloody effective at Pangaea."

Ben nodded. "Agreed, but it caused a few problems as well. The good news is Admiral Hartmann has signalled. She's on the ship *Admiral de Ruyter* and will join us in twenty-four hours. I'll get my people to signal course and head to the rendezvous." He grinned. "We gain some punch, and I lose my independence again."

"The penalty for being Flag Captain," laughed Gamal Weitz.

Harry strode into the Wardroom, dropped into a seat across from Ferghal, and accepted a drink from the android steward, who knew his preference by now. He'd just enjoyed a fabulous half-hour holocall with Mary and was feeling on top of the world.

"Back from your tour of the *Zukov* already?" he said to Ferghal.

"These repair ships are amazing. The repairs were so fast—all because we could be pulled into a bay and the work done under atmosphere."

The *Marshal Zukov* was a giant in every sense of the word. Having drawn the *Daring* into her huge repair bay, the securing arms embraced her as swarms of workers cleared her damaged sections. Ripping out entire modules, they manoeuvred new ones into place and quickly had the ship back to full fighting strength within a matter of days.

"Indeed," replied Harry. "And the ship reports that she is fully functional again—even better, she tells me, since she has also received some upgraded programming and new components to her neural net."

Ferghal laughed. "And to think that not very long ago, you and I had never heard of living machines or networks or artificial intelligence—much less ships which voyaged in the vastness of space."

"Just what Mary was teasing me about! She says my letters are full of how *Daring* says this, *Daring* says that, and new music I have discovered, thanks to *Daring*, and she knows *Daring* is female." Harry grinned.

"She's jealous! Who can blame the lass? You think more of the ship than of her!" Ferghal had the enjoyment of seeing his friend blush.

"Scoundrel. I do not! Mary is always in my thoughts."

"And in your dreams, I'll wager!" Ferghal deflected the cushion thrown at his head.

"What are you two laughing about?" Rasmus joined them. "Another of your jokes that play with words?" His expression was rueful. "It is something I will need explained, isn't it?"

"Not at all." Harry smiled in greeting. He had discovered that many of the jokes he enjoyed depended on wordplay and puns— and these did not always translate into another language. "We were laughing at ourselves and the fact that it is hardly four years since we were plucked from our sailing ship and a life of hardship to this age of wonders with all its conveniences. Until then we had never even considered the possibility of travelling beyond the sky in ships such as this."

"Oh." Rasmus studied them for a moment. "It is true, we forget that you are not, as you say, from this time. Yet you fit in so well and have adapted beyond everyone's expectations, exceeding our own abilities in some things."

"Well ..." said Ferghal, glancing at Harry. "We do have an advantage, but it came at a price, courtesy of the Johnstone Group and their dungeon lab on Pangaea."

"Yes, I know." Rasmus broke eye contact for a moment. "But look at how you work with the ships now. No one has been able to reproduce your ability, so there must be some other factor that has not been identified." He grinned and changed the subject.

"Oh, have I told you that some of our tests have been very helpful for my project."

Harry smiled. "I am happy to have been of assistance to you, Rasmus. I confess it has been most interesting—and some of the experiments were fun."

"Aye, and of some concern to those of us who must repair the equipment you two so happily damaged with your explosions," Ferghal added with a hearty guffaw. He had built an apparatus to allow the mixing of a variation on gunpowder that Rasmus concocted and Harry tried to make. A small miscalculation on Harry's part, unusual in itself, had resulted in the mixture igniting with a flash and a bang that had set off alarms in compartments adjoining the lab.

Rasmus laughed. "I apologise—we have miscalculated on occasion, but your work has been most helpful when we have done so." He was being tactful. Harry had, in fact, been careless because he was enjoying it so much, and the explosion and fire could have been much worse—not to mention, his eyebrows would take some time to grow back. He was lucky not to have suffered permanent damage.

"Captain Maia," said the Base Admiral as he greeted *Daring*'s Captain. "I've a new assignment for you, a bit of a haul across the sectors, I'm afraid."

"Yes, sir." The Captain nodded. "We're ready."

"I want you to carry out a sweep through this sector then pick up a group and take them to Pangaea. You can also drop off your semi-permanent resident scientist there, Rasmus I think is his name." He indicated a long patrol line through a sector on the borders of the area controlled by the Consortium. "There is another matter—they have a base or possibly a command centre equipped to intercept our signal traffic. We think they have cracked some codes and can work out deployment positions from it. We need to find it and put it out of action fast."

Captain Maia nodded again. "I heard that buzz. A leak in our Coms Branch is suspected. Just one question, sir. If this base is so important, why are they allowing the independents to operate on its doorstep?"

"Probably because it provides them a degree of cover for what they're up to. They may be after some alien tech as well. There's reported to be a lot of preserved cities on the planet and a primitive population that defends those cities but doesn't live in them. We think they are just on the border, and a couple of planets would support such a base in that general area. Your force is small enough to look for pirates yet big enough to carry the scan gear you need, and fast enough to outrun anything you can't out shoot."

"Yes, sir. Any hope of progressing my request yet?" The Admiral's quizzical expression prompted her to add, "— concerning Lieutenant Clarke's possible transfer."

"Ah, yes, that. I'm afraid not. I've read your report carefully and can see the problem, but we're very short of qualified navigators at the moment. I hope we'll have someone by the time you reach Pangaea though." Hesitating, he added, "I shouldn't tell you this, but the Lieutenant has, shall we say, some rather senior support. They don't want him moved for some reason."

"Mr. Gunn." The voice of the ship's Chief Warrant Officer was crisp. "Report to the Admiral's Command Centre, sir. You're assigned to her staff from today."

"Aye, aye, Chief." Danny grabbed his jacket and made for the door of his cabin tugging it into place and making sure he was smartly turned out as he hurried to obey. As he crossed the Gunroom, he passed his friend Midshipman Rob Shaw. "I'm summoned to Admiral Hartmann. I wonder what she's like to work for?"

"A real dragon," said Rob with a wily grin. "She eats Midshipmen for breakfast—poor old Spike Rajput is nearly a nervous wreck after only a month in her company. Good luck," he called as Danny shook his head laughing and exited the compartment.

His stride purposeful and brisk, Danny negotiated the several passageways and decks that led to the Flag Command Centre. Though this was not the first time Danny had seen this space, or the almost identical one on his guardian's flagship, *Vanguard*, he still found it awesome.

He spotted the Admiral conferring with her senior plot officers and the Flag Lieutenant. Approaching the platform, he waited until the Flag Lieutenant glanced his way as the other officers left to return to their own positions. Snapping a salute he said, "Midshipman Gunn, ma'am, reporting as ordered."

"Good." The Lieutenant acknowledged the salute. "You'll be on my team for the next few days, Mr. Gunn, handling signals and codes."

"Aye, aye, ma'am." Danny was conscious of the Admiral's penetrating gaze in his direction.

"Mr. Gunn, is it?" she demanded.

"Yes, ma'am." Danny stood to attention.

A flicker of a smile crossed the Admiral's face. "One of Admiral Heron's ancient mariners, are you?"

It seemed she intended this to be amusing, but Danny didn't want to second-guess her meaning and get it wrong, especially because her comment had dented his pride somewhat. Stiffening his back, he replied, "I have that honour, ma'am."

Admiral Hartmann laughed suddenly, turning heads. "You'll do, young man. James warned me you were inordinately proud of your association with Sub-Lieutenants Heron and O'Connor."

"They saved my life, ma'am, when I was a wee lad." He winced inwardly as soon as the words were out, and hoped he hadn't been too forward by interrupting her.

"Ah, yes, I recall the story—brave young men, all three of you. Now, as Mr. Radetski will tell you, I expect quick wits and accurate work. You'll be with my staff for a month, and I expect you to measure up."

"Yes, ma'am."

"I hear you are very good on targeting, and you're a fine musician," she added.

"I find the targeting quite easy, ma'am, and I enjoy the music."

"Well, I may require your company one evening, Mr. Gunn. I have a small group who join me for musical sessions. From what I'm told, you would make a good addition to our number. " Her link chirped, and she nodded a dismissal to Danny with a crisp, "Carry on."

Danny stood flustered, not sure what to make of her last remark.

The Flag Lieutenant signalled him. "This way, Mid. I've a pile of signals for you to process."

Danny found himself seated at a console and absorbed in processing the endless stream of signals between Fleet HQ and all the scattered squadrons, fleets and individual ships. Among the stream of orders, he saw one requiring *Daring* to complete her repairs and to sweep an enemy sector. He felt a twinge of envy. How he wished he could be with Ferghal and Harry instead of stuck on the flagship!

Touching his jacket pocket, he smiled as he felt the letter nestled there. Harry was such a fantastic friend and a real gent. Even when they had served on HMS *Spartan*, it had been said on the lower deck that Harry was a real officer, one who really cared for his people, and Danny had good reason to know that was true.

He still sometimes woke from a dream convinced that his elevation from illiterate powder monkey aboard a "wooden wall" sailing ship to Midshipman aboard a spaceship was just that, a dream. In a sense it was.

He snapped back to the present as he spotted a signal that looked out of place.

"Sir," he said to the Flag Lieutenant. "There's something odd about this signal. Message zero eight zero seven at eleven hundred stop zero five ordered *Daring* and *Diamond* to Sector NG Fifteen. Why would anyone repeat that signal to a base in Sector Four?" He frowned. "That's one of the bases we evacuated four months ago because the Consortium had overrun that area."

The Flag Lieutenant was at his side. "Show me."

"Mr. Heron." Lieutenant Clarke sounded even more irritated than usual. "The course you plotted doesn't comply with the standard routes for this Sector. I've told you before. You must not deviate from the Pilot Manual."

"Yes, sir." Harry's temper boiled at the Lieutenant's rudeness, and he had to force himself not to snap in response. "But there is a Fleet amendment in Pilot Note Four Zero Four One which directs that as the standard route is compromised, Fleet ships should adopt a course variant, and it provides options on five variations, sir. In plotting our present course I adopted Variants Three and Five."

"Pilot Note? What are you talking about?" Clarke reddened when he realised he'd just revealed his ignorance. "Oh—yes, yes, of course. Nevertheless, because I am your senior officer, you should have confirmed this with me before you adopted any variations." Even to himself Lieutenant Clarke sounded rattled. He glared at Harry. "Your independent attitude is a major problem, Mr. Heron."

"I beg pardon, sir." Harry's fists were tightly balled, and his knuckles were white as he struggled to hold his temper in check. "I shall refer all my course plots to you in future if that is what you require of me."

"What? No, that isn't what I meant." The Lieutenant seemed to be struggling with himself. "Damn it, Heron, just follow standard procedures in future."

"Aye—yes, sir." Harry watched the Lieutenant walk away and wondered what had occasioned this outburst. Surely, the Lieutenant had seen the Pilot Note and the warning that the standard courses were compromised and known to Consortium forces. *To hell with him*, Harry fumed, and he made his way to the laboratory. Rasmus was waiting to test a new mixture that promised to be even more powerful than anything they had tried so far.

Ferghal looked up as he was joined by one of the other Engineering Officers. "Hello, Hannes, what brings you to my forge?"

"A fascination," the newcomer replied. "I heard you hammering and came to see what you're making this time."

"Well, you had better put on some ear protection then," said Ferghal replacing his own. "This will be noisy—I must reform this blade, and that requires considerable hammering." He drew the glowing metal strip from the furnace and placed it on his anvil. Then, after a moment to study the metal, he struck it with the hammer, the blows seemingly random until the eye picked up the pattern. He finished and plunged the long strip into a tank of oily liquid. "There, it is done for now." He grinned at his visitor. "I can shut down the furnace and give your enviro systems a rest."

"Yes, we can always tell when you're using it." Hannes Lange grinned. "We get a real spike on our atmosphere controls as soon as it fires up." He nodded toward the smoking blade as Ferghal wiped it down. "And no wonder. That must get pretty hot. What is it, anyway?"

"A cutlass blade. I could get the replicators to make it, but the steel from them is a bit brittle, so I thought I'd forge one myself." He showed it to the visitor. "And it has turned out well."

Hannes opened his mouth to speak but was interrupted by the urgent sound of the general alarm.

In the Navigation Centre, Lieutenant Clarke settled into his seat, his heart racing. "Navigation Officer in post. I have the Con."

"Acknowledged, Pilot. Plot an intercept to the contact."

"Interception course. Yes, ma'am." Aral Clarke entered the coordinates then selected the standard manoeuvre options from his menus. Quickly he plotted in the manoeuvres for this system and the type of engagement suggested by the reported contact and sent them to the helm.

At his console, Harry watched as the coordinates streamed through the network. The ship jumped toward its target. Not for the first time Harry thought these manoeuvres were safe only as long as the ship's movements remained unpredictable. The trouble was that the enemy could, if they had access to the program or the Manual, predict exactly where a ship would emerge from the microtransits.

The shudder and the sensation of pain the ship felt as she emerged from the third sequence told Harry they had taken a heavy hit. He hoped the shielding would hold. He contacted Lieutenant Clarke. "Sir, I suggest a variation in the manoeuvres. The Consortium ships are using predictive shadowing, I think."

"You concentrate on your work, Mr. Heron, and I'll do mine," Lieutenant Clarke snapped even as the ship shuddered again. "I have the con, and we will do this exactly according to procedures!"

Harry acknowledged the order, but even as he did so, he spotted that they were about to jump into a possible trap. He flagged this up to Targeting, as he knew it would be futile to say anything to the Lieutenant. As expected, the ship dropped into the gap between three Consortium ships. Fortunately, thanks to Harry's alert, Weapons got in the first body blow, but the enemy returned fire, and *Daring* took a mauling.

"Navigation." Captain Maia sounded angry. "What the hell are you playing at? Give me some unpredictable evasions, please! I don't feel like being a sitting duck today."

"I'm doing my best, ma'am, but they're following our standard manoeuvres." The Lieutenant sounded nervous. His forehead glistened with sweat.

Captain Maia had had enough. "I've told you for the last time—throw that bloody book away and do something unpredictable! Use some initiative and get us clear of them!"

The Lieutenant looked at Harry, uncertainty in his eyes. "Suggestion, Mister Heron?" His sarcasm was poor cover for the desperation he felt. "You heard the Captain. You always have something clever to suggest."

"If I may suggest adopting a reversal of the La Grange, sir," said Harry. When he saw the Lieutenant's confusion, he added, "Shall I?"

"Do it."

"*Daring, remember the manoeuvres we used last time? Repeat them, but adjust them for this system.*"

The ship danced rings around her enemies, leaping in and out, throwing off their targeting completely until the five small attackers withdrew into hyperspace.

"Pilot." The Captain sounded angry. "I want to see you and Mr. Heron in my quarters once we have secured the ship and I can relieve you at the con."

The interview with the Captain was one-sided and brief. Neither Aral Clarke nor Harry was spared her tongue-lashing.

"You spotted the trap, Mr. Heron, and alerted Targeting—yet you let us enter it. Why?"

"Ma'am, I did not feel it proper to intervene with the con. Lieutenant Clarke had control, and he is my senior officer."

"Did you suggest anything that might have avoided this?"

"I did suggest that we deviate from the standard manoeuvres, ma'am."

Her gaze locked on the Lieutenant. "And did you consider this, Mr. Clarke?"

"No, Captain, I did not." He actually sounded proud of himself. "I feel very strongly that we should follow the procedures. They are intended to give targeting the best option for tracking the enemy."

"And does it occur to you that this particular enemy might have a copy of the standard maneouvers?" she snapped.

"That's not possible, ma'am." The Lieutenant looked shaken.

"Not only is it possible—it's the only explanation for the way they can track our evasions so accurately. This is the second time I've had to warn you about this. It stops now! You'll throw that manual away and use your initiative from now on." She held up a hand as the Lieutenant made to protest. "That's an order. Dismiss."

In the Consortium Base on Planet Lycania, Colonel Rees studied the strange buildings through his binoculars. This was the fourth of these alien cities they had tried to secure for the research team. Like all the others, the buildings looked like they had grown organically and not been constructed, and there were no furnishings or any indication of their function or use. Even more eerie, they were in perfect condition but unoccupied—until anyone attempted to examine them. Then the native population, nicknamed Rottweilers or Rotties by the Consortium troops because of their canine appearance and willingness to attack, swarmed into them and chased the intruders out.

"You say the Rotties attacked you as soon as your team tried to set up your equipment?" the Colonel asked a researcher.

"Correct, Colonel. As soon as we tried to take samples of the structural material, they swooped in seemingly out of nowhere. We tried to use a laser cutter to open a panel. Next thing they were all over us, and they weren't gentle about it, either."

"Your equipment?" The Colonel refrained from expressing his opinion. The xenobiological team had captured several 'specimens' and tried to run tests on them. They'd learned a little about these hominids that resembled rather savage bipedal wolves, but the specimens had escaped, and now they shunned contact, or were extremely forthright in repelling any attempt at contact or capture.

"The Rotties smashed everything. We were lucky to get away with our lives. I don't know what they're hiding in their cities, but it must be important. Damn, if we could just figure out how they grow these structures, imagine what we could do with that technology. These buildings self-regulate for temperature and interior lighting, they're weather- and stormproof, non-combustible in the main, and they can adjust to translucency."

The Colonel paused. He could imagine what some of the Board would do with it, and how they'd exploit it. "Right, well, my orders are to see that the Rotties are cleared out and that you and your people get what you need. I can give you a few hours. That will have to do. We can't take on the entire population even if they apparently have no modern weapons."

Chapter 6

Hopeless Position

———————————

Midshipman Daniel Gunn looked up when he heard his name called. Sub-Lieutenant Richthofen entered the Gunroom and made his way to where Danny stood waiting.

"At ease, Danny." Arno Richthofen grinned. "Your musical talents are required. The Admiral requests your company this evening. Take your flute and the rest of your favourite instruments with you, especially the ones you use for your folk music."

"Yes, sir." Danny returned the smile, but he was nervous. "I hope she's not wanting me to do a solo act for her."

Arno laughed. "No, she has a small group of officers who join her in a musical jamboree when she can spare the time. She plays the cello, but I expect you know that. The rest of the group includes Flags, her Writer, the Royal's Bandmaster and the Executive Commander." He grinned at Danny's expression. "And one of them seems to have shopped you and your ability with instruments—so now you are bidden!"

Danny grinned. "Any idea what she likes to play?"

"You name it—anything except pop music, I'm told."

"Pop music, sir?"

When Arno saw Danny's puzzled expression, he realised the young man didn't understand what he was referring to. "Never mind, you probably don't play any of that anyway. I hear that she's very good on her cello, so expect a real workout."

"Thanks." Danny gave a brisk nod. "I'll be prepared, sir."

Arno spent a few minutes discussing a change to the duty roster with another Midshipman, and then he left.

Immediately the Gunroom senior called across to Danny. "Don't go getting a big head now, Gunn. Playing music for the Admiral isn't going to get you any slack from the rest of us."

"I wouldn't dream of it," Danny retorted. "Should I play badly, do you think? Then, maybe she won't invite me back."

Several of the other Midshipmen hid smiles at this. Danny might be the youngest member of the Gunroom, but he had several times demonstrated his courage. They had begun to admire his refusal to succumb to the deliberate campaign of intimidation that Midshipman Gareth Arbiel waged against him.

Not once had Danny acknowledged the older man's constant barrage of insinuations. He had shown himself well able to deal with any attempt to intimidate him. Like Ferghal, he could be very direct in dealing with anyone who tried to rough him up, and similar to Ferghal, he usually had the aggressive edge needed to turn the tables in his favour. He hadn't spent his early childhood as an orphan on the rough streets of Portsmouth without learning some survival skills.

If only you knew what I endured in the lower decks of the Spartan *when I was just a boy*, he challenged the man inwardly. *I held my own, and I did so on the* Vanguard *when the Marines captured us.*

"Ignore him, Danny." Spike Rajput stood up. "He's just jealous. Don't worry, the rest of us will be praying for you tonight, especially now that you've survived a month as Flag's doggie without getting bitten by her too. Hard luck, old fellow."

"Thanks, Spike." Danny grinned, though he didn't feel happy about the baiting or the order to attend the Admiral's jamboree. He found the sniping from Arbiel tiresome, and sometimes wished he could talk to Ferghal or Harry about it. But that, in his eyes, would be to admit failure that he couldn't handle the men in the Gunroom on his own.

When he returned to his cabin, he collected his flute, a tin whistle, a small harp, his set of Celtic pipes and the music scores he thought might be appropriate.

The Consortium's assault on the chosen city site was going well.
"The Rotties don't have plasma weapons, sir. Just those dart bows
of theirs and those axe things they carry."

"They're not giving up though." Colonel Rees watched his
battle display. "A pity our stun settings don't seem to work on
them. They're damned determined to keep us out."

"Yes, and they're learning not to take us head-on." The
Captain watched his advance troops storm another building.
"They wait until we're inside, then somehow appear behind the
lads. Always have to watch your back, and they're bloody murder
up close."

"I see the troops are using grenades before entering any space.
The researchers are worried it might damage the sentient
buildings and make it difficult to get the samples they want."

"They'll damn well have to work with it," the Colonel
snapped. "This has cost us over thirty casualties already, and we've
killed a hundred or so of the Rotties for less than half this damned
city!"

The Captain shrugged. "They wanted one of the Rottie
corpses for research. We got them three. If they get nothing else,
that'll keep them busy."

"At least a dead one can't let itself out of the cage, overpower
three guards, release its friends, and walk out of the damned
facility!"

"Mr. Heron!" Aral Clarke sounded more than usually angry. Ever
since the Consortium destroyer had surprised the ship, he'd
become nervous and perpetually short tempered. "These latest
chart corrections—why didn't you check with me before you did
them? This means I have to change all my course calculations for
the next stage. If you'd told me, I could have saved myself the
effort."

Harry looked up in surprise. "I beg pardon, sir. I believe I
notified you through the correct procedure. I posted the notice of
changes as per the procedures on your console and the tablet. If
you prefer, I can do the adjustments to the courses. It won't take
me long."

"I'll do them myself," snapped the Lieutenant. He bit back a
further comment, but old habit made him unable to restrain
himself. "Damn it, Mr. Heron, I can't do everything and check on

your work too. You've really got to work with me—I must know before you take any action in future."

Harry was stung. His efforts to 'work with' the Lieutenant had so far earned him more hostility from that petty little man. "I always do my best, sir. I have followed your instructions and the procedures carefully in an effort to work with you, sir."

The Lieutenant frowned as he busied himself with his tablet. "But you still insist on working through that link of yours. How can I check your work if you refuse to do it the way the rest of us do? And your insistence on deviating from the standard manoeuvres has created all sorts of problems for me. Do you realise I have to rework all the LaGrange calculations so that we can take non-standard evasive action in future without reference to the Manual? Have you any idea how difficult that is?"

Harry opened his mouth to issue a snarky 'yes, I do in fact know how difficult it is to do it manually—do you?' but he restrained himself and took a deep breath instead. He had no doubt the Lieutenant was struggling to find the correct calculations. Harry had already found several that needed recalculating after the Lieutenant entered the data. The *Daring* herself had flagged up a number of serious errors.

Taking the respectful approach, Harry said, "I could assist you with those, if you prefer—I do enjoy the calculation of such tables, as you know, sir."

"So you can take even more credit from the Captain? No, I'll do them myself." The Lieutenant seemed to be running out of steam. In truth, he knew he had made several serious mistakes in the calculations, and he was terrified his inadequacies would be revealed. He sat down heavily. "Ever since you convinced her the standard manoeuvres were compromised, she's been giving me a hard time for using them. How the hell did you know the enemy could track our manoeuvring?"

Harry was surprised by the question. "It is obvious, sir. They managed to predict every move we made. They must have used the same standard manoeuvres we used. This was proved as soon as we changed the pattern. They couldn't match us move for move as soon as we deviated."

"So you say," the Lieutenant flared. "But it's also possible they would have lost the sequence if we had continued—but you had to interfere."

"I regret I cannot agree with you, sir." Harry stood his ground. "Mathematically, the odds of their having followed our movements so closely without being able to read our manuals are extremely remote. I have calculated ..." He broke off when the door opened and Commander Nielsen entered the office.

"Ah, good, you're both here." He nodded in acknowledgement. "The Captain is very pleased with your work, Mr. Heron. Now, to business: Mr. Clarke, the calculations on the alternative manoeuvres—I want them completed today for our next visit. The Peiho system is the last on our list of checks, and there's every chance we could run into trouble when we start that survey." He looked directly at the Lieutenant and held his gaze. "The Captain is very clear on this. The standard manoeuvres are to be abandoned. She wants it understood once and for all that they are not, under any circumstances, to be used in future. Am I clear?"

Aral Clarke felt the sweat prickling. He daren't admit that the replacement calculations were a long way from finished, or that he had not, as yet, removed the standard evasion programming from the system.

The best he could offer was a subdued, "Yes, sir," and get the hell out of there as soon as he was dismissed.

The Captain activated her comlink as the display of the Peiho system sprang into focus. "Scan, check for any signs of mining activity in system, especially in the ring systems round the inner planets." The system lay just ahead of the ship, the various planets each showing a marker against the background starscape.

"Yes, Captain." Lieutenant Barolong nodded to his senior ScanTech, who was already on it. "Some anomalies are showing up around the fourth planet. Could be auto mining equipment, but we'll get a better idea when the drones can be moved closer in."

"Okay, as soon as we complete the outer circuit." Captain Maia watched the data scrolling across her screen then looked at the starscape displayed around her. Something was out there, but where? To herself, she added, "And more importantly, what?"

"Sorry, Captain?" Commander Nielsen looked at her.

"Talking to myself, Anders. Sorry." The Captain flashed a smile. "We've swept through four out of five systems looking for the proverbial needle in a haystack. There has to be something—but where? And what the hell are we looking for?"

"Good question—a Consortium base, according to our orders, but what sort of base? I've checked and double-checked. All HQ can tell me is that it is on a planet, and they are now reasonably certain it's in this sector." He indicated a small bright dot in the display. "My bet is it's there, on the fourth planet. It's got a population, some sort of anthropoid life form. A mining survey was done before all this started, and the Johnstone Group applied for permission to establish a research station there to investigate some new species and alien artefacts. It was granted, and I think they put a construction team in. It's reported to be evacuated. If I were looking for a place to build a base in a hurry without arousing suspicion, I'd choose someplace like that."

Captain Maia nodded, her face thoughtful. "You're right. Thanks for putting your finger on it." She activated her link. "Navigation, prepare to move us into orbit mimicking the usual track of the planet Lycania, but keep us far enough out to avoid raising any alarms."

"Yes, Captain," said Lieutenant Clarke. "I'll have the course laid in a few minutes."

"As fast as possible, please." The Captain turned to the Commander. "If we're right, there may be a hostile reception. Sound action stations."

Harry dozed, his book open in his lap. The alarm startled him. Leaping to his feet, he made for the door, his book forgotten in his haste to depart. Behind him, Rasmus picked it up and placed it on the table, and followed the last of the officers as they exited the Wardroom, but he headed to his laboratory.

In Engineering, Ferghal slid into his seat and linked himself to the ship. "Daring, *tell me what happened.*"

"*The Captain ordered Action Stations as a precaution. I am moving into position in the fourth planetary orbit so we may observe the fourth planet without being too close.*"

"*Thanks.*" Ferghal was relieved to hear this. They had seen more than enough action lately. He focused on his screens and checked his team. The ship shuddered as she dropped out of the brief transit and decelerated.

"Scans on Planet Lycania, Northern Hemisphere, all electronic signatures and any signal beacons." The Captain's orders were quietly given, but her face was taut as she stared at the image of the planet on the view screen. "Focus on the major landmass in the eastern half of the Northern Hemisphere."

"Yes, Captain." Lieutenant Clarke seemed distant and pre-occupied, but the Captain tried not to let that worry her.

An alarm blared, jolting everyone to action.

"Ship in system, closing fast. She's firing on us!"

"Return fire." Captain Maia gripped the arms of her command chair. "Navigation, commence evasive action. Coms, send the Under Attack signal and our position."

The ship shuddered as it received a devastating hit.

"Damage report," barked the Captain.

"Two hyperpods destroyed," Commander Nielsen reported from the Damage Control Centre. "Manoeuvring is restricted, but we can still fight the ship."

"Our signals are being jammed—hypercoms are out," reported the Coms Officer.

"Damn. Engineering, keep us moving as best you can. Weapons, hit him as hard as possible—keep firing no matter what happens." She winced as another shudder rippled through the ship. "Navigation, bring us about and head toward the planet. Let's try to pull him into the ring system round Lycania."

In the Emergency Helm position, Harry checked the manoeuvring orders and grimaced. He could not believe it. Lieutenant Clarke had reverted to his beloved LaGrange Manual again, and this time in direct disobedience of the Commander's orders. No wonder the enemy was all over them. Even worse, Harry was no longer in the Navigation Centre with the Lieutenant, so there was nothing he could do to correct it. He winced as the ship cried out in his head. *"Aaaah! I can't hold together much longer, Harry."* The *Daring* sounded strange in his ears. *"My signals are disrupted and do not reach the relay. I can no longer transit."*

"Hold up, old girl. The Captain is doing all she can to shake him off."

"But I cannot transit, Harry, and we are approaching a dangerous orbit path that will bring me within the orbit of the larger moon." The ship shuddered again. *"And I have just lost the last environmental lung space."*

Harry ran a check. It wasn't reassuring. The ship had suffered major damage, structurally as well as mechanically. He could feel the AI losing its capacity to reason, and he realised the ship was dying even as he listened. Feeling helpless and rather alone, Harry fumed. Why couldn't Clarke understand that most situations were nonstandard at best? He felt very uncertain of what to do now. He couldn't find Ferghal through the system and was worried that something had happened to him.

"Abandon ship. All hands, abandon ship. Muster at the life pod stations and commence evacuation immediately." The Captain's voice was calm as she spoke over the comlinks. She switched to a personal channel. "Engineering, transfer propulsion to my console, please, and evacuate your station." She switched channels again. "Navigation, switch helm to my station, then clear out."

There was no response.

She tried again. "Navigation. Lieutenant Clarke, transfer control to my station."

Again, there was no response. She switched channels and contacted the Emergency Helm Station. "Mister Heron, do you have the con?"

"No, ma'am, but I can acquire it. Has the Lieutenant fallen?"

"He doesn't respond. Transfer the con to my console and get to a life pod." She felt tired. The helm information joined the propulsion data on her console. She punched in her orders and waited. The last life pod indicators signalled their departure. "Good," she said to the empty Command Centre. "All our boys are away. Now we'll take at least some of the bastards with us as we go, old girl."

Leaving the Emergency Helm position, Harry hesitated. Should he run to his cabin to retrieve the letters he'd written to his family? There were at least three, and paintings for Mary among the several waiting to be shipped home. "No time," he told himself, making his way swiftly to the life pods. It had been two weeks since his last call to his sweetheart. The embargo on personal communications while they were in enemy space irked him. This deep in hostile territory, the ship had been running with communications in receiving mode only. He thought of the unfinished letter to Mary and to his Aunt Niamh as he made for the life pods.

He dove through the last door and entered the life pod station just in time to see the last hatch seal. Fear clutched his heart as he realised that the other bays were already empty. He raced to the next station and found those already gone. Turning, he retraced his path across the dying ship and collided with Abram Winstanley, the ship's Coxswain.

"All the life pods seem to have departed in this section, Swain." He gasped for breath. "Any left on the other side?"

"None, sir," replied the Coxswain grimly. "And several of us are still aboard, including your scientist mate."

"Rasmus? How? Where's Lieutenant Clarke?"

"Gone, sir. Didn't hang about. Soon's the abandon ship was ordered ..." Abram Winstanley left the end hanging. "I stopped to help a couple of the lads, sir."

Harry had a thought. "The hangar deck. Quickly. There may be a barge or a launch left. Round up everyone. Let's go!"

A motley collection of survivors joined Harry at the access to the hangar. A red light flashed above the door. Glancing through the glass panel, he stepped back and ordered, "Rig in EVA. The bays are open to space, but one of the launches is still intact by the look of her." As an afterthought, he added, "Make sure you take all your normal kit with you. We'll need it on the surface."

A scramble to obey ensued, and in record time everyone, including Rasmus, was rigged and cycled into the hangar, each one clutching a bundle of clothing to his suited chest. The launch proved to have some damage, but this was not in a vital area and would not affect re-entry—or so they hoped.

"Hope we're right, sir." The Coxswain grimaced as the Engineering TechRate finished the checks a bit too methodically for his liking. "Run a check on everything else—quick as you can," he growled at the man. "We don't have time to spare, and if she breaks up on re-entry, we might as well have stayed aboard."

"Right." Harry glanced around the group of suited figures. "Which of you is a pilot?" There was silence.

The Coxswain glared at the group. "Come on then, don't be bloody shy. What about you, Skoronski? Hodges?"

"Not me, Swain, Propulsion Operative, that's my line," said Skoronski.

"ComOp, Swain," said TechRate Maddie Hodges. "Sorry, no can do."

With a shock, Harry realised the TechRate was a woman when he heard her voice, something he hadn't expected because she was nearly as tall as he was and strongly built, and much of her shape was hidden in the bulky suit. When he took a surreptitious closer look, he could see her womanly figure, though she was very muscular and athletic. Adding to his confusion was her rather androgynous face and very short haircut, shaved on one side of her head with long dark-black bangs. Capping off this look, she had several ear piercings in the exposed ear, which he could only liken to the adornment of pirates in tales he'd read as a boy. She was altogether fascinating, and for several moments, Harry felt so flustered he couldn't think straight.

Snapping out of his lull in thinking, he remembered the urgency of the situation. "Take the Engine position then," Harry said to Skoronski. "We'll have to figure this out quickly. The Captain is planning an ambush. She thinks the ship's clear of everyone." He slipped into the pilot's chair of the launch and secured himself. "This will be rough, so strap in!"

He linked to the launch's AI. These were less sophisticated versions of the AI network on the parent ships, and he hoped this one would be intelligent enough to give him the help he needed.

Harry thought of the most logical command he could give the launch. "Delta Two Four, *start your lift engines and disengage your docking ties, please. Then move us clear of the bay.*"

After a brief delay, Delta Two Four responded. *"Please engage the navigation yoke and guide me through the docking bay doors."*

"Very well." Harry already felt impatient. He grasped the yoke and moved it gently as he had seen pilots do on numerous occasions. The launch responded, swinging dramatically and heading toward the bulkhead next to the door. Harry swore under his breath and swung the yoke in the opposite direction. Three or four attempts saw him successfully turning the nose toward the opening.

"Hold a steady path through the opening, please," Harry ordered.

"I cannot see the opening," came the response.

"Use my eyes." Harry was irritated at having to give the most basic, obvious commands to the launch. Clearly, some parts of its

AI network weren't working correctly. He wondered what damage might be lurking undetected.

"You can see what I see," Harry explained. *"Now move us out of the ship."*

"Is this how humans see? I usually use my scanners. If you engage them to auto, I can use them instead."

Harry threw a desperate glance at the console. He couldn't see anything that resembled a switch for the scanners. *"Engage your scanners to autopilot,"* he ordered the launch. *"You know how to do it!'*

They cleared the bay just as the *Daring* swung toward the enemy cruiser. Captain Maia had timed her move to perfection, and the enemy cruiser lost almost its entire forward end as the dying *Daring* smashed into her. The distraction allowed the launch to descend into the atmosphere of Planet Lycania undetected by the Consortium scan operators, who marked its descent as a large piece of debris, one among many in the storm of ship sections that rained into the atmosphere for the next several hours.

Aboard the *Delta Two Four*, Harry had the bemused thought that communicating with the launch's very basic AI was like explaining something to a child. *"Now, just keep level and straight. I think there is a good landing place on the plateau."* Harry sought the coordinates and identified them to the launch. He hoped his rather hasty survey was right when *Delta Two Four* complained that he was not piloting it properly.

This was going to be damnably difficult, but they had no other choice. How long could they survive on this planet? They had no real knowledge of it and almost no survival gear. He wondered if anything on the surface would serve as nourishment. Deciding to deal with that problem when it was relevant, he focused on landing the launch.

"This is going to be a bit rough, I fear," he told his passengers.

"It's a bloody miracle you've got us this far, sir," Coxswain Winstanley chipped in. "I reckon we only need to land once as long as it's in one piece!"

"I'll do my best, Swain." Harry managed a grin, adrenalin and bravado making him reckless. "But I'm no pilot, and the launch isn't being helpful."

"Well," Rasmus cut in, "I'm told any landing you can walk away from is a good one!"

Everyone laughed at that comment.

"Remind me of it when we're on the surface, Rasmus," said Harry with a grin. He coaxed the launch to bring them down gently and level on a narrow strip of open ground as he guided it with the yoke and the rudders.

Barely fifty miles to the west of where Harry was attempting to land, Lieutenant Clarke mustered the survivors from the twenty or so life pods that had landed as a cluster. He looked about him anxiously. Heron wasn't present, so there was a good chance he was dead.

Several other Lieutenants were present, but none more senior than he. The senior officers were either not present or not in a state to take command. This meant he could take charge—and he had already decided his course of action.

"Right. Mr. Barolong, Mr. Matthews, organise the Rates please. I want all weapons handed in. I'm pretty sure the Consortium's people will be here soon, and we aren't going to resist. Our people have had enough. We'll surrender as soon as they get here, then our wounded can get treatment and shelter." He frowned as Paul Barolong made to protest. "No arguments, Paul. I'm the senior!"

"Yeah, right," came the retort from Lieutenant Matthews, who gave him a cold look. "So you're ordering us to surrender, are you? Will you also be assigning our cell block numbers when we're prisoners of war?" He shook his head in disgust.

Clarke ignored that last comment. "We have wounded men and scarcely any supplies to feed or treat our people. I don't like it either, but we have no other option."

"Like hell you don't—*sir*." Paul Barolong snapped a perfunctory salute and followed his fellow Lieutenant to carry out the order, his brow furrowed with grim reluctance.

Chapter 7

Survivors

Ferghal came round to find himself lying on an inflatable bed. His head hurt, and his left arm felt numb. He tried to push himself up, but pain lanced through his left arm and leg, and he fell back with a gasp.

"Easy, sir." The soft voice of the MedTech penetrated the fog in his head. "You've got a broken leg, and your elbow was dislocated. You're lucky your people got you into a pod for EVAC. Trouble is you need a spell in a med-unit, and we haven't got one. I just hope the Consortium people have."

Ferghal gathered his wits and asked, through gritted teeth, "Where's Harry? Is Mr. Heron here?"

"He's not come down, sir. They say he didn't make it off the ship." She eased him into a more comfortable position. "Now take it easy, sir, and I'll get you something for the pain."

Harry, you can't be dead, old friend! You can't leave us like this. I won't believe you've gone—I'll keep looking for you until I find you.

He felt a needle in his arm, and the world darkened again, and he drifted into an uneasy sleep disturbed by confused dreams of his and Harry's boyhood, which morphed into dreams of their adventures on HMS *Spartan* and the recent events that had landed him here. He was completely unaware of the arrival of the

Consortium force and the discussion between Aral Clarke and the Consortium Major, who accepted Clarke's surrender.

The launch dipped then steadied as Harry concentrated on coaxing it into as normal a landing as possible. The ground was coming up fast now.

"Brace yourselves," Harry called over his EVA comlink. "I don't think we're going to land softly."

He was right. The landing was rough, not only because the launch's AI chose the moment of touchdown to lose a large part of its circuitry, but because the ground, covered by short, rough vegetation, wasn't exactly level. The undercarriage collapsed, dumping the launch onto its belly and throwing the occupants hard against their restraints as it crashed through the vegetation shedding chunks of itself. It finally came to rest at the end of a trail of wreckage, the fuselage miraculously still in more or less one piece.

"Everyone okay?" The Coxswain was the first to recover. "Get the doors open."

"Thanks, Swain." Harry made a quick check of the AI and discovered it had become just a simple programmable circuit, its self-awareness apparently gone. He levered himself free of the seat and turned round to look at his crew. "Everybody out. I think our launch is unlikely to be useable from here on."

"Well, mein freund, at least we walk away. A good landing, I think."

Harry laughed. "If you say so, Rasmus." He cast his eyes about the landing area. "Anyone hurt?"

A chorus of negative responses was reassuring. Instinctively, Harry checked the group for ComOp Hodges, having been raised to protect the safety of women first. She was joking with one of the men and seemed to be enjoying some banter.

"The pods will have been programmed to make a landfall close to one another," said the Coxswain. "I think they must have come down in a bunch to the west." He glanced at Harry. "Engineering took a real beating, sir, but I think most of them got away. Their control room is close to a cluster of life pods."

"I hope you're right, Swain. I hope you're right." Harry sent a prayer heavenward. *Lord, look after Ferghal. If he be dead, keep his soul, and if he be alive, grant that we may be reunited speedily. If it be your will that I lead these brave souls, grant me the wisdom to do so wisely and the strength to do it for as long as need be.*

"Well done, Major." Consortium Brigadier Newton was pleased. "Are you sure you have all the survivors?"

"Yes, ma'am, Lieutenant Clarke is certain that all the survivors are accounted for. He seemed almost eager to be taken prisoner." He grinned. "Couldn't wait to hand over a complete list of everyone he had with him, and some of his fellow officers aren't too pleased about that." He shrugged. "It might have been very different if Commander Nielsen had been in a position to take command. I've put him in separate accommodation, if one can call it that. His injuries are stable now. He should make a full recovery."

The Brigadier nodded. "Good thinking. Perhaps we can get some useful information from them individually. Separate all the officers and NCOs from the rest and from each other. You never know what we may learn if we get them talking by playing them against one another."

"Already in hand," the Major replied. "And there's a bonus. We have one of that pair the Board had put out an all points bulletin on—the ones supposed to be from the nineteenth century. He's in a med-unit, quite badly beaten up. According to Lieutenant Clarke, he can manipulate any AI without using an interface."

"Now that is something. Which one have we got, Heron or O'Connor?"

"O'Connor is the name I have here." The Major looked up from his tablet. "The Lieutenant seemed to think the other one died on the *Daring*. He's not among the survivors."

Ferghal's head felt much better when he awoke. His attempt to move was frustrated by his enclosure in the med-unit, though it took him a few seconds to recognise it, and that sent his thoughts hurtling back to his awakening on *Vanguard* almost four years previous. He lay still, his eyes shut tight as he tried to steady his thoughts. Where was this place? And where was Harry? He tried to link to the AI and discovered that he could only connect to the med-unit he was lying in. Everything else was nothing but a garbled buzz in his head.

"Good, you're awake, Mr. O'Connor." The voice came from out of his line of sight. "As I'm sure you've discovered, you can't access our network—a simple precaution to ensure you don't escape."

"Where am I?" Ferghal opened his eyes and tried to make out the details of his surroundings. "Where are the rest of our people? How do you know who I am?"

"The rest of your people are in the main camp." An attractive woman moved into view. "You're in our special lab. Your Lieutenant Clarke was kind enough to supply us with all your names. He identified you when we recognised your name and service number on the list."

Ferghal snorted. "Typical. Bloody traitor."

"Depends on your point of view." The woman smiled an empty smile that didn't reach her eyes. "You see, we couldn't take the risk of you getting into the network at the base. You're in an isolation lab, and we have a special screen to prevent you linking to anything outside this space."

"What do you intend to do with me?" Ferghal kept his voice level.

"Some of our top scientists are on their way to examine you and find out why you are able to interact with AI networks through your thoughts alone." The woman seemed a little annoyed. "Several of us here are trained to do all the tests and investigative procedures, but you will make someone's name famous."

"You spáilpíns will get little enough from such tests," Ferghal snapped, using one of his favorite Irish insults. "Your people did their worst on Pangaea."

She ignored his comment. "I must say you're quite a fine specimen." That comment rankled, but Ferghal chose not to respond. He didn't need her twisted form of flattery. "Your leg is healing nicely, and your arm is almost back to normal. You had a rather nasty dislocation of your elbow and a massive contusion— but it has all sorted itself out rather better than I thought it would. You must have taken a very hard knock to do that damage."

"I suppose having a console land on you can be counted as a hard knock."

Ferghal vaguely remembered what had happened. The last thing he could recall was an explosion and then searing pain as a bulkhead collapsed and a console fell and pinned him to the floor.

He made another attempt to link to an AI and succeeded in accessing the medical network, but this time he ran into a problem he had not encountered before. The system demanded he submit his security access code. He wondered what this might be, then he had a stroke of luck. Through the network, he watched someone in the building enter a code and gain access. That was all he needed.

Badly shaken by the narrowness of their escape, Harry wrestled with the inconceivable thought of losing Ferghal. He was certain his lifelong friend had died in the *Daring*, and he felt utterly alone now, bereft of hope and ill equipped for the task ahead of him.

He pushed his anguish aside and set to thinking while studying the terrain.

Twisted spires of rock glistened with silicates and pyrites, the eroded shapes forming fantastic sculptures that gave a hint of ferocious winds and extreme temperatures of heat and cold. The vegetation was spiky. Leathery foliage furled or turned to catch the light of the bluish sun that gave the landscape a cold florescence.

The wrecked launch made a forlorn sight in the devastated vegetation littered with its debris.

Their situation seemed hopeless. They had few weapons, no transport and very little in the way of food. Harry looked around at the people with him, a motley collection of twelve men and one woman, excluding himself. There was Rasmus, who had no business being with them anyway, and the rest of the crew represented almost every department of the ship. Three had minor wounds, one a sprained wrist and all of them were tired, shaken and hungry. He stood up. He was the officer, and officers had to lead their people. He put his doubts and uncertainties aside.

"Right, Swain," he said. "We can't stay here, and there's nothing salvageable of the launch. Set the demolition charges, and then we'll get everyone moving. We'll use the lift packs in the suits to go into those hills. I want to get off this plateau and into some shelter before sundown in case anyone comes poking around the wreckage. As soon as we're clear of this place, we can stop for refreshment."

"Right you are, sir." The Coxswain turned to the group. "Right, you lot, you heard the Lieutenant. Keep below the treetops and stay together. Turner, Singh, Maroti, Kemp, you're carrying the kit packs for now. We'll change round at the next leg."

Harry walked over to Rasmus. "I meant to ask, have you had any training in the use of the EVA suit you're wearing?"

Rasmus grinned. "Nein. But I think I am about to learn very quickly."

Harry said, "I fear it might be a crash course if we are not careful. Allow me to assist you." He entered a set of coded instructions into the control panel on the suit. "Very good. Now, it should only be necessary for you to press the enter command, and the suit will lift you. Once airborne, you will need to emulate our actions." He attached a long tether. "This will allow us to keep you in our wake until we can teach you to fly the suit yourself."

Rasmus was not impressed. "So, you do not trust me to do this myself?"

"On the contrary." Harry tried to be diplomatic. "It's just that we do not have time to show you properly. This is merely a temporary fix. I will ensure that you are given the proper training as soon as we are safely away from here."

Rasmus laughed. "Okay, tow me away, Mr. Heron."

Harry grinned in relief. "Thank you, Rasmus." To the Coxswain he said, "Very well, Swain, let's get airborne."

Almost a hundred miles to the north of their landing position, Harry spotted what he hoped would be a shelter they could use. The plume of smoke that marked the destruction of *Delta Two Four* had long since faded from view. "There, Swain." He pointed. "Follow me down."

The small party made a slow descent onto a wide ledge that sloped toward an opening in the shoulder of a steep ridge. Below it, a long steep slope of broken rock stretched down toward a gentler incline dotted with low-growing bushes. A stream poured itself over a series of steps to the left of the opening, which Harry investigated with careful attention. It showed signs of having been occupied at some time, but there was no indication of recent habitation.

"Move our people into the cave, Swain. This planet is subject to sudden and very violent storms according to what little I managed to learn of it. This cave has water and a good vantage point, both of which are necessary while we establish where we are and what we can do about it." He glanced at the men. "Get our equipment under shelter. I want a sleeping area set aside, and a clearing where we can cook and work."

"Aye, aye, sir." The Coxswain grinned and threw up a salute.

Harry returned it with a smile then spoke to the scientist. "Rasmus, I think you'll have to take charge of our food supplies and the cooking." He grinned. "I know—it is not your normal line of work, but I fear we will all have to learn some new skills very rapidly if we are to survive this scrape."

Rasmus shrugged. "I shall try not to poison anyone. Maybe my skill with chemical concoctions will come in handy making a stew of some sort."

Harry grinned. "Good. Sounds like you've got that under control. I'll trust you to it."

"I'll give Mr. Rasmus a hand, sir." A TechRate named Turner interjected. "I can cook some of the basics anyways."

His companions laughed. "You? Cook?"

The Coxswain returned. "I suggest that we shut down all our electronic gear, sir. The enemy will be able to track us if we use anything electronic in any location where they don't have settlements or patrols. It'll be a dead giveaway."

"You're right." Harry gave himself a mental kicking. "I should have thought of that. Shut down everything electronic immediately."

Aboard the *Vengeance*, Admiral Hartmann checked her messages again. "Contact with the *Daring* has been lost. Do we have a plot on her last known position?"

Danny Gunn's heart skipped several beats as he listened.

"Yes, sir. Her last contact position was at Sigma Sol. She left there a week ago in transit to the Peiho system, her destination being Planet Lycania. She was due to send her Mission Completed Report two hours ago. Her location beacon went offline as per standard procedures when entering enemy space, and we can't make contact."

"What have we got in that area?" The Admiral was brisk as she got out of her Command Chair and made for the huge display that showed the dispersal of her forces.

"Nothing within less than a month, and most of it small stuff."

"Damn. Very well, order the nearest ships to do a sweep of everything along the line she would have taken." She paused to consider her next decision. "Order Task Group Bravo to get underway to Sigma Sol, and get my Command Team in here immediately. I'll want the search extended. If the *Daring* has run into a superior force, I want to know where and why. That area is supposed to be only marginally occupied—no traders, no bases— so what are we missing?"

"Er ... sir?" Errol Hill, TechRate First Class and Weapons Specialist, sounded concerned.

"Yes, Hill?" Harry looked across to where the TechRate stood staring out at the cavern that was their temporary home.

"We have company, sir, non-human, and I think they may be hostile."

"Don't show any weapons. We don't want to provoke them. Everyone stay as you are, but be ready to respond if they attack." Harry moved to stand beside the sentry. Glancing about and seeing nothing, he asked quietly, "Where away?"

"Over there, sir." Errol Hill indicated a rocky outcrop. "There's two at that outcrop and another four or five lower down the slope."

"Ah yes, I see them, but I don't see any weapons." Harry grabbed his ranging optics and surveyed the strangers. He could see that they carried packs of some sort and what appeared to be rather sophisticated metal tools, which could also be used as weapons.

The creatures stood on two feet, but that was the limit of their resemblance to anything human. Their forearms were longer than a man's and much thicker, joined to wide shoulders and a thick neck. A distinctly canine head topped a heavy body supported on short powerful legs. They were clothed head to toe in garments that had a rubbery appearance, blue-black in color and form fitting like a scuba suit. It was apparent, by their mannerisms and the obvious sophistication of their clothing, that they were intelligent.

Harry watched as one signaled the others, who then retreated into cover.

"Stay here and don't make any threatening or sudden movements," he said to TechRate Hill. Stepping forward several paces to the lip of the ledge, Harry kept his hands clearly in view. He eased down and unbuckled his weapons belt, and placed it on the ground beside him. Moving his hands to where he could put them on his knees, he nodded his head to the leading alien. Behind him, he could hear the Coxswain telling the others to keep still but be ready to move in Harry's defence.

"Is he mad?" Rasmus whispered.

"Absolutely bloody certified, sir, but I'd rather work with him than some of the others I've had to serve under. He's mad in a very intelligent way, and gets it right most of the time."

"I know he led a crew that brought back a captured freighter about a year ago," said Rasmus. "There was something about him and Ferghal using swords to attack the ship's crew."

"That's the story, sir." The Coxswain's voice was taut. "And if he can keep us out of the jug here, I reckon we might be in for some interesting times." He tensed. "Be ready, people—the leader's moving this way."

Harry tensed as the leading alien approached. As it got closer, he could see just how powerfully built it was. It moved with the stiff-legged motion that a dog or perhaps a wolf might use when approaching an enemy. Full of menace, it conveyed the impression of being ready and willing to respond to any threat.

In that moment, it clicked into Harry's memory: he had read about these creatures known as the Canids, and now he understood why that name had been chosen to designate them. They reminded him of very powerfully built dogs, or possibly wolves, that stood and walked upright. When he made that correlation, and remembered that they'd been nicknamed the Rotties after the fierce, powerful breed of dogs known as Rottweilers, he knew that he needed to approach them with a great deal of caution and respect. The record said they were nomadic, unsophisticated and possibly a degraded remnant of a more advanced species.

As the leader approached, Harry forced himself to relax, his artist's eye recording details of the Canid's clothing and physique. It was obvious these beings had access to sophisticated materials and tools. The thought crossed his mind that he and his men might benefit from this, or better yet, gain access to the uniforms, suitably adapted, of course, to human physiognomy, to help them survive in this alien environment.

The Canid leader stopped a few yards in front of him and sniffed the air, its upper lips curled back baring the tips of a powerful set of teeth. He appeared uncertain, and Harry knew that uncertainty could lead to a sudden and dangerous response, so he turned his hands palms up to show he had no hostile intent— praying that these creatures would understand the gesture.

Now that he could get a better look at the tool belt, he noticed it had a manufactured appearance. Nothing suggested a primitive species. He wondered whether the report was wrong, or worse, if it had been deliberately falsified.

Harry's tension eased when the Canid's lips relaxed and closed over its teeth, but he tensed again when the massive creature moved closer.

"We mean you no harm," Harry said in a calm, steady voice, just as he would use when speaking to an animal whose instincts were on full alert. "We seek only shelter from our enemies."

The Canid fixed him with its gaze, and Harry had the feeling that he was caught in a weapons sight as the eyes locked onto his. A series of growls and what sounded like a whine responded to his speech. Then, with a gesture to his companions, the leader backed away. When he had put some distance between himself and Harry, he turned and joined his fellows. Minutes later the entire group dispersed into the scrub.

Rasmus and the Coxswain walked over to Harry when it was safe to move from their positions.

"That was certainly an encounter of the unusual kind," Rasmus remarked. "Do you think they'll be back?"

Harry replaced his weapons belt. "I should think we might see them again. I do not think they are as primitive as the record suggested, and we will need allies if we are to survive on this planet until we're free of this place. We must find a way to communicate with them." He looked along the valley below. "I rather think they will watch us closely until they make up their minds whether we pose a threat. In the meantime, I want no one to make any threatening move should they return—unless, of course, they attack us."

"Cut a section around this area." The scientist indicated the area he wanted removed. If he was right, a specimen from one of the buildings on Lycania might reveal the technology that was concealed on this planet. "It appears to be some sort of node," he added as he watched the extraction. "Steady there ... if we can remove it intact, we can make a detailed examination of it in the lab."

The Consortium soldiers watched with bored disinterest. These tech geeks seemed to think they were superior to everyone, and this detail was a major pain in the ass, especially when you had to fight off the Rotties so these nerdy berks could poke and pry looking for their 'hidden tech,' whatever that meant. It got damned unpleasant if the Rotties got close enough to go hand to hand. The buggers were powerful and could bite a man's arm off when threatened, and the knives they used in close combat were serious weapons. An 'exciting adventure on an intriguing planet' as their orders had described it—yeah, right! This was a lousy detail, no matter what these boffins thought it was worth.

Firing up the laser cutter, the technician stepped forward and applied the laser. Smoke erupted, and a stench of burning flesh filled the room. The stench caused the operators to make a rapid retreat, but not fast enough. The opening sealed shut, and the walls began to contract in the manner of a foam that filled the space and engulfed the scientists and the soldiers guarding them.

Desperately the Captain tried to contact his superiors. "Alpha Leader, we're trapped in location Delta 5. Do you hear me?"

Silence greeted him. He repeated the call. Nothing.

The foam enveloped him, and everything went dark.

Chapter 8

Consortium Ascendant

――――――――――――――――――――

"**W**e've recovered all the survivors and bodies from the *Daring*, plus our own casualties from the *Sirte Global*," the Colonel reported to Brigadier Newton. "The only unexplained bit of debris is a crashed launch. It came down around fifty miles beyond the life pods. It's a remote area of little interest to us, occupied by the Rotties. There is no sign of survivors, but there is also no trace of human remains in the wreckage."

"Have you had the area searched?"

"Yes. It turned up a couple of groups of the Rotties, but nothing human. There were some tracks around the wreck itself, but we found nothing to indicate who or what made them. We've done an aerial scan covering everything in a five-hundred-mile radius, but there is no sign of any survivors and certainly no sign of anyone using any of the tech that humans need for communication, transport, food or weapons." He paused. "Of course, it's possible that the launch crashed after being ejected from the wreckage, but we'll keep looking."

"Could the Canids be hiding them?"

"It's possible but unlikely, especially since our research team tried to cut out a section of a building, and found nothing in the process." The Colonel glanced at the Chief Scientist who held his peace for once.

"Excellent work. I see the list includes *Daring*'s Exec, Commander Nielsen, three Lieutenant Commanders and most of the Lieutenants and junior officers, plus quite a crop of Rates and Warrant Officers. Yes, very well done."

Colonel Rees gave a curt nod to acknowledge the compliment. "Thanks, ma'am, but it's a pity the CS *Sirte Global* was almost destroyed. *Daring*'s Captain Maia stayed aboard the wreck and rammed her into the *SG*."

"I knew her at one time, a brave and determined officer of the North European Confederation Fleet and a damned good commander. Not like her to get caught the way the *SG* did." The Brigadier shook her head. "You recovered the *Daring*'s beacon and relocated it as I ordered?"

"Yes, ma'am. It's been shipped to the Ceti system and reactivated. They'll not be able to track it back to here."

"Good." The Brigadier hoped this would give them time to crack the secret of the technology that seemed hidden in the cities. The first research teams had failed and been replaced by the much more aggressive Johnstone Xenoarchaeological Research Group, experts at extracting and adapting alien technologies.

Their arrival had coincided with Brigadier Newton taking command of this garrison and the signal interception unit, and marked a new phase in relations with the Canids. Up to this point, the Canids had largely ignored the human presence, satisfying themselves with compelling anyone who tried any physical action inside the structures to vacate them as fast as their legs and vehicles would carry them. That changed with the JXRG team's demand that at least one of the sites be secured and their workers protected.

What the Canids lacked in weapons and protection, they more than made up for in determination, strength and aggression, which they used as and when needed. Each attempt to secure a site had been bitterly contested and cost a lot of casualties on both sides. This convinced the JXRG chief scientist that the technology to be gained from the Canid cities must be acquired at any price.

"Then all that's left is to hope our military forces on this and other planets, and the blockade of resources can bring about the surrender of the North European Confederation and the World Treaty Organisation."

The Chief Scientist cleared his throat. "Before that happens, Brigadier, I want double the number of guards for my teams. We are very close to getting our hands on this technology. It is of immense importance—far greater than perhaps you military people appreciate. We can't afford to waste time, especially after what occurred the last time my team tried to take a sample from one of the buildings."

Brigadier Newton frowned. "What happened to your science team is not the sort of response I'd expected, given the casualties we've inflicted on the Canids in pursuit of this tech. It doesn't mean any runaways won't get something similar either. Have we scanned them?"

"The tech in these cities interferes with our scans." Colonel Rees glowered at the Chief Scientist before he added, "And the researchers haven't found anything that will do it. Before you took command, they tried to tame the Rotties and train them as one would a pet dog, a laughable attempt considering these creatures are most definitely not dogs. Obviously, the effort failed. I doubt a bunch of Fleet flyboys would have much chance of survival. They won't be able to communicate with these Canids, and they could well end up on the menu."

"Hmm." The Brigadier nodded, her attention focussed on a map. "Keep a watch on this area, please. If anyone has survived and is roaming around out there, I want them found and brought in. I don't like uncertainties, and I don't like the thought of Fleet personnel roaming free just waiting to cause us problems when we least expect it."

She turned to the Chief Scientist. "What progress are you making? What did your other team find in the city?"

"We're still working on it. Part of the problem is it deletes the data from any equipment we take into the structures. Some instruments are literally fried in there. The samples we got are silicone based, rather like a fungus. Trouble is, it decomposes very rapidly as soon as it is removed from the original. It resembles some sort of nanotech. That's all we've determined so far. I'd like to try occupying one of the buildings as soon as we can figure out how to disable its defence mechanism." He paused. "We think these are not built cities in the usual sense, meaning they weren't constructed. Rather, they appear to be a sort of life form, one we've not encountered before, and from its response to us, it has a form of sentience. We plan to examine that more closely."

"You mean these structures are not intended for occupants?"

The scientist looked uncomfortable. "The responses suggest it, but there may be some technology that would do it as well. We just need to figure out how to get it to drop its defences."

"I think you'll need to work on that as a priority. The next time a team is trapped in one of these buildings, they might not be so lucky." The Brigadier drummed her fingers on her desk. "And none of those it caught last time can recall a damned thing after the walls closed in on them, as they described it."

"At least we got them back, more or less unharmed."

"True, but they were stripped of our very expensive weapons and equipment, and the Chairman wasn't too pleased about that." His tirade was practically ringing in her ears still. She sighed. "Besides, we only found them because of the search for the survivors from the Fleet ship."

"Yes, but at least we have one of the lab rats from Pangaea now."

"A good catch indeed. What have you learned from examining him?"

"A little, although we can't start the real work until Doctor Wan's team arrive. O'Connor's healing properties are remarkable. And we were absolutely right to put him into the remote unit, install the virtual screen, and isolate it from the Base."

"Just remember he's a Commissioned Officer in the Fleet, and a range of protections must be observed with him. We don't want to do anything outside of international law, as that will cause prying eyes to take a closer look at everything else we've got going on."

"Exactly," said the Colonel. "These tests have to stay within the range of what's permissible."

The scientist shifted in his seat. "Well, those restrictions make it very difficult for us to find out how the work on Pangaea could have caused this. You do realise that, I hope."

"That is your problem," said the Colonel. "As it is, our use of non-commissioned Rates to build and establish this base and to operate the equipment to manufacture the kit for our structures and finance our operation here is barely legal under the treaties.

We can't afford to be accused of allowing unethical research—look at what happened when the Pangaea lab was exposed."

"I am fully aware of the constraints," the scientist snapped. "And Doctor Wan is too. I remind you that O'Connor's abilities are a direct result of the experiments we did on him at Pangaea. In one sense, he is the product of our work. We have a right to the result."

Brigadier Newton leveled a gaze at the scientist. "His rights don't seem to have counted for much on Pangaea. Surely, as a citizen, he has a right to benefit from the use of his DNA, or am I simply being naive?"

"In our view, his rights as a citizen of the Confederation are debatable. The manner of his arrival in our society is questionable, and the original grant of protection and citizenship given to O'Connor and Heron was challenged by the Department of Science and Technology itself."

"Yes, and the challenge was dismissed by the Supreme Court of the Confederation. I will not permit any test or examination that infringes his rights. Is that clear?" The edge in the Brigadier's voice was unmistakable.

"Abundantly. But Doctor Wan has the authority of the Board to undertake all necessary procedures to discover why O'Connor and Heron—if we had that one in our lab—are able to communicate with any available AI network through their thoughts alone. That may involve surgery. You will have to take it up with the Board."

Restless and bored, Ferghal paced the small chamber that was now his home. His leg was a little stiff, but it had healed, as had his elbow. He had worked his way into the network in this building and learned how the security screen worked. He had also learned that the connection that normally existed between the laboratory and the rest of the Base had been deliberately disconnected, and the lab isolated.

He prowled the room. Sparsely furnished, it offered very little by way of comfort. The only chair was utilitarian and fixed to the floor, and the entertainment console had a limited store of games, which he considered useless child's play, and movies, boring in the extreme. Some even made a laughable attempt at capturing Britain in the 1800s, and a few did a plausible job of portraying life on a sailing ship during the Napoleonic Wars. Having lived through the reality of that experience, he'd toyed with the idea of accessing the network to have a go at tweaking the movies, but then he realised this was possibly one of the ways his captors planned to study him, so he left them untouched.

And so he used his active mind to entertain himself, and constantly worked out how to escape this imprisonment. He'd learned what was planned, and it worried him, but that made him even more determined to have his own revenge as soon as the opportunity arose. Listening to the AI, he became aware of a new voice in his head. He paused to listen more intently.

Slowly a smile spread across his face. Then, remembering he was under surveillance, he suppressed the smile and resumed his pacing—but he was working out a plan furiously in his thoughts. Someone had brought into the lab a portable interface to the main Base network. He made full use of the opportunity it gave him.

Chapter 9

Hunted

Harry faced his group. "We need to make a decision. I do not intend to surrender to the Consortium. Some of you may understand why. But I cannot ask the rest of you to follow me on a path that, for all I know, will lead to a lonely and unpleasant death. The facts are these: We have very little food and must soon experiment with eating what we can hunt, catch or gather. That has certain risks, as I am sure you are aware. We have few weapons and can do little to defend ourselves until we can manufacture something to meet the need, or capture some weapons from our enemies. We are being hunted—you've all seen the search teams and aerial sweeps. Those are the facts. You must decide for yourselves whether you are prepared to stay with me and attempt to disrupt their operations or give yourselves up and become prisoners of war."

He let his eyes sweep the group before he stood up.

"I shall leave you to discuss it among yourselves. You may call me when you've decided."

"I'll join you." Rasmus stood up too. "I am not a soldier or a cosmonaut, so I am not under your orders, Harry. I will go with you." Taking Harry's arm, he steered him out of the firelight.

Once they could no longer hear the men at the campfire, Harry and Rasmus found places to sit. Above them, the blaze of stars cast a ghostly light on the harsh landscape.

"Thanks for that, Rasmus. I appreciate your offer, but I really must tell you I do not know what to do or how we will survive. I remember reading that the winters on this planet are extreme, and I have no idea how long we may be able to keep ourselves alive and free—or even if."

"Harry, you have done very well for us so far, and I think you will continue to do so. Do not let fear creep in and rob your intelligent mind of possible solutions. There is always a way. We must simply find it." Rasmus grinned in the gloom. "Besides, I have a fancy to see what it is like to live off the land." He broke off as the youngest TechRate, Rahman Watson, joined them.

"Mr. Winstanley's compliments, Mr. Heron. Would you please come back to the campfire? You too, Mr. Schulte-Lubeck."

"Certainly, Rahman." Harry stood up. "I'll come immediately."

"Thanks, sir." The TechRate threw up a salute, a broad grin on his face. "We've decided—we're with you all the way."

And with that, the future seemed much less bleak. It would be tough, and Harry worried that this decision placed his people in danger, and could even get them killed. Sabotaging any of the Consortium systems would intensify the hunt, and evading their patrols would prove difficult and dangerous. On the other hand, they had little with which to do any damage anyway. His best course of action was to stay free and keep as many of the enemy's troops occupied in searching for them as possible.

Admiral James Heron listened to the scant information the briefing officer shared with him.

"*Daring*'s locator beacon was recovered in System DGS673, sir—twenty light years from her patrol and reconnaissance routing. There's no other wreckage—no bodies, no debris, nothing that shows she was destroyed there. The conclusion is that the beacon was planted deliberately."

James was visibly angry. "So we still have nothing to tell us what happened to her or where?"

"No, sir."

"Well that's no damned help at all. What's been put in hand to find her? I understand at least one other ship has vanished like this in the past."

"Yes, sir. There've been five. The *Argus* disappeared in very similar circumstances five months ago. Her beacon was also recovered in a remote system with no other wreckage." The Lieutenant Commander felt he was on safer ground here. "The *Argus* was also on a patrol and reconnaissance mission. The *Daring* may have been caught in a similar trap."

His fingers drumming the desk, the Admiral frowned. "These ambushes are far too frequent and too convenient to be coincidence." He stood up. "Thank you for your time. I'm on my way to my flagship. Keep me informed of any developments."

"Yes, sir." The Lieutenant Commander sounded as relieved as she felt. She stood thinking a moment longer after the Admiral departed. She knew the *Daring* carried two of the men the Admiral regarded as sons, and in the absence of any news, it seemed likely they were dead.

Her link buzzed and she answered it. When she read the message, her eyes widened, and she hurried after the Admiral.

She caught up with him at his transport module. "Sir! I think we have something. Intelligence sources report that the Consortium's research teams say they have one of the men they call the lab rats. A specialist team is on their way to examine him."

The Admiral's face turned stony. "Thank you. See if they can find out where and who."

Watching the Admiral's expression, his Flag Lieutenant bit his lip. *God, he thought, someone is going to pay dearly if anything happens to Harry or Ferghal.* And then another thought hit him. *If only one was captured, where the hell was the other?*

"We have a problem, sir." The Coxswain studied the Canids blocking their way to what looked like a series of buildings. "They don't look friendly," he said in a low voice, and in truth, they looked ferocious. "Shall we arm our weapons?"

"No." Harry was quiet but firm. "We don't want to provoke them. I'll try to parlay. We need the shelter of those buildings they're guarding for a few days at least."

Rasmus shook his head. "They do not look as if they want to talk, mein freund. Be careful you are not on their menu."

"I shall." Harry unbuckled his belt and dropped his weapons. "Be ready to defend yourselves. If I fall, do not try to rescue me—save yourselves."

Moving forward step by gradual step, he held up his hands with his palms facing the Canids.

The leader of the pack immediately made an aggressive display of charging forward and gesturing with what Harry realised was a pair of vicious looking knives. The bared fangs were alarming, and so was the deep rumbling snarl that accompanied the charge.

He stopped. "We intend you no harm. We seek only food and shelter." Pointing to the nearest building, he made the motions of putting food in his mouth and laying his head on his folded hands to indicate sleeping. Other members of the group were moving to encircle them. That they didn't trust humans was obvious—probably, he thought with disdain, because of some action by the Consortium troops. *I don't blame you,* he said inwardly, remembering all too well what the Consortium-backed Johnstone Group did to him. *You have every right to be wary of humans.*

Harry waited to see what response he would get to his pantomime of eating and sleeping. The leader seemed unfazed and repeated his aggressive display.

Harry had an inspiration. Taking a freshly caught fish and his fire-making tools from his backpack, he bent to the ground and laid the fish on a flat stone, one of many that littered the ground in this region. He gathered a few twigs within reach, and set about making a small fire. This caused the leader to withdraw, his weapons raised and ready. The Canids focused on the smoke rising from Harry's kindling as he blew gently on the tinder and slowly fed it twigs and chips until the flame grew into a blazing campfire.

As he worked, something seemed to be tugging at his subconscious, a sensation he couldn't identify, but it felt like when another person you know really well says the same thing you're thinking. He didn't have time to mull over it, so he pushed the thought out of his mind and busied himself skewering the fish to set about cooking it.

The leader edged closer, nostrils scenting toward the fire and the humans. Then he turned, barked sharply and withdrew, and his people followed him.

Rasmus and the others joined Harry.

"That was interesting," remarked Rasmus.

"I don't know about interesting," said the Coxswain. He gazed across the empty landscape. "What made them go like that?"

"Must be the Lieutenant's cooking," joked Maddie Hodges, relief making them all a little crazy.

"Well then," Harry said with a chuckle. "You'd better take over the cooking. I'd not wish to be accused of poisoning you all as well." Privately he wondered what tried to access his mind. It felt like his link was being tested. He dismissed the thought and made the conscious choice to focus on the fact that at least they now had shelter in the empty structures for a few days, a welcome relief.

The Consortium's searches intensified, forcing Harry and his crew from their comfortable refuge in the empty city. The ensuing weeks had taken them deep into wild and broken country. They watched and avoided Consortium vehicles and ground patrols that seemed to be conducting a systematic search of the area. For protection at night and shelter from the wind, they slept in caves or hollowed out notches in rocky outcrops. On one occasion, they came close to being caught by one of the violent storms that swept this land. A number of times they had to take shelter as aircraft patrolled the area.

They came across another empty city, completely deserted but in perfect condition, as if the inhabitants had simply packed everything and left minutes before.

"Damned spooky, these places, sir. Don't the natives live in them?"

"I have no idea. Maybe they do in the winter." Harry hesitated. "That's a good question though. Where do the Canids actually live? We've encountered no other habitations, and they certainly don't live in the caves we've used, but why? Has the Consortium attacked them? If so, why would they do that?"

"They need a reason, sir?" The Coxswain saw Harry's expression and knew what it meant. "You think we're being watched, don't you, sir, as if we're not alone here."

Harry had the feeling something was trying to hack into his neural link. He nodded. "Tell the others not to damage or touch anything unusual. We'll move on as soon as we're rested."

It was the Coxswain's turn to prepare a meal for the group. "Damned if I know how the natives cook," he complained, waving smoke from his eyes. "We've seen 'em eating, and it doesn't look like raw stuff. More like ration packs."

"I've noticed that too, Swain. I wish we could actually talk to them. I've seen tools that would make Ferghal envious, but never any sign that they live in these seemingly perfect towns and cities."

"And their weapons are odd, sir. Look like some sort of crossbow and those nasty knives they can switch into play. Bad news at close range, but not if someone's got something with longer range."

Harry nodded in silent agreement, lost in thought. He was concerned about the condition of his crew. With their uniforms and boots showing the effects of hard wear, he wondered where they might get replacements. The Canids wore something that looked like the sort of rubbery suit divers wore, and their boots looked like they could withstand just about any terrain and weather condition imaginable.

Harry grimaced. Thoughts of uniforms and boots reminded him of his painful feet. "How are the men's feet, Swain? Mine are not used to this terrain."

"The lads are struggling, sir, make no mistake. Our boots weren't made for this." The Swain laughed. "We don't normally wander around planet-side, and what's good on the ship doesn't hold up to this sort of use. Good thing we grabbed the boots that go with the EVA suits."

"And they aren't really up to this either, Swain. Mine chafe badly."

"I can't feel what I'm walking on anymore, sir." The Coxswain grimaced. "It's like my feet are on fire most of the time."

"I know the feeling." Harry sighed. "My boots are all but destroyed. We'll have to find some replacements."

"Mr. Heron." The lookout's voice cut across their conversation. "I think you had better see this, sir."

Harry hobbled to where the Rate was crouched in a sheltered spot observing something in the distance.

"What is it, Will?"

"An armoured transport vehicle is coming this way, sir, some sort of patrol."

Harry focused his binoculars on the transport. The crew didn't seem to be paying much attention as their vehicle skimmed towards Harry's position. "Damn," he said. "Warn the others to get into hiding. They'll be on us in ten minutes. No one's to move unless I give the order—but be ready to defend yourselves."

"Got you, sir." Will slipped down from his perch and joined the Coxswain who moved the others into hiding after dowsing the fire and covering it.

Watching the approaching vehicle, Harry realised that it was headed for a large pool just downstream of their position. It pulled up and the crew disembarked.

"They're either bloody sloppy or they don't expect to find anyone." The Coxswain's quiet comment caught Harry off guard. He had crept up close and crouched next to Harry.

"You're right. Maybe we can surprise them. There's only eight of them, maybe one more in the vehicle."

"They're setting up camp, and they've got a food replicator." The Coxswain licked his lips.

Harry's stomach grumbled as if in reply; their rations were desperately low. Food was the single biggest problem they faced. There'd been nothing in *Daring*'s record of what this planet had in the way of food that was edible for humans. The risky process of tasting small quantities of the animals they hunted or the berries they found to determine whether the food was edible meant they were often hungry if it produced a bad reaction in Harry, who always volunteered to be the guinea pig. One such experiment had produced such a violent reaction that he had almost killed himself eating the meat of a small animal, which turned out to be toxic.

"Swain," he whispered. "They're settling down for the night, but I have a plan that will get us some fresh supplies and new equipment. I will enjoy riding something other than Shank's Pony for a few miles at least."

"Shank's Pony?" The Coxswain looked baffled. He was used to Harry's old-fashioned euphemisms, but this was a new one on him.

Harry chuckled. "It means having to walk because you're too poor to afford a horse—yes, I know, my Irish roots are showing." He cleared his throat in slight embarrassment and became serious. "We want their boots, the food replicator and everything they use for communication. I don't want them calling up help until we're miles away."

"Okay, sir, I'm on it. I'll get the rest of the crew."

As they crept closer to the Consortium camp, Harry and TechRate Will Turner were surprised at the casual attitude of the camp's occupants. None of the men seemed to be keeping any sort of lookout, though all were soldiers.

Harry and Will stood motionless when a voice called, "Razi, report us in place and camp set in."

"Gotcha, Corp," came the response from the vehicle.

"There is one in the vehicle at least," Harry whispered. "And the rest seem to be enjoying their supper." Focusing his mind, he found himself linked to the vehicle's rather simple-minded onboard computer. Listening carefully, he tracked the message the operator sent out and realised this was one of a chain of search teams. It alarmed him to learn that he and his crew were surrounded.

"We're inside a ring of these patrols," he whispered. "Trapped." The conversation of the group reached him.

"What do you reckon, Corp?" said one of the men at the replicator. "Do you think we'll find these guys?"

"Nah, their corpses maybe. It's been eight weeks now. They haven't got the equipment to survive this long, and their ration packs will have run out weeks ago. Besides, if they're still alive, they're most likely camped on the easier ground to the east."

"What are the chances they're hiding out with the locals?"

"What, with the Rotties?" There was a sharp laugh. "What do you think? No one's managed to tame them or even get close enough to talk to them. Nah, they'll stay well away from them if they're clever. The Rotties don't like us humans—especially with us trying to take control of their towns. Anyone running into them could be in trouble."

"Heard the scientists aren't having any luck with their examination of the material their buildings are made out of, either. Seems those things have some sort of artificial intelligence. Any electronic equipment they take inside goes haywire, if that makes any sense."

"Ha. Not a lot. We killed a lot of Rotties for nothing. Too bad—I was hoping to tame a few for pet dogs." He gave a snort of laughter and a sarcastic grin.

"Good luck with that!" said the other. "You'll be in his supper dish before you can say, 'Good doggie.'"

Harry had stopped listening to their banter when he heard the comment about electronic equipment being fried when taken into those buildings. *That explains a lot*, he mused, and put the thought in the back of his mind for now.

Turning to Will Turner, he whispered, "Okay, Will, tell the Swain to be ready. I'll disable the coms system first then make my move. As soon as I have their attention, I want you fellows to take them."

"Got you, sir." Will moved away without a sound.

Harry focused his attention on the vehicle's AI and discovered that each vehicle—twenty of them—emitted a signal that reported the vehicle was operational and on its station. *Damn*, he thought, then realised that he could make that work to his advantage. He adjusted the program and watched as the next cycle of call, response and confirmation went through. Then he intervened again, telling the AI to log but not send any communication other than the automatic signal.

The AI resisted, but Harry overrode this, taking the precaution of disabling the connections between voice com and the uplink, and he ordered the computer to disable the personal comlinks that depended on the vehicle relay for long distance communication. He couldn't trust the computer and didn't have time to persuade it to accept his intentions, so he disabled the parts of it that posed a threat. When he caught the Coxswain's hand signal, he drew a deep breath and stood up. He reached the first survival dome without being spotted, and then he stepped out into the open.

"Bloody hell." A soldier dropped his tray and reached for his weapon when he saw Harry stagger toward him gasping for breath before he collapsed. When the other soldiers caught sight of Harry, they grabbed their weapons and kept him in their sights as they advanced.

As he had hoped, the soldiers clustered round him wondering if he was dead or alive. The Corporal dropped to his knees and lay down his weapon to turn Harry over.

"Bloody hell" was all he managed to say before Harry's plasma projector made contact with his chest, paralysing him.

Before the other men could react, the Coxswain's voice rang across the clearing. "Freeze! The first man that moves will be charred where he stands."

The soldiers froze.

"Step back from my officer," the Coxswain ordered. "And put down your weapons—easy, there! My lads will fry anyone who moves too quickly."

"You won't get away with this," the Corporal snarled, having recovered from the initial stun. "My ComOp will have sent out our distress call already." He gasped for breath at the effort it took just to speak.

"I don't think so," Harry said, rising to his feet as soon as Ranji Singh restrained the Corporal. "I took care of that before we interrupted your little dinner party."

The Corporal cursed as the ComOp dismounted rather violently from the vehicle, the burly figure of Errol Hill emerging behind him followed by a grinning Maddie Hodges.

"He was a bit distracted, Corp. Funny that," she added, adjusting her tattered jacket.

Harry's proper upbringing meant he didn't quite get her meaning at first, or the reason for her impish grin, but it made him feel rattled nonetheless, so he quickly turned to address the Corporal.

"I'm afraid we have greater need of your equipment and transport than you have," he said. "I'd be obliged if you ordered your men to strip. We need your coveralls, boots, and comlinks. We're in a hurry, so quick as you can, please." He caught the crafty gleam in the Corporal's eye. "And before you try anything clever, we'll start with you. Sit down and remove your boots, all of you—now!"

"You'll have our people swarming all over you soon, mister," the Corporal snarled, even as he obeyed Harry's order. "Our vehicles are monitored constantly. Any failure to report at regular intervals is taken as a call for assistance."

"Thank you for telling me that, but it's old news." Harry smiled, his projector unwavering. "I've already dealt with it."

"Impossible. No one can alter that system unless they can get into the program itself."

The Corporal seemed very confident, so Harry checked the network to make sure. "Maybe someone did." He grinned to rub in the insult. "Now, Corporal, I very much regret that we cannot leave you or your men free, even in your underwear. I'd be obliged if you would all fit yourselves into your survival shelter, please. We have good reason to know how cold the nights are at this altitude, and I would not wish you to die of it."

"This way, Corporal." The Coxswain was firm. "Stennet, Brydges—full body search on everyone. No tools and definitely no comlinks—make sure none of them have anything hidden."

"No way are you going to get away with this," the Corporal protested angrily. "Its against the Convention!"

"Haven't noticed any of your lot following the Convention," snorted the Coxswain. "Morati, anyone resists, you know how to deal with them."

"I got you, Swain." The big man grinned broadly and flexed his shoulders then smacked his fist into his opposite palm. "Okay, friends, get in line. Let's see what you're hiding. Go on, I've got a few complaints I want to settle with someone."

Harry decided he shouldn't be watching this and moved to the transport, leaving his crew to sort out their prisoners. He knew he could trust the Coxswain not to break any of the Convention rules, but felt he shouldn't be there to see any 'bends' the Chief Master Warrant might put in it. He busied himself interrogating the Consortium's transport systems, and learned a great deal about the terrain and the disposition of their pursuers—and, best of all, he managed to hack into a database that gave him valuable information on the native population and their habits.

He was feeling a lot more confident of their survival as they crammed themselves into the transport and headed off into the night.

Chapter 10

Ferghal's Fury

_____

Ferghal was tired and angry. Doctor Melville Wan and his team treated him like the lab rat they considered him. Strapped to a padded table, his head in a brace, he was inside a scanning machine, unable to see anything except the polished metal of the tube.

The latest series of tests involved an attempt to trigger his cyberlink by sending it a stream of data, all of which he concentrated on blocking.

"It's not working," said the doctor. "Let's try sedating him. Maybe then it won't be so easy for him to resist our commands."

Ferghal swore violently when he felt the needle penetrate the vein in his heel. "Be damned, the lot of you! I'll not tell you a bloody thing, ye black-hearted scum." His accent descended rapidly into the slightly harsh tones of his homeland, the lush hills of north County Down, Ireland.

Ignoring the protests of the MedTech operating the scanner, Doctor Wan ordered, "Commence the trial again. The drug will take a few seconds to take effect. Start the test sequence."

Inside his prison, Ferghal fought to stay conscious as the drug coursed through him. His hands and feet went numb, and the paralysis crept up his legs and arms. His body went limp, and to his embarrassment, he lost control of his bladder. This sparked his fury. They had humiliated him, and he would not give them the satisfaction they sought. His roiling anger helped, and his mind cleared of the creeping fog that had been seeping into his consciousness. Now he'd bloody well show them.

He linked to their equipment.

"It's working." Doctor Wan studied his display, a note of satisfaction in his voice. Then everything went haywire.

"Shut down the network!" the laboratory supervisor ordered. "Quickly—he's altering the programs!"

"I can't." The technician sounded desperate. "He's blocked all exit and input commands, and now the power seems to be on the emergency supply, which I can't shut down from here."

"Don't do anything," the doctor ordered. "This is fascinating. I want it recorded." He gasped as the screen flashed up a message.

THERE WILL BE NO RECORDING, YOU BASTARD.

The stench of scorched and burning electrical components filled the room. "Put the fire out!" shouted Doctor Wan. "Do it now! The data must be saved!"

Ferghal's fury knew no limits. Now that he was inside the lab's network, he was hell bent on destroying it and everything it contained. For a few seconds it put up a fight, but it was no match for an angry man who had learned to build these systems. He knew exactly how to cause its failure, and he set about doing it. The AI was reduced to gibbering idiocy within minutes.

The laboratory staff were close to panic as everything around them failed. The replicators spat out useless rubbish, offal, stinking goo and anything else they were instructed by the commands that Ferghal ordered. The lights flickered and failed, necessitating a scramble to find portable lights since the emergency circuit could not be activated.

Finally, someone had the wits to drag Ferghal out of the scanner and cut the power cable to it. Unbeknownst to his tormentors, however, Ferghal was still linked to what was left of the AI. Even better, the restoration of feeling in his limbs told him the drug was losing its grip, something his tormentors wouldn't know if he had anything to do with it.

The doctor was beside himself. "What have you done?" he shouted at the immobilised figure on the table.

"Paid you back in spades for what ye've done to me and my friend Harry, you scum," Ferghal spat back. Now his cunning kicked in, and he feigned paralysis for several long seconds. Then, amping up the drama, he faked a violent tremor. When the "tremor" eased, he lay gasping for breath before he shot a fierce look at the doctor. "Why can't I control my limbs? What have you done to me, you vile tormentor?"

"The drugs are taking effect at last," breathed one of the technicians.

"Too late," snarled the supervisor. He turned to the doctor. "I warned you this could happen." To his assistants he said, "Get him out of that damned scanner and into his cell. I'll have to contact the Base and get the AI people over to sort out the system. It's basically fried." He stamped out of the room, and his assistants set about freeing Ferghal, thinking him paralysed.

No sooner was the last restraint released than he exploded off the table. One man went down with a broken jaw. Another landed on the floor seconds later clutching his groin and retching in pain. The third had more sense. He dodged Ferghal and tried to push a console between them. It didn't save him.

Vaulting the obstruction, Ferghal landed like a cat and grabbed the nearest technician, using the unfortunate man as a weapon. The doctor found himself the target of the enraged Irishman's fists and suffered a broken nose and a concussion as his head made contact with the wall. He would have suffered even worse if the guards hadn't arrived at that moment.

There was a flash, and with a grunt, Ferghal folded and collapsed. The guard eased out of his crouch in the doorway and surveyed the lab, his stun pistol at the ready. The laboratory was a scene of devastation. Ferghal had taken out his rage and frustration on everything and everyone. No one seemed to have escaped his fists or his feet.

The guard grinned. *Hell, I don't even want to know what he would have done if he'd had a weapon!* He wiped the smile from his face and made way for the rest of the guard.

Brigadier Newton listened in cold fury to the reports of the events in the research laboratory. These researchers seemed to have no consideration for anything or anyone. Their 'research' overrode every other consideration, moral or ethical. Doctor Wan sat opposite her, his face showing the effects of Ferghal's assault. A surgical splint covered his battered nose, and both his eyes were puffed up, the area around them dark with bruising.

Doctor Wan spoke first, wanting the upper hand. "I must insist that we be allowed to take him back to a research facility on Eritrea Five." He winced in pain. It took every bit of effort to speak without jolts of agony shooting through his face. "It's obvious we will have to carry out an investigation by vivisection. There is no other way to ensure he can't resist our investigations."

"No," the Brigadier snapped. "He's a prisoner of war and entitled to my protection. I won't allow another damned Pangaea situation. He stays here! We can control his access to the AI and prevent him doing anything like this again—and I must remind you that we warned you this could happen. You ignored it. Now you've come very close to compromising everything we're doing. That I won't allow."

The doctor grunted in protest. "Then let us take him somewhere else. Once we have him in our laboratory, he isn't your problem."

"Hasn't it occurred to you that if he gets on a ship, he'll get into the AI network, and you won't get to your destination? You saw what happened to the lab network when he went berserk inside it. There's no way I can let you put a ship at risk like that." Her expression told the doctor not to push his luck.

The doctor shifted in his seat to find a more comfortable position, but everything hurt. He let out a shaky breath and decided to take a placatory approach. "Brigadier, at least allow us to continue our observation of him. Perhaps if we can get him to lower his guard we will be able to get some idea of how exactly he is able to work inside a closed, secure AI network."

"Very well, but there will be no further risk of his getting anywhere near our main system in any way whatsoever. Am I clear?" She fixed the doctor with a cold stare. "Just one more thing. No drugs, no invasive procedures, and definitely no attempts at any form of torture, physical or mental. Any hint of any of that in future, and you had better believe me when I say that I will personally put you and your team in a place no one will ever find you."

"I don't like being threatened." The doctor tried to sound tough, but it wasn't very effective given his bandaged head.

"I'm not threatening you, Doctor. I'm making you a promise."

"But ..."

The Brigadier held up a hand. "And what's more, I am placing this on record with the Board. I will not tolerate any experiments on any POW under my jurisdiction."

"But he's a valuable research asset, and we need—"

"He's a human being, not some laboratory specimen! Your experiments broke every line of the damned Convention. Just who the blazes do you people think you are? Do you have any concept of what you almost derailed here? That man is an officer of the North European Confederation Fleet. Have you any idea what a half decent lawyer would make of your experiments?"

"Brigadier, you obviously don't appreciate the importance of this research. If we can replicate this man's ability, there are immense benefits for all of us. Sometimes one individual must be sacrificed for the benefit of many." The doctor would have said more, but the Brigadier stopped him.

"Don't continue, Doctor." Her voice was harsh. "That argument has been advanced in the defence of every atrocity and injustice in human history. It is not going to be used here to allow you or anyone else to abuse prisoners of war. Now, I have work to do even if you do not. Good day."

Ferghal woke, a gradual process that took some effort to crawl from the deep sleep of exhaustion to the reality of lying on a hard mattress in a cold cell, and remembering why everything hurt. He ached all over, and his mouth was dry. His knuckles were sore and swollen, but he felt a grim satisfaction as memory returned.

A cheerful voice greeted his stirring. "Good, you're awake. I was a bit worried for a while. Some people don't react well to a stunner."

He groaned and struggled to sit up. For a bleary moment, he wasn't sure if a person had asked that question, or if it was more of the annoying chatter of the network burbling happily to itself in his head. Its functions were garbled and utterly mindless after the abuse it had suffered.

"Did I kill the bastard?" Ferghal said aloud.

"No, but you came close." His visitor chuckled, and lowered his voice. Ferghal turned his body to face the man sat on a chair in the corner. "The rest of us reckon you did a bloody good job in there, sir. And the Brigadier has given orders that you're to be left alone in future."

"That so? Well, I hope it means I can have some tools and a few things to work with." He focused his eyes on the man's face. "You're new. What happened to the old guard?"

"Brigadier's orders. They've all been relieved. I'm afraid you have to stay here, though. We can't take you to the Base." He gestured around him. "Not after what you did here." He stood up. "I'd better get going. Give me a list of things you'd like, and I'll see what I can do. Just wish I'd been here to see you take that lab apart," he added with a grin.

Ferghal shrugged, returning the grin. "Just doing my duty as an officer of the Fleet, but I'll confess I had some pleasure in giving those bastards something to remember me by."

Ferghal's mind was already working out a solution. Someone would come and repair the damage. They'd have a portable system or something with them. He could wait his chance, especially now that he knew how to get past the security programs.

The guard laughed. "They'll remember you, all right—every time the doctor looks in a mirror, I should think!"

Ferghal grinned in reply, but his thoughts were elsewhere. During this brief conversation, he had noticed that the door to his cell had a makeshift mechanical lock. When the time came, he knew exactly how to deal with that.

Chapter 11

Refuge

Harry disembarked from the transport they'd confiscated from the Consortium soldiers. He and his crew had taken a very circuitous route to reach their new camp, a route planned by Harry to give a completely false trail to any pursuers. He had chosen this spot precisely because it was in the midst of a large complex of abandoned yet remarkably preserved buildings. Through the vehicle's data links, he'd managed to learn a great deal about the activities of the Consortium and their interest in these cities. Now, he finally knew why the Canids responded with such wariness toward humans, but this opened a new puzzle for him. Why did they allow him and his crew to occupy one of their buildings?

He stood next to the Coxswain overseeing operations. "The Consortium research team gathered information on these sites, but it seems they could not scan them because some manner of shield prevents it." Grinning, Harry added, "It suits our purposes perfectly, Swain."

"Damn right, sir. Think we'll be able to take some time out now, sir?"

"I hope so, Swain. We need a little rest, and this will be luxurious after living in caves."

"Strange that the Canids have not attempted to prevent our entering the city, though," Rasmus joined in.

Harry nodded. "More important, why do they not live in these cities? Is there some hazard to doing so, or a taboo against it, which we are breaking without realising it?"

"Perhaps these buildings have some other purpose," Rasmus mused. "Why have you chosen this site?"

"The data files I accessed on the way here indicate that this area is as far as possible from the site the Consortium drove the Canids out of for their own selfish gain. These buildings block our scanners, so we may hide here for the winter, I think." The nagging sensation that something was trying to connect to him dragged at Harry's subconscious. He studied their surroundings, but could detect nothing unusual or out of the ordinary.

"Sounds good to me, sir," said the Coxswain. He gazed at the building Harry had selected. "Looks pretty alien, don't you think?"

Harry nodded. "It does, like nothing on Earth at least."

Rasmus stepped closer to a wall to examine it. "These walls are completely organic—grown, not built. Amazing."

Up close, the organic nature of the structures was obvious. Even their shape and layout suggested a living organism rather than a purpose-built structure. The material used to create them was unknown to Harry, and Rasmus simply shook his head when asked.

"Weiss nicht. No clue my friend. One day, when you get me back to my laboratory, perhaps I can tell you."

"In the meantime," said Harry, "tell our people not to cut or pierce any of the walls. The reports in the Consortium files say any attempt to do so causes the Canids to attack." He frowned remembering something in the record he'd accessed. "Strange, but the Consortium research team think these buildings may not be buildings at all, but rather some strange life form."

Rasmus touched the wall, careful not to nick it. "Interesting. The surface has scales. They remind me of very small photovoltaic cells."

Harry glanced at Rasmus. "Photovoltaic? Do you think they are a form of electrical generating system?"

Rasmus shrugged. "It would explain the orientation and the internal structures. With these surface areas, you could generate a very large charge. I would need to examine it much more closely though."

"Do you think they still occupy these cities?" asked the Coxswain. "Maybe they're just gone temporarily, like it's their hunting season or something." The thought of being the hunted occurred to him and made him go silent.

"No one knows where they live," said Harry. "They're seldom seen in the structures or in the streets. But as soon as there is any attempt to damage one of these structures, they arrive, seemingly out of nowhere, and get very aggressive about defending it."

Conxswain Abram Winstanley studied the entrance to the building. "You said you had a second reason for choosing this site, sir."

Harry smiled. "Yes. It's roughly three hundred miles from where we were and a long way from where I shall send the vehicle when we have unloaded it. There's a reason for that. Since the Consortium people have examined other cities, it seems unlikely they will visit this one—and we are well to the west of their base and far from the area they will expect us to hide in."

The Coxswain indicated the long inlet that stretched across the front of the building dividing the city in half. "And we've a sea of sorts. Wonder if they've got any boats we can use."

"At least we can fish in this water—I think," remarked Will Turner to laughter from the rest.

"Right, your job then, Turner," the Coxswain shot back. "Any more volunteers?"

"Get everything off the transport, Swain," Harry ordered, his attention on the task in hand. "We'll make ourselves at home here for now. It won't be long before someone discovers the vehicle's tracker signal is just the transponder at our prisoners' location. I want to send this vehicle to a false destination well away from here before then."

"Good thinking, Harry," said Rasmus. "This will give us some breathing space—provided they don't find the transport anywhere near us."

Harry nodded. "That is the one difficulty. I plan to program it to take itself to a point in the far south. According to the maps it carries, there are canyons and difficult terrain in that region."

"Is it far enough that they won't come sniffing around here?" said the Coxswain.

"It will be at least five hundred miles from our starting point there and six hundred from where we are here. There is too little time of darkness left for it to reach that destination before dawn, so I will direct it to conceal itself by day at an alternate destination to the south east and to go on to its final destination tonight."

"I suppose we should be thankful we have longer nights," Rasmus commented. "But I'm not looking forward to the six weeks of perpetual night that will engulf this part of the planet soon when the winter snows hit. Even though it'll mean the Consortium won't have patrols out during that time, it will make hunting and fishing impossible."

"Yes," Harry agreed. "I'm hoping we'll find shelter and the means for heating ourselves among these structures during the severest weather. The sharp tilt of this planet's axis certainly creates some very severe seasons. From the manner in which the nights are lengthening, I think we must be entering the autumnal period." He glanced at the inlet. "If there are any boats, we may find one useful."

"Transport's clear, sir," Errol Hill reported.

"Thank you, Errol," Harry acknowledged. "Right, Rasmus, I'd better get this done. ComOp Hodges, perhaps you'd assist me. I want their coms monitored while I'm doing the programming."

"Yes, sir!" She grinned, eager to get started. "Anything in particular, sir, or just the general traffic?"

"Just the general traffic, but particularly anything that suggests they know we've got away."

With their stolen transport sent off to mislead any pursuit, Harry and his motley team made themselves at home. As Maddie Hodges watched the armoured transport skim away on the route Harry had programmed, she reported, "No signals about any missing squad, sir. Pity I couldn't strip out that com unit. We'd have been able to monitor them."

"True, but it was an integral part of the AI. We will have to find another way." Having made that pronouncement, Harry turned and hurried into the building, hoping to distract himself. Maddie awoke feelings in him he wasn't at all sure how to deal with. Best to get on with the business at hand.

Inside the building, Harry noted just how unusual its structure was. "There don't seem to be any right angles," he remarked to Rasmus.

Rasmus peered at it more closely. "I've never seen anything like it. Light and warmth come from within, and both are uniform."

"Could an electrical charge cause it to give off this kind of soft, muted light?"

"Maybe." Rasmus stood back and studied the walls. "It appears to be a form of photoluminescence." He looked at Harry. "But it is unlike any I know. This is the first I have encountered that illuminates when you enter the space."

"I thought it strange," Harry said. He touched the wall again, aware of its warmth, and had the impression that it was like a computer screen. He also felt a peculiar sensation inside his head when he was near it.

"The temperature seems very regular," said Rasmus. "In here it is quite comfortable."

This had been puzzling Harry. "So it seems, but why, and for whom? Those who examined this place on previous excursions thought it might be used by the Canids, but they could find no specific source for the heating or the lights."

He decided not to comment about the sensations in his head.

Lieutenant Aral Clarke seated himself in the small makeshift office used by Commander Nielsen. As senior surviving officer in captivity, the Commander was now the man to whom the prisoners and their guards looked for any matter of discipline or guidance.

"You wanted to see me, sir?"

"Yes." The Commander's eyes seemed to drill into his visitor's. "As you know, there'll be a court martial when we are freed from here. The loss of the *Daring* will have to be explained. As senior survivor, it'll be me in the dock, and I'll need all the information available concerning the ship's final moments. You were the last officer to leave the Nav Centre, I believe."

"I think so, sir." Aral Clark relaxed. Maybe this wouldn't be so bad. "I had the order to clear Control and abandon ship from the Captain. So I took all the surviving people in the Navigation Centre and loaded them into the remaining life pods. Ours were the last ones to leave the ship."

"You checked to make sure the Emergency Helm Control was cleared?"

"No, sir. I assumed Mr. Heron would clear it." The Lieutenant wondered what had prompted this question. "Of course, it was quite difficult by that stage. The coms were failing, and I had to get the people with me clear—and only a couple of pods remained."

"So you can't be sure that everyone was accounted for. I understand the Coxswain didn't make it. Was he killed before you left the Nav Centre?"

"I don't recall, sir. I thought he was with the others when we left."

The Commander's face was unreadable. "Very well. Tell me about the manoeuvring from the moment we were attacked please. What evasive manoeuvres did you adopt?"

"We ran variations of the standard La Grange patterns, sir." Aral Clarke felt his uncertainty rising. "As I've often pointed out, they offer targeting the best options for tracking an enemy while we manoeuvre."

"Variations on the standard manoeuvres? What sort of variations?" The Commander's voice was quiet.

"I recalculated the standard manoeuvres, sir, to allow Targeting to follow and remain within the best parameters for battle conditions ...." Aral Clarke faltered, the expression on the Commander's face a mix of rage and contempt.

"That would certainly explain our inability to shake them off. Didn't Captain Maia give you a direct order on a previous occasion never to use the standard manoeuvres again?"

"Sir?" Lieutenant Clarke could see the trap yawning before him. "I varied them as much as possible ... yes, sir, I mean ... there was no time to calculate a different set, sir."

"No time to calculate? You had several weeks! Did you task Mr. Heron with any of it? No, I thought not."

Clarke swallowed. The Commander's expression said everything.

"So I may record that you used standard manoeuvres despite knowing they could be tracked and predicted by the enemy." The silence was deafening. "And then you abandoned ship leaving a number of your people aboard."

The Lieutenant's face told the Commander all he needed to know, but he needed a clear, verbal answer for the record.

"I take it you are aware our captors believe a small group managed to escape by some unknown means, and that it may include at least one of our fellow officers."

"Sir?" Aral Clarke swallowed. "Er, no—I mean, yes, I have heard the rumour, sir." He felt cold. Some of his fellow prisoners already treated him like a pariah because he had insisted they surrender without a fight. Certainly none of them would forgive his betrayal of Sub-Lieutenant Heron.

"It is more than a rumour. There is a group out there on the loose, and by the sound of it, they're causing our captors considerable concern. And we know that they didn't use a life pod to escape the ship." The Commander stared across the table. "So how did they escape, Mr. Clarke? As senior Lieutenant, perhaps that is something you should have checked before making your own escape."

"I did my best, sir." Lieutenant Clarke shifted in his seat and took a defiant posture. "The ship was falling apart, and you were injured and unconscious, and being evacuated by your team. I waited until all the other departments had cleared the ship!" His voice rose in desperation.

"Apparently not. Someone remained on board long enough to plot the helm orders for the Captain to ram our attacker. Was it you?" The Commander glared at the now white-faced Lieutenant. "No, I thought not. So whoever it was is also the person now leading a group of survivors on this godforsaken planet without equipment or survival gear. And yet this group and their officer are making enough of a nuisance of themselves to the Consortium ground forces that they've got all their spare troops out searching. Any idea who that officer might be?"

"No!" Clarke exclaimed. He coughed and cleared his throat to cover his abrupt response. "I mean, no, sir." He thought quickly. *Heron! It had to be Heron, but how the hell did he survive?* Clarke was absolutely certain there had been no life pods remaining when he'd triggered his own.

The Commander leaned forward and looked Clarke straight in the eye. "Well, I can make a stab at guessing, and I wish him and his team the best of luck. I'll do everything I can to support them, and I expect—no, I'm damned well making it an order that every officer here does everything in their power to prevent the Consortium from finding out who it is, and if they do find out, to render assistance to the officer if there is a chance to do so. There will be no further assistance of any sort to our captors. Is that clear?"

"Yes, sir."

"Very well." The Commander paused. "I am aware I was not in a position to carry out the evacuation checks myself, but the Court will not consider the fact I was unconscious when evacuated by my team as mitigation of my responsibility for the loss of our ship. I doubt they will take a light view of an officer such as yourself failing to ensure those in his care were evacuated before he departed to safety. No further discussion is needed on the matter. Dismiss."

Lieutenant Clarke felt the bitterness rising within him. It was all so damned unfair. He hadn't wanted this posting. He knew he battled with the mathematics, but his uncle had insisted he had to do at least one commission in this role to get the promotion he so badly wanted. And Delle—she just didn't understand. Well, he had time. He'd find an excuse for using the standard manoeuvres. There would be a Fleet Order covering them, and the surrender could be argued round.

Maybe if Heron were 'accidentally' killed...

Lieutenant Clarke rose to his feet and saluted, a perfunctory gesture at best. As he walked out of the office and made his way to the exercise area, he was acutely aware of the averted glances of his fellow officer prisoners. He had a lot to think about.

Chapter 12

Waiting and Wondering

James Heron cringed at the angry torrent from his sister. They'd had no word about Harry and Ferghal's whereabouts, and she was beside herself with worry and fear.

When she paused to take a breath, James took the opportunity to speak. "Niamh, there is no evidence that the boys are dead. In fact, the contrary—I have every reason to believe Ferghal is alive and well. And if he is alive, I am pretty sure Harry is too."

He knew he had nothing but the flimsiest evidence to support this statement. The only thing he had was an intelligence report that a team of scientists had been sent to a special lab to investigate someone known to the Consortium contact as 'the lab rat'. The reported description could have been either of the boys, but was most likely Ferghal due to the mention of the young man having very red hair and a violent temper.

If I had to face one of them in a real rage, I'd rather face Ferghal. Harry's temper was far more dangerous because it was backed by cold calculation. Ferghal's was less focused and, while destructive, it lacked the real venom Harry could muster. It was as well Harry recognised this as one of his character flaws and kept a tight rein on it.

A family trait, James acknowledged as Niamh fired at him.

"You're not even listening to what I'm saying, are you, James? Have you no feelings at all? Do you ever stop to consider anything other than your precious duty and the Fleet? Do you ever consider what those of us who care for you and the boys go through while you swan around the universe?"

The Rear Admiral was stung by this comment. "Yes, I do, and you should know it, Niamh, better than anyone. I'm doing everything I can to find the boys. But it's not just them—it's every one of our people, including all of you at home and everything the Confederation represents, corrupt damned politics and all. That is what I am under oath of allegiance to defend, even when it means giving up my own flesh and blood. Do you really think I find it easy?"

Niamh's face paled as the fight drained out of her. "I'm sorry, James. It's just so hard. I love those boys as if they were my own sons."

"So do I, Niamh. So do I . . ."

Admiral Katrina Hartmann, Commander in Chief, Fleet One, strode into her Command Centre.

"Flags, this report suggests our opponents have an edge on us in ships and troops." Positioning herself at the Flag Lieutenant's console, she activated a holographic display. "Our three starships with their six cruisers and twenty destroyers and frigates could be up against four starships, four cruisers and three landing ships with an equal number of frigates and destroyers. If the Consortium choose to fight, it'll be a tough match."

"It'll be close, ma'am, but two of their starships are conversions. The specs we have suggest they may be less effective than they appear."

"Get Captain Curran on the link for me." She moved to her Command Console. By the time she took her seat, Ben Curran's face was visible on her holographic screen. "Morning, Ben, this is going to be a tough call. They have our garrison on Planet Regulus cut off, so I have two choices—order the garrison to surrender, or go in and break the siege. The only problem is the size of their reinforcing fleet. They easily match us for firepower."

"I've been looking up the stats myself," Ben replied. "Though it looks uneven, I think we have an edge. Our intel says they have the *Khamenei*, *City of Richmond*, *Corporate Trader* and ICL *Conveyor* with them. According to the assessments, the last two are quite a bit less powerful than they appear. Neither has the protection and compartmentation of a purpose-built starship. They're also a lot weaker, in terms of weapons, than our oldest ship, so the balance may be a bit in our favour."

Admiral Hartmann nodded. "Assuming our information is correct, that will even things up. All right, we have to go with that, so let's see what our options are for a plan of attack. I don't intend to give them a chance to organise a defence if I can help it, and those three landing ships are my priority. I want them disabled or destroyed. I'm expecting to be joined by two more LSPs of our own in the next two days. Command wants us to get them into position to reinforce the garrison as soon as we can."

Ben nodded. "I agree. If we can prevent their landing force from being withdrawn, that will give them a real problem somewhere else."

"Right, let's look at our options." The discussion turned to the overall strategy and tactics of an engagement and the disposition of their forces as they dropped out of transit. "What do you think of the latest intel assessments?"

"The balance looks marginally in our favour, but it is close." Ben paused. "The *Khamenei* is Admiral Gratz's flagship, and she's based on an earlier design of ours. They will have upgraded her systems, but possibly not her layout and structure."

"Good. That gives me a basis to work around. Conference in my quarters at fifteen hundred. We can start putting some flesh on the bones." Cutting the link, she ordered, "Flags, I want to game some options. Get me some players, please."

Danny joined Spike Rajput in the Gunroom. "I managed to out manoeuvre the cruisers while simulating the enemy cruiser force command." His grin broadened. "Gareth wasn't happy—he was commanding our cruisers. The Admiral gave him a real chewing out for his interpretation of her orders."

"Watch out, my friend." Spike leaned closer. "Gareth doesn't like losing on the simulator. You'll make an enemy of him if you're not careful."

"Then he'd better learn to be less predictable," said Danny, brushing it off. He wasn't easily intimidated by anyone. Changing the subject, he asked, "Is there any news on the *Daring*? Do they know if she's been found or if there are survivors?"

"There's a rumour she was destroyed by the Consortium's *Sirte Global*. The intel is that cruiser is now in repair dock having her fore end rebuilt after a run-in with a destroyer, possibly the *Daring*. I hear there were survivors, but I haven't heard anything else." Spike glanced at his friend. "I know Harry and Ferghal were on her—I hope they're okay."

"So do I," said Danny. "I pray for them every day."

Brigadier Newton of the Consortium Fleet tapped the desk, her thoughts on the elusive survivors. Her search teams had turned up nothing more since the theft of the transport. The vehicle was intercepted and destroyed when it refused to stop or surrender, but no human remains were found inside it. Where had the escapees abandoned it? More important, where were they now?

The security arrangements for a visit by the Chairman and several Directors were going to complicate things. Her forces were already stretched due to the need to send a strong military force with every scientific team working in the cities. The Canids simply would not give up, and now that they'd learned that direct attacks on Consortium troops only led to multiple deaths, they employed guerilla strikes against targets of opportunity—any group or individual not being very, very careful. Even then, the Canids had the ability to hide in plain sight, and they used it very effectively. Her troops were suffering mounting casualties from it, and the researchers weren't immune either.

On top of that problem, with a group of Fleet personnel on the loose creative enough to escape her patrols, and with the boldness to walk right into her soldiers' campsite and take them off guard, she had reason to be worried. They might just be capable of pulling off a surprise stunt and endangering the Board members, especially as her troops' best efforts had so far been unable to discover any trace of where the runaways had gone to ground.

When the room was silent, she spoke. "We know they can't leave the planet, and they don't have transport." Standing, she paced. "So where the hell are they? Could they be in one of these cities? The Canids seem to have withdrawn from all the cities near our Base."

Colonel Rees responded. "It's possible, but we'd have to search each city individually. We can't scan them. We've tried. No result. Some sort of field blocks our scanners, and we don't have the time or the resources to visit every site and search it."

The Brigadier was thoughtful. "But we can concentrate on the ones within the range of our Bases. We can check as many as possible in the immediate vicinity of where the transport vehicle was recovered, and fan out from there. At least we can make sure they aren't within striking distance."

The Colonel nodded. "I'll get on it. If we don't find them, it's unlikely they'll survive the winter unless they find some way of eating the stuff these Rotties manage to digest—and they'll need heating and shelter, which might be a challenge, but that will help us locate them." He paused. "We may just have to destroy the cities completely if we can't smoke the Fleet fugitives out by any other means. We have the capability."

"As a last resort. I don't want to use fission weapons unless we have no other choice. Besides, that would destroy any chance of cracking the secret of these sentient structures, and could impact on our other operations here. No, we need to find another way."

Chapter 13

Discovery

———————————————

Autumn gave way to winter in a series of violent storms that brought an end to their ability to find food in the environs of the abandoned city. The replicator they'd acquired was unable to produce the quantities of food they needed, and they had to conserve its power pack to keep it functioning as long as possible. They could look forward to a very lean time. The only consolation was it also brought an end to their enemy's efforts to find them.

For Harry, the downtime allowed him to wonder what was happening in Mary's life. Thoughts of his sweetheart at home brought other feelings now, made more difficult by the fact they embarrassed him, and sometimes invaded his dreams. His mood was worsened by the fact that Maddie Hodges and Errol Hill had formed a relationship, which the others tacitly accepted. This posed another dilemma. He struggled to understand why that made him jealous. After all, he truly loved Mary, didn't he?

He decided he'd wrestle with these thoughts another time, and went in search of Rasmus. He was always good for intelligent conversation that challenged Harry's mind and distracted him from relationship worries.

He found Rasmus pottering about in his sleeping quarters. Harry seated himself and plunged right in with the other matter that concerned him lately. "I cannot escape the feeling we are being watched at all times, Rasmus. I wish I knew who or what was doing the watching. It has troubled me from the beginning. Do you feel it too?"

"Yes, but not all the time. It seems as if something or someone is studying what I do—a ghost perhaps!" He hoped to lighten Harry's mood.

Harry laughed. "I do not think we have ghosts, but we must be vigilant nonetheless."

The Coxswain tapped on the doorframe. "A moment, sir? I think we've solved the cooking problem. Hill and Skoronski have cobbled together a stove of sorts, and Hodges converted a power supply from some kit she took off that transport. Means we don't have to make a fire to cook the fish we catch."

"Well done." This was something that had troubled Harry. "So it's fresh fish for supper, is it? Where have they rigged the stove?"

"Right this way, sir. It's more a sort of heated plate, but it works. Now if we could just get a nice beef culture, or a bit of bacon..."

Laughing, Harry and Rasmus followed the Coxswain to where the TechRates had installed their stove. The unit was a crude but satisfactory cooking plate. They'd also contrived a workable pan in which to cook.

Harry surveyed the work. "Well done. That solves the problem of lighting fires, which I suspect is how our enemies have identified our location on previous occasions."

The feeling of being watched came to a head when Harry woke up to find himself covered by a cloth of the sort the Canids used. There was no sign of anyone having entered the chamber and got past the guards, and no one of his party had brought in the cloak-like garment to put over him. Searching his memory, he recalled he had felt cold, and then had felt much warmer after someone had placed it over him. As he lay in the darkness in that hazy zone between sleep and wakefulness, he was awash with memories of his mother doing the same thing on cold nights in their big stone house in Ireland when he was a boy.

That put him in an introspective mood on this cold, bleak day.

"Good morning, Harry," Rasmus greeted him with his usual cheer as Harry joined the others in the chamber they used as a dining hall. "Coffee?" Rasmus held up a steaming pot.

"Thank you," Harry replied absently. Then the oddness of the situation struck him. "Coffee? We haven't had that for a while. Please tell me how you managed to obtain coffee."

"Didn't have to look far, sir," commented the Coxswain. "Our supplies doubled overnight—look for yourself."

"Not just the food either," chipped in TechRate Hill. "Someone got in during the night and left us a load of stuff—like these cloaks, sir. I was nice and snug once someone put one over me while I slept. Thought it was something else at first." He glanced at Maddie Hodges and winked. She gave him a sly grin.

Harry frowned. He had a sudden guilty feeling for not having demanded to know who had covered him with the cloak the moment he felt it in the middle of the night, and now realised it was identical to those worn by the Canids. If those creatures could bypass their sentries so easily, then perhaps the Consortium troops could too. "Where were our sentries? What did they see?"

"Ahead of you, sir," rumbled the Coxswain. "I've already grilled the boys. None of them were asleep at their posts. Whoever got in and out didn't go past them. I think we may have to shift positions so that we don't get caught again—or we need to post sentries inside and out."

"All the more reason to worry," snapped Harry. "If anyone can just walk in and out without being seen, we had better find out how!" He hadn't meant to sound so gruff. "Very well, we'll shift our position. There's another suitable building across the street. We must do so immediately—and this time we'll make sure we control every entrance."

Settled in the new location, Harry noticed what appeared to be a network interface. He peered at it then stepped back, startled, when the device emerged from the wall.

"What the hell is that?" growled the Coxswain.

"Damned if I know, Swain." Harry shook his head. "But it looks like some sort of interface. I wonder what for?"

"I know this place hides something from our scanners, and I wish I knew what." The Coxswain scowled at it. "Gives me the bloody creeps. It doesn't even look like it's meant for humans."

"It must serve some purpose." The unusual patterns on the surface confirmed Harry's assumption that it was an interface. "That looks like the palm scanner we use for security access." Placing his hand on the surface, he said, "See, it contains an outline of something like a hand."

"More like a paw," remarked Rasmus who had joined them.

Harry felt a momentary tingle in his hand, and lifted it clear of the surface. "Strange!" He stared at the device, a frown creasing his brow. "I think it scanned my palm. See? There is luminescence in the place where my hand was." He staggered slightly as his ears filled with strange sounds. He clapped his hands over them in a useless effort to make it stop, but the sounds were inside his head, having entered through his neural link.

"We've had to call off the work on the cities, Brigadier. The weather makes it impossible to continue." The leader of the Consortium scientific team shook her head. "We've made a little progress, we think. We have at least managed to keep a sample from the latest one we examined. It does confirm our earlier conclusion that it is a life form."

"At least that's something." Brigadier Newton studied the scientist. "Are you any nearer figuring out the power sources? The lighting system?"

Missing the sarcasm, the scientist paused. "We're pretty certain the lighting is a form of bioluminescence, but why it reacts to any physical presence and isn't constant, we haven't managed yet. A pity your troops can't keep those Rottweilers out of our hair. We could make much more progress without their interference."

"If you could tell us how to see them before they attack us, that would help," snapped the Brigadier. "What is happening with your tests on Lieutenant O'Connor? I trust he's not been allowed to get into the AI?"

"Definitely not! We've taken every precaution to keep him isolated." She looked up. "Doctor Wan is very frustrated by your orders. He plans to raise it with the Board when they visit."

"He may do as he pleases, but remind him that what happened was a result of his refusal to accept our warning, and I shall be saying so to the Board."

The scientist opened her mouth to retort, then thought better of it. "Yes, well, what happened is unfortunate. However, we are pursuing a new line, one suggested by a conversation with that Fleet Lieutenant – Clarke. He tells us that, with Heron, sometimes he's unable to control the link. The AI 'reads' his mind. It's an avenue we'd like to try using a portable system such as an android servant. If we fit one with a recorder, we can—"

"I'll stop you right there. You do know the androids are all in direct link to the Base AI, right? If one linked to O'Connor, that would automatically connect him to the Base." She paused. "No. I can't allow it."

In his cell, Ferghal watched the small group of scientists as they conferred out of his hearing, or so they thought. Hiding his grin by cupping his chin with his hand, he listened to them through the remnants of the AI, using its reconfigured audio pickups to eavesdrop on their conversation. It had taken him some time to adapt bits of the neural network for his purposes. He'd taken care to make it look as if the damage to the system precluded his using it. The last three months had certainly been productive from his perspective, albeit lonely. At least he had made friends with some of the guards.

"The Brigadier refuses to allow us to make any physical examination, and she's vetoed using a droid," he heard the leader say. Ferghal recognised him, the unfortunate doctor whose nose would forever show his encounter with Ferghal's fist. "But when Dr. Johnstone gets here with the Board, we can get that reversed. In the meantime, I suggest we carry out the planned trials with portable equipment—but make certain it's isolated and hidden from the main system."

"Well," began another of the party, his arm still in a sling thanks to Ferghal, "after the damage he did to this dome's system, we'll need to make sure there is no contact at all with the comlink. It seems dangerous to allow him to enter a network that is linked in any way to another system."

"I agree," said a woman, who Ferghal recognised as the one who'd attended to him while he was in the med-unit. "But I am curious to know exactly how he could do the damage he did. He managed to override the power regulation to large parts of the circuitry, and blew out key components in the process."

"That's supposed to be impossible," another of the team interjected. "If I hadn't seen it with my own eyes, I wouldn't believe it—"

"And he managed to prevent our attempts to shut down his link," said the lab supervisor. "I suggest we move very cautiously with this one. The firewalls and proxies we had in place were useless once he got in."

"Then you need to lock down the network and make it inaccessible to anyone but us." Dr Wan sounded impatient. "How hard is that?"

Not hard at all, Ferghal answered him inwardly. *If you give me another chance, my friend, you'll find out just how much damage I can do. And if you rig up another system, I'll hack into it and find out what else you're up to.*

"I hear the troops think there's another group of survivors. There was talk of one of them being able to do things to the computers on their vehicles. They say he overcame their locator beacons and the failsafe system for infiltration and attack."

"Yes, I heard that," said one of the others. "A group of troopers were ambushed and stripped of their clothing and equipment, then left sealed in a portable dome in their underwear. The attackers took their transport but left its locator beacon giving the auto responses the rest of the patrols expected while making their getaway. They destroyed the transport near one of the alien cities about six hundred kilometres south of here—but there was no trace of the escapees in the wreckage, and those vehicles aren't normally capable of unmanned manoeuvring."

The response to this was lost to Ferghal as his heart leapt with joy. Harry! He had to suppress his desire to laugh out loud. This was just too good. He should have known his friend was alive and well, out there somewhere causing havoc for the enemy. Now he had even more reason to frustrate everything this shower of spáilpíns attempted. Somehow, he would find Harry and his team. Somehow, he would find a way to get out of here. For the first time since he had awoken in this damnable place, Ferghal found hope and, with it, the determination to escape.

Chapter 14

Engage the Enemy

———————————————

NECS *Vengeance* and her fleet dropped out of transit on the edge of the outermost asteroid field encircling the system. The star at its centre formed a brilliant image on the Admiral's display, and the scattered planets circling it showed varying shades of brown or red as they reflected its light.

One of the inner ones was a small bright jewel, a home away from home for a small human colony and garrison under siege by a powerful Consortium force. The system provided a valuable source of minerals and ores and a place for emitter satellites and scanners for at least one side in this conflict.

"In position," Captain Curran reported from his Command Centre. "I expect their monitors will be sounding the alert."

"I would be surprised if they weren't already at action stations," Admiral Hartmann replied. "We have four starships, five cruisers, nine destroyers and twelve frigates on scan with three landing ships in orbital positions."

"Confirmed. Our ships are deployed as ordered. This will be close, though, and they have at least four more ships than we do, but the extras appear to be conversions. They don't belong to any known class."

"Good." The Admiral paused. "Well, we have no choice now—the garrisons are under sustained attack, and won't hold out much longer if we can't break this siege. Initiate Variant Twenty-One of my attack plans."

To her Flag Lieutenant, she said, "Give me a link to all ships."

"Online, Admiral," responded the Lieutenant.

Aboard the CS *Khamenei*, Admiral Bob Gratz studied the scan reports. Satisfied, he nodded. "Good. I expected this. We've a slight edge with the upgrades on the *Trader*, and the *Reitz*, *Albacore*, *Francini* and *Asia Star* give us some extra strike capability. Deploy for battle in accordance with my orders. The landing ships remain in orbit to support our forces on planet."

"Deploying as ordered," the Flag Lieutenant reported, watching the display.

The Consortium's senior Admiral was a bold commander. His plan split his forces into two equally balanced groups, his intention being to divide the attacking forces to allow him to concentrate on the weaker elements of his enemy. He knew Admiral Hartmann well. They had been Midshipmen together in the Fleet, and she was a superb tactician, a skill she had demonstrated early in her career.

But he was also aware of her weakness—a reluctance to sacrifice ships or men when faced with a choice between pressing home an attack and risking heavy casualties, unless it meant a chance to inflict heavier damage on an enemy.

His deployment and the minefields he had laid meant his opponent would have to approach along a route his forces could predict, which gave them the chance to target ships dropping out before their scanners and targeting arrays could clear. He was confident his ships could hold off this attack and prevent the relief of the local garrison. His expression was one of grim resolution. The die was now cast. His opponent's tendency toward conserving her forces would work against her, he was sure.

Aboard the *Vengeance*, Admiral Hartmann watched the enemy deployment with a touch of satisfaction and relief. Good old Bob, predictable as ever. She frowned when she noticed the flashing patterns that indicated the minefields and the position of his ships. She leaned forward, her eyes on the screen. "Deploy the anti-mine countermeasures ships in quadrant Alpha, and let's see how he responds to that."

The Flag Lieutenant checked his plot. "Mine clearance force responding."

"Good. First cruiser squadron, prepare to support the mine clearance approach. If the opportunity arises, transit through the gap and take the landing ships. *Victorious* and *Emden*, move toward the Southern Polar division, but be prepared for my signal to join us when I strike at their flag division."

Admiral Gratz was mildly surprised when a small group of strike craft and mine clearance ships dropped out and began to destroy mines on his extreme flank. He ordered a counter strike by his frigates and watched as a cautious skirmish commenced with the two groups playing a deadly game of cat and mouse in and around the minefield. He ordered reinforcements to the area when it became apparent that the mines were being neutralised.

"They have something new to use on the mines," he snapped. "Send a squadron of strike craft to tackle their clearance ships."

"Their Flag Squadron is closing on the predicted path," the Scan Commander reported. "They'll be in range in three minutes."

"Prepare to engage. Division Two—move on my signal."

Admiral Hartmann breathed a sigh of relief as her scan team noted the enemy ships firing up their drives. "He's taking the lure. Signal *Victorious* to launch her strike and join us as soon as the enemy responds. We'll launch our strike fighters and missile carriers once we're within their strike range, and then we'll withdraw. I want to pull him away from his defensive position."

"Do we know he'll follow us, ma'am?" The Flag Lieutenant sounded uncertain.

She grinned. "Bob Gratz has a tendency to chase, and I want him to chase me."

"The cruisers have gone into the gap in the minefield," reported the scan officer. "They've engaged the enemy's frigates and have them on the run."

Another voice cut in. "Enemy cruisers moving toward the *Parramatta* and *de Ruyter*."

"Keep me informed. Captain Wright knows what I want him to do."

The ship shuddered, and Captain Curran's voice cut into the Admiral's comlink. "Engaging the enemy—two starships and two cruisers. Strike craft launched and frigates engaging."

"Thanks, Ben." The Admiral turned to her Flag Lieutenant. "Warn our ships—prepare to disengage and pull back to the rendezvous for our formation. If I know Bob Gratz, he'll take the bait. Are the LSPs in position?"

"Confirmed. They are in place with their escort, awaiting our signal."

"Good. Where is his second division now?"

"They're closing on us, in range in five minutes."

"At one minute give the order to pull back and send *Victorious* and her group into their flank." She concentrated on her screen. "I'm counting on you now, Gratz, my friend. I hope age hasn't taught you caution."

At his station, Danny Gunn watched his targeting screen, concentrating on tracking the ship identified as the primary target for the weapons clusters he controlled. On either side of him a pair of TechRates kept the weapons locked to the target. He couldn't help recalling a fleeting memory of his former role aboard the *Spartan* during sea battles with the French, running between the magazine and the guns with his powder charges. That led to thoughts of Harry and Ferghal. He focused again with renewed vigor. This was for them.

"Fire on my mark." The voice of the Weapons Commander was calm.

Danny activated the fire command and waited, his fingers poised on his interface pads. When the order was given, he fired on command. Bright bursts of incandescence illuminated the image on his screen as his weapons hit their target.

"Shifting target," he said through gritted teeth as tremors in their own ship told a story of hits received. He focused again on the target, selecting a cluster of weapons pods near one of the ship's stubby fins. He stabbed the command switch, and again, bursts of incandescence told of satisfying hits. An even brighter spray of plasma burst from the enemy ship carrying with it large sections of her hull.

"Shift target to the damaged area." The Commander's voice was sharp. "Don't give him a chance to recover."

Other weapons pods joined Danny's as he poured fire into the gaping hole in the stricken ship. Further bursts of fire erupted from the enemy vessel, and the Commander ordered, "Shift target—next in line. Lock to weapon arrays and launch bays."

Once again, the target scanners adjusted and focused, and plasma erupted from their weapons. Danny's team tracked the other ship's broadside launch bays and caused a tremendous amount of damage.

"Cease fire. Disengaging. All targeting stand by for reengagement. Track previous target. Don't lose contact as we move. Link to navigation to maintain relative positions and range." The orders flowed in a calm, almost bored, yet nonetheless compelling stream.

Danny made sure his scan was linked to the navigation system. He watched as the ship accelerated out of range then regrouped with her division in the Admiral's chosen position. Through the comlink, he could hear the reports flowing back and forth on damage and casualties, and hoped that his friends were safe.

Admiral Hartmann smiled as she watched her battle plot. "He's taken the bait," she said. "Warn Captain Kessler to stand by to attack their cruisers with his group. One of their capital ships seems to be lagging. She took quite a mauling. Tell the destroyers to harass her—missiles if they can."

"Acknowledged," came the response. "The LSPs and their escorts are in position and ready to move on your order."

"Good. I don't want them to move yet. I want their main fleet clear of the planet first. Warn Captain Wright to be ready for action as soon as we have their capital ships engaged."

"Enemy fleet in range in seven minutes."

"On my mark then." The Admiral felt calm. "Time to close our little trap." She watched the display then keyed her comlink. "All ships reverse course and engage. His minefield has just become our ally."

Aboard the *Khamenei*, Admiral Gratz realised his danger the moment the *Vengeance* swung rapidly through a turn that caused the ship's structure to groan with the strain. For those at the extremities, the swing caused a momentary discomfort as the motion temporarily disturbed the artificial gravity. The ships closed rapidly and far too quickly for any attempt to use micro hyper bursts for evasive manoeuvres.

The opposing ships opened fire almost simultaneously. Admiral Hartmann glanced at her Flag Lieutenant. "Tell Captain Wright and the LSPs to strike now. Whatever else happens, I want their landing ships destroyed and our LSP troops landed."

Alone at home, Niamh listened with growing anxiety to the news. "We have a report that a Consortium fleet has been engaged in battle by a WTO fleet under the command of Admiral Hartmann in the Regulus system. The engagement is still in progress, and we will bring you updates as soon as we receive them."

"That's Danny's admiral!" Niamh exclaimed. Then the rest of the news report hit her. She considered calling her husband then decided against it. Theo had enough on his plate.

An idea came to her. She found her coat and slipped out, instructing the transport module to take her to the ancient church that bore the plaque commemorating Harry and Ferghal's disappearance in 1804, and their presumed death.

In the quiet of the ancient church, she ran her fingers over the worn brass of the plaque, tracing the lettering as she read its inscription.

In loving memory of Henry Nelson Heron,
Midshipman, serving aboard His Most Britannic
Majesty's Ship Spartan 74 guns.
Lost at sea in a sea-fight with two frigates of the
French Fleet the 30th day of November in the year
of our Lord 1804.
Born 20th May 1789.
Died at sea 30th November 1804.
Also to the memory of Ferghal O'Connor, Boy
Seaman, and sometime stable boy in this Parish,
friend and companion of the aforesaid Henry, lost
in the same sea-fight.
Born 11th February 1787 and
died at sea 30th November 1804.

She murmured a prayer for their safety, and said, "Not yet. Please not yet."

Chapter 15

Contact

———————————————

Harry awoke from a dream of walking with Mary along a deserted beach, and had the distinct feeling that he was not alone. In the months that he and his crew had been living in these buildings, they had learned that any movement activated the lights in their living quarters, but there must have been no one moving about on this night because the interior was dark—unless whoever was here was invisible to the sensors, or the sensors were programmed not to respond to their movements. He tensed and listened then rolled off his bed and dropped into a crouch with his weapon ready. The lights came on at his movement.

He stared about the room. There was nothing other than his own belongings stored where he had placed them. Everything seemed normal, but the feeling of someone or something in the room was overpowering. Then it registered—there was something. He could smell it. But what was it? And more importantly, where was it?

A memory tickled his consciousness and clicked into place. He replaced the plasma projector in its holster and sat on his bed. He placed his hands palms up on his knees and spoke in a quiet voice.

"Show yourself, please. I know you do not understand me, but I hope you understand that I mean you no harm, and I think you have a peaceful intention as well."

A large Canid materialised near the wall. Harry recognised him as the leader he had interacted with previously. For several moments, they assessed each other. The Canid placed a small object on the floor and pushed it toward Harry. As the creature moved, Harry noticed its cloak, and realised that must play some part in the Canids' apparent ability to vanish from sight and reappear.

"You want me to have this?" Harry asked. He reached for it cautiously, and when he picked it up, he felt a tingle in his fingers. It was compact and lightweight, and its surface shone with a luminescence from within. Harry looked up and smiled, hoping the Canid would correctly interpreted this as an expression of friendliness.

"Thank you. But why do you bring it to me?"

A series of growls, barks and other sounds issued from the device, and startled him so completely that he almost dropped it.

The Canid growled a rapid response, and a voice from the device said, "I am Grakuna. Attend me. We go to the pack den."

The Coxswain crowded into the doorway with TechRate Hill close behind. "You okay, sir? We've had visitors again." When he saw the massive Canid leader, his jaw set in a hard line.

"How'd he get in here?"

The device in Harry's hands growled and yipped.

"What the hell?" yelled the Coxswain, and he moved to advance.

"Easy, Swain," Harry said as the Canid adopted a threatening stance and produced a weapon. "My visitor brought this device, a most useful one, I think, for it serves as a translation tool."

The visitor uttered a series of canine-like yips and barks.

The device spoke again. "We serve the Provider. We are instructed to help you. You must come to our den. Your presence here is a danger to us."

The Coxswain sensed a trap. He'd grown up in the rough parts of Manchester and was nobody's fool. "You'll take a couple of the lads with you, sir." It was a statement rather than a request.

"Very well, Swain, and I shall want you to keep track of where he takes us and how we get there. Make sure you take particular note of the entrance." Harry thought for a moment. "Let Errol and Hodges come with me. I shall want the rest of you to make sure we are ready to move at a moment's notice when I return. Apparently, we must relocate. Have the men ready." The device growled and yipped a translation.

The Coxswain looked unconvinced. "I'm not sure you should do this, sir. Maybe I should go."

The leader responded with a rapid-fire series of sounds, which the device translated as, "You must all come now. You cannot delay."

Harry frowned. "Why can we not remain here? Why the hurry?"

"Those who seek you are close. If you remain, they shall find you and discover that which is not for them." The visitor adopted an aggressive tone. "They cannot be permitted to cause further damage to our Provider." The gesture took in the entire structure around them. "We will assist you if you assist us in protecting the Provider who shelters us."

It took Harry a moment to consider this. His people were safe and comfortable here. True, they were short of suitable clothes and food, but they were warm enough and able to survive. Then again, this help could give them the means to do more, perhaps even to strike at the Consortium forces that shadowed their every move.

By now the rest of the team were grouped in the corridor outside, alert and ready with the few weapons they had. Taking in their ragged appearance—he was the only member of the group still beardless—he considered his options. So far, he had been unable to think of anything more than defending themselves if they were attacked, and to keep running. Perhaps now they had a chance to take a proactive role in the battle against the Consortium.

He reached a decision. "Very well. Swain, clear the decks. We're all going. If the Consortium has a patrol nearby, we cannot linger." He grinned at a sudden thought. "They must be having a bad time of it in this brutal weather."

Harry was not wrong. Outside the temperatures were very low, and the winds carried fine grains of ice at speeds that stripped coatings from metal surfaces. Men moving about in these conditions needed protective suits, a necessity that had all but trapped Harry and his men inside the buildings since the snows arrived.

"If you're sure, sir." Coxswain Abram Winstanley looked dubious. Turning he gave a series of rapid-fire orders, and the men scattered to obey.

Two miles away, a Consortium patrol commander deployed his search teams into the first of the alien structures. This was the fifth city they had searched. To his second in command he remarked, "These bloody places are creepy. Every time our tech teams set up their equipment to examine them, the Rotties appear from nowhere and chase them off. Where the hell they come from is a good question, because they don't live in them. They just defend them as soon as anyone tries to cut a wall or force anything open that looks like a sealed door." Indicating the cluster of buildings, he added, "Just look at these structures—nothing like anything we build, and just standing empty, but they're well maintained. And what the hell are they made of? According to our people it's some sort of organic material."

"Yeah." His second in command nodded. "I heard about that. There's something hiding here, and they say it is some sort of life form, but also some form of advanced tech that the Board can't wait to get their hands on."

"Be worth something if they do. No one knows what generates the power these buildings run on. It's nothing like anything we use," agreed the senior. He spotted the signal indicating the building was clear. "Next one over, Sergeant," he ordered on his link. "Funny that there's no sign of the Rotties either."

"Maybe they've finally given up."

"Doubt it. The Colonel says we'll be making a full assault to take control of several of these places so the tech geeks can do their thing as soon as summer comes." The vehicle shuddered in a sudden blast of wind. The Commander grimaced. "I'm sick of this search. It's tying down two battalions of our troops, and besides, I don't think the Fleet runaways are still alive in this weather. If they are, they won't be any sort of threat when we find them shivering and huddling in some dank cave, miserable wretches."

"I hear you," said his second in command. "And from what I've heard, one of them may be Heron, best friends with that prisoner O'Connor they're holding in the Iso-lab." He glanced at his patrol commander. "I heard that wild Irishman made a real mess of their system."

"What, did they let him loose or something? Idiots!"

"No, more like he broke loose. They say he got into the AI in his head while they were trying to find out how, and he altered vital parts of the program and made it fail."

"That so?" The Commander chuckled. "There must be something in it. Our orders are clear that if we capture this lot, and there's a Sub-Loot with them, we're to make sure he gets knocked out and kept out until we get him to the Base lab, so if he's really that unchained, well, let's hope one of the other squads finds him first."

Harry and his team followed the Canid leader down a ramp into the bowels of the building, struggling to carry their possessions and everything they had acquired during their long stay on this planet. Before departing their campsite, they tried to eradicate every trace of their presence, but time was against them, and they had to move out quickly. As they followed their guide, Harry was conscious of the fact that evidence of their stay would be visible to any reasonable search.

Reaching a chamber they'd explored several times, they were surprised to find there was now a circular door leading into a tunnel in one wall.

"Bloody hell," exclaimed the Coxswain. "Why didn't we see that before?"

"More important, Swain, where does it go?" said Harry, giving him a sidelong glance.

"It resembles the Unterbahn," remarked Rasmus. When he caught Harry's baffled look, he added, "The sub-surface transport system in our major cities."

"Ah." Harry nodded. "I thought that might be what you meant. But the question, my friend, is where does this go, and how can we be certain our pursuers will not follow us?"

"There will be no pursuit." The voice startled Harry. He glanced at the device in his hands then looked at the Coxswain and Rasmus. It took him a moment to realise that only he had heard the voice.

"You're an AI?" He concentrated his thoughts, as he would have done to converse with the *Daring*.

"I am the Keeper, Protector and Provider of the ones you call the Canids."

"Why are you helping us?"

At first, there was no response, and Harry had time to wonder if he had asked the wrong question, but then, in his thoughts, he heard the deep voice of the Provider's reply.

"They plan further attacks on us. You must help my people stop them."

Harry took a moment to digest this, conscious now that everyone was staring at him, including the Canid. He let his question form. *"Can you help us to free our friends and provide the means to destroy the enemy?"*

"I may conceal you and provide you with the means of shelter, food and movement to your destinations. I cannot provide you with weapons. Those you must construct yourselves, though I can provide the materials."

"Very well," Harry acknowledged. *"Then let us make our escape from here. We will need a great deal if we are to defend you."*

To his companions he said, "It seems we have a task to perform in return for our safety and comfort. I will explain it as we go."

The Coxswain glanced at him, uncertain of what was really going on, but he kept his thoughts to himself. To his men he said, "You heard the Lieutenant. Move it! We haven't time to hang about."

Chapter 16

A Near-Run Thing

Danny concentrated on his targeting screen. The *Vengeance* was taking a lot of damage. A number of systems were inoperable, and several of their weapons emplacements were damaged. Within the Weapons Control Centre, several consoles were out of action. The smell of burning metal tinged the air with a metallic taste.

One of the operators had suffered burns when her console failed and she was caught by the flash; another had serious wounds caused by the destruction of a display screen.

Danny locked his array onto the enemy flagship and warned his TechRates to stand by. "They are in range in twelve seconds," he added. "Prepare to fire."

"Ready!" came the responses.

"Fire! Concentrated bursts on my aiming point."

The bright bursts of incandescence lanced from the projectors, their focus on a damaged section of the enemy ship's hull, which blossomed in a flare of destruction as a large section of the hull tore away. Danny's targeting shifted to a cluster of what he took to be communications antennae.

"Shift target," he ordered. "Fire on my command."

"Ready."

"Fire."

The array disintegrated and large chunks of the other ship erupted as the bolts tore into her hull.

"Admiral, we've lost the inter-ship coms array. We are trying to reroute through the long range system, but we can't contact the Fleet." The Communications Officer's voice betrayed his desperation as his team struggled to reroute their communications. Severe damage to all systems was making it increasingly difficult to keep in contact with all the Fleet components. Without the inter-ship link, Admiral Gratz had lost the ability to direct his fleet.

"Prepare my barge. I'll shift to the *City of Richmond*. At least from the barge and the *Richmond* I can talk to the Fleet."

"The launch bay for the barge is inoperative, sir. We can get a launch away from the after hangar though."

"Make it so. The *City of Richmond* has a command suite I can use. Tell Captain Ahmadi to provide me with cover for the transfer. I'll alert the *Richmond* from the launch."

"Yes, sir." The Flag Lieutenant hurried away to make the arrangements.

Admiral Hartmann of the North European Confederation Fleet studied the dispositions of her fleet and their enemy. "Give me the latest on the position with the landing ships."

"Our LSPs have been inserted, ma'am. Our cruisers have knocked out two Consortium landing ships and damaged a third. The troops are on their way down, and they are being engaged by the rest of the enemy's cruiser squadrons—it's fairly evenly matched now."

"Very well. Have we any resources to support them?"

"Not at present, ma'am." The Plotting Officer ran a check on dispositions. "We can give them some small stuff, but nothing more."

"Ma'am!" exclaimed a Lieutenant. "Their flagship has just launched a barge—someone heading for the city class ship beyond her."

The Admiral stood and stared at the display. "Hmm ... that may be the break we need. Order *Victorious* to close with her and engage them with everything they have. We must have knocked out something on the *Khamenei*. Gratz is trying to shift his flag!"

"They're recovering the barge." The voice of the scan operator cut through the Control Centre. "And they're trying to disengage. Do you want us to pursue?"

The Admiral considered this. "Negative. They're moving behind another minefield. Order our ships to regroup. We've achieved our first objective to get our troops on the ground and to knock out their landing ships. Once we've regrouped, we can tackle their minefields again." She paused. "Get me the damage status on our ships, and send the LSP force some assistance."

Captain Curran spoke through the link. "Admiral, the enemy is reforming and making for the LSPs' position. I recommend pursuit and engagement."

"Very well, swing us past the minefield and resume attack formation please, Ben. This isn't over yet."

A new voice on the comlink caused the Admiral to pause. "Flag from *Constellation*. Captain Hopkins of the NASF joining with my escorts, Admiral. Where do you require our services?"

"*Constellation*, you're very welcome. Assist the *Parramatta* and her squadron defending the LSPs—they have their hands full." Hearing Captain Hopkins' acknowledgement, the Admiral turned to the Flag Lieutenant. "That's unexpected but welcome. The *Constellation* was with the North American Fleet at New Washington. Admiral Howland must have detached her and sent her on." She flexed her shoulders to ease the tension. "It looks like they've finally declared themselves active for the WTO."

"I'll signal our thanks," said the Lieutenant, but no sooner had he got the words out than the ship convulsed and an alarm sounded. "Damn! Hull breach. Everyone into survival suits—now!"

Danny felt himself lift from his seat and land heavily, first colliding with one of his TechRates and then with a console as air whistled out of the compartment. Dazed, it took him a moment to realise what was happening. When his head cleared, he struggled to get his survival suit on. Immediately he discovered he had a problem—his left arm dangled at his side, broken and useless. Desperate, he forced the suit onto his body, ignoring the pain.

"Here, sir, let me help you." A TechRate steadied him, wrestling the suit closed. The man bundled Danny into the escape hatch and followed to cycle them through. Already the smoke was thinning as the immediate fires died from lack of oxygen. He looked at Danny's pain-pinched face through the visor. "I'd better get you to the medics, sir—your arm doesn't look too good."

Danny gritted his teeth, the pain intense as he replied in a strangled voice, "Thanks. I think I can manage. Just give me a minute to get my breath back," but as soon as he said that, he fainted.

The small troop of Consortium soldiers reached the building that Harry and his crew had occupied barely an hour ago. Acutely aware of their danger and knowing the Fleet fugitives were armed, the searchers followed combat procedures rigorously. Searching room by room, floor by floor, they worked their way in following a much-practiced routine, bursting into the chamber, weapons hot and ready. They relaxed when it proved as empty as all the other rooms they'd searched in this building. If the Fleet survivors had been here, they were gone now, but they couldn't have been gone long. The smell of cooking and unwashed humanity was pungent through their breathing filters.

Lifting his visor, the sergeant sniffed. "This place smells worse than a backed-up latrine."

"Someone's been here, Sarge. Look at this bit of rubbish, and food scraps from a fish."

The squad leader approached the Lieutenant. "Sir, something or someone's been using this building. We found these." He held up a pair of very worn boots and a small toolkit. "Looks like some of our kit, but none of our people have been in this area."

"You're right." The Lieutenant took the toolkit from the sergeant. "This is one of ours. It has the unit ID on the case." He handed it back and glanced around him. "Okay, there's someone here then. I want this area searched. Take the damned buildings apart if you have to, but find them." He activated his comlink. "Captain, we may have a contact with the runaways from the *Daring*. I'll need more men to search this area properly."

"Stay where you are. I'm on my way over with the troop. Secure the area and make sure all your equipment is secure—especially the coms and the vehicle's AI."

Harry gazed about the large round chamber with its high domed ceiling and passages leading out in several directions. Galleried walkways circled the perimeter. The ground floor had the appearance of a park with a fountain, ponds and flowering plants.

The tunnels were lit, and it was obvious that many of the chambers opening off the galleries and tunnels were dwellings. A large number of Canids were present, most of them staring with fierce intent at Harry and his men.

The Coxswain grimaced. "Hope we're not on the menu."

"No cauldron or roasting spit in sight," Harry bantered, his mind taking in all the details as he followed the guide. The translation device growled and chirped in his hand while in his ears, the voice of what he assumed was an AI explained that they would be given their own living area. It occurred to him that he needed to share this information with the others.

"According to the AI that runs this place, we are to be given our own space. They will assist us and provide everything we need."

"It would be helpful if they could provide us with some coarse sulphur and potassium nitrate—" quipped Rasmus "—assuming you still want me to create some black powder. The replicator can't produce enough pure sulphur, and I can't make a good explosive without it."

"Some decent clothes would be useful, sir," said one of the men.

Harry had thought of that, but was spared the need to answer when their guide stopped and gestured, then growled something that the device translated. "Here is your place. Tell me your needs and I will fulfill them."

Harry bowed his acknowledgement, an unconscious gesture from his eighteenth century upbringing. "My thanks for your assistance to us. Allow us to settle ourselves, and we will certainly inform you of our needs when we know what we may require."

Harry told his group, "The Canids and their Provider are offering us protection. The Provider is, I think, some kind of AI system. Like our ships, it is capable of logical intelligent thought."

"An AI, sir?" said the Coxswain in an uncharacteristic interruption.

"So it appears, though it may be something else. It tells me it is the servant of the Siddhiche, and that we are to assist in protecting it. I assume it means protection from the Consortium, our mutual enemy. In return, we will be provided everything we need."

"Some new clothes an' boots would be great," remarked one of the men.

"That would certainly be useful," said Harry. He noted the expressions of their Canid watchers, which ranged from skeptical to hostile. "I think not all of them welcome us. I've been told by the AI that until they were attacked and driven out of their cities, they had no need for the sort of weapons we and our enemies employ, which means they have nothing with which to fight back. We will help them to create some and acquire others, I hope."

Rasmus nodded. "It will serve them well to be able to defend themselves properly. I will need some specialised equipment. Do you think they can provide it?"

Harry nodded. "I'm certain the leader trusts me now, and he knows that I mean him and his people no harm, but we must be careful of everything we do in the presence of these Canids. Do nothing that might provoke them or be misinterpreted as a slight upon them or theirs. Those wretched Consortium troops, never satisfied with enough, have killed and injured many of them in attempts to seize their structures. We must show the Canids that even though we are human, we have no such intention."

In his cell, Ferghal explored what was left of the lab's AI network. He was bored, primarily because the materials and tools he had been promised by the guard had not been provided. The network seemed to be as mindless as it was when he finished his angry assault on it. It was practically useless now, but that didn't worry Ferghal.

He had discovered that whenever anyone brought a portable interface near the facility, he could use it to enter a larger network that, he assumed, must be in a separate building nearby. Someone had one today, and he used it to enter the larger mind, which accepted him as a mobile node. He explored the data for anything that might confirm his belief that Harry was alive and free.

Chapter 17

Tipping the Scales

———————————————

"Someone was here recently." The Consortium Major frowned as he studied the rooms Harry and his men had occupied. "These places give me the creeps. You always feel as if you're being watched." He glanced at the troopers, all in combat ready postures, all with their backs to blank walls as they guarded their officers.

"Glad I'm not the only one that feels it." The Patrol Commander looked around. "The men have been through every building now, sir. No other signs of habitation, and no sign of the Fleet personnel we're looking for."

"Well, if they left before this storm started, they're likely dead, unless they found shelter. It's bloody awful out there."

The Lieutenant hesitated. "If they're dead, then problem solved, but my people were certain they hadn't been gone long when we found the stuff they left behind. You can still smell the food they cooked—some sort of fish, I think. Smells like it anyway."

"They can't have gone far then. But where the hell are they? Tell the Sergeant to search again. I want a floor by floor search, and I want them to look for anything out of the ordinary." He stared at the large panel embedded in the wall. It was difficult to tell, but he was sure it was less prominent now than it had been when they'd entered. "Put sentries at the access to all the surrounding buildings, and double guard on this one."

Harry's desire to take the fight to the Consortium came down to mobility and weapons. He and his men lacked transport, but Rasmus, aided by Coxswain Winstanley and TechRate Hill, worked tirelessly to manufacture some crude but effective grenades.

"We're working on a sort of landmine and a smaller version you wanted—a torpedo, I think you called it."

"Yes, a Bangalore torpedo, one that can be pushed beneath a barrier and detonated remotely. That will be most useful."

"We have plenty of them grenade things now, sir," said the Coxswain. "And these little buggers." He grinned and held up a tube, gazing at it almost lovingly. "This little rocket may be small, but it's a mean little bugger when it hits something, and with Mr. Rasmus's special mix as propellant and the charge when it hits— boom!" He grinned, and the others laughed when he added the sound of an explosion to make his point.

"Trouble is the rocket is unreliable," said Rasmus. "The nozzle needs work. It doesn't develop the thrust it should, and the directional stability is erratic, to say the least."

"If nothing else, the grenades will be useful for our own defence," mused Harry.

Rasmus nodded with infectious enthusiasm. "Then we shall keep at it and develop them. I will persuade our hosts to provide the materials we need for a more sophisticated explosive. It will increase our effectiveness." He was practically bursting with energy to get back into the makeshift lab he'd set up in his quarters.

"Then I will ask the Provider. I would be happier, I confess, if the explosives were in a secure store."

TechRate Skoronski stood to attention just inside the door. "Sir, we have visitors."

"Visitors? Oh." Harry stood and bowed to acknowledge the large Canid at his doorway then grabbed the translator. "Welcome. To what do we owe this pleasure?"

A translated response issued from the device. "Greetings. We have clothing for you and your pack."

Puzzled, Harry said, "Thank you, that is generous. Where should we collect these?"

"Yours are here. Your packmates will receive theirs in the outer chamber." The Canid stood aside and two smaller ones entered, who had the distinct look of adolescents, to Harry's mind, their arms filled with bulky bundles, which they presented to Harry and Rasmus. "We will wait to ensure they fit correctly," said the elder one.

The jackets, which varied in colour from olive green to brown, gave the wearer a slightly bulky appearance due to it being heavily built up to protect and insulate. The collar encased the neck and supported the back of the head, which emerged through a close-fitting opening. The collar was a sort of hood that could be pulled up to cover the head and protect it in extreme weather. Stout and surprisingly comfortable boots encased their feet and lower legs, and provided incredible grip and support for their ankles. "Everybody comfortable in these outfits?" Harry asked.

"A bit tight on the chest, sir," Maddie commented. "And no support!"

Errol Hill grinned at Maddie and gave her a wink. "Yeah, I can see that. My only complaint is they're a bit warm. I'm almost too warm, if you know what I mean."

"Cheeky bugger!" said Maddie. She gave him a playful push, and everyone had a good laugh.

Torn between stifled laughter and embarrassment, Harry struggled to maintain composure, always the staunch leader. "Er, right. Here, Miss Hodges, use this translator to explain your ... the problem ... to the Canid there ... the elder one." Finally he just handed it to her.

Amid a storm of banter, Maddie grinned. "Thanks, sir." Turning to the guys, she retorted, "Alright, you lot! So they don't know the difference between human men and women. Oh!" she exclaimed as the device yipped and growled.

"Just talk to it, Miss, um, ComOp Hodges. It'll translate to the Canids whatever you say." To the others, Harry ordered, "If you're all fitted and comfortable, we'll leave ComOp Hodges while she explains her needs."

Still laughing and joking, and Maddie enjoying the attention with her typical good humour, the men filed past Harry, with the last one out being the Coxswain, who confided, "You'll have to persuade this Provider chappie to make a change to these outfits, sir. The shirt, for one—it traps sweat."

Harry had noticed this himself. "Good point, Swain. I'll do it as soon as Ms. Hodges is finished."

It took several attempts to explain the need of a permeable material for shirts and underwear.

"They don't understand the whole perspiration thing," Harry explained to Rasmus.

"Perhaps they don't have pores and don't perspire as we do." Rasmus paused. "Perhaps I should explain this."

The Provider finally understood the need for human skin to 'breathe' and perspire. The shirt and underclothes were changed to a lightweight material that wicked away moisture while keeping the body a comfortable temperature.

"It's confirmed," said Consortium Brigadier Newton. "The Chairman and some very important board members will arrive in twelve days. We need double security and a five-mile total exclusion zone around the Base perimeter. Aerial surveillance, and shoot on sight anything that looks like a threat."

"What about the natives?" asked Colonel Rees.

"Divert them. I want no threat to the Board while they're here." Brigadier Newton turned to another Colonel. "Your patrol found evidence of human use in a building. Have they found any trace of who, and when they were there?"

"Not yet, ma'am." The Colonel looked uncomfortable. "As soon as our troops tried to force their way through some of the barriers, the natives attacked us. In close confines like that, they have a big advantage."

"So? A few of them against armed and armoured troopers?"

"There were too many of them, and in a confined area, discharging our plasma weapons is very risky. Our people had no option but to withdraw and wait for additional forces. By the time the reinforcements arrived, there were more of them, and it got messy. We took casualties, and so did they. They take violent exception to us doing anything at all to their precious structures, whatever those things are."

The Brigadier nodded. The fight had escalated very fast, and the Colonel was wise to withdraw. "Then we'll keep a lid on them there. They're five hundred miles from here. We'll deal with them after the Board has left." She turned back to her Chief of Staff. "Assign additional surveillance. Order our forces to shoot on sight if they spot anyone or anything leaving that area."

"What about the Johnstone situation? Lieutenant O'Connor will have a legitimate complaint about his treatment. With Dr. Johnstone arriving with the Board, we'll have a problem on our hands if they try to do any further experiments on him. The damage to the AI nodes is so bad there is only one way to fix it—a total replacement."

"I have the Chairman's word no one will attempt anything on him." She glanced around the table. "Has he been given the recreational tools he wanted? We have a duty to ensure his welfare. Since we can't put him to work with his companions, we'll have to find some other way to make him useful."

The Colonel nodded. "I'll see to it. The researchers have blocked his request so far—they say they need him to get frustrated and bored. I think they're hoping he'll try something they can track."

Lieutenant Aral Clark stared at the ceiling above his bed. With his fellow prisoners restricting their interactions with him to business only, he felt isolated. Not that this was a new feeling. It had been a hallmark of his childhood, with his father always away on a ship to some remote outpost, and his mother busy with her own life. An exclusive boarding school had seemed a good option, but unfortunately, it had turned into a nightmare due to his desire to be popular with his classmates. That had backfired, as everything always did, and he'd become the butt of some rather cruel jokes.

He knew his intellectual limitations, but tended to overcompensate by being very rigid in his methods of work. *Why won't they admit I was right to insist we surrender? They know we were outnumbered and couldn't fight off a bunch of ground troops!*

Even as he thought it, he knew the other officers would've countered by saying they should've at least put up a fight and forced the Consortium's people to work for it.

His mind wandered to his wife. Delle was the love of his life, but she never seemed satisfied, always pressing him to do better, to push for accelerated promotion, ask for a better posting. Nothing seemed good enough for her, even when he'd briefly held a post as Flag Lieutenant. Then she carped because he wasn't mixing with the 'right' people, the ones who could make his career or break it, as the case may be.

Well, he'd taken this post as Navigating Officer on the *Daring* because it would be, as his uncle said, a steppingstone to a planet-side post and a promotion—except he could barely handle the mathematics. And then along came Harry bloody Heron, that annoyingly perfect Irishman who had somehow landed in Clark's world all the way from the nineteenth century, and if that weren't bad enough, he just happened to be related to Admiral Heron of the mighty Fleet, to add insult to injury.

"I hate him," he said aloud, and startled himself. He hadn't meant that to come out. He looked round guiltily in case he'd been overheard, but no one seemed to notice.

His thoughts continued to plague him as he lay in the darkness. How the devil had Heron survived? Where was he? And how would Delle react to the news that her husband was a prisoner of war? Maybe she thought he was dead already. Maybe she had already contacted the life insurance company and demanded they pay up on his deceased ass. He wouldn't put it past her. He'd have to try to talk to one of the Consortium officers, see if he could get a message out to her.

When he was too exhausted to think, sleep finally claimed him.

Harry stared at the busy scene. "Unbelievable, Rasmus! The Consortium's team of xenologists and archaeologists evidently knew nothing of this. How could they not have wondered at the tools these people carry, or these astonishing garments? There is no suggestion in their reports of any attempt to discover any of this." Hesitating, he added, "But this past summer, their research teams examined some sites. The Provider says they damaged his surface nodes, by which I understand he means the cities, and they killed many Canids who tried to prevent it."

"Surface nodes?" Rasmus' eyes widened. "Do you mean the cities are—?"

"So it seems. These are not cities, as we understand them, but they have some function in relation to the Provider, the AI on this planet, in terms of supplying nutrients and photovoltaic power." Harry smiled. "And, of course, these structures provide shelter to those who guard them, and to strays like us who blunder into them seeking a hiding place. And now we find ourselves in the very heart of a society and civilisation our enemies have no notion exists."

Rasmus nodded. "We're fortunate indeed that they accept us."

Harry watched several large Canids, somewhat ferocious in appearance, setting up the machines provided in response to Rasmus's request and specifications. He stepped closer to examine one. "These machines are new. There must be a manufactory somewhere."

As if in response to Harry's musing, one of the Canids stepped forward and spoke to him through the translator in his powerful paw-like hand. "They are made to your exact requirements. Do you wish to see where?"

Glancing at Rasmus, Harry checked his urge to nod, having discovered this had a very different meaning among the Canids.

"Thank you, we would."

The tour left Rasmus and Harry astonished. Their hosts were certainly not backward in any sense of the word, yet it was obvious they lacked any sort of modern weaponry.

"We had no need of weapons until the other humans invaded. We have only our cloaks and our ancient weapons. Now the Provider tells us we must learn from you to create the weapons we need to defend him."

Harry considered this. "The weapons I had in mind would be crude but suited to our use until we could capture more powerful ones." He glanced at Rasmus. "I do not have sufficient knowledge of the more sophisticated devices our enemy uses."

"But you have some weapons of that sort. We have seen them."

"Indeed we do, but to replicate them and manufacture more is not within our expertise, unless you have the machines, equipment and materials we would need to do so." As he spoke, they moved into a new chamber. Larger than the previous one, it held a range of machines Harry vaguely recognised as the type that formed and shaped metal. "Ah, yes! If my friend Ferghal were here, he would be delighted to put these to work on the task. Sadly, I think he is either a prisoner or dead."

The Canid studied him before speaking. "Instruct us in the making of your explosives. We have seen their effect, but we think they can be better used. Tell us what you need, and we will assist you."

Harry considered. "Very well. We had best make a start. Rasmus will show you how to make the explosive, and Mr. Winstanley will set some of our people to work making the devices for it. Show us where we may work."

Ferghal had found a way to connect to the Base AI through a portable unit brought in to run the lab systems. Now he found himself reading, in his mind's eye, a lengthy list of names and duty positions. He was about to move on to something else when he recognised a name and a posting.

Memory clicked into place of an obstructive bureaucrat at Pangaea, and suddenly the list made sense. He found the transmitters and watched the signal protocols until he was familiar with them. Then, he created a signal package and sent it to an address in Fleet Security that he'd been given after he and Harry had succeeded in bringing home the cargo liner *Twee Jonge Gazellen*. With that done, he erased the record of the signal from the auto log, but failed to notice that he'd just diverted the Consortium's encryption keys to the address he'd used.

He stretched out on his bed and grinned with satisfaction. *That'll give someone a bit of a start*, he thought, as he 'watched' his captors watching him on their supposedly secret monitor. One of these days, he'd give them something to watch. Until then, he'd try to send a message to the Admiral, but he'd have to be careful.

At home in Ireland, Admiral James Heron received the report he'd been waiting for. He contacted his sister Niamh via holocall. She would never let him hear the end of it if he wasted a single moment to give her an update.

True to form, she accepted the call immediately. "Any news, James? Please tell me you have good news for once."

"Fleet Security think they know where Ferghal is. They're sure it's him because they got a message with his tag in it."

"Good! When are you or someone going to pick him up?"

Well, that was faster than I expected, thought James with a sigh. His sister was not an easy woman to deal with.

"Not anytime soon, I'm afraid." James Heron cut off his sister's protest. "We can't. It's deep in Consortium territory. At least we know he's safe, and very likely Harry is too."

"But if he can send messages, why can't you make contact?"

"Niamh, much as I'd like to, the message was, shall we say, unusual, and not from a Fleet transmitter. We think Ferghal must have used his cyberlink and tapped into one of theirs." He laughed. "We got a bit more than he perhaps realised when he sent it."

"What did he send you?"

The Admiral smiled. "Something that gives us a tremendous edge. Security are delighted, and plan to use this to our advantage." A notification in the corner of his holoscreen flickered. "I'm needed. I'll be in touch as soon as I have more."

Harry tried to settle his mind to say his prayers, a nightly practice, but he found it challenging on this night because there was much to think about. The day's activities had been productive, and the Canids were quick to learn, innovative and far more dexterous than they appeared. Harry now had a large stock of grenades, mines and Bangalore torpedoes to attack the prison so they could free Ferghal and all other Fleet personnel held captive by the Consortium. Rasmus's tube-launched rockets were also being produced, now with a reloadable launching tube.

To focus his thoughts, Harry started his prayer as usual, asking for safety and protection for his family and friends, especially his guardian, Admiral Heron, as well as his 'Aunt' Niamh, his sweetheart, Mary Hopkins, and Ferghal and Danny, wherever they were.

The entire time he prayed, he sensed that the alien Provider watched and listened, even though his prayers were in his thoughts. Unlike the Fleet and Consortium systems, he could not shut the Provider out of his head

He concentrated with more effort as he reached the intercession of his prayer. *Provide me with the courage to face the enemy, Lord, and give me the knowledge I need to keep safe those who are entrusted to my care—*

The Provider spoke. *"I do not understand your request for this material you call courage or this safety you want for the individuals you name. Please clarify your request."*

"I did not address this request to you," Harry said in his thoughts, startled out of his prayer. "I am praying to my Maker, and do not expect you to provide these things."

"But you are an organic life form as I am, as are the Canids. You are not a machine like the electronic entity your enemy uses, yet you say you have a Maker. Who is this Maker?"

"You are a life form? But are you not the creation of the Siddhiche?"

"No I am not. I am the result of their manipulation. I am the nodes your people refer to as cities, and more. I am an integral part of everything on this planet, a watcher for the Siddhiche. The cities, to use the word familiar to you, are parts of my nutrient assimilating organs and shelters for the Canids when they need them. Our relationship is symbiotic. I provide for them, and they serve my needs. Now you humans are among us and threaten the balance in our partnership."

Harry considered this carefully. "Why then have you adopted me and my team?"

"Because you and another in the camp of your enemy are different. You have been touched by the Siddhiche, and we are linked."

Now wide awake, Harry's heart quickened. "Where is this other? Is his name Ferghal? Can you communicate with the network where he is being held—or better, with him?"

"Of course. The artificial mentality does not know I am part of it. Everything it does, I know. But a part of it has ceased to function. The one like you has destroyed parts and reduced the remainder to imbecility. They are afraid he may enter their main network and discover the things they hide there."

Harry's interest was now fully engaged, sleep forgotten. "Can you let me speak to him? What do they hide?"

"You may speak to him directly. I will show you the way. As to your second question, they have a strange project that concerns other intelligences not of this world. This project is protected with the highest level of security."

Harry considered this. What sort of secret project could the Consortium be hiding on this planet? What was their AI doing that was so important that it had to be hidden on this outlying planet far from the reach of the North European Confederation and the North American Union? He would have to seek the answers somehow. Finally, he asked, "Can you check if Ferghal is sleeping? I wish to speak to him, but I don't want to disturb him."

"He is awake. Follow my directions."

Chapter 18

Found

TechOp Cam Khodro grumbled to himself. His Lieutenant was a bully and quick to blame him if anything went wrong. He started a routine check of the signal transmission logs, a nuisance task because it meant travelling to the remote transmitters and downloading the data then analysing it line by line.

"Waste of bloody time," he muttered to himself as he scrolled through it. He reached to increase the scroll speed then blinked to see if he had really seen what he thought he'd just seen. He stopped the scroll and peered more closely. There was a gap in the log. For almost seventy-two seconds the transmitter had been idle—if the log was correct—and there should never be a gap. The transmitter should be sending a constant carrier signal to the hypercom satellites. He checked the rest of the log. There were no other gaps.

Leaning back in the seat, he thought about it for several minutes before reluctantly activating his comlink. "Lieutenant Barclay? Sir, there is something odd in the signal log. There's a gap in the transmissions of seventy-one point eight seconds."

"So what?" The surly response was typical. "Why the hell are you bothering me with it? You know what to do. Get back here, write up a defect report, and log it. Don't expect me to do your job for you."

"Welcome to Lycania Base One, Chairman." Brigadier Newton saluted as the Chairman of the Consortium disembarked in the massive hangar. "If you'll follow me, the garrison is ready for your inspection."

The Chairman smiled. "Thank you." His gaze swept the vast hangar. "You've done well. Even with the tech you have at your disposal, you seem to have built a great deal more than we expected."

"Yes, sir. As directed, I've kept the Fleet prisoners busy with hard labour. Naturally we can't use them on anything sensitive, of course, but the physically demanding work keeps them occupied."

"Good thinking." The Chairman nodded. "They know we are intercepting sensitive information, but they don't know how or from where—and we want it to stay that way."

"We appreciate that and have kept their TechRates and Officers well separated." She hesitated. "I've had to put a block on the research team's experiments with the man O'Connor— especially after they allowed him to get into the facility network."

"So I heard." The Chairman frowned. "Dr. Johnstone bombarded me with demands all the way here. What happened?"

"We're not exactly sure, and neither are the researchers. Their drugs didn't have the effect they expected. He fried some of the AI nodes with power surges, and he deleted or altered large parts of the program. The AI is now a simpleton, not even capable of running basic functions without manual intervention."

The Chairman was fully attentive now. "That bad? Is there any danger of his getting into the main system?"

"It's isolated, and there are security screens in place. With our coms monitoring operations, we can't afford his disrupting it." Emboldened by the Chairman's concern, a departure from his usual bored half-interest, she added, "I must insist he remains isolated from all nodes of our AI network. I'm not at all happy about the suggestion they perform surgery on him to find out how he connects to it."

The Chairman's frown became pronounced. "Who suggested that? You have my assurance I will permit no such thing, not now, not ever. And your decision to keep him away from any AI has my full support."

"Thank you, sir. It was suggested we allow the Johnstone Group to take him aboard a ship and send him somewhere else, but I've blocked that as well. If he was able to get into a ship's network before, I don't even want to think what could happen now that he's been held captive for some time. I'm sure he would employ his pent-up anger in ways we can't even imagine."

The Chairman nodded. "I agree. He remains here until we bring this to an end. His own people can deal with him then. The news from Admiral Gratz is good. We didn't get the outright victory we wanted, but he held off a force of equal strength and has drawn their forces away from this sector very successfully."

"That gives us a bit of space."

"If we can stall the Fleet long enough in the Regulus system, we will have the WTO on its knees before they can deploy in this vicinity again."

With their conversation finished, the Chairman climbed the few steps to the stage and stood behind the podium that had been set in place for his use. Behind him, the other members of the Board sauntered into position. The vehicles and aerial patrol craft that normally occupied the floor space of the brightly lit hangar had been drawn to the sides or removed to other shelters. Outside, the weather had turned cold, and flurries of needle-like ice particles were scouring the structures.

Brigadier Newton surveyed the assembled workers, military personnel and support staff, noting with annoyance that the researchers were conspicuous in their absence. She would have some strong words with them and the guard commander if they made any attempt on the young man in their care.

On watch in the communications support control, Cam Khodro noticed a new login from the Isolation Lab. He checked the ID for the terminal and noted it was a portable interface. "Damn," he said to himself. "One of the damned researchers again. Bastards don't bloody think about the security at all."

He recorded the ID and the location in the security log and made a note to point it out to his supervisor. With the Brigadier's orders in mind, he flagged it and put it on the list of random checks to pass on. For a moment he considered contacting

Lieutenant Barclay, then rejected the thought. His response to the last report of an unusual event suggested it would be dismissed anyway. Out of curiosity more than anything else, he memorised the ID and decided to run a trace when he next had the opportunity to do so.

Ferghal had to suppress a shout of joy when he heard Harry's voice in his head. He sat bolt upright in bed then remembered that he was being watched, so he put his hands to his face as if waking up from a nightmare then sat on the edge of the bed with his back to the cameras. *"Harry, you scoundrel! You've had me so worried— where are you? How do you speak to me through this AI if you're not here?"*

"Easy, old friend. I am a long way from you—I think—and I speak through an unusual form of AI that is resident here, called the Provider. Is all well with you? What have they done to you?"

"Nothing I couldn't handle. I'm doing good and hanging in there, as our friends say! These bastards tried to drug me and scan my head, but the drugs failed and I destroyed their AI for sweet revenge. Had fun doing it too."

"That's the Ferghal we all know and love! Never fear, my friend, we will find a way to get you out of there. I have a number of our people with me, and the Canids will assist us—those are the native inhabitants of this planet. They're really amazing. They walk upright like men but have a close resemblance to canines. But I need to ask you something. Have you been able to figure out what the Consortium is hiding at their Base on this planet? There is some project they guard heavily, something to do with networks off this world. It seems of great importance to them, from what I can gather. Have you discovered such a thing?"

"There is one. I do not understand the mechanics of it, but I can show you the manner in which it can be found." Ferghal paused. *"Harry, it must be important, because their Board has come to observe it in operation. They are here now, as is that fiend Johnstone, the one who has pursued us from the beginning. He rails against the Chairman's refusal to allow him to dismantle my head or to remove me from this planet."*

Harry leapt to his feet. *"What? Johnstone is here? There is not a minute to lose—we will find you and secure your release as soon as I can discover a means to do it. I will ask the Provider to keep us linked. Night or day, if they attempt anything, you must tell me. I will tear them apart with my hands if I have to, but you will be free, Ferghal. You will be, and that right soon."*

He had to check himself as he hurried to find the Coxswain and Rasmus, a plan forming in his mind with every step. He needed to talk it through with his companions. He would also need the grenades and other explosives they had made.

Admiral Hartmann received the signal with relief. The standoff with the Consortium Fleet could have gone either way, but now she could bring it to a close.

"Reinforcement at last—and ahead of theirs. Signal all ships. Battle group will assemble in accordance with my Deployment Order in Formation Twelve. Cruisers on the wing position and destroyers to seek targets of opportunity once we have engaged their battle squadron. The *Tromp* and the *Parramatta* will remain in reserve to protect the LSPs. We move as soon as the newcomers have joined and been brought up to date with my orders and formations."

"Very good, Admiral." The Flag Lieutenant and his staff were already carrying out orders.

"Signal just in. Rear Admiral Heron intercepted a Consortium force and damaged or destroyed most of their ships, and is driving them away from this region."

"Enemy ships have powered up their drives, Admiral." The scan officer's report cut across the Command Centre even as, throughout the ship, the action stations began to sound.

"Enemy ships are going hyper, sir."

"Track them and maintain scanning," the Admiral ordered. "All ships prepare for pursuit."

"They're entering transit—looks like they've had enough."

"Damn!" the Admiral exclaimed. "Order the pursuit. I want to finish this."

Aboard the *Khamenei*, Admiral Gratz watched the scan reports for any sign of pursuit. He was annoyed that his reinforcements had failed to arrive, but he realised their delay was due to having been intercepted by the superior Fleet. How that had come about would have to be investigated since the ships had been routed through a sector that Fleet ships did not use under normal circumstances.

"No pursuit, sir," reported the scan officer. "The decoy drones have worked. We've given them the slip."

"Alter course. Make for the repair base at Archaelos. We've achieved our purpose. We pulled them away from the Peiho System and New Babylon. Our Assault Group succeeded in getting troops onto the planet and capturing it. It's a bonus that the ships we took on will have to be put into repair." He stood up and made for the door. "I'm going to get some rest. Signal our course and destination to the Chairman's office."

Aral Clarke settled at the workstation and applied himself to the task given him by the Consortium's lab supervisor. It was boring and unrewarding, but it was something that at least broke the isolation from his fellow survivors and took his thoughts off his concerns about his wife and their future.

"New set of samples for you, Aral." The supervisor pushed some vials across the worktop. "How was the last batch?"

"All tested within the parameters you gave me. I've filed the report." Pulling the sample tray toward him, he glanced at the label. "These aren't for a fuel cell system. What are they?"

"Something we more or less scrape off the surface in some of the driest areas. Damn good for making plants grow, so we hydroponics nerds take all we can gather. It's the most useful thing we've found on this planet. It's very rich with it. The agri-haulers ship it away for use on some of the worlds where the soil quality is too poor for crops."

"Good to know I'm doing something useful then." Clark could barely suppress his snarky tone. The supervisor ignored him and chose not to reply, and left him to his task.

Placing the first of the samples into the machine, he entered the material code and waited for the unit to run its checks. The Consortium had set up some huge manufactories on this planet to build fuel cells for their strike craft, weapons components for projectors and a few other things, plus this fertiliser the planet seemed to have in abundance, which he'd heard was great for growing plants but was poisonous when ingested.

His mouth stretched into a smirk that accompanied his snort of derision. With a bit of luck that damned Heron and his gang would poison themselves eating it.

Chapter 19

Explosive Reunion

H arry found Rasmus preparing to turn in for the night. "Rasmus, I'm sorry to burst in on you like this, but I know where Ferghal is held, and we must rescue him now. I have a plan, but we will need all the explosive devices we can carry." He grinned impishly. "And we will need them to be the most easily used, not the overly sensitive sort you have tried, if you please. They must be safe to carry upon our persons."

"They are, mein freund. We have made the powders and the fuses. Herr Winstanley has a large supply of the devices. All that is required is to insert the fuse." He looked puzzled. "Why now? Can't this wait till morning?"

"There is not a moment to lose. The Consortium has researchers on their way to try some new experiment on Ferghal, and I cannot permit it."

Harry and crew assembled in the transport chamber. They were short of sleep, but the grenades, mines and torpedoes would give them the edge in the assault—he hoped. To his surprise, several of the Canids were present, and evidently intent on accompanying them.

Turning to the Coxswain, Harry announced, "Mister Winstanley, I am told we will be travelling by the below-ground transport to a place near the structure in which Ferghal is held. We shall arrive at dawn. You all understand the use of these grenades? Once you have struck the fuse, it cannot be extinguished. You must place the bomb and take cover."

"We get you, sir," the Coxswain replied. "But it'll be a learning on the job exercise for us. This business of starting a fuse and then chucking the bomb isn't what we're used to."

"I know, Swain," Harry said. "It's a bit old fashioned, but it's all we have for now besides the few weapons we took from our enemy, and you know the reason we must be careful of those. Who has the charges I want placed?"

"Me, sir," Josh Moroti responded. "And I have the igniters as well."

"Good. I'll want you to stay close to me once we get there."

Their Canid companions gathered their packs and assembled at one end of the room. A few minutes later, the leader growled in Harry's direction followed by a series of yips, whines and guttural sounds. The translation device did its job from within the pouch Harry carried, and said, "Follow us. The vehicle is here."

An opening appeared in the wall where the Canids stood. In Harry's mind, it was rather like the iris of a great eye, or some sort of gullet opening to swallow them. They boarded the large tubular vehicle, which sealed once they were inside. As on their previous journey, seats emerged from the floor, and they seated themselves.

In his thoughts, Harry heard the host saying, *You will be transported to your destination where we will guide you toward your friend. Tell your companions they must secure themselves—the distance requires speed.*

"Secure yourselves in the seats," Harry instructed his team. "I am warned this journey will be swift."

The team looked for straps but found only appendages that sprouted from the seats and embraced them in the manner of belts. The seats moulded around them to provide support for their backs and heads, and the vehicle accelerated.

A new group had arrived at the lab with their aggressive and overbearing leader. Ferghal could hear the man demanding that the Guard Commander remove Ferghal from his cell and transport him to the laboratory so that the man and his team could immediately begin a series of experiments on the specimen, as he referred to Ferghal. The guard was equally determined he would not permit any experiment without the authority of Brigadier Newton.

"The Brigadier doesn't have the authority to stop us," snapped the man, who Ferghal realised was the infamous Dr. Johnstone. "I tell you, the Board have sanctioned it!"

"So you say, but I have written orders from my commanding officer that I must have her authority before I can allow this."

"Damn your orders! I want that man in my lab now," the doctor stormed. Turning to the technicians, he snarled, "Take him out of that cell and get him into the lab."

"Sentry!" the officer barked. "Shoot anyone attempting to remove the prisoner."

"You wouldn't dare!" shouted Dr. Johnstone. "This is vital research."

"Don't push your luck, Doctor." The Guard Commander had reached his limit. "Under my orders I have the authority to lock up you and your staff—and I don't give a damn who you're connected to on the Board. I'm not going to stand by while you commit murder."

The doctor's appeal failed to work because Ferghal had told the Guard Commander what had been done to him and to Harry on Pangaea by Dr. Johnstone's scientists. It disgusted the Guard Commander, though he kept this to himself.

Ferghal, listening to the argument between the two men, was startled to hear Harry in his head.

"Ferghal, you wished to speak to me?"

"That I did, but how did you know?"

"It seems our new ally, the Provider, knows your thoughts and mine," Harry told him. *"What is afoot?"*

"Harry, no less a person than Johnstone himself is here and demanding my removal. Thus far, my guard is refusing his request, but I am not certain they will continue to do so if the orders are changed. It seems the Consortium's leaders are here as well, and this spáilpín has the ear of at least some of them."

"We are nearing your prison and, with luck, will be with you before they act. Courage, my friend, we will be there soon."

"I have no choice," Ferghal responded. *"But if they seize me with that stun weapon again, I am lost, I'm thinking."*

"Then help us—tell me what you know of the facility and its defences so that we may strike effectively before they can prevent us."

Ferghal gave Harry all the information he knew, and then he added, "I am able to use the monitoring part of the system to locate their people, and I can guide you to my cell."

"Better and better," Harry replied.

After emerging from the vehicle inside an artificial cavern, the group checked their equipment. Like the city they now lived in, this place had a similar structure and arrangement, though it was much smaller, and the population evidently engaged in different activity to those at their home base. The Canid leader signalled that they must follow. Obeying, Harry told his team what he had learned from Ferghal.

Following the Canid guide, they arrived at a position from which they looked down on the small fenced facility. They lay on their stomachs for camouflage against the ground.

"Daylight's going, sir." The Coxswain joined Harry and the leader of the Canids. "They've got surveillance on those towers. Be tricky evading them."

"I see them and the defence system." Harry turned his head to address the Canid. "We need to destroy that power plant and the cables to those defence emplacements." He waited while the translator yipped and growled.

"You wish to use these devices on the poles beneath the power unit, and at the weapons? What of the other systems?"

"My people will insert the torpedoes under the cables and the masts. The power unit will need a different approach. They are familiar with these systems, and know how to neutralise them."

The Canid grunted. "We will observe. We must learn to use these devices."

"Thank you." To the Coxswain, Harry said, "Swain, when I give the signal, your people may fire the igniters. They will have two minutes to clear the field. Please ensure they understand it is vital they are behind substantial cover within that time." To the Canid, he added, "Your people should fall back once the devices are planted. I do not want them injured by the explosions."

"We will use the opportunity to acquire some of their weapons. Go well!" The Canid growled into his translator, listened to a reply, slid back, pulled a cloak over his head and vanished.

"Bloody hell, that's creepy." The Coxswain stared at the place where the Canid had been visible moments earlier.

"It is rather unnerving," said Harry. "Right then, Swain. Now we discover how well our grenades work." Pointing out the dome they needed to access, Harry outlined his plan for the strike. "I want you to lead your group to create a diversion. If you cause a great disruption and blow up those facilities there, they are the main barracks. The administration and accommodation domes and the power supply are located there. As soon as the torpedoes explode, commence your attack."

"Right, sir. Where will you take your team in?"

He pointed out a smaller structure. "From that side." He indicated the perimeter closest to the dome he knew Ferghal to be in. "And try to take them by surprise to release Ferghal."

"They'll put up a tough fight, sir. Those guys are regular troopers."

"I fear it may be a no quarter situation. We have little choice in the matter. We must not fail."

"I follow you, sir." The Coxswain nodded. "I suggest you and your team get going. I'll move my people into position and make a start on getting our bombs planted as Mr. Rasmus showed us. Is there any sort of electronic perimeter?"

Harry chuckled. "They think there is. Ferghal assures me he has disabled it. Take care, though, as there may be other devices. I would certainly not rely entirely on a single system if I were the guard officer. There may well be patrols."

"Those I can deal with, sir." The Coxswain grinned. "That kind of thing is my field—not this poking around in the network's head, if you'll pardon my saying so." He looked at Harry and grinned. "See you on the other side." He slipped down the slope signalling his people into position.

Harry was puzzled by that expression, and had a flashback memory to when he went from 1804 to 2204 in the midst of a blast of gunpowder, not unlike what they were about to unleash. "I hope not," he said under his breath, pushing his fears aside.

The twisted shapes of the leathery plants that grew in this area concealed clusters of eroded rocky outcrops that covered the terrain they had to cross. Patches of snow and sheets of ice covered the ground. Against this backdrop, the stark vegetation made fantastic patterns. The cover was sparse, but their clothing helped them blend into the landscape, and they were able to move quietly toward the Consortium Base, their belts and pouches filled with explosives.

Some of the Canids accompanied him, and a larger group went with the Coxswain. Well within the time he had allowed, they were in position. "Ready?" Harry said to his team. "You have the igniters to hand?" He received their assurances. "Very well. Ferghal promises to have the entrance open for us and the other chambers secured. We will go directly to his position, but there is an antechamber adjoining it where a number of guards and researchers are gathered." He sketched a rough plan on the ground. "All are armed with the stun weapon. We take no chances—I think one of the grenades should disable them, but have a larger device ready if it does not."

He tried to contact Ferghal to discover what was in progress inside the dome.

"Ferghal?" he said. He waited, wondering whether he had lost his connection to the Provider. When it finally responded, he asked, *"Is Ferghal still available?"*

"I am here, Harry." Ferghal sounded anxious.

"Good. We are in position. Can you see anything on the monitors guarding the perimeter? Can you manipulate them so they do not see us?"

"Nothing. Wait—I see some movement at the other end of the compound. There, I have altered the vision on the guard's monitor. They will not see anything now. What is afoot?"

"Mr. Winstanley is ready. There will shortly be some explosions— at least I hope there will be. Once your guards respond to these, we will strike into your position and release you from your prison. How are you secured? Are you kept in irons? How is the door secured?"

Watching, he caught the signal from the Coxswain's side, and responded with his own.

"I am secured only by the door, and it is a lock so simple I can open it in a trice." Ferghal seemed very excited now. *"As to the access to the cell block, I will disable the entry port and secure the doors accessing the rooms entering upon it. Beware, though —Johnstone and his people are all in the chamber where they can observe me."*

"Very well. We will use one of our bombs on them. When you see a grenade flung into the room, take cover behind something solid. We do

168

not know how powerful these will be. Is there somewhere you can take shelter?"

"When I see you entering, I will go to the toilet! I shall hope the saints preserve me from your device there." Ferghal thought quickly. "One thing I ask, Harry—the Guard Commander has been most concerned for my welfare. Spare him if you can."

"How will I know him?"

"He is the only man here with the markings of rank upon his uniform. There are three guards. The others are not of any rank that is visible."

"I cannot promise, my friend. You know I cannot risk our people in trying to show mercy to our enemy, kindly disposed or not. And, as their officer, he must be prevented from rallying his people."

"I know that, Harry. Do your duty."

As soon as he finished speaking, a massive explosion at the far end of the compound shook the ground. It was quickly followed by several more. Lights flickered then died as the power plant disintegrated amidst a brilliant flash.

Leaping to his feet, Harry shouted, "Now! Quickly, before they recover!"

He charged through the opening as the low level emergency lights flickered into life. It occurred to him that there could be a problem if someone was waiting on the other side. His blood up, he thrust the thought aside. Errol Hill beat him through the door and was at the far end a few steps ahead of him, the fuse on the cylindrical grenade in his hand already spluttering.

The door opened on a group of people arguing. Their voices stilled as the cylinder sailed into the room and bounced off a wall before it careened toward the furious Dr. Johnstone. Without thinking, he caught it.

In the passage, Harry and his team flung themselves to the floor a millisecond before the grenade detonated. The shock wave bent the half closed door in its frame and deflected the blast from their prone forms, though they felt the shock through the floor.

Harry was the first to his feet and leapt through the door, his ears ringing as he bawled, "Ferghal, if you hear me—join us quickly!"

His feet skidded in blood and he almost went headlong. Struggling to maintain his balance, he collided with the only person to have a weapon drawn. A brief struggle saw the injured soldier disarmed and helpless in the grip of one of his crew. The blast had thrown everyone in the room from their feet, and no one seemed to have escaped injury.

The door to Ferghal's cell had been blown almost off its hinges, and Errol Hill combined his strength with Ferghal's to rip it open. Ferghal emerged, his expression exuberant.

"That was some device," he said above the rising sound of moaning and whimpering from the injured. "Have I not said before that you are the most destructive man I know?" He looked for Dr. Johnstone and grimaced. "One, at least, will not pursue us any longer—I fear he must have taken the full force!" He knelt down and relieved the Guard Commander of his weapons, something the other members of Harry's team were already doing to the other wounded.

"Is this the one you asked us to spare?" Harry said, joining his friend.

"Yes, and by the goodness of the saints, it seems he has suffered no worse than the concussion." Ferghal clasped his friend and said, "Oh, Harry, how I have missed your company these months, but we must hurry! Their people will be on us if we linger. We need to get out of here now."

The team threw their remaining grenades into open doors as they departed, causing enormous damage and further confusion. There was no pursuit as they retired back to the cavern, the Canids materialising around them and chattering in their strange mixture of growling and yipping as they did so.

Settling into the transport vehicle, Ferghal studied the Canids then looked at Harry. "You have a strange way with those you encounter, Harry. First the Lacertians and now these dog men are your allies. What is your charm?"

"You ask me?" Harry laughed. "I do not know why you have followed me or stayed my friend these many long years." He wiped his eyes to hide his emotion. "It is so good to have you returned, my friend—I cannot say how it has been to have you gone from my company."

"And I you." Ferghal's grin was lopsided. "But perhaps on the next occasion our reunion can be less explosive, though that does seem to be our usual way of doing things!"

Around them, the team collapsed in laughter at this remark, to the puzzlement of the Canids, who watched this strange human behaviour with expressions of interest.

The response team surveyed the devastated Iso-lab site with amazement. The barrack and administration domes were torn apart, and scenes of complete devastation met their gaze in every structure. The powerhouse nearby was nothing but a crater, and the destruction in the laboratory block left no doubt that something extremely violent had happened here.

"What the hell did this?" The officer commanding the rescue team demanded to know. "I've never seen anything like it—plasma bolts don't throw debris around like this."

One of his sergeants picked up a twisted bit of metal, evidently part of a cylinder, and sniffed it, his nose wrinkling. "Stinks, that does. Smells like burnt chemicals."

The survivors from the attack gave a very confused range of impressions of who had attacked them. Some thought it had been the natives, but others said it was humans in Canid clothing. The attack had been well planned and executed. It was obvious to the investigating officer the attackers had a detailed knowledge of the facility.

The weapon described by the survivors made no sense to any of the team though. A cylinder with sparks coming from its end didn't seem to be much more than something with an electrical short circuit—and that couldn't possibly cause this level of devastation.

"Must be something they got from the Rotties," the officer reported to the Chairman and the Brigadier. "Never seen anything like this—some sort of blasting device. Dr. Johnstone must have been holding one or standing right next to it when it detonated."

"The medics say it caused massive trauma." The Chairman's voice was impassive.

"It isn't pretty. The others were lucky, only blast injuries or broken bones when they were thrown down by the blast. Some of them will be permanently deaf. If it'd had a fragmentation element, they wouldn't have survived. Other domes were hit by fragmentation versions, and ... well, I don't need to go into detail."

The Chairman's face was inscrutable. "Brigadier, I'll assign more troops to you. We can't afford to have this group jeopardise our operations here. Hunt them down and destroy them. If these, er, Rotties are involved, take them out as well. No more playing around. I know the research teams will want them captured, but we can't afford another incident like this. I'll leave it to you. See that it's done."

Ferghal's former guard lay confined in a med-unit, which gave him plenty of time to think about the event that put him here. Chiefly, he recalled, or thought he recalled, the care his former prisoner had shown in ensuring he survived. But he had some grisly memories too. The image of Dr. Johnstone catching the explosive would remain with him for life.

Only his own lightning reflexes had saved him. His instinct for self-preservation had been triggered by the realisation the prisoner and the attackers were taking cover. His survival was miraculous nonetheless, his injuries the result of not being fully on the floor when the bomb exploded.

He had much to think about while he recovered.

News of the attack and Ferghal's escape soon reached the other Fleet prisoners. The TechRates were the first to hear, as was always the way. Then it filtered through to Commander Nielsen and his group.

"Whatever the attackers used tore the place apart," he told the others. "It blew that bastard Johnstone to bits. He was holding the bomb when it detonated."

"Bloody good show," one of his listeners replied. Glancing at Aral Clarke, he raised his voice. "It seems that Mr. Heron and at least some of our people survived and have managed to come up with some weaponry."

"They got Mr. O'Connor out then vanished," Commander Nielsen remarked, watching Lieutenant Clarke's expression as he sat alone nursing a mug of hot coffee.

"Our guards seem to be quite stirred up," remarked another Lieutenant.

"The Chairman is furious," said the Commander. "They're tearing the place apart looking for them. I hear they have orders to destroy those abandoned cities and shoot down any of the Canids who try to stop them."

"I hope to hell they give us an opportunity to get out of this dump," one of the others commented. "I'd love to have a crack at disrupting this place a bit more."

"We'll have our chance," the Commander agreed. "Soon, I hope."

Aral Clarke bit back a response. What did it matter? Heron and his lunatic activities had put them all in danger, but the Commander and the others refused to see it, as usual.

"Why wasn't this anomaly reported immediately?" The Communications Major was furious. "And these portable interface accesses from the Iso-lab? There had better be a damned good explanation, mister."

"The signal was probably just a power blip," protested Lieutenant Barclay. "At least that seems the most logical explanation, sir."

"Except it happens to coincide with someone accessing Top Security files in the database from a portable interface in the Iso-lab!" The Major glared across the desk. "The security code is one that has never been issued—so who the blazes do you think was using it?"

"But the researchers were always using portable interface units there, sir. How was I supposed to know it wasn't them?"

"Did you check? I thought not. In future, I want all unusual or unexplained events logged and investigated. Clear?"

Cam Khodro could see from Lieutenant Barclay's expression there was a rough ride ahead. He wondered if it was too late to ask for a transfer to another station.

Alone in his berth Harry wrestled with his thoughts. His people had performed well and come through the raid unscathed, and for that he was thankful, but he was certain they would not be so lucky again. The death of an enemy was regrettable, and he was all too aware of how many he had killed and injured. It didn't sit well with his faith, but he was also trying to come to terms with the Canid culture. It was hard to understand why several of the more hostile ones now seemed to look on him as some sort of war leader. He also had to consider whether further assaults could be justified now that Ferghal was free and safe. They needed weapons and med-units. Full assaults would be costly and very risky with little reward unless there was some hope of rescue by their own people. With these thoughts running through his head, he eventually fell into an exhausted sleep.

Chapter 20

No Backing Down

The weather turned vicious, not that Harry and his team noticed, for they were deep below ground within the subterranean city that was their living host. Ferghal, Abram Winstanley, and Rasmus put this opportunity to very good use and built up a stockpile of grenades and larger charges. Maddie Hodges proved very adept at constructing the fuses Rasmus designed, and under her tuition, a team of several of the smaller Canids built more. The Canids learned fast, and had a few innovations of their own to offer.

"Not such savages as our people think," Harry remarked to Rasmus.

"As you say." Rasmus gazed at one of the larger workspaces. "No wonder they could provide all that we asked for so quickly."

Ferghal threw himself into the task of making a form of mortar that could be used to project their grenades onto an enemy. It was as well they had prepared these, for when the weather did ease, the Consortium struck, leaving Harry no option but to fight back.

And it rekindled the hostility of the Canid leaders.

Harry surveyed the scene. The once intact and surreal buildings had been reduced to rubble for the most part. Smoke billowed from one area, and the stench of burnt material filled his nostrils. The Consortium's aerial attackers had withdrawn, but their ground troops moved cautiously among the wreckage.

Slipping back into cover, he turned to his group. "There are far too many to take head on, so here is my plan. We will use our Bangalore torpedoes to destroy their vehicles. Mr. Winstanley, your section will move to this point and infiltrate the area where their vehicles are parked. I will take Moroti, Hill and Ms. Hodges. We will use the shoulder tubes to draw their attention. Ferghal, when we open fire, use your bombs to keep their searchers busy."

"Aye, aye, sir. Come on you lot, let's get going." The Coxswain and his companions followed a gully that led to their infiltration point. Ferghal studied the area ahead then moved off to find a position with the remaining people.

"Ready?" Harry glanced at his team. "Let's go." He took two steps forward when Errol Hill touched his arm.

"Still, sir." Errol's voice was quiet but urgent. "One of them is coming this way."

The group stood still as the Consortium trooper, obviously alert, advanced, his weapon ready. Conscious that their cover would be useless soon, Harry prepared to use the shoulder-launched rocket he carried. Untested, he had no idea whether it would be effective or accurate.

The trooper tensed and stopped.

Looking in the direction the man was peering, Harry realised he could see Ferghal setting up his mortar. Reacting quickly, Harry aimed his rocket tube and ignited the missile. Briefly enveloped in smoke and a shower of sparks, he lost sight of his target, but heard a shout and a loud bang as it detonated.

"We better move, sir!" Errol Hill called. "He got off a report before your rocket blew him off his feet."

"Here they come," called TechRate Moroti, indicating a group of troopers fanning out in an arc toward them. Hefting the plasma rifle he carried, he sighted it and sent several bursts toward the advancing troopers, sending them diving for cover.

"Damn," Harry muttered. He assessed the situation. "Fire our rockets at them. Pick your target carefully, but don't let them get close. Use the grenades to slow them down if you can." Loading his tube, he picked a target.

The smoke and bangs of the rockets drew more attention, including Ferghal's. A group of soldiers advancing to join those attacking Harry's group found themselves diving for shelter as the bigger bombs from Ferghal's team rained down among them. Then a series of larger explosions from their vehicle park drew their attention, and as the troops hesitated, Harry and his team retreated, meeting up with the Coxswain and then Ferghal as they ran to their hidden escape entrance.

Harry was the last to dive through the opening just as the entrance sealed.

"That was too close for comfort," he said, dusting himself off. "We will have to find other ways to strike at them."

Harry studied the faces of the Canid leaders gathered in what he thought of as their council chamber. The Consortium's attacks on the cities continued despite the desperate defence put up by the Canids and Harry's team. Their explosives gave the Consortium troopers good reason to be wary now, but they could not counter the aerial bombardment.

One, an elder of the group who had been hostile toward Harry's party from the start, held forth at some length. From Grakuna, the elder who had brought them into the city, speaking through the interpretation device, he learned that this elder, called Rathol, was advocating that the survivors should be expelled and their explosives and weapons used to destroy all human occupants on the planet, including Harry's crew. Others disagreed, and the debate became heated as Harry tried to find an opening into which he could speak.

Finally, he bellowed, "If you wish to discuss me and my people, we have a right to be heard in this debate!" That bought him a moment of silence, and he took his chance. "Rathol wishes to seize the weapons we have created and shared with you, and use them against us while annihilating our mutual enemy. Is this the Canid way? Should not we work together against our common enemy?"

There was a growl of dissent. All eyes were focused on Harry.

"Our people are different in many ways, and my friends and I did not seek to be here, nor did we seek to make this war. Yes, my people have created weapons, but they are crude, and the weapons of those we fight are much more powerful. We need to work together if we are to succeed."

A chorus of growls and barks interrupted him briefly.

"Yes, you are all more powerful than we are, but is that the way you treat guests? It is not our way. We are your friends. We are not like those we fight. If our people succeed in our war, you will not have to be afraid that we will interfere in your peaceful way of life as our common enemy has done. On that you have my word as an officer of the Fleet." He knew he was taking a chance, as he really did not know what the North European Confederation would do to back him up, but he was pretty sure they would not treat the Canids the way the Consortium had done.

Grakuna took the floor. His words seemed to convey a more authoritative and less aggressive tone. Following the discussion as best he could, Harry was reassured to learn that the majority of the Canids shared Grakuna's view, but as the meeting drew to a close, he realised there was some contention among the leaders.

The small outpost looked ideal for an attack. A mining operation with a very small population of technicians maintaining the machines, it was lightly defended.

"Perfect," breathed Harry. "Only a dozen guards and no electronic defences. If we destroy that conveyor structure, it will bring the operation to a halt, and that processing plant cannot operate if it is not fed a continuous supply of ore."

The others studied the site carefully. Unlike their previous assault, this one would not see them attacking a much larger group of battle-hardened soldiers.

"My group will set the charges along the conveyor, sir. We can set the fuses as soon as you give the signal."

"Good. Remember, Swain, the flying fuse we've devised is uncertain in its timing. Once lit, you need to run for cover immediately. Those mines have Mr. Rasmus's special powder in them. It is considerably more powerful than our original."

Ferghal joined them. "I have my mortars ready. I will target the guardhouse first. Will you deal with the AI and block the comlinks?"

"I am already linked, my friend." Harry grinned. "Let us begin." He watched as Mr. Winstanley led his team toward the long conveyor system held aloft by its gantry towers. This close he could see how tall they were. If they wrecked enough of them, perhaps they could disrupt this operation. At the very least it would force their enemy to defend their outposts at the expense of their attempts to destroy any more of the cities.

Immersing himself in the AI, he watched its routines as he sought the comlink controls. Finding them, he watched the communications stream, for the most part routine orders, instructions, requests for information and reports. If he disrupted it too soon, it would alert the enemy, so he waited, taking the time to learn as much as he could of the activities of this and all the other AI systems it was linked to.

He started as he caught a movement in the direction of the conveyor, then relaxed. Mr. Winstanley had completed laying the charges. Carefully, Harry raised the long stick with a coloured cloth attached to its end, and waved it. The Coxswain waved in reply then ducked from sight. When he reappeared, he and his team were racing toward Harry, ducking from cover to cover.

Harry shut down the AI comlink, raised his signal pole again, and waved it in a figure-eight motion.

The reply was immediate. The ground-shaking bang of the first Bangalore torpedo was followed by several more that announced Ferghal's crude mortars sending their explosive grenades toward the buildings. The explosions brought the occupants streaming out, looking for the attackers. They took shelter again as more of the bombs burst in the air, on the ground and behind them.

With a deafening roar, the first of Mr. Winstanley's demolition mines detonated, then two more simultaneously, and finally the rest. The conveyor collapsed, the final section falling onto the processing unit, just as a larger explosion tore that building apart.

The Coxswain chuckled as he joined Harry. "Had a spare charge, sir, so we put it on the conveyor as soon as we fired the other fuses. Looks like it hit the right spot!"

"So it does." Harry fired the rocket flare to signal. "Time to go, Swain. I'll wait for Mr. O'Connor. Get the rest of our people to our tunnel, please."

Harry was feeling resentful. Their raids had brought the disruption he'd wanted, but not as much as he'd hoped. His twelve men and women—he didn't include Rasmus because he was not a warrior—could only do so much, and they were outnumbered and outgunned. Their mines and Bangalore torpedoes were too difficult to position and use with ease, and the shoulder-launched rockets were inaccurate and unreliable. They needed a more accurate mortar and an improved rocket launcher; something against the aerial craft as well. But he lacked the people, the equipment and the means to do everything he knew they needed to succeed in this miserable conflict.

His resentment was in part a reaction to his feeling guilty for the damage and injuries the Consortium had inflicted on the Canids because of his attack on them to free Ferghal, and the response to his attacks on their installations and mining outposts.

On top of all that, it was his twentieth birthday. *What a wretched way to spend a birthday,* he thought grimly. *If only I could be with Mary and not here in the middle of all this.* He really missed their regular holocalls. He wished he could find a way to talk to her. *But no, as usual I'm stuck on some godforsaken outpost with no way to communicate with her or anyone back home.*

He let himself fume for a few minutes then pushed his angry thoughts aside. His crew needed his attention, and moping wouldn't solve anything.

His men had suffered in the attacks and raids on the enemy, and that didn't sit well with him. Ranji Singh was out of action and needed more medical attention than they could give him. Even Ferghal's birthday greeting and his gift of a small forged replica of the Fleet insignia had barely lifted his blue mood.

His resentment was fed by the knowledge that everyone looked to him for leadership, and he was feeling very unequal to the task. The recent attacks had shaken his confidence. He'd turned in on himself, searching his soul and wondering whether he should give himself up to the Consortium to put a stop to this madness.

Despite his brave words to the Canid leaders, he knew the continued conflict would be costly in terms of lives and injuries—yet the alternative no longer seemed to be an option either.

He felt very alone as he considered their situation. He was unable to stop the Consortium's attacks on the living nodes of this strange life form that had provided him and his team with food, clothing and shelter through the ferocious winter.

His anger made him determined to find some way to make them pay for their assaults on the Canids.

He looked up with weary eyes as Ferghal entered the small room Harry used as his personal retreat. "What new problem have you for me, my friend?" he asked.

"None I am aware of—save you, Harry. Your mood concerns us. This assault on our host is not your fault. They have been trying for a long time to discover the technology they believe is hidden in the Canid cities, and they have made many attacks upon our friends to secure that tech. This latest assault was inevitable as soon as they realised how you've survived this whole time, and where you've been hiding—not to mention your bombardment of their Base to set me free, for which I am eternally grateful." Ferghal grinned with his usual good cheer.

"However you want to frame it, I must accept responsibility for this. When I attacked their outpost, I did not consider the possibility of reprisal—and I have visited their AI, thanks to our host, and learned that they have ordered our destruction. We are, it seems, a greater threat than the Fleet itself to their operations here."

Ferghal frowned. "That's a lot of operations—the manufacture of fuel cells for interceptors and strike craft, projects that examine and attempt to replicate technologies they have seized from others, a listening post for Fleet and other encrypted signal traffic, and one that attempts to interact with the Fleet communications systems."

Harry considered this. "I wonder if this is the thing they guard so jealously that we must be killed in case we disrupt it. If so, then perhaps that is our retaliation." He smiled and stood up. "Thank you, my friend. I think we know exactly how to cause them distress. Show me this secret and let us see what we can do to amend it so that it works against their plans."

Ferghal didn't comprehend at first, but then a smile spread across his face. "That is the Harry I know. Join me in our host's mind and I will show you the project, and when we have done that, we have dinner and drinks prepared to celebrate your birth anniversary." He laughed suddenly, adding, "And now you are officially permitted to take alcohol."

Lieutenant Clarke stood before Commander Nielsen, his feelings very mixed. "So you want me to supervise the Rates doing this construction work for the Consortium, sir?"

"Correct, Mr. Clarke, and to ensure our people are not being abused. Naturally I expect you to keep your eyes and ears open for any information that might be useful to our side." Commander Nielsen kept his expression neutral. He suspected Lieutenant Clarke of aiding the enemy, and he wanted to check his suspicions. "This work detail is technically within the Convention on the use of POWs, but I suspect it is also to be used to harass the Canids."

"I see, sir." Aral Clarke felt sure there was an ulterior motive to this assignment. Could the Commander suspect him of collaboration?

"You'll have several Master Warrants actually running the detail, I'm told. You are there purely to ensure the Convention is observed."

"Yes, sir." Aral Clarke felt his pulse quicken. It would give him an opportunity to show his captors that not all Fleet Officers were obstructive and bent on sabotage.

Commander Nielsen noted the look of anticipation that his visitor couldn't hide. "Make sure our people aren't abused, Lieutenant. You'll be collected after Roll Call tomorrow morning. Carry on."

The Commander hoped Clarke lacked the imagination to see through his motive in giving him this assignment. He didn't trust Clarke, and the two Master Warrants assigned to the group would be keeping a very close eye on the Lieutenant.

"We cannot—indeed we have not the means to attack our enemy directly," Harry told his companions. "Therefore I propose that we continue to make attacks of opportunity on them and their installations wherever and whenever we can."

The Coxswain concurred. "Makes sense, sir. If we force them to defend their own places, they'll have to ease up on their attacks."

"I agree." Harry turned to Rasmus and Ferghal. "We will need some new weapons for this, and more powerful mines. I have in mind carrying out unpredictable attacks in small groups at a distance from any of our host's surface nodes and without direct contact with the enemy."

"What do you suggest?" Rasmus asked.

"A large mine that might be remotely triggered to disrupt one of their patrol convoys. I would like to have a device that will fire off multiple mortars, as if a ground assault were to follow, but which can be triggered and then left by those that place it so they can make their escape."

Ferghal nodded. "It will not be difficult to create one, but that will leave something for our enemy to find."

"Typically it would, but not if it were to include a final device that destroys it."

"I will work on it." Ferghal hesitated. "What of their manufactories? Can we not attack those? Or disrupt their off-world activities with some recoding of their signals to associates?"

"I intend to discover how we might do that, my friend. Leave it with me. If you can give us the means to retaliate where they do not expect us to, that will be a mask for everything else we hope to achieve. I wish to find a means to access their hypercoms emitters to send a message to the Fleet as a backup to what you have already sent."

Coxswain Winstanley looked across to where Harry sat staring into the distance. "He's been like that two days," he murmured to Rasmus. "I'm worried about him. He seems to have shut himself into the AI. What the hell is he doing?"

Rasmus looked up from the device he was working on. "According to Ferghal—Ich meine Leutnant O'Connor—he is studying a project in the enemy's AI. I think, when he finds a way to turn it against them, it will go badly for them."

The Coxswain nodded. "Right. And when he does, it will be bloody creative." His chuckle shook his frame. "God help them if he finds a way to pay back what they did to Mister O'Connor."

Deep in the Consortium AI, Harry gathered information and forwarded it to Fleet HQ. He knew he needed to be careful, as he had already discovered that at least one ComOP was aware of his intrusion, and was monitoring the emitter logs.

Ferghal joined them carrying a long tube and a pair of shorter metal rods. Behind him, a Canid carried a device that resembled a large drum with three adjustable legs with spikes on the ends.

"I think this will work as a launching tube for our grenades," Ferghal announced. "But I will need to test it on the surface where we can see how great a charge it can withstand."

Rasmus examined the tube. One end of the cylinder was closed and somewhat thicker along the lower third. A collar, two thirds of the way up from the base, housed a pair of sockets into which the adjustable metal rods fitted and supported the tube at an angle of roughly forty-five degrees. "The propellant charge will need to be calculated carefully, but I think this will be effective—albeit inaccurate."

"Aye," Ferghal agreed. "It will be best used to put down a barrage of fragmentation bombs, I'm thinking. As for this beastie—" he indicated the drum-like device "—if it works as I hope, it will fire twelve mortar bombs then blow itself to pieces." His grin widened. "But I have left out the final charge so we may test it."

"When do you want to do that?" asked the Coxswain.

"As soon as possible," replied Ferghal. He glanced at Harry. "He's still busy, so I will not disturb him. We can take them to the surface at the city-node the enemy destroyed. They have withdrawn from there to search another site some distance away. Perfect for a test-run among the wreck they left."

Aral Clarke sat alone in the mess lounge that officers of his rank were allowed, even former members of the Fleet such as himself. An attractive woman came into the room, poured herself a cup of coffee, and glanced in his direction, holding the carafe with a question in her eyes.

"Coffee?" she said.

"Sure, why not," replied Clarke. *Let a woman wait on me for a change*, he snarled inwardly, as if arguing with his wife Delle.

She joined him at the table and pushed the steaming cup toward him. "I've seen you around here and there," she said, easing into the conversation with a light tone and a friendly smile. "I believe you worked with Sub-Lieutenants O'Connor and Heron. That must have been interesting, with them bouncing into the twenty-third century from the nineteenth, or something like that! I can only imagine the challenges faced by whoever brought them up to speed on our way of doing things."

Lifting the cup, Clarke glanced round to make sure they were alone in the room. "Yeah, tell me about it. I worked with Heron, or should I say, he worked for me. He was supposed to be my assistant, but he's an arrogant little prat and far too clever by half."

"Bit of a pain to work with, was he?" She chuckled and leaned across the table, eager to hear more.

"Bloody impossible! Always argued with me, and knew better on just about everything, or thought he did." His resentment burning, Clarke continued unfettered now that the floodgates of his wrath had opened. "Very clever with the maths, and so pretentious with that old-fashioned accent and way of speaking. Really annoying little bastard."

He finally took a long slurp of his coffee. "That's good coffee, thanks," he added, not sure what to say next. He had never been able to make small talk with women, for some reason.

Taking a sip from her cup, the woman, a psychoanalyst and Dr. Wan's right hand, encouraged him to continue.

Clarke's resentment boiled over. "I put him on a charge twice for insubordination, but the Commander refused to take it forward. He and the Captain thought the sun shone out of Heron's—well, you know what I mean."

"Does he have the same ability as O'Connor?" she asked innocently. She'd been present when Ferghal had got loose in their attempt to trigger his link, but absent when Harry had freed him.

His tongue now loosened by the apparent interest of a beautiful, intelligent woman, Clarke continued his rant. He was on a roll now. "Yes. If anything, Heron's better. His ability with mathematics and calculus means he gets right into the algorithms. He doesn't need an interface—just lets the AI read his mind, any AI. And you should see him with the servant droids. They act on his every bloody wish! 'Yes, Mr. Heron, right away, sir,' and they scurry off to do his bidding when he hasn't uttered a damn word."

With careful prompting, she encouraged him to pour out everything he knew about Harry and Ferghal's ability to immerse themselves in any AI network they had access to. Despite herself, she was fascinated by Clarke's account, and she was rather sorry when a Fleet Master Warrant Officer came into the mess lounge and interrupted the flow with a reminder to Lieutenant Clarke that he was supposed to be checking on the work of a group of fellow prisoners instead of taking a coffee break.

"You check on them, Warrant!" snapped Clarke. "I'm not a bloody nursemaid." Clarke caught the expression of contempt the Warrant Officer failed to hide. "I'll be there when I'm finished."

The psychoanalyst rose. "I'd better get going anyway. Thanks for the chat, Aral. You're a very interesting man." She smiled. "Let's hope things get sorted out soon, and we can all be friends again."

She slipped past the Warrant Officer and exited the lounge. Mr. Clarke would get a talking to from his senior officer, but she didn't care. He wasn't worth worrying about. Heron and O'Connor, on the other hand, were choice research subjects. There was plenty to examine later and discuss with Dr. Wan, and she had recorded it all.

When Harry emerged from his mental link to the AI, hungry and tired, his head abuzz with ideas for future disruptions, he finally noticed Ferghal and Rasmus, who were laughing at a shared joke with several others of their team.

"Hello, Harry." Ferghal grinned. "Welcome back to the real world, ceann urra. Let's get down to it. You wanted a device that would throw our bombs some distance, right? Well, now you have it. Look at this beauty." He gestured like a showman toward the heavy tube that Errol Hill was cradling to his chest. "Behold, our mortar."

"Excellent." Harry studied all of the explosive devices. "You have tested them?"

"Yes, and we have discovered the mortar will throw the bomb a little over two hundred yards." Ferghal gestured toward the drum. "As for this beast—well, a few of these and our enemy may think the Fleet has arrived!"

"I'll be honest, sir." The Coxswain shook his head. "I didn't think they would work, but those bombs certainly fly out of the mortars. Just one problem as I see it—the fuses are a bit uncertain. Some burst in the air and some on the ground."

"But that isn't such a great problem," said Ferghal. "Rasmus has an idea to fix it, and he has created a chemical igniter that does not require the use of a match to set the fuse burning."

"Good." Harry nodded. "But now I have another idea. We need an aerial shell to deal with their flying craft." He looked at Rasmus. "A larger rocket will be required for this—one that bursts at the top of its flight and throws fragments into the path of any flyer."

"Ja, that is possible," agreed Rasmus. "It requires only the creation of a nozzle to direct the gas stream, and I will amend the powder mixture to give the correct burning rate. The fuse may be more complicated."

"If you give me a drawing of what you need," said Ferghal, "I will make them and show the others how to do it. Maddie can—" he caught Harry's look reminding him to maintain decorum "—I mean ComOp Hodges will get her team busy making them."

The others dispersed to get in the supper queue, and Harry and Ferghal were alone. Ferghal slipped into the ease of joking with a boyhood friend. "So, now that you've crawled out of Alice's rabbit hole, what have you learned about the Cons?"

"Alice's rabbit hole?" Harry was so flushed and flustered that Ferghal let out a huge guffaw of laughter.

"Your look was priceless! It's this thing everyone says based on some book written sixty-one years after we were hurled from the deck of the *Spartan* and dumped into this century. We were too early to read it, and now we're too late to know what the hell they're talking about." Ferghal gave a lopsided grin.

"Right then, I'll take your word on it," Harry said, regaining his usual stoic demeanour. He didn't take too well at being the butt of the joke, even a good-natured one from his old friend Ferghal. "Now, back to matters at hand, I learned a great deal of information that will be useful to our Admirals if I can find a way to send it to them. Since your signal, they have made the separation so complete that the hypercom transmitter is entirely independent of the Base AI."

Ferghal nudged him and gestured toward the lengthening supper queue. "We don't want to miss the food, whatever it is." They stepped to the end of the queue and grabbed their supper trays. When they'd found a place to sit apart from the others, Ferghal picked up the thread of conversation. "When I was their prisoner, I overheard the guards' conversations more often than they realised. I learned that our officers are kept in separate holding cells from the rates, and they use our TechRates to run their manufactories. Did you discover anything about the rest of our crew from the *Daring*?"

"Aye, that I did." Harry's expression was hard. "And I learned where they are. When we're ready and our weapons are thoroughly tested, we will obtain their release." He looked up as one of the Canids joined them. Gesturing toward an empty seat at the table, he said, "Greeting, friend. Please join us."

The big Canid placed a translator on the table and said, "Greeting. We desire to learn how to use the device you use to throw weapons at an enemy."

Harry nodded. "Excellent, but we must work in concert, else our enemy may strike against us with even more fury than before. And we will need to manufacture many, many more than we have. Can your people help us do that?"

The *Vengeance* dropped out of transit and slowed to join the squadrons of her enhanced fleet. "Impressive array," Captain Curran remarked to his Executive Commander. "Now that's what I call a fleet. Looks like the politicians have finally decided whose side they're on."

"Sure does, but it looks like we've a large contingent of the North American Union fleet here too. I'm counting five of their starships and at least ten cruisers plus a lot of escorts and smaller ships."

"Looks as if half our starships are here. The rest must be spread between other concentration points." Ben leaned forward and activated the inter-ship communication link as the incoming message signal flashed. "Good evening, Admiral Hartmann, quite a party you have here."

"Good to see you, Ben. Everything back to full operation on board?"

"Fully repaired and fully operational. We'll be ready to welcome you back aboard whenever you wish, ma'am."

"I'll make the transfer at twenty-one hundred. My Command Staff will accompany me. We have some reinforcements, and I'll be receiving Admiral Kersage tomorrow so he can meet your team and mine."

Ben exchanged a glance with his Executive Commander. Nodding in response to the Commander's acknowledgement, he said, "We'll be ready for them, Admiral."

"Excellent. I'll fill you in on the plans once I'm aboard. It's good to have you back. I was beginning to think you'd be held up somehow and miss the rendezvous."

"No chance," Ben acknowledged. "We told the repair crew that if they dragged out their work, they'd be finishing on passage."

The boardroom of the Consortium's cruising headquarters had all the luxurious appointments of the corporate headquarters they'd had to give up on Earth. The chief executives sat with their respective Directors round the great U-shaped table.

Admiral Gratz listened as the Chairman's deputy presented the situation report. Militarily, the conflict was still marginally in their favour, thanks mainly to the support of the Sino-Asian Imperium. But the superiority was wafer thin, and any reverse could throw the balance in the opposite direction.

"The blockade on raw materials and resources is having an impact, but the Confederation and their allies have found alternative sources. We have our management team looking at the suppliers. Where possible, we will take steps to deal with them." The deputy continued his briefing, informing the meeting of the initial approaches from a section of the World Treaty Organisation Commission for a truce. He smiled. "I wonder whether the peace lobby will appreciate the irony of having appointed one of our agents as their ambassador."

The Chairman interjected. "I doubt it. Mehmet has worked hard to sow defeatism." The deputy sat down and turned to the Admiral. "What is the state of our ships and troops?"

"Morale is good, but our reverse at Regulus shook some of our commanders. I have put in hand a range of developmental exercises to build confidence and initiative. Our ships have proved to be as good if not better, in some classes, as those of the Fleet and the North American Union."

"Don't you have the advantage of the scan disruptors?"

"They've found ways to see our ships even when screened, so we no longer have that advantage." Gratz paused. "Brigadier Newton reports that there has been no further contact with Sub-Lieutenant Heron and his merry band of runaways, though there is evidence they're still on the loose. Her forces have reduced three of the alien cities to burned-out shells, and think they may have killed or injured some of the group."

"Is there any indication Brigadier Newton's tactics are having an effect?"

"It appears she has it under control, sir, but she reports the Canids have become very aggressive and are using weapons, some of which they captured from our troops, and some they seem to have made themselves, a sort of crude explosive device. The Brigadier's policy is to drive them away from our installations. She reasons, and I support her view, that we can deal with them once the war is settled."

"So we may assume she has the situation under control?" The Chairman paused. "Or should we consider replacing her?"

"It appears she has it under control, sir, but there are a number of anomalous logins and gaps in the transmissions log from their hypercom transmitter. As a precaution, the transmitter is now completely separated from the rest of their systems. Her AI specialists are working to find the problem, and she assures me the isolation of the hypercoms guarantees there can be no unauthorised access."

"I don't like the sound of that, guarantee or no guarantee. Order her to ensure these ghost logins are traced and dealt with immediately."

Harry gathered his crew around him, a mix of humans and Canids. "Our plan is to capture weapons with this raid, and to cause the Cons as much inconvenience as possible. They will not expect us to attack them at this site because they think we surrendered it, but we must expect them to defend themselves. Grakuna and Rathol will set up the bombards. Once those begin firing, we will strike against their perimeter sentries. Remember, this is to cause them discomfort and to test our weapons in an assault. Do not risk yourselves if they respond in force."

The Coxswain grinned. "If those bombards and the mortars work as planned, sir, it will be damned unpleasant for them. We're ready. Let's do this!"

Chapter 21

Project Ruin

The Consortium camp had been sited with care, dominating the obvious approach to the small city that their scientists were struggling to examine. Harry studied the perimeter through a pair of range finders. "They have patrolling sentries set up, Mr. Winstanley, and an intruder detection system further out." He handed over the optics. "Take a good look. I think the Command Post is there, in the centre."

The Coxswain studied the indicated cluster of vehicles. "Looks like it, sir. You want me to target it with the mortars?"

"Yes, Swain. Even if you don't take it out, it will disrupt their response." He caught a brief flash of light from the ridge on the far side of the encampment. "Grakuna signals he's ready. We will move as soon as their barrage commences."

Moments later, bright flashes signalled the firing of the first of the self-destroying mortar clusters. Seconds later, more fired with thunderous bangs along the sides farthest from Harry and the waiting assault team.

Harry and his men ran to the enemy perimeter and were inside the first line of defence before the sentries spotted them.

Dropping to one knee, Harry aimed his rocket launcher at a troop of soldiers advancing toward him. The rocket ignited and the missile hurled itself from the tube in a shower of sparks, joining several more fired by others in his group. Fitted with a contact fuse, the rockets exploded as they struck armour, vehicles and domes, sending the troopers diving for shelter. Taking cover himself, he hastily fitted a second rocket then peered round the corner and noted that several of the troopers were down or seeking shelter as the Coxswain's mortars joined the barrage.

"Set the mines and incendiaries!" Harry shouted to his team. Taking aim with his rocket tube on a pile of equipment cases, he activated the igniter, and the rocket whooshed away. He changed position and slipped another into the tube. The mortar barrage kept the defenders pinned down. Firing another of his missiles at a pair of Consortium troopers sheltering beneath a vehicle, he changed position again.

A larger explosion hurled parts of a power generator around, and when the noise ceased for a few seconds, Harry heard the whistle signal that he'd been waiting for. Grabbing his own, he blew it, as did his team members in the cacophony of exploding missiles and the scream of rockets. Racing from one scrap of cover to the next, he followed his people to their rendezvous point.

"Everyone's clear, sir," Errol Hill gasped, diving into a hollow almost on top of Harry. "The fuses will go any moment now." He stopped as dirt and debris spattered down around them. "Bugger, that one was a bit early!"

Harry's response was lost in the rolling succession of explosions as more of the charges detonated. Grinning like a lunatic, he leapt to his feet and signalled the others to follow.

The Consortium Brigadier surveyed the wreckage. "You say they fired explosive shells from a distance? Where the blazes did they get them?"

"They must be making them somewhere. Pretty crude design, a sort of rocket with an explosive head on it, but effective. We found a few that didn't detonate, though. We think the fuses failed." The Colonel offered one of the recovered missiles. "Not very big, but absolutely deadly if it hits a person. Our armour is designed to deflect and diffuse a plasma bolt, not something like this."

"Seems unlikely anyone could do so much damage just with these."

"They had some bigger stuff as well, charges their people must have placed while the rest held us down with these. They took out our Command Unit and the Commissariat with some sort of shell fired from cover, and managed to carry off a container of medical supplies and another of weapons spares."

"That doesn't sound like the Rotties." The Brigadier paused. "So that damned Fleet group must be responsible, those savage fugitives led by Heron. Don't know when to surrender, do they, but there aren't enough of them to cause this much damage—or have we been losing prisoners as well?"

"No, we still have all the prisoners we rounded up. According to our troopers, it was the Rotties—at least all the attackers they saw were dressed the way the Rotties dress."

"Right. Well, pull our people back for now. I'll reinforce your unit and put extra guards on all our outposts. I want a full reconnaissance from the air as well. I want to know where the hell these people are hiding, and where they are making these weapons!"

Despite the extra patrols, or perhaps because of them, Harry's hit-and-run raids took a serious toll on Consortium morale. He had been right. Small parties equipped with the self-destroying mortar packages stood a much better chance of reaching their target undetected. The Canid teams were exceptionally adept at setting these up, aided by their screening cloaks. They set up batteries of the mortar cakes, as Mr. Winstanley dubbed them, and cleared out of the strike zone. When triggered, these did considerable damage and gave the impression of a major assault. While the Consortium force attempted to counter the assault in one direction, a raiding party infiltrated, seized what they wanted, planted some of their demolition mines, and ran for cover.

Grakuna expressed his satisfaction to Harry as he surveyed the damage to one of the Consortium outposts. "Your strategy is effective. Our enemy is forced to defend their own dens now, and leave the Provider unharmed."

"True, Leader of the Packs, but now they seek to harass your people." Harry turned to ComOp Hodges. "Signal Mr. Winstanley to withdraw."

"Aye, aye, sir." She stood, held a pair of coloured flags above her head, and made a sweep with one. When she spotted a response, she swept the flags in a series of positions on either side of her body. Watching the response, she said, "Message acknowledged, sir."

"Well done." Harry had realised early that they needed the means to communicate quickly and easily between groups when carrying out these attacks. Without the means to use comlinks or to create them, he'd recalled the semaphore system of the British Royal Navy he'd joined four hundred years earlier. ComOp Hodges had proved an apt pupil. She improved on his system and taught the others, drilling them to perfection. Now he had a signaller with each group, and the Canids had learned to use the flags as well.

Grakuna watched the signaller, and growled his concern. "Our enemy is wary now. They have learned that to follow too closely is to invite a trap." The big Canid studied Harry. "They seek you. We have heard them declare that you must be destroyed—you and the fox-haired one."

Harry laughed. "Then we must take care they do not have the opportunity. I shall look as much like a Canid as is humanly possible."

The big Canid managed his version of a smile at this comment, and Harry had a distinct flashback memory to the happy expressions of his faithful dog back home in Ireland when he was a boy.

Ferghal's small team of Engineering Rates had been enhanced by a number of Canids who watched their work and copied it, and even made some improvements. The manufacturing expanded rapidly, and Rasmus took over the supervision of the operation, which gave Ferghal time and space to create a larger missile for defence against the aerial strike craft.

"I have developed a fuse which will be triggered by a scanner pulse. It is a simple device, and has no electronic signature itself." Rasmus glanced at a workbench where several small Canids were engaged in detailed work. "I think it will work with Ferghal's missiles, though we should include a self destructing charge to detonate it when the propulsion ceases."

"That would be wise. Is it not possible the new fuse might detonate the charge too early?" Harry asked.

"Yes, so I have tried to ensure it will need the maximum power of a pulse—the strength it would encounter at close range." Picking up a completed fuse, he showed it to Harry. "Beautifully made. These people are very dexterous, despite appearances."

"A pity then that we must use them to create devices of destruction." Harry disliked the idea that the Canids had been a peaceful race until pushed to defend themselves and their Provider by the human invaders. "I have it in mind to release as many of our own as we can from their imprisonment camp and to seize some weapons while we're at it."

"That will certainly increase the problems for the enemy," agreed Ferghal. "What say you, Rasmus?"

"It will be a risky thing, my friends, and there's a chance of betrayal if any of those you release decide to play the informer. It will very likely provoke another major strike against our host."

Harry nodded. He valued Rasmus's opinions. "It is a risk we will have to consider. I have discussed it with our host and will do so again before we make any such move. How does the rocket design progress?"

"Very well, though we still can't get the height we want. It needs a longer tube, and the stabilisers leave a lot to be desired."

"That's an understatement," Ferghal interjected. "We had one chase us in the last test—it shed its tailfins soon after firing and looped several times before it turned and came after us!" The errant rocket had only just missed them as it tore past to bury itself in the ground close by. They had all been showered in the debris of earth, stones and fragments when it detonated.

"Not the best thing to happen then," said Harry, grinning at the image Ferghal conjured. "Can we improve it?"

"We already have," said Ferghal. "It's more stable now, but we need to work on the range. It bursts beneath the altitude of their aerial craft, but never you fear, we will resolve this too."

Harry was encouraged. "Then I think our chance may come soon. My interventions in their AI are having an effect, though they attempt to repair what I do as soon as they detect it. I'm building in sub-routines that initiate as soon as they alter something. I'm waiting for a good moment to launch a coup d'état and take it away from their control—or turn it against them."

"We're approaching dropout," announced the Weapons Commander. "Prepare to engage as soon as we get a clear lock. The intel is that they have four cruisers defending a repair ship. That's our primary target. Leave the escorts to *Warspite*, *Doorman*, *Dresden* and *Bremen*."

Danny waited while his targeting screen showed the usual burst of static as the ship transited the singularity. When it cleared, he identified the target and focussed the scanners on the vast bulk of the repair ship. The range was still too great for his batteries, so he tracked and locked on to the target, seeking to identify key installations or openings on her huge hull that would provide an opportunity to deal her a crippling blow.

The range closed rapidly and was almost within the parameters when Danny noticed that the aspect of the other ship had changed. This presented him the opportunity to fire directly into her vast open docking bay.

"Target the open bay. Lock on the interior and fire on my order," he directed his team.

"Ready."

"Fire."

Danny watched as the bolts of plasma traversed the intervening space and vanished into the dock, lighting up the interior spectacularly. Plasma bolts and beams engulfed the huge ship as she desperately tried to manoeuvre out of danger. A fire erupted in the repair bay, and a great flare burst out of the open doors, evidence of an escape of oxygen and fuel.

"Cease fire!" The command rang through the Centre. "They're abandoning her. Well done, Mr. Gunn, your batteries found her liquid oxygen tanks. She's a dead ship now. All batteries, shift target—we're engaging the lead cruiser next."

Outgunned, the escort cruisers broke off the engagement and vanished into transit. "Secure the batteries." The order was matter of fact. Danny watched on-screen as the ship launched barges and other small craft to recover survivors from the rapidly disintegrating repair ship.

"Well done," the Weapons Commander called out. "Great shooting, guys. That's one less problem for us to worry about and one more for the Cons."

The Consortium's AI monitors learned Harry's manoeuvres and reprogrammed themselves to trace every attempt at access. In return, he monitored their activity and altered his accordingly. It was extremely useful being able to hear the enemy's plans and movements, but also frustrating because he could not access their off-world communications. Those had been very effectively isolated, probably on the assumption that he and Ferghal were able to send messages to their Fleet commanders.

"I do not know how much longer I will be able to escape their traces," he told Ferghal. "They have come close to finding my entry link. Only the Provider has prevented their discovering it so far. For now, I have to be content to listen to their plans and spoil what I can." He grinned. "Here's a bit of fun for you. I found Dr. Wan's research on you and replaced it with all the tales of Fion MacCumhaill that I can recall. I hope he enjoys it."

This elicited the laugh from Ferghal that he was hoping for. Stretching his arms and flexing his shoulders, he said, "What have you there?"

Ferghal stood and, with great dramatic flair, he shook out a folded silver-grey garment, swept it over his shoulders, and wrapped it around himself.

"A gift from the Council of Leaders, one of their special cloaks. There's one for you too." Grinning, Ferghal said, "Now you see me." His grin widened. "And now you don't!"

Harry laughed as Ferghal's body vanished, leaving only his disembodied head visible—nothing but a mass of thick red hair, two blue eyes, and a wide grin. "It doesn't quite work like that, Ferghal, unless you've a desire to emulate some phantom of legend. I wonder if they have Halloween on this planet?" They both laughed at that wisecrack, and Harry added, "I think you're supposed to cover your head too. How does it function?"

"Now that, my friend, is the secret." Ferghal took a stance and launched into his best salesman's voice. "The fibre is made from the silk of a moth native to this place. It bends the light and deceives the eye of the beholder. An onlooker sees everything around it, but does not perceive the cape itself or the wearer. How many would you like to order today, good sir?"

Harry laughed again and walked round Ferghal, examining the cape in detail. "Astonishing, and very useful. The Council gave you this?"

"Yes, and several more. Enough for a few of us to accompany their raiders undetected. They are very valuable and only given to a select few. There is one other feature—it only works in contact with our Canid garments. To any other user it is no more than a cloak."

"That explains why our pursuers have not found the means to counter it." Harry smiled. "We have an advantage we did not appreciate, my friend. Now to find the opportunity to exploit it."

Chapter 22

Juggernaut

———————————————

Opportunity, Harry believed, was what you wanted it to be, or when you created it. Having studied his enemy's dispositions and the scattered nature of their operations, his next move was to intensify the raids and capture more of the Consortium's weapons. This plan was not without risk, but that had never stopped him before, and now Ferghal was with them again. The two of them together, with this fine team, were an unstoppable force.

He grinned as he looked at his assembled squad. The human element was almost indistinguishable from the Canids except in size and carriage. Like Harry, their hair had grown long, and the men all had beards. Careful styling made them appear, to a casual observer, like their hosts the Canids. Even the Coxswain's balding pate now had the characteristic mane and ear tufts of a Canid. He suppressed a laugh when he thought of his girlfriend, and wondered what she would make of his wild scruffy appearance.

"I have seldom seen so despicable a collection of irregulars," Harry told them. "Our appearance is probably enough to frighten our opponents to death—if our phantom visitors don't."

"I have to agree that this lot are pretty despicable," the Coxswain growled. "I wouldn't want to have to stand down wind of 'em or get too close in a fight."

"I fink the Swain says we stink, sir," Jim Stennet quipped. The youngest member of the crew except for Harry, he had proved very adept with loading and firing the mortar tubes. He sniffed his underarms and added, "An' 'e's right!"

"Speak for yourselves," said Maddie with a cheeky grin. "We women think of these things, even when we have to pack in a hurry to catch a launch to the back of beyond in five minutes. But I'm not sharing my precious deodorant and shampoo with you filthy lot, so don't even ask!"

They all laughed at that remark, and Harry grinned as Rasmus got in a comment. "Heron's Hellions. That's what we should call ourselves now. I always wanted to be a rogue, if only for a short while!"

"Very well, if we must give ourselves a name, that's as good as any!" Harry grinned. "Right, it is time we were on our way. Have we all the equipment we need for this excursion? You have the rockets, Ferghal? And your section have the mortars and the mines, Mr. Winstanley?"

"Yes, sir," the Coxswain confirmed, and Ferghal nodded.

"Very good. We will deploy as I have outlined. Mr. Winstanley, your team will move in as close as possible to fire on the guard. We wish to cause disruption and to divert their attention from the magazines. Ferghal, you and your team seize the summit and prepare to fire on any aerial craft that attempt to close us."

"We will do our best to distract them," Ferghal responded.

"Remember," said Harry, "this is a small outpost, lightly manned, but it has much we can make good use of. We want their transport and their weapons. Once your mortars commence, Mr. Winstanley, my team will infiltrate the disengaged side and secure the stores we need. Watch for my signal for the cessation of firing—I will fire a port fire to signal my intentions. Blue smoke to retreat, red to cease firing and join me."

He felt pleased with himself. The plan was an excellent one, and the attack would be supported by Grakuna and Rathol, the latter having been won over by Harry's careful tact and diplomacy, and by their grudging respect for his courage in standing up to his enemies.

This assault on a Consortium outpost was the result of Harry's exploration of the Base computer and the military communications network it supported. He had chosen this outpost because it was lightly manned and defended, and a considerable distance from any of the node cities that might suffer from retaliation. His listening to the Base AI had paid off. He now had a clear idea of the troop deployments, strengths and search orders. He'd also learned of this small depot and rest station, which occasionally housed some of their colleagues.

His intention was to capture more weapons with which to supplement their homemade bombs, mortars and rockets, and some med-units. They needed the weapons to counter the Consortium's aerial craft and allow them to meet the enemy on more equal terms.

Ferghal caught Harry's attention. "I suggest an amendment. Let my batteries remain apart until you have retreated to safety. Then, if their aerials should intervene, we may yet drive them away and avoid their seeing anything we do not wish them to."

The Coxswain nodded. "That makes sense, sir. Better to have the ability to scare off any intervention before they can see what we're doing."

"Excellent. I trust you to carry it out." Harry glanced at each member of his crew. "Everyone ready? Good. Let's get into position and prepare for our attack. I wish to strike as soon as they go to their breakfast. Speaking of, they probably won't like it today." He paused for effect. "I programmed liquid soap to be added to their food replicators. They might spend the morning in the—what do you call them?"

"The port-a-loos!" the others said in unison, and everyone burst out laughing, and after a round of rowdy chatter to ease the tension, they got into position to wreak havoc on the enemy.

Checking the dispositions of his people, Harry considered his next move. The early light was enough to distinguish the terrain, and they had reconnoitered the ground and prepared a way through which they could seek cover. The changing light and the colour contrasts caught his artist's eye, and he wished he had time to sit and paint the scene before him.

The Coxswain's mortars were in position and the ranges checked against where they would land on the commissariat and sleeping quarters, and the surrounding area. His interference with the automated defence system at the laboratory had resulted in this being detached from the AI systems, and now it was directed manually.

Catching a movement near the perimeter, he saw the signal he hoped for. The charges had been placed beneath the electronic barrier projectors. This meant getting very close to the perimeter and risking triggering an alarm, but several cloaked Canids achieved that with no problem.

The second part of his team was well concealed and would emerge once the Coxswain and his team had the Consortium troops pinned down. Harry's group was in place ready to storm the weapons store, their primary target. It was a risky plan, but the terrain worked in their favour, and he hoped to block any Consortium signal to reinforce their troops before he neutralised his team's initial target.

A final check confirmed his lookouts were in position. Ferghal was ready to fire the placed charges and take care of their rocket battery. Abram Winstanley and his assault team were poised for action. Behind him, his own team waited to rush the armoury. It would be a close contest, but he knew their explosives would be sufficiently unfamiliar to the enemy to cause confusion.

They might have a problem if the garrison called in air support. Their anti-air rockets were little more than dangerous fireworks. Though unlikely to do more than make their enemy wary of approaching too closely, he hoped they would deter any attempt to intervene.

The increasing light from the rising bluish sun threw a harsh glare across the landscape. From his concealment Harry watched as the guards changed and dispersed to their guardroom and then, to their commissariat.

"ComOp Hodges, signal Commence to Mr. O'Connor and the Coxswain, please."

Grinning, Maddie stood, got a 'ready' response of a single exposed flag from both, and quickly sent the alphanumeric code for the Commence signal.

Diving into cover next to Harry, she called, "This is much more fun than my usual Coms role, sir!"

They heard a satisfying thump from the first mortar, and the subsequent ones were almost drowned out by the roar as the placed charges that detonated and hurled fragments of the perimeter projectors skyward.

Harry laughed in triumph. It was a glorious sight. As the mortar bombs landed, some exploded above the ground and others detonated on it.

Harry stood. "Follow me," he ordered his group. "Hodges, stay close. The rest of you know what to do. We go in fast on the blind side, get what we came for, and get out."

The mixed group of Canids and humans acknowledged his order, drew their cloaks around them, and vanished. Keeping to cover, Harry led the way down the slope.

The mortars were causing mayhem. The position in which the shells exploded made little difference as the shrapnel, stones and debris hurled out or upward, flung in all directions by the bursting bombs, perforating the commissariat and the barrack domes. Men emerged from the structures, some obviously roused from their beds, some falling under the hail of shrapnel or diving for cover.

At the perimeter they removed their cloaks to ensure they did not run into each other. Racing forward, their weapons ready, they focused on their objective. Members of the team peeled aside to plant their bombs on the emplaced weapons defending the perimeter and just coming into action.

A guard, who had been facing the assault on the far side of the camp, turned and saw them. Raising his weapon, he fired at one of the attackers, and missed. Dropping to one knee, Errol Hill fired a tube-launched rocket from his shoulder at the armoured man. Whether because the man did not realise what the weapon was or had not recognised it as a threat, he made the mistake of remaining upright and attempting to sight his weapon on one of the figures running toward him. The rocket struck him on the side of the head and knocked him to the ground. That saved him further injury as it careened between the domes then burst and perforated the structures around it.

Harry reached his objective and found, to his relief, the lock could be operated by his cyberlink. His team took all the weapons they could carry. Others gathered equipment and any supplies they needed.

"Stennet, place the charges, then go!" Harry ordered. "Take the things you can carry with you. I'll fire the fuse as soon as you're clear."

"Done, sir," the young TechRate called, gathering up a heavy plasma projector and several smaller weapons in a container. His arms loaded, he staggered as he ran for the door and hurled himself after his companions.

Harry lit the fuse, gathered the bundle of weapons, and bolted out of there.

Sprinting for the cover of the escape path he was surprised to see several vehicles approaching along the track. A burst of plasma on the path ahead of him made him change direction and lent speed to his legs as he ran for the cover of the narrow cleft in the rocky hillside. Behind him, the armoury erupted, the crude charges sending chunks of the dome and its contents high into the air.

"All units—close up on the Camp. Prisoner transports, withdraw and fall back to allow Units Two and Three to close up." The Captain's orders were rapid, his attention on the figure running diagonally toward them. "Gunner, target that man!"

The operator trained his turret weapon on Harry, but the automatic targeting system, designed to target stationary or very fast moving objects, refused to lock onto the weaving figure. With attention focused on trying to obtain a clear lock, the operator failed to see the object that flew toward the open-topped vehicle in a high arc trailing a thin stream of smoke.

The Commander did see it, but failed to recognise it—until it burst above and slightly beyond their vehicle. The shower of fragments and small stones with which it had been filled smashed into the vehicle's top, sides and exposed equipment. A stone smashed the visor of the turret operator and caused him to stab the firing command key. This, in turn, sent a blast of plasma searing past Harry as he plunged through the gap in the outcrop then stumbled and fell flat.

That saved him. A little to one side of Harry, Maddie noticed a pair of troopers trying to cut Harry off. Dropping her flags, she snatched up her rocket tube, loaded it, took aim and launched it, then loaded another and sent it at the second man. Without waiting to see the effect, she grabbed her flags and ran to where Harry was gathering the fallen weapons.

"Come on, sir. Some of the bastards are ahead of us."

Behind Harry, a second grenade burst inside the vehicle closest to him with devastating effect, but now, the second, third and fourth vehicles were deploying and bringing their turret weapons to bear. Warned by the burning lead vehicle, whose surviving crew were struggling clear, they belatedly closed their upper hatches.

From his hilltop vantage point, Ferghal watched in mounting frustration as more vehicles joined the first group. Troopers began to spill from these, deploying rapidly to pin down Harry's team as they scrambled for cover. Trapped, Harry signalled his people to use their recently captured weapons.

Using the shoulder-launched projector, he disabled a vehicle and sent the troopers racing for cover. A hail of grenades flushed these men and several more he had not seen on his flank into a rapid retreat, and he made a run for new cover to join the rest of his small team in their escape route.

"Quick!" Ferghal ordered, when he saw Harry's predicament. "Adjust the launchers to fire down the slope. The projectiles will cause them damage even if they do not burst as planned."

His team leapt into action. Raising the base of the tube to his shoulder and aiming the device at a vehicle, TechRate Brydges lit the fuse. He yelped as the rocket erupted, the wash of burning sparks and the acrid smoke engulfing him as it did so.

The effect on the troops below was dramatic. The missile arrived trailing fire, struck the ground en route, and lifted to soar into the centre of a group of troopers crouching behind a rocky outcrop.

The explosion threw two of the troopers over the outcrop and killed two more outright, leaving the rest bleeding from their wounds. The survivors looked round in desperation to determine where this new attack was coming from, just in time to see another of these lethal projectiles land. It struck a vehicle and fell to the ground, hissing viciously and still in motion as it slid about erratically. The motion ceased as the rocket ran to an end.

There was a moment of silence and then a flash and bang that rocked the nearest vehicles and showered a large area in debris and lethal shrapnel.

Harry and his team took full advantage and melted along their pre-planned route, joined now by the heavily laden Canids as they fled toward their well-concealed access to the transport tube. The Coxswain was close with Ferghal not far behind when Harry ran full tilt into a Consortium trooper. The two of them fell to the ground in a tangle of arms, legs and weapons.

Harry recovered first and clubbed the unfortunate man into unconsciousness, grabbed his weapons, and flung himself into cover. The rest of his team opened fire on the Consortium troopers who ran to cut off Harry's escape. The Coxswain's team ran straight into the middle of the fight and joined in the desperate struggle that had become a hand-to-hand battle between individuals.

Harry and his people were outgunned, outnumbered and outclassed, but they put up a desperate fight. The troopers gained the upper hand, and Harry was almost at the point of ordering his men to surrender when Ferghal arrived with a large group of Canids. Rapidly the position was reversed.

The Sergeant now in command of the surviving Consortium troop called, "Call the Rotties off! We surrender."

"Cease fire," shouted Harry as the man he had been grappling with looked round in confusion. "Throw down your weapons and we will not harm you," he added in a quieter tone as the tumult stilled. "Swain, disarm them all, please, and see to the wounded. Ferghal, thank you, my friend—another minute and we must have surrendered to them."

"So I could see." Ferghal's face was tense. "But I fear we must hurry. They have called for air support and beyond yon hill are two of their vehicles containing some of our people." He indicated the Sergeant. "This was their guard, I'm thinking. What should we do with them?"

Harry thought quickly, not easy to do because he was badly shaken by just how close the fight had come to being lost. "We take them and their transport with us—come, we will have to move fast. Use our link to disable the beacons on the transports. I will deal with the release of our comrades and attempt to divert the airmen." He mopped at the blood running from a cut on his scalp then tried to ease the pain in a twisted ankle. "We have no choice but to keep you with us as prisoners," he told the Consortium Sergeant. "But we will require you to wear blindfolds when we reach our destination."

Maddie Hodges limped up to him, her face smeared with dirt and blood oozing from a scalp wound.

"Hodges, are you wounded? Thank you for your defence— those troopers would have had me without it."

"I'm fine, sir. The bastard that gave it to me isn't, though. And now I'll need to replace my flags." She waved the bloodied stick in her hand and grinned. "I said being your signals op was more fun than my usual role, sir, but I didn't realise it could be this much fun!"

Chapter 23

Heron's Hellions

———————————————

Colonel Rees was furious. "How the blazes did this go wrong? How did a bunch of runaways manage to take on armed troops in armoured vehicles and not only steal our weapons and get away, but take some of our people prisoner?"

"It was very well planned and executed." The Major struggled to keep his own temper. Like the Colonel, he had had a disturbed night. "They took Camp Two by surprise, and knew exactly how to disrupt the perimeter defences. The transmitters were blocked, which prevented the Commander from sending out an attack report. Charges knocked out the perimeter barriers and the emplaced weapons, as well as the projectiles they used against the troops when they responded."

"But that doesn't explain how they managed to take out the four assault units. What went wrong there?" The Colonel consulted a tablet. "We have over sixty killed, injured or taken prisoner, and all we have to show for it is one of theirs dead and several possibly injured. On top of that, they've now got another forty on their side since they got away with our prisoner detail, and a lot of weapons—in our own transports!" The tablet hit the table with a thud.

"There was confusion when our air strike got there. The prison vehicles were signalling their normal code and following the route as if returning to Base," the Air Commander responded. "And we had to deal with some form of missile—both of my strike craft were damned lucky to return."

"What kinds of missiles? Bloody bows and arrows?"

Ignoring the sarcasm, the Air Officer replied, "They took damage as they made a low sweep to investigate a suspicious contact. One took a direct hit when he flew into the missile, and the other was peppered with projectiles, which seem to be mainly small stones. We've never seen anything like the weapons they used, and they have no electronic signature, thus the surprise attack. Our scanners picked up no signals beforehand."

The accommodation deep underground, though comfortable, provided no direct means of observing what was happening on the surface. With his ankle badly sprained, Harry was more or less confined to his quarters while Rasmus and the others attended to the replenishment of their rockets, mortar bombs, and the development of some improved missiles. Several weapons specialists among the Fleet prisoners that Harry's team had freed from the Consortium compound were helping set up a factory to build copies of the captured plasma weapons under Rasmus's supervision.

Alone, he had time to consider the results of their assault, and the consequences. They'd had a lucky escape, but it was far too close a call. Unfortunately, all of the medical equipment and many of the heavier weapons, the main object of the raid, were lost. On the positive side, they now had two transport vehicles hidden in their host, and the weapons captured would give them an additional capability.

What weighed most heavily on Harry's mind was the loss of one of his men. Will Kemp had fallen in the close hand-to-hand engagement just before Ferghal intervened. Harry was troubled by the deaths on both sides. Losses were to be expected in battle, he told himself, but he took no pleasure in it, even in the death of an enemy.

Ranji Singh suffered a burn from a plasma bolt that thankfully brushed past him but did not hit him with full force, and nearly everyone was nursing some cuts or bruises from the desperate fight in the scrub.

Then there had been the air strike. Efforts to interfere with the Consortium's airborne AI network had failed. They simply could not hold the link to them long enough. Ferghal had managed to launch five of his missiles in rapid succession, striking one of the aircraft as it passed low over the battery. The other aircraft had sheared off only to be caught by the shower of debris from two bursting charges.

Now they had two dozen prisoners to care for and an additional forty of their shipmates.

Luck had been far too much of a factor, and Harry was deeply aware that any future operations would have to be much better planned.

He looked up as Ferghal joined him and settled into a chair. "That was too close run for comfort," he said, rightly deducing Harry's thoughts.

"I know it, my friend, and Will has paid for my oversights. I will have to consider carefully what we do next, for they will now be alert to us and our weapons." He indicated his swollen ankle. "I have little better to do at present than to create more mischief in their system."

"They will enjoy that!" Ferghal laughed. "I have put the Coxswain to work on screening our new comrades, and Jim Moroti to caring for our Consortium prisoners, who seem mightily disquieted by our alliance with Rathol and his people."

"The prisoners are another consideration. We must take care they do not see or learn too much in case we must turn them loose again."

"They did not enjoy the blindfolding while they were taken below ground and transported to a separate holding area where they can see nothing of importance." He glanced at Harry then down at his hands, not wanting his emotions to show. "You were close to being killed, my friend. This start has won us a respite, but it was too close—altogether too close for our comfort."

"I am well aware of it," Harry acknowledged. "I do not intend to make another attempt unless we can be much better prepared. Your rockets did tremendous damage, though, and show a need for some cannon. Our mortars are effective, but we need something which throws our projectiles horizontally, or, better still, can fire grape shot."

Ferghal eased back in his chair and stretched out his legs. "I have an idea for another type of rocket—one that can be fired from the shoulder like the small one we already use, but bigger and more powerful. I shall explore it." He stopped as a rather petite Canid entered the room and placed a bundle before Harry. She indicated that she wished him to open it.

He did so, not sure of what he might find.

"A portable med-unit. Excellent!" He looked up to thank her, and saw that his visitor had stepped back in alarm at his raised voice. "No, no, it's alright. This is just what we need." He smiled to ease her tension, and she visibly relaxed. The device was similar to a type used in the Fleet to heal small wounds on the extremities such as the arms and legs. "Here, Ferghal, I say, where is our translator?"

The growls, yips and grunts emanating from the equipment stored on a shelf to one side revealed its position. The Canid waited as Ferghal retrieved it, and then she replied. "Raki sends you this. It was found in the Chambers of the Healers. He thinks you have need."

"We do indeed," replied Harry. "My thanks to Raki."

The Canid gave a slight bow of her head and departed.

Harry said, "I think this will help Ranji and the others heal more quickly. I must take it to them and ensure it is put to use. How is Maddie ... ComOp Hodges doing? She fought like a wildcat. I think she actually gored one of the Cons with a signal flag, it was that bloodied, but I hesitated to ask."

Ferghal chuckled. "Our Maddie is in fine fig, and has been joined by several others of her gender—among them three more ComOps and two Medics. Maddie has them well in hand." He grinned. "And you're right about her skill with flag weapons. I am told there is a Consortium trooper with a portion of the semaphore staff embedded in his thigh."

Harry chuckled at the image that conjured. "His thigh, you say? A close one, then."

Ferghal laughed. "The way she tells the story, he walked away from that confrontation with some difficulty, or should I say limped, and he's lucky she missed her aiming point!"

Harry winced at the mere thought of such a direct hit, but a smile tugged at his mouth. "Is he among our prisoners?"

"No, we left him and their other wounded for the Consortium to sort out."

The attack ran smoothly despite the stiffened opposition. The extra men gave them enough people to mount a serious assault, especially when combined with the growing number of Canids proficient in the use of the weapons acquired in their raids of the Consortium Base. Reaching his objective, Harry operated the doors. Warrant Officer Kellerman tossed in a grenade, and the Rates stormed into the dome as soon as the grenade exploded.

Harry entered to find his men dealing with an injured Consortium trooper and several others in the process of being disarmed. A voice brought him up short even as his men began to strip out the equipment they wanted.

"Heron? Are you insane? You could have killed our people!"

He would've known that whiny nasal voice anywhere. He turned to face the speaker. "Lieutenant Clarke," he said, greeting his erstwhile superior as politely as he could. "I trust that you are not here as a patient of their sawbones, sir."

"What the hell are you playing at? You're endangering everyone, not just the fools who've followed you in your idiotic escapades. All guts and glory, aren't you?" His nose wrinkled, and he sniffed in disgust. "And by your unkempt appearance and filthy stench, you've not bothered to maintain civilized standards either."

Harry enjoyed watching the Lieutenant's face register his shock at his wild appearance. "A little difficult under the circumstances, sir. I'm afraid we have had to make do without showers and the luxuries that you've no doubt enjoyed immensely." The Warrant Officer joined them. "Warrant Kellerman, get the equipment we came for, and let's get out of here before the garrison can reorganize themselves." To Lieutenant Clarke, he said, "We have need of some of their med-units. I trust you will help us requisition them."

A renewed uproar outside warned of an attempt by the Consortium to retake the initiative, and the distraction gave the Lieutenant a chance to waffle in his response, so he said nothing.

Harry felt as if he were dealing with a stubborn child. "You are welcome to accompany us and to seize your freedom, sir. I assume, of course, that you have not given your parole to the Commander here. If you have, I will not ask that you break your word."

"You must be mad!" Clarke looked genuinely alarmed. "There's no bloody way I'll come with you lot! They're hunting you and O'Connor and everyone with you, and they have orders to shoot first. It's bloody madness to go on like this. You're putting everyone in danger with your stupidity, but why should that surprise me? That's what got us dumped onto this shithole planet in the first place!"

Harry was tempted to respond with his words and fists when the Warrant Officer returned and intervened. "Leave Mr. Clarke to me, sir. He'll bloody sell the lot of us out to save his own skin. You get the lads out and the weapons away. I'll make sure that this—" he snorted in derision, his eyes locked on the Lieutenant's chalky face, "—this officer doesn't betray you or help his Con mates outside."

Harry understood the Warrant Officer's disdain for Clarke, but he had to set an example. "Mr. Kellerman, I am sure that Mr. Clarke will take care not to assist our enemies. Move our people out. Take the weapons and as many of these med-units as you can carry, but spare one."

The Warrant Officer hesitated, and in that brief pause, Lieutenant Clarke's personal demons spilled out into a tirade. "So, now it's Warrant Kellerman is it? Well, you can be sure I won't forget your insubordination and your threatening a superior officer. I'll have you on a charge as soon as this business is settled. You can count on it."

"Then you'd better watch your back every moment, sir! Bloody sold Mr. O'Connor to the Cons as soon as they laid eyes on us—and you couldn't wait to surrender the rest of us either. Well, we're giving the bastards hell while you hide out here in your cushy quarters. My lads and yours have been working their asses off manufacturing stuff for the Cons while you've sat back and enjoyed yourself. Don't give me the 'respect your rank' bit. The rank and uniform, yes, but the bastard wearing it? Not unless you earn it, you twat, and you're a long way from doing that—ever!"

"Warrant Kellerman!" Harry barked. "Enough. If you continue this verbal assault, the charge will be mutiny. You will hear from the Coxswain as soon as we return to our base. Now get our men out of here and back to the transport. Immediately, if you please!"

For a moment, it looked as if Warrant Kellerman would disobey him, but he snapped to attention and saluted. "Yes, sir."

Harry looked at the outraged Lieutenant, whose face was an unhealthy florid red at this point. In a calm, level voice that betrayed no emotion, Harry said, "I apologise for my Warrant Officer's disrespect. I shall ask that you give me your word that you will not reveal our encounter to the enemy or the directions you may have heard as we worked. Do I have your word, sir?"

The Lieutenant hesitated, his darting eyes betraying his thoughts. He gave a curt nod. "Yes, okay, whatever. Just get the hell out of here and leave me alone, but I won't forget your insolence or your defence of that man either. You can count on it when we're released."

"If you say so, sir." Harry knew there was no way he could trust this man. "I suggest that you get into a med-unit, sir. We will be detonating some charges as we leave, and that will be the safest place to keep your body parts intact." He waited to see the Lieutenant hurriedly insert himself into a unit and then instructed the medical AI to administer an anesthetic dose.

Harry joined his retreating group and made his escape, firing the fuses for the placed mines and charges as he did so. The Consortium troops followed at a cautious distance. Experience had taught them that following Harry's raiders too closely resulted in casualties. Even so, the explosions caught them unaware and discouraged further pursuit.

Harry was surprised to find that they had acquired several new recruits, though these all seemed to be nursing partly healed injuries.

Warrant Kellerman acknowledged his question with a grin. "Couldn't leave them behind now, could we, sir. They wanted to come, so we liberated the lot of them. Sorry about Mr. Clarke, sir. Old story—him and me have a history, but I'll place myself on a charge as soon as we get back, sir."

"That will be best. You must realise that I cannot overlook your having threatened the Lieutenant, whatever the provocation. He is, after all, a senior officer, despite his odious ways. See the

Coxswain and give him a full account of it. I'll see him as soon as you've done so. It will have to wait, of course, until we are reunited with our proper authority, but make a record of it now, please."

"I will, sir." He studied Harry for a moment. "And I'll say this now, sir, you and Mr. O'Connor are something else, not like the normal run, and light years different to Mr. Clarke's sort."

"I'll take that as a compliment, Mr. Kellerman. We'd best leave it there, if you please, but thank you." Harry was flattered, but wary of inviting familiarity.

The outburst had unsettled him, but it also reminded him that the command of men depended on trust and respect. He hoped he would never lose the trust or respect of anyone under his command.

The Hellions took perverse pleasure in the disruption of Consortium operations. After the near fiasco of their first attack on the small Base, Harry confined operations to ambushing mobile forces, the bombardment of larger installations, and blowing up remote mining sites.

"We released another fifty of our comrades on this raid," Ferghal informed him. "Most are our former shipmates from the *Daring*." He grinned across the room at Rasmus. "The latest fuse from our mad scientist here is a beauty. We downed two of their flyers with it."

"I'll take that as a compliment," said Rasmus, slurping a cup of what they called coffee, for lack of a better term. It wasn't as bitter as coffee, and had more of a nutty, plant-based flavour.

Ferghal took a seat at the table next to Rasmus, where Harry and a Canid pack leader were nursing their own steaming mugs.

"The weapons certainly were effective," Harry mused. The raids and attacks had consequences. Patrols were increased in strength and escorted by high-flying air support. It became difficult, if not suicidal, to engage in ambushes. Even so, this actually worked for their next excursion, as the increase in patrol personnel meant the guard squads had to be reduced on the prison details.

"The enemy now has fewer of their number protecting the prison." The Canid gave them a detailed report of his pack's observation of the secure facility used by the Consortium for their prisoners of officer rank.

Harry considered the implication. "That is good. It may offer an opportunity to release some of our senior officers."

Rasmus took a long sip as he processed this. "If they have reduced their guards in the effort to catch us, have they not also withdrawn people from their landing field for the strike craft? Perhaps we can deliver a serious blow if we attack that while another team releases the prisoners."

Harry nodded. "That is worth exploring. Certainly if we can destroy some of their aerial craft, that will assist our efforts and perhaps bring an end to their attacks."

"Then let us ask Grakuna to conduct a reconnaissance of the landing field defences so we can plan our attack," said Ferghal. "Do you think the Provider can establish a link so we may examine their layout?"

"Yes," said Harry, "and having the layout will give us an advantage. But I do want to obtain the release of at least some of our officers. They have knowledge and experience we lack, and as our enemy becomes more determined, we need that if we are to defeat them."

Rasmus gave him a surprised look. "We have done very well without it."

"We have," Harry agreed. "But as our numbers have grown, there is a need for leaders of suitable rank and expertise. We four cannot do it all, even with the help of the Coxswain and the Warrant Officers."

Harry leaned forward, his arms folded on the table as he gathered his thoughts. It wasn't often that he relented from his usual stiff posture, but he felt comfortable with his fellow leaders. "Some of our success has been luck and a reluctance on the part of our enemy to accept that such crude weapons could be as effective as they have been. Now they have the proof of their losses, and we enter a new phase. If our group grows any larger, we will need to divide into squadrons. For that we must provide leadership." He looked at them each in turn. "It is our duty to free all Fleet personnel from captivity."

Chapter 24

Tipping Point

H arry greeted his visitor with a smile. "You delivered the note to Commander Nielsen?"

"It is done as you required," said the young Canid named Regidur, translator in hand. "Here is the reply."

Accepting the folded paper, Harry opened it, frowning to read the hastily scrawled note.

> *Keep up the good work Mr. Heron. You fellows make me proud. We will do everything we can to support you. Be warned, though —this place is heavily guarded. Don't waste lives and equipment on us unless you are sure of a win.*
>
> *Commander Nielsen*

"Thank you, Regidur. Were you able to see anything of the facilities?"

"Yes, Leader. As you required, I examined the defences. I obtained entry by waiting for one of their patrols, and I left the same way. It was simple for me because I was alone. It would be challenging for a team to get in."

This confirmed what Harry suspected.

Harry scanned the camp, noting the positions of the new movement monitors and the patrolling troopers. The successes had brought renewed attacks on the sentient cities. In response, Harry and the Canid leaders stepped up their own attacks on the Consortium bases and installations.

They decided their first target for a larger assault should be the camp to which the factories were attached, and that had a specific goal in mind: to release as many imprisoned TechRates as possible. Contact had been made with the inmates, and they knew exactly who was where and which of the POWs could be relied on to join them, and more importantly, who could not.

Easing himself back into cover, Harry ordered, "Signal the Coxswain—Commence attack."

"Aye, aye, sir." Maddie Hodges grinned as she raised her flags.

Errol Hill was waiting with his group a few yards away. "Here we go," he said when he saw Maddie's signal. "Stay low and stay sharp. We go in, blow the barriers, and get the people out. Warrant Mercer and his team will watch our flanks and take on the guards." He caught the signal from Harry. "Right! Move, people. Stay in cover until the last minute. Wait for the Swain's lot to start the ball rolling then draw them away."

When the group reached the cleared perimeter, they paused. The fading light from the low-lying sun was barely sufficient to see the obstructions and defences, but enough to allow the enemy to see them as they raced across the clearing.

Watching from his concealed position on a rise, Harry followed the movement as his people approached. He connected with the camp's AI. Focussing on the monitoring system, he tried to make sure it didn't reveal his people as they approached.

"Replay the last hour of the view on the monitors," he instructed it.

"This is contrary to normal protocols."

"It is a test to see if they notice anything amiss. Do it now, please."

The AI complied, not least because Harry used the Consortium Commander's interface identity for access. He knew he would have to monitor this and be ready to cancel any order to defend the camp. Everything hinged on the timing of the attack, though there was some room for slippage.

Below him, Errol Hill's squad of grenadiers and Warrant Mercer's skirmishers, as Harry thought of them, moved forward, hidden by their shared cloaks. Between them and the Coxswain's position, most of the Hellions waited, ready to strike when the defenders tried to face the Coxswain's assault. They intended to pull troops toward the manufacturing area and commence a second assault on the prison block. He hoped the third group, including a number of Canids, would be able to drive a wedge between the two sections of the camp and split the enemy's forces.

A series of explosions and the flash of weapons fire announced that the Coxswain's group had commenced their attack. The effect was immediate, and the perimeter defences sprang into life, the weaponry tracking back and forth as the operators sought targets.

Alarms sounded across the camp, and armoured troops hastened into pre-arranged positions. At the point of attack, the activity intensified, and Harry watched as troops were called away from his end of the camp, leaving a thin screen of defenders in place. Now he could see the mortar fire that the Hellions aimed at the factory domes. Several were ablaze, and a larger explosion than their mortars could produce saw another large dome slowly collapse as flames leapt above the ruins.

With the light fading rapidly, he could just make out Errol Hill's troop at the perimeter. He held his breath as one of the defence towers swung, apparently responding to a detected movement.

Harry maintained the monitoring system on its replay, leaving the perimeter defence weapons operators to track phantoms not visible on their screens. One or more of the operators realised what was happening and attempted to correct the system. Eventually, losing patience, Harry ran a shutdown command.

In the camp Command Centre, the Guard Commander swore in exasperation as the towers remained blind.

"What the hell?" The Defence Commander got nothing when he tried his comlink. "All troops, stand by to defend the perimeter." He tried the uplink to the main Base and discovered it was dead. He swore again as several explosions rocked the dome and debris rained down from the ceiling, warning him that one of the enemy's crude bombs had scored a hit.

Satisfied, Harry watched as Errol Hill's team made it through the perimeter without mishap. So far so good. The flash of plasma fire drew his attention to troopers racing to positions where they could pin down his people.

To Maddie, he ordered, "Signal Warrant Mercer—Enemy position on the right." He watched as the signal was acknowledged and the Warrant's team moved to pin down the defenders. Explosions from the position of Errol's targets gave him the signal he needed, and movement in the camp signified the rush of defenders drawing back to assist the pinned down troops. "Signal Colour Sergeant Arbinder—Attack."

He'd timed it nicely. The Colour Sergeant's assault was a textbook example of an infantry attack—not surprising, as his group were Marines. They drove a wedge into the enemy and brought complete chaos to the defence.

Reaching the prison dome, Errol Hill signalled his people into position. Thanks to Harry's ability to access these AI systems, he knew the layout and what to expect once they entered. He also had the access code for the main entrance. When his team was ready, he entered the code.

The door slid aside, and two of his team entered, lobbing grenades into the Guardroom and over the counter that stood duty as a reception desk and partial barrier. Caught by surprise, the man on reception duty was slow to react. Not so the occupants of the Guardroom. Two erupted out of the room ready to fire on the attackers as the first grenade detonated.

"Rani, get the doors open, and shift the prisoners out." Errol Hill consulted a note. "Leave the buggers in cells 20 and 23. We don't want them."

Rani and three others raced into the corridor activating door codes while Errol retrieved the guards' weapons and checked their condition. Two were dead, as was one more in the Guardroom; the third was badly wounded, but there was no time to deal with him. Errol applied a dressing to staunch the bleeding from the worst of his wounds then stood to direct the prisoners filing into the entrance toward the waiting Canids. "This way. Quick. Follow the guides."

After a momentary hesitation, the leading Rates obeyed, but one had to get in a comment.

"Bloody hell, mate. Don't know where you guys came from, and as for your mates—"

"Just do as they say and move it, chum. We haven't got all day, and you'll soon find out where we're from."

"Hey, Errol, where'd you spring from, shippers?" One of the prisoners punched Errol on the shoulder, a big grin on his face. "You guys are a sight for sore eyes. Who're your pals? Wouldn't want to tangle with them in a dark alley."

"Mind you don't, Ty, or you'll come off worse."

When Rani and the others joined them, Errol said, "All out? Good. Let's go."

From the promontory, Harry watched the progress marked by flashes and explosions. When he saw the signal that the prisoners were clear, he ordered, "Send the withdrawal signal."

The rocket flare soared aloft and burst. In his position, Chief Master Warrant Winstanley saw the flare. He nodded to the men around him. "Blow the mines, then let's get our people out of here."

Brigadier Newton surveyed the damage. "They knew exactly what to hit. This will take months to repair. Get all the finished fuel cells and the rest of the components moved to the main Base. Move the remaining prisoners too." Her frown deepened. "Obviously, our systems are completely compromised. They knew exactly who was a plant for us and where they were located. They've left them in their cells."

"It certainly looks that way," the Colonel replied sourly, "but how the hell did they know which of our people were plants? Even the AI doesn't know that—only you, me and our Security Chief have that information."

"They must have insider intel," said the Brigadier. "We'll change tactics. Concentrate all our forces and make them come to us in our chosen locations." She indicated the wrecked factory units. "Salvage as much as possible and get it moved. I want it done quickly. Then set this place as a trap. See to it."

"Yes, ma'am." The Colonel activated his comlink and gave a series of orders. "That'll get it moving." He hesitated. "But from what the Guard Commander says, something made the AI monitors malfunction. Without them, the towers were useless. I suggest we look to manned defences and cut out the AI altogether."

"Good idea," the Brigadier replied. "According to my briefings on Heron and O'Connor, they shouldn't be capable of getting into a system without being close to it. Ours is screened, so it should shut them out entirely. Either our briefings are wrong, or something else is at work here."

"You wish to communicate with your own people off this world?"

Harry sat bolt upright. The Provider had read his thoughts. *"Yes, but how? Only an AI network can encrypt the messages for these hypercom emmiters. Can you do it?"*

"I have created a link. It is not through the intelligence of our enemy, but it will allow you to make contact with your own people if I am given the encrypted message."

Harry hesitated. Thinking furiously, he said, *"I need to send a package I have created in our enemy's system. It is already encrypted in anticipation of your finding a means to enable it. Can we retrieve it and send it?"*

"Direct me. I will retrieve it and send it when you show me the path."

"Then follow me through the system."

And with that, the package was on its way—crude, possibly corrupted in part, but hopefully recoverable. He grinned. He'd sent it to Captain Brandeis at Fleet Security, and could just picture the uproar when they realised what it contained. He laughed at the thought of what the Consortium would do if they found out he'd just sent their entire Code Book to the Fleet with their latest deployment intentions.

Admiral Hartmann keyed her comlink. "Flags, get a secure link to Rear Admiral Heron—immediately, please."

"Yes, Admiral." The Flag Lieutenant moved to the Signals Master. "Flag to Flag. Gold Code."

"*Vanguard* online now, sir." He looked up as the hologram formed. "Morning, Tom. Gold Code. Flag to Flag, for your Lord and Master from ours."

"Morning yourself, Franz. Rear Admiral Heron standing by. On the mark, three." He gave a curt nod. "One, two, three." The pair touched keys, and the secure channel between the Admirals was a private connection.

"Good morning, James," said Admiral Hartmann. "I have a mission for your Fleet. You're aware that the signal interference was being directed from Planet Lycania. If the Security people are correct, your ward, Sub-Lieutenant Heron, has just sent us a message from that planet."

"At least we know where he is now. Presumably, he's safe and still free. Is that correct?"

"Very much so. He sent us a complete list of all the prisoners held there, and marked up the ones now freed and fighting with him, plus an inventory of the stuff they're manufacturing and mining on that planet." She paused. "Through the efforts of Harry and his crew, we've pushed back the Consortium and got them stretched at the moment, so this is an opportunity to launch a direct assault on their Base. You will take out the installation they were using to orchestrate their activities in that sector, and release all of our people held prisoner there. It'll turn their most vulnerable flank. I'm assigning three extra squadrons to your command. You'll get the USS *Constellation* and her support group, the *Karl der Größe* and her task group and the first heavy cruisers. You'll have six assault ships with full complements of troops. Your orders are to land forces on the planet and clear out the Consortium installations and personnel. There's a native population to consider, a canine-like people known as the Canids. If possible, we want no collateral damage to them, though the intel suggests there is some sort of resistance movement at work against the Consortium that involves the natives. We're not sure if that's Harry's group, though it is possible. We will want to make an alliance with the Canids as soon as we have the opportunity."

"Right." James Heron acknowledged the order, his mind already assembling the things he would have to include in his plans and orders. "The intel says their fleet are massed in the Merovian sector, but they still have three squadrons near enough to Lycania to put up a stiff resistance and be reinforced quite easily."

"Leave that to me. My task is to make sure they don't interfere with you. I have a couple of personal scores to settle with my old friend Bob Gratz."

"So I hear. The latest report says they've sent reinforcements for the garrison on Lycania, and their mining and manufacturing operations there are crippled." He smiled. "That rather suggests my wards are causing something of a stir."

"That's true," said the Admiral. "The intel reports have been a bit puzzling on that score. One report suggested something explosive was being used in attacks on the Base there. Would that be your pair?"

"I'd be prepared to take a bet on it. I just hope they don't come unstuck before we can get everyone out of there."

Chapter 25

Hunters and the Hunted

The guerrilla raids meant the Consortium garrison could not operate with impunity. Coupled with this, the Hellions' ability to appear unexpectedly just about anywhere on the surface then vanish again without a trace frustrated all attempts to find their Base.

Harry and Ferghal surveyed the Consortium soldiers they'd conscripted into service. "We need more leaders," said Harry. "There are now more than a hundred of us, and we cannot oversee everything."

"There are a number of Warrants and Senior Rates among them," said Ferghal. "We've Colour Sergeant Arbinder and thirty Marines. Let him take charge of the infantry. I could train the Warrants to command the rocket battery or the cannon."

Harry nodded. "Sounds like a good plan. Their Base AI is now so confused that it aids us." He laughed. "It even tells us where the Consortium troops will search next."

"True," Ferghal responded, noting Harry's smile. "And our Canid friends have become proficient at laying traps and misleading their aerial craft. Some of their raids rival even your attacks for boldness."

"Aye, they do," Harry acknowledged. "But we are still unable to make use of the off-world communications directly."

"Then we must find a way to get past their screens." Ferghal collected the device he was working on. "If you allow, there are several among the Rates I may trust to manufacture the engines for these new rockets."

Harry smiled. "Inform the Coxswain. We need all the rockets you can manufacture." He adjusted his jacket. "Now I must see Grakuna and the other pack leaders. We need to know the movements of our enemy, and the Canids are better able to undertake this than we are."

Brigadier Newton now had twice the number of troops the Base had started out housing, but the increased force seemed to have little impact on the raids. The accommodation was cramped, and the AI had caused another problem.

"Have you made any progress figuring out how the AI is being accessed and what is happening to the files that have been tampered with? How about the risk of a security leak?"

Major Willis shook her head. "It's developed a sort of paranoia. These advanced AIs are a damned sight more aware than most people realise." She rubbed her temples in a fruitless effort to ease the headache that had plagued her for at least a day now. "When they blew the science team's AI, there must have been some connection between the two. There wasn't supposed to be, so I'm not sure what it was, but the Base AI suffered the equivalent of traumatic shock. When we fix one problem, it produces another. These ghost visits could be symptoms of it." She paused. "At least we found most of the files and restored them, so that's something."

The Brigadier wasn't impressed. "So in the meantime, we have a demented AI running the Base systems."

"Not demented—more like a frightened child."

"Well, these damned ghost visits are not funny. If it's the AI playing silly games, I want it stopped. Morale is plummeting, and we're all getting edgy." Signalling the interview was over, she added, "It's bad enough that the doors and lights function on a whim, or so it seems, but why must I endure these ridiculous concerts that go on for bloody hours? And why always classical music or this damned Celtic music? I can't stand the classical stuff! The Celtic is fine in small doses, but three hours of it?"

The Major hid her smile. "I've got someone working on it. I'll chase him, and take him off the routine shifts. If anyone can figure it out, Khodro is the man."

Cam Khodro sucked his teeth. Going over the signal log for the hypercoms wasn't his favourite occupation. Doing it after Lieutenant Barclay had already supposedly done so was more than a pain. He ran his private checking program, and stiffened when a ping announced an anomaly.

"Damn." He stared at the display then reached for his comlink. "Major, we have a problem—a big one."

"I'm on my way. What is it?"

"Another gap in the signal log. All of three minutes."

Brigadier Newton looked up as her Adjutant joined her. She wasted no time on pleasantries. "Sit down, Barry. So, what news do you have for me? Have our patrols had another run-in with the Canids?"

"Not today. Major Willis found a problem with the hypercom logs. There was a three-minute gap in transmissions, but when she ran more checks, it appears to be part of the problem with the AI. Her people can't find any evidence of a signal going out or coming in during those three minutes. She's working on it though."

The Brigadier nodded, but the frown didn't leave her face. "I don't like this at all. What about the ground situation? You've suspended airborne strikes?"

"The Canids are all over the cities and won't let our people near them. The missiles they're using to defend against airstrikes are getting bigger and a lot more lethal, so I've had to curtail aerial strikes. We haven't got the resources to take on a straight fight with them, especially now their weapons are getting better. Their vanishing trick makes it damned difficult to target them, though we have found out how it's done. It's some sort of screen, but we haven't been able to unravel how it works yet."

"How did we discover that?"

"Luck. Our platoon commander managed to grab a Canid that his men had killed, and he brought it back for research. It's a sort of cloak, but the material is the key to its invisibility." He smirked.

"The researchers are delighted—compensation for losing their star exhibits, Heron and O'Connor, and their research records on those two."

The Brigadier nodded. "The Chairman thinks the WTO is almost ready to negotiate. I hope they do. If they don't, we have a problem. The allied Fleet is increasing in strength, and several of the colony worlds we control are getting rebellious."

The Major grimaced. "Yes, things could get ugly if we don't get a settlement soon. My sister is one of the Chairman's aides. The Board wants a ceasefire and control of all the worlds we have at present. They believe this will buy time to consolidate, build up our forces and undertake a propaganda campaign to get the rest of their objectives through the back door."

"That's for the political types to sort out," said the Brigadier. "Our job is to eliminate these Fleet radicals, subdue the Rotties, find the tech they're hiding and secure our position. The weapons they're using are crude, but our systems don't recognise them, so they don't respond. What suggestions have the patrol commanders come up with?"

"Not much. So far, the only real defence is to make sure they keep their hatches closed while moving, but that means our people are driving blind, to a certain extent. Those savages have found a way to cripple and disable our vehicles by detonating devices underneath them. We're working on solving that problem by mounting an imager to monitor the view behind."

"Good. At least they haven't tried another major assault, but these tip and run raids are tying down patrols and straining our resources."

"Those aerial projectiles are a major headache for the strike flyers. The shrapnel is lethal. The last flight team that encountered them were lucky to get back to Base. Around a third of our strike force is out of action with perforation of the airframes, systemic damage to equipment and propulsion systems, and three pilots with wounds."

The Brigadier frowned. "How the hell are they getting their hands on these weapons? They can't have a limitless supply!"

"There's another development. The med-units are full of troopers who tried to chase a bunch of Rotties and ran straight into some sort of artillery barrage—short range, unguided, but it showers a large area with projectiles, mostly small stones. The wounds would be far worse if our troops weren't equipped with armour, but even that doesn't offer complete protection."

ComTech Cam Khodro struggled to make sense of the access log. "Ma'am," he called to Major Willis. "According to the log, no one on the Base has had access to the databases or the operating controls for the last twenty-four hours."

"Impossible." The Major peered at the screen. "I'm logged into the Defence System right now—check that."

"There it is, ma'am. Nothing. According to this, you're not in the system at all."

"Here, let me try something." The Major took over the interface and entered a string of commands.

After a brief pause, the display revealed a completely different version of the log. The Major frowned. "This is ridiculous. It's as if the system is rewriting the logs to match the query." She straightened up. "That proves it. We've got a serious problem with the AI. Do a full sweep of the system and ask it to show you who has accessed what, when and how."

"Yes, ma'am."

"And do it now. I've got a feeling this is not just the AI suffering a breakdown. This is something else."

Chapter 26

End of the Beginning

Rear Admiral Heron looked up as his Flag Captain, Richard Grenville, entered. "Good evening, Richard, take a seat." When the Captain was seated, he continued. "It looks as if we have a major task on our hands. I want a conference of all Captains at fourteen hundred so we can work out the strategy and tactics and get to know one another. We'll have the *Karl der Größe* and her escorts and a US squadron alongside our own, and there are several independents to integrate as well."

"Good." Richard nodded. "I was going over the Fleet list and figured we'd need to make sure our communications and manoeuvring procedures are standardised, or we could have a problem."

"I agree. I plan to run the simulators with the Commanders to get everyone used to the way we operate. I've had Flags prepare info packets with our coms procedures and manoeuvring standards. Commodore Dewey of the Constellation has been exercising with the main Fleet already, so his people should be ready."

The Admiral looked up when the door opened and the Flag Captain entered. "You look worried, Flags," said the Admiral. "What's happened?"

"Intel briefing just in, sir. The Consortium has a larger force than we believed, and they're on the move to Planet Lycania. Intelligence Services haven't been able to discover why."

Once more exploring the Consortium network, Harry monitored the signals flashing back and forth between the various units of the ground forces, a daily task for him. This allowed him to monitor the movements of patrols and to circumvent the traps they attempted to lay for him.

He was feeling very tired and sluggish, bored with the routine, when a priority signal from off world streamed in, decoding as it arrived. He sat up fully alert. The message electrified him. A Consortium Force was on its way to the planet to intercept an invasion force by the Fleet. Worse, a decoy was being set up to disguise the movement and lead the Fleet into believing the planet was only lightly defended. Somehow, he had to convey this to the Fleet.

He addressed the Provider. *"I have urgent need of your assistance."*

"In what matter?"

"I need to use the emitters, but our enemy must not suspect it or find evidence I have done so. Can you create a distraction?"

"It shall be done. Is your message ready?"

"Give me a few minutes. Perhaps you can start misleading him while I do it."

It needed less time than Harry anticipated. He quickly considered how to word his message so that he remained anonymous to the enemy but recognisable to the Commander-in-Chief. With a burst of ingenuity, he chose the name The Ancient Mariner to signify himself as the sender. It took ninety seconds for the hypercom emitter to transmit the message, which made him glad he'd added his guardian's signal address as well.

"It is done, Provider."

Harry shared his discovery with Ferghal, and insisted they monitor every off-world signal to and from the Consortium Base from now on.

"But what will we do with this information?" Ferghal protested. "It is all very well us knowing it, but that will not help our friends."

"We will find a way," Harry insisted. "The Provider can distract their ComTech who seeks us in the AI. We may then have little time to convey our knowledge to the Fleet."

"Very well," Ferghal agreed. "Better they have some information that assists them—even if it is at the last minute."

Harry gathered his senior people for a meeting. He had already consulted the Canid leaders, and they awaited his proposals for a campaign.

"A Consortium fleet is on its way here," he began. "They've been ordered to engage or trap us any way they can. Mr. O'Connor and I have been monitoring their communication, and we have warned our people. I propose that we prevent them from using their landing facilities either to land their people or to send aloft their strike craft. It will not be easy, and carries with it great danger for us all."

He paused to look at the group before him. "We will have to reconnoitre the perimeter, but I intend to make use of our mines, mortars and everything else we have in our arsenal."

"What about the officers they're holding there, sir?"

"We know where they have them in the main camp and will take care not to target that area. They also have fuel cells somewhere on the base, and those may be of use to us eventually. Our task now is to gather our ideas and consider how we may best achieve this. I welcome your thoughts."

"Tell us how you want to do this, sir," said the Coxswain. "Maybe we can come up with some ideas if we know what you think can be done to disrupt their plans. If it's just to scare 'em, this lot standing on a hill nearby ought to do it." There was a laugh from the others as he pointed his thumb in the direction of a Warrant Officer's scraggly mane of hair.

"I think a full assault is out of the question," Harry said. "But I hope we can do enough to prevent them operating from their landing and launching area—perhaps prevent them deploying until our people can land, as I feel sure they will attempt." He glanced around the group. "It is a big task—a hundred of us against the thousand or so they have—and not all our people are really suited to this kind of fighting."

Many of those they had liberated were technicians or had served in administrative roles, and had not the strength or stamina for the arduous operations they were engaged in.

Harry saw the nods as his point went home.

A Warrant Officer at the back of the group asked, "Couldn't we try to get inside their perimeter and mine the landing bays and launch pads, sir? Seems to me that we would only need to wreck a launch or something to make them unusable."

"Good idea," Harry acknowledged. "How would we get inside? They now have a triple screen, and even Grakuna's people can't get through it." He made a note. One of the pack members, the young Regidur, had succeeded in getting a note to Commander Nielsen. Perhaps there was a way inside.

"We've still got a couple of their transports, sir," another Warrant spoke up. "Couldn't we modify one to carry a big bomb and then send it through the perimeter?"

"That is feasible," Harry replied. "A sort of fire ship on land." He nodded. "Yes, I like that idea. How many of their vehicles do we have now, Swain?"

"Six, sir. Though at least one is only just usable, and they're pretty much scattered. We'd have to get them all back here and then over to the Base if we do this."

"Let's do it," Harry said. He looked at the Warrant Officer who had suggested it. "Mr. Heuer, is it not? Please see Mr. Winstanley about arranging to bring them all here so we can put your idea into practice." He acknowledged another member of the group. "You have an idea, Mr. Van Duren?"

"Yes, sir. I reckon we could set up batteries on three sides overlooking their launch and landing bays, and lay down a barrage that would discourage them from moving while a path was cleared to get into the perimeter. If we combine that with some of Mr. O'Connor's surface-to-surface rockets, we could pin them down long enough for our people to land and join in—if we can time it right."

"Yes, that accords with my own thoughts," Harry acknowledged. "But, as you know, they will deploy field pieces against us unless we can find positions they cannot target, yet within our range." He nodded to the Coxswain. "Your thoughts, Mr. Winstanley?"

Watching his friend, Ferghal marvelled at the manner in which Harry was engaging the Warrant Officers, many of whom had never been asked to contribute to strategic planning before. It was obvious they were finding it a novel experience, and the discussion got lively as ideas were dissected, some discarded while others were developed.

By the time the meeting broke up, everyone had a task to prepare some part of the overall plan.

Harry gave them one final directive. "Gentlemen, keep in mind that whatever you are tasked with must not conflict with any other part of the operation. You must consult one another at every step."

A chorus of 'yes, sirs' erupted, and everyone dispersed to set about their work. Ferghal clapped Harry on the back when they were the only ones left in the room. "Masterful, Captain. You inspire them with your confidence in them. Heaven help our enemy with such men in opposition."

"But we are the few against many, my friend. It will be like the wasp against the elephant. We can only hope to discomfort them and distract them. If the Fleet doesn't succeed in breaking through and landing, I fear it will be the end for us." He hesitated. "And the cost in lives is likely to be heavy. No easy thing to accept, for it rests on my head alone."

"Then I have some good news for you. While you were engaged in your planning, I monitored a message to the Consortium fleet. Rest easy, our ships are now alert to the danger they face."

Chapter 27

Stir the Hornet's Nest

———————————————

Rear-Admiral Heron studied the intel report. To his Flag Lieutenant, he said, "Contact all Captains—holo-conference in half an hour. This intel changes the situation. I'll want to run a series of simulations to determine the best dispositions against what we now know they have waiting for us. HQ say they're concerned about the source—they suspect a ruse because there's conflicting intel from other sources."

"Yes, sir." The Lieutenant enjoyed working with his Admiral. His respect had deepened for the way his superior worked closely with his team yet never surrendered his position as leader. "Shall I set up the Flag Command Room for a Captain's exercise?"

"Not yet." The Admiral paused to consider. "We're still five days from dropout. Get me a team of our own people— Lieutenants and Mids—and let them run some battle sims with our ships and the Consortium's. Let's see what shakes out of that. Here is the deployment to use for the enemy, and if you come back in ten minutes, I'll give you my deployment for the exercise."

The Flag Lieutenant grinned. "Who do you want in command of each side?"

"Hmm. Their commander is Leandra Enescu. I was at College in the same year as her, and she was a weapons specialist. Let's fly a kite here—Commander Polzanov from Weapons Branch can lead the Consortium Team. Get Captain Grenville to take the lead for the home team. Once we've tried out some sims with our own people running them, I'll get a Captains team in, and we can try it again with everyone fighting their own ships in the sim." He stared at the signal on his tablet again, noting the phrases and words used, and the sender of the message. "The Ancient Mariner." He grinned. "I think this is genuine. Right. We'll go with it!"

Striding into the Briefing Room, Brigadier Newton launched straight into her brief. "Our fleet is assembling outside the Peiho system, two hours ahead of us in a hyperjump. They will move closer when we've confirmed that the Confederation Fleet is approaching. Admiral Enescu intends to drop out right behind them to engage them before they can deploy. Our forces will be boosted by additional troops—and the Board hopes that a victory for our ships will be sufficient to get the WTO and Confederation to the negotiating table."

The Colonel grimaced. "As long as everything goes to plan. Our runaways seem to have gone to ground, and the Rotties with them. Strange, there have been almost no sightings of the Rotties for a week now—and those we have seen have been walking alone or in small groups heading away from this area."

"Keep monitoring them," said the Brigadier. "We'll deal with them once our people have sorted out the Fleet. Our immediate task is to provide a surface base for the interceptors that will land here in four days. They will need additional fuel cells and charger units for the interceptors' weapons. That will be your task to sort out, Major."

"I'll get onto it, but we don't have the capacity. Our own strike force is pushed for space, and there are only twenty-five of them. How many are we expecting?"

"Here's the signal. Says one hundred and twenty to be landed and prepared for air defence."

"That's pushing beyond the limit. I'll have to enlarge the landing area and put in a dispersal system. I'll need earthmovers and clearance to switch production to interlock platforms for them to sit on. Three to four days' work at the least."

"Take whatever you need. You've got three working days, so you'll need additional labour forces as well—use the Rates from the prison camp if you have to."

"I'll need to," the Major acknowledged. "And the sooner I get this started the better. I'll also have to change the perimeter defences, and that will diminish their effectiveness."

"Agreed." The Brigadier nodded. "We'll have to accept that the extra troops and fighters will strain it, but they'll also give us an edge. Admiral Enescu has given her ETA for the interceptors as four days from now. They'll be delivered by a pair of cruisers. They'll drop out, launch their payloads and remain in orbit as the bait." She looked around the table. "They'll be accompanied by four landing barges carrying the troops to boost our garrison. I propose to station them at the Sinclair Base and use them as a mobile force to support us if we're attacked."

"That doesn't give us a lot of time to prepare," the Colonel remarked. "At least at Sinclair we have the accommodation to house them. Since we moved the officer prisoners from there, our bandits haven't gone back to attack it. Hopefully, they'll see it as being only lightly defended and have a go at it if we are busy. They'll get a nasty surprise if they do."

"Harry," Ferghal interrupted his friend as he discussed their plans with several pack leaders. "The enemy is to be reinforced in preparation for our Fleet's arrival. The Brigadier has received orders from her Admiral."

"Then it is as well we have warning of this."

A senior Canid spoke. "We must penetrate their barriers and prevent this."

"There will be an opportunity." Ferghal glanced at Harry. "If you agree, of course. They are enlarging the landing field, and the defences must be moved. It will give the chance to place some of our devices inside their field and perhaps some of your people too."

"An excellent suggestion," said Harry, and the Canids signalled agreement. An hour later, the group parted to consider their options.

To Rasmus, Harry said, "I have learned they are preparing the Base they name Sinclair to receive the additional troops they expect. We cannot engage the principal base and that one at the same time, and we run the risk of being caught between the two no matter which one we attack. On top of that, I'm worried about the presence of the additional interceptors. With so many on hand, our plans will be extremely difficult to execute."

"Unless you can prevent them from becoming airborne in the first place," said Rasmus.

"And how would we be doing that?" Ferghal asked, lapsing into his Irish lilt, never far from the surface, but always more pronounced when he was under pressure. "Sure and they would be aloft within minutes of our striking—unless they be very tardy in their response."

"It's true," Rasmus replied. "But it doesn't require a great deal of damage to disable these atmospheric craft. The best time to strike at them is as soon as they land and are occupied with maintenance and refuelling. Each craft must be recharged and checked before it can fly again." Spreading his arms in a characteristic gesture, as if he were pronouncing a blessing on them all, he smiled. "So my friends, if you strike as soon as they are all on the ground and being serviced, you may remove their advantage." He grinned at the surprised expressions of the group. "See, sometimes modern knowledge is useful—even when you plan an old-fashioned war."

Ferghal responded first. "Of course! Atmospheric entry requires an enormous expenditure of power, so their fuel cells will be drained, and the stress of entry, even with the shielding, requires a full inspection before flying again. Even the barges and launches cannot immediately take off again. It is why we always carry Engineer Rates on them." Ferghal grinned. "You're a sly one, Rasmus, that you are, and no mistake about it."

The chaos of the construction work on the Consortium Base enabled them to slip in with their devices and plant them undetected. For this, the Canids used their screening cloaks. As agreed, some took up positions inside the landing area perimeter.

The completion of the extensions saw their plan for disrupting the grounded aerial craft in place.

"We're ready, Harry. Now it is in the hands of Fate," Ferghal reported.

"Well done, my friend." Harry pulled on his jacket and adjusted the equipment harness worn over it. "It is time. Their reinforcements will arrive in six hours according to their signals. Let us take up our positions. That will give us a brief period to rest before it begins."

"My team are ready. We will be in position within the hour." Ferghal rose to join his batteries and arrange their transport.

"Good. Mr. Winstanley, have the others move out immediately." Harry hefted his own packs and acknowledged the response of their Canid coordinator. "Ready, CO Hodges?"

"All set, sir. Even got some spare flags in case I wear these ones out!"

Harry laughed as he turned to go. "I shall bear that in mind."

Outside he addressed all the Warrant Officers tasked with leading groups. "Are all your targets clear? Good. Then let us get into place. I have sent Leading Rate Aiken and Pack Leader Namreh to the pass in the mountains between the second base and this one. They are to plant the land mines and delay any effort at relief or support."

Ferghal followed his friend. "A good move. It will not be difficult to hold that." The surface route between the two depended on the availability of a single pass through a jagged mountain range. A relatively small party could hold it and prevent any passage through it.

Concealed beneath a rocky outcrop, Harry surveyed the landing field. Overhead a steady stream of interceptor craft howled in to land on the prepared pads on the plain below them. Through his connection to the Provider, he knew Ferghal was ready with his rockets and mortars. The Canid pack leaders and their people were also in place for their part in the strike. Cautiously he scanned the area before him, looking for the small tell-tale marks to indicate the positions of his teams.

To Maddie Hodges, he said, "We will stir the hornet's nest here today—enough, I hope, to disable this armada sufficiently for our people to land."

"You're right there, sir," said Maddie. "Just wish I was with the team setting off the fireworks. I've a few scores to settle down there." She hesitated. "Pardon my asking, sir, but how sure are we the Fleet will be here today?"

Harry stared at the view, listening to an exchange through the hypercom emitter. Then he grinned. "I'm very sure. In fact, from the signals they're exchanging, within the hour. They are in the system and approaching this planet as we speak. We may even see some of the engagement from here." He paused as the howl of engines subsided. "It's time to strike! That is their last interceptor just disembarking its pilot, and by the looks of the thing, they have just learned of the Fleet's arrival. Make the signal to attack, if you please!"

Maddie stood and raised her flags, watching for the acknowledgement from the eight positions below and on either side, and then, in several swift movements, she sent the numeral seventy-nine followed by "The Fleet is here." She dived into cover as the world erupted. Harry's signal meant "Engage the enemy," and the added spur of knowing that their own were about to arrive lent a determination to the attackers.

Mortars, rocket bombs and mines burst among the maintenance crews running for cover in a tangled mass of confusion and panic. From his vantage point, Harry could see activity, which assured him his Canid friends were in position and doing their part. Three unmanned transports advanced into the perimeter screen and immediately attracted the attention of the outer projectors. Several beams hit the first vehicle, but it continued moving, even as it burned, the nearest turrets tracking the blazing carrier. Then it detonated spectacularly, destroying the closest turrets while the second vehicle ploughed on, slightly off course, into the second tier of defences. Like its leader, it was soon ablaze, and so was the third, but their detonation had the desired effect, and Harry's Hellions were able to penetrate the perimeter.

A direct hit on an interceptor ruptured its fuel cells and scattered debris among several other craft. Men fell under the hail of shrapnel, which also damaged the interceptors. Several more joined the first in exploding violently, and even those furthest from the assaulting force suffered.

The initial chaos was rapidly replaced by a determined response. Harry's people came under furious fire from ground troops. Several interceptors lifted off and targeted the attackers. Harry realised that the fight was about to become very bloody indeed. He managed to say a quick prayer for all those who would fall or be injured in the fight, and then he focused on his task.

"Incoming strike!" Ferghal yelled above the din of the mortars firing as fast as their crews could load. "Bearing left, closing—fire a barrage commencing—now!" Errol Hill and his team changed the bearing of their rocket tubes and ignited the fuses, the first of the big aerial rockets hurling itself from the tube with a vicious hiss and roar as it gathered speed. Already one of the Canid batteries was sending its missiles aloft as another flight attempted to target them. Ferghal watched as the aircraft sheared away trailing smoke and shedding parts as the barrage intensified.

The approaching interceptor pilot saw the trail of smoke as the first rocket soared toward him, though it appeared to be well clear. More rockets soared into his path, and he made the fatal mistake of ignoring them. One of the new arrivals, he had not been warned of this archaic device or of the effect it had on an airframe if it got too close.

Six burst above, below and in front of his speeding interceptor. His canopy shattered, and he lost control as several vital stabilisers were shredded. He had time to exclaim, "What the hell?" before his speeding craft slammed into the ground in a great burst of flame and shattered airframe.

His wingman had just enough time to register the effect on his leader before he desperately sheered away as more of the deadly devices soared around him. He evaded the worst of the damage and managed to keep his craft aloft long enough to attempt an emergency landing some distance beyond Harry's command post.

Other pilots found themselves facing a similar barrage as they attempted to target the mortar posts, one suffering the fate of having a rocket penetrate the thin skin and detonate inside it.

"I got nothing on my scanners," a frustrated pilot snarled. "All I can see is smoke trails, and I can't get a weapons lock on those. Nothing shows on the ground either. What the hell is this?"

Seconds later his speeding craft was rocked by several near bursts, and to his fury, his cockpit alarms sounded a major malfunction. He did the only thing left to him; he aimed the interceptor toward the position of the incoming rockets, and ejected from his craft. Unfortunately, that sent the dying craft into a steep dive before it crashed almost on top of his forces.

From his position, Harry saw the Consortium's ground forces grouping for an assault on one of his positions. To Maddie he ordered, "Send a message to Mr. Winstanley—Enemy regrouping to your right—number twenty-three."

Maddie leapt into action then ducked down again after noting the acknowledgement. "Sent, sir. They've seen them, and it looks like they're ready for them."

"Good." Harry was concentrating on his link to their host mind. "I have asked Pack Leader Rongar to send some of his force to assist them. Now, send a message to Mr. O'Connor—number eight, if you please."

Ferghal looked up as the signalman called, "From CO, sir. Number eight!"

"Good." To his team he called, "Shift to our forward position mortar by mortar, Warrant! I want you to target their inner defence line. Rocket battery, relocate on their wings, half battery load, and commence firing contact bursts."

It was not going so well for all of the Hellions. On two of their positions, Harry's teams were taking heavy casualties, and the remaining members of the key team had been forced to withdraw, compromising his plan to release the officer prisoners. From his vantage point Harry watched in frustration as a team led by one of his recently released Warrant Officers was driven back by a determined defence then surrounded. "Signal Sergeant Oribi—number thirty-six—Enemy to your right."

As the signals went back and forth, Harry felt a surge of concern when he saw the high-level contrails of a large number of craft entering the atmosphere and descending. At a distance, there was no way of knowing if they were friend or foe. He could make out that there were a lot of small craft, but these seemed to be escorting a number of very large landing barges.

"We seem to have others about to join us," Harry said to Maddie, "but I know not if they are our friends. Send this message—Prepare to withdraw. New forces descending toward us."

Maddie frowned. "Pardon me, sir, but that's a bit of a long message, isn't it? Is there a corresponding number?"

Harry grinned. "I'm afraid you will have to spell it out, ComOp Hodges. I devised no number for this eventuality."

"If you say so, sir." She returned the grin. "I hope the other buggers on this detail can read it properly is all."

Harry smiled again. "Yes, that might be a challenge for some of them, but I have full faith in your ability to send the message clearly." While she flagged the message, Harry used his link to access the Consortium hypercoms in the hope of discovering whose forces were coming on the scene. It proved frustratingly difficult, but he did manage to pick up a signal going out and calling for assistance. That was confirmation enough for him; the descending barges had to be from the Fleet. A surge of jubilation coursed through him, and he felt more hopeful than he had in a very long time.

"I am certain they are ours, Maddie. Signal number twelve to all our teams, and follow it with the signal 'Render all assistance'."

"Aye, aye, sir. I'm on it!" Maddie gave him a wink and a big smile, and that made Harry blush.

He would've flushed an even deeper red had he realised that in his exuberance, he had slipped protocol and called her Maddie and not ComOp Hodges, but she would never tell.

Chapter 28

Final Assault

Locked down in their quarters, the Fleet officers could hear the carnage outside but had little idea of what was actually happening.

"That fool Heron must be behind this!" Lieutenant Clarke fumed as yet another explosion rocked the dome. "He's a danger to us all. He's abandoned all pretence of civilised behavior, and—"

"That's enough, Lieutenant." Commander Nielsen's stern tone brought Clarke's whining to an abrupt stop. "One more word and I'll have you restrained pending court-martial. Heron is doing what you haven't the guts or the ability to do. What's more, I've had about as much as I can take of your whining and complaining, and don't think I'm not aware of how much you've passed on to the Consortium's scientists and indirectly to their commanders. Now shut up or get out of my sight and my hearing."

Dumbfounded, Aral Clarke flushed beet red. He was stunned that the Commander knew of his underhand dealings and had never let on until now. This emboldened him, and he considered a retort then thought better of it, very aware of the fact that he had no supporters among the officers present. With as much dignity as he could salvage, he left the small lounge and retired to his quarters nursing his sense of outrage.

Commander Nielsen fumed in frustration, it being little comfort to him that he knew, or at least suspected, that Harry's siege on the Consortium Base was an attempt to release him and the others. Harry had sent a written note to him using one of the Canids as messenger, warning him of the plan, and so he had some idea of what was in progress. He touched his pocket again, the unfamiliar feel of folded paper somehow reassuring. This was the second time he had been contacted like this, and it had not been easy to hide the translator device from the regular inspections for contraband denied the prisoners.

He paced back and forth, forcing himself to remain outwardly calm as he tried to work out what was going on from the snippets of conversation he could overhear as the guards took up defensive positions in the cellblock. The battle seemed to be intensifying with new explosions sounding bigger and closer than before. Withdrawing the note he opened it and read it again, once more admiring the beautiful handwriting he found so difficult to read.

Commander A Nielsen Esquire

Sir,

I trust this finds you and our colleagues in good health. I write to advise you that I have learned that our forces will be attempting a landing soon. My men and our allies will launch an assault upon this Base in an effort to disrupt the defences. We hope that the opportunity will arise to secure your release in the course of that action.

Of course, should it be the case that you and our colleagues have given their Parole to the Commander of the Garrison, I will not ask you to break it unless you are in a position to withdraw it voluntarily.

I remain your humble servant,

H Nelson-Heron
Sub-Lieutenant, NECS Daring

He looked to where the other officers were gathered then took a seat. It had been damned difficult to persuade everyone to assemble in what he hoped was a protected place without revealing what he knew was coming. All he could do was wait.

He smiled suddenly when he realised Harry would not have known that Gentlemen's Agreements were no longer permitted between enemies unless for mutual protection from another force. He'd have to explain this to him somehow, and could imagine the look of surprise on the young Lieutenant's face on being told.

ComRate Cam Khodro checked the signal emitter logs again. There was definitely a signal sent from the transmitter that had no origination code from their system. He checked the current logins and found he could identify the Brigadier, the Com Officer and the Air Strike Commander's codes, but there was an additional login which gave him no code, and when he tried to trace it, the code refused to identify itself.

When he tried to block the intruder, his terminal screen cleared and his access was locked.

"What the hell?" He keyed his comlink. "Major Willis, I've got a problem. Something just shut me out of our system. I think we have a serious bug. Something is logged into the emitters, and when I tried to trace it—I got shut down."

The Major hurried over. "Here, let me see. What were you logged into when it happened?"

Cam showed her. Using her login credentials, they checked the system carefully. The strange login had gone. Neither realised the Provider was using the Major's own login and watching exactly what she could see.

"Try to log in again," the Major told Cam. She called to another member of the staff. "Is anything odd turning up on your systems?"

Cam logged in on his alternative ID and checked his system record. It was intact, so he scrolled down to the location of the mystery signal. It had vanished.

"It's gone!" he exclaimed. "And the logs have—"

He got no further. A series of explosions rocked the Communications Centre, and smoke filled the compartment. Several of the workstations went offline, and the Rates manning them tried frantically to restore the functions. More explosions shook the building, and the smoke thickened.

The door slid open and a smoke-stained and shaken Lieutenant peered in. "Everyone okay? Sorry, Major, we took hits from several explosive bombs, and we have a fire in the building. We've got it isolated and under control. Are your systems still operational?"

The Major glanced around at her team. "A couple are down, but we'll have them back ASAP." As the Lieutenant withdrew, she said to Cam, "Leave that for now. Get the internal coms back up then see what you can do to restore the movement sensor system."

Admiral Enescu seethed with anger when she received the news of the Fleet landing force. Her carefully prepared trap seemed to have been circumvented.

"How did they insert a landing force without escorts or landing ships?"

"They came in close to the planetary atmosphere on the blind side, Admiral. Fast drop and back into transit. The Base reports they were attacked ahead of it happening. Something took down our defence satellite monitors as well."

"So we don't know where they came from?" Surging out of her seat, she gripped the rail and peered down at her staff. "Where the hell is Hartmann? She has to be close. Send in Scout Force One with a troop carrier. Let them launch the troops on a low orbit pass. Insert interceptors in support and attack any landing ships in the vicinity. That should flush out Hartmann. Warn all ships to stand by to drop out the moment we know where they are."

"The Base is taking a real beating, and according to the latest report, the air wing have taken a hammering." The Captain referred to some notes. "What's strange is that we can detect only personal weapons in use, yet the uplink imaging shows heavy weapons of some sort. Whoever is leading this attack is using something our scans can't detect."

"Is it some form of alien tech?" demanded the Admiral.

"Apparently not. Brigadier Newton says it's self propelled—or some of it is—and explosive. It has no electronic components or guidance. That's why it doesn't show up on scan."

"So it's crude and unreliable," snapped the Admiral. "What the hell is wrong with our people? Can't they deal with a bunch of primitives using the next best thing to a bow and arrow?"

Her Chief of Landing Forces, a Major General of long experience, bit back a retort. "If it was just the escapees, it would be contained already. The local aliens have joined forces with escaped prisoners, and the people leading it are the pair that escaped from the Johnstone lab on Pangeaea—not to mention, one of them, O'Connor, escaped the holding cell on Lycania, set free by the other, Heron. Newton reports they have been interfering with our AIs and causing absolute havoc."

The Flag Lieutenant announced, "Support Landing Force deploying and going in, Admiral," as he listened to a private signal com. "Our cruisers have been attacked by a force of three cruisers and ten destroyer class vessels pursuing our transports." He stiffened at what he heard next. "Two starship class vessels have dropped out and are launching interceptors!"

"Got you!" Admiral Enescu growled. "Typical Hartmann, she's adopting a defensive strategy—send in Divisions One and Two, and support them with Cruiser Groups Hotel and Juliet. She'll have to send in the rest of her fleet, and when she does, we'll jump them!"

Aboard the *Vanguard*, Rear Admiral Heron watched the developing engagement on a visual display populated by relays from his ships. He saw the sudden appearance of the additional starships and cruisers and their host of escorts. To his Flag Lieutenant he said, "Signal Destroyer Groups One to Four and Commodore Dewey to take his ships into action."

His simulations had come up with a number of predictive responses to his insertion of the landing ships and their troops—and it seemed his opponent had adopted the most obvious. Better, she had assumed he had committed all his ships in response to her gambit. He watched the dropout of the new swarm of ships and the enemy response.

The Scan Officer reported, "All the enemy ships listed in the C-in-C's intel report and that Ancient Mariner message are on scan and closing to engage. They've taken the bait, sir."

He nodded, satisfied. "Signal all groups—Engage the enemy." He keyed his personal link and ordered, "Take us in, Richard. I want to neutralise their flagship if we can. Leandra Enescu can sometimes be provoked into reacting without thinking things through."

Raki's pack fought with cunning, but the sheer number of forces against them began to tell. Even with the weapons taken from the enemy in their raids, they soon found the soldiers had the advantage in their use.

Reluctantly the big Canid gave orders to retire and regroup, and began to extricate his people. His signal flashed to his fellow leaders and to Harry's position as well.

With his teams in the thick of the fighting, the numbers against them were telling. Harry gave the order to Maddie. "Send the signal to withdraw to the southern boundary. Then send to Mr. O'Connor number four. I want him to lay down a barrage with everything he has left."

Receiving the signal, Ferghal ordered, "Load with contact exploding heads on the rockets and mortars. Batteries, maintain fire with what you have."

He watched as the first rockets soared away, followed minutes later by the mortars. The ground-shaking thump of the mortars as they sent their shells sailing over the enemy's heads added to the excitement his team felt. The flash and bang as these landed sent the defenders diving for cover, exactly what Harry had hoped for.

No one noticed the errant rocket as it roared to its apogee then began its descent, twisting and wavering as it did so. Those who did see its arrival didn't have time to run anywhere as it hurtled into the vent shaft that led into a bunker filled with fuel cells and purified materials awaiting shipment to the agricultural worlds and satellites.

In the noise of the battle, no one outside the underground store noticed the initial flash and blast of debris ejected from the entrance to the big bunker. The subsequent eruption got everyone's attention.

The Base Communications Centre took the full force of the explosion and the debris of a damaged strike craft. The wreckage smashed into the external wall and hurled debris through the compartment.

ComRate Cam Khodro never knew what hit him. Seconds before the blast, he had finally traced the source of the interference, but now he would never report it.

On his hillock, Harry and his team saw the debris hurled skyward, and seconds before it reached them, saw the shockwave. He had time to yell, "Everyone—down!" He threw himself into the depression as the ground leapt beneath him, and debris and heat blasted over them.

Harry picked himself up, shaking a layer of filth and debris from him as he did so. He first checked that everyone with him was uninjured. Then he scrambled up to the ridge and stared at the scene of devastation. Nothing stirred below him, and an eerie silence hung over the entire panorama.

A cold hand clutched his heart as he cast his gaze to and fro. Where was Ferghal? Where were the rest of his people? Turning to several men who had joined him, he snapped, "Signal all our positions. Check status and ask who needs assistance."

Maddie used her flags to attract attention, her concern tempered when she got a response from Errol Hill's position.

"Seven responses, sir. Nothing from Warrant Kellerman. He and his team were close to the blast."

"Team Six needs assistance, sir. Same with Team Four," called a second signaller.

"Mr. O'Connor says his people are all fine, just shaken, sir."

"Thank you. Signal Team One, repeat to Five—Render assistance. Add the location of the teams needing help. Direct Team Three to assist Warrant Kellerman."

"The Cons are regrouping, sir."

Studying the enemy positions, Harry lowered his binoculars. "They're falling back and taking up positions closer to the main structures. Signal all the other teams to regroup on Mr. O'Connor's position. I think our part in this is almost at an end." He indicated the mass of contrails and bright bursts of fire overhead. Below him, smoke and desultory flames issued from a huge crater, all that remained of a large part of the hastily prepared landing dock area.

"Message from Sergeant Timlik of Team Three, sir." The signalman sounded subdued. "No survivors from Warrant Kellerman's team. The Sergeant asks for orders, sir."

"Tell him to secure our dead and join us as soon as possible." Harry suddenly felt very tired and very alone. These were his men, and he had led them to their deaths. How many others, he wondered, had he lost in his determination to stay free of his enemy's clutches and cause them injury?

A party of Canids joined them on the hillock. "How have your people fared, Raki?" Harry asked. "That explosion was unexpected. Did it kill or injure any of yours?"

The Canid leader stared at him for a long moment as if gathering his thoughts, then growled a lengthy response. From the translator Harry learned that the Canids had lost a large number of their fighters. Then he heard, "Rathol and his warriors say there are more coming, strangers we do not know. What is your intention now?"

"Some will be our friends," Harry replied. "But these ones"— he indicated the new contrails—"may not be." He thought quickly. "I think we must do our best to prevent those that hold this place from joining their comrades, and we must release our officers if possible."

"Then we will assist you. But warn those who come that they must not attack our cities or buildings, as your people call them, because these are living nodes of our Provider."

"I shall do my utmost," Harry promised. "But now, let us join Ferghal and the others so we may plan our next actions."

The blast registered on the scanners of the descending Fleet landing barges, and seconds later, so did the shockwave on those nearest the source.

"Someone's touched off something big," commented the pilot in charge of the Command Launch. "And there was some sort of firefight going on around the location of the target area, but against someone using something that doesn't show up on the scanners—and now this."

The Colonel leaned forward to study the screen. "What the hell? That looks like a volcanic blast."

"Unlikely—this area is seismically inactive," replied the barge Commander. "It doesn't register as a reactor failure, but there is something else. The atmospheric analysis is showing up chemical products. Some of it could be ruptured fuel cells, but there are other things in there I've never seen before—high levels of nitrates and carbon, and some metal salts." He stopped talking as his helmsman signalled a course change and a potential landing site. "That's our landing zone—put us down."

"Right." The Colonel warned his team. "We're going in. I want the CC set up as soon as we are on the ground. Coms, signal the others. I want them down in an arc across the agreed drop zone. Air Support, stand by to repel their landers. The second wave will have to take them on. I want our people to advance on the target ASAP. That blast should have disorganised them enough for us to take them out before their cavalry get here."

The roar of the landing engines announced the final phase of the flight, and there was a slight bump as the landing gear touched the ground. Within seconds, the cargo of Marines discharged and set up their defensive perimeter. Right behind them, the Colonel's team disembarked and unloaded their sleds full of equipment for the Command Centre. Spread over several miles in a great arc facing the semi-destroyed Base, other barges touched down and disgorged their forces. Before the Colonel's team had finished deploying their equipment, the first units were advancing toward the great pall of smoke and dust hanging above the Base.

Admiral Enescu of the Consortium fleet studied her visual displays. Her opponent was playing a wily game. The opposing fleet was either smaller than she had been informed, or elements of it weren't yet committed. This was not the sort of deployment she had anticipated. Could Admiral Hartmann have changed her tactics? No time to worry about it now; she'd shown her hand and would have to play it through. To her Flag Captain, she said, "Identify the *Vengeance* and engage her."

"No sign of the *Vengeance*, Admiral," came the response. "We identify the *Valiant*, *Ramillies*, *Constellation* and *Karl der Größe*."

"Damn, has she changed flagships as well?" She paused. "Very well, target the American ship. Let's give them a reason to regret siding with the North European Fleet and not us." She listened to the flow of orders and tracked her ships as they closed the enemy.

Something nagged at the back of her mind. Could their intel have been wrong? It had always been accurate until now. Where were Hartmann and her flagship? Why were there only four starships on scan? She'd expected five. "Run a check on our intel sources. Is the *Vengeance* reported in any other system?"

Her Intel Officer ran a check then cross checked. "Admiral, this report states that she's with the main fleet in the Regulus sector. And it's confirmed—she's there. Our intel must be flawed."

"Then who the hell—?" She stopped as the alarms sounded and the ship lurched when it took a hit from behind. The Admiral stared in disbelief at her display.

"Starship *Vanguard* engaging," announced the Control Officer. "Rear Admiral Heron's flagship, and she's got six heavy cruisers and her frigates with her. Admiral, we're outgunned and out manoeuvred. Orders?"

"Damn that James Heron! Damn him!" She struggled to control her anger. "We'll have to fight our way clear. All ships to disengage and turn away. Execute a battle turn on my mark. Make for the sixth planetary orbit and regroup. Launch missiles and mines as we turn."

Why did it have to be Heron? He had been her nemesis in battle simulation training, and she was sure he knew that it was she he was up against.

James Heron watched the display, his eyes missing nothing. His intervention had been well timed, though the enemy flagship was handled with finesse and extricated from the attack with what seemed to be minimal damage. Now he expected his opponent to regroup her forces. Though they were evenly matched, his fleet had a slight edge in that all its ships were purpose built. His one doubt was the recently joined independent vessels. This was, after all, their first engagement. His analysis of his opponent's tactics and his assessment of the system's possible options for manoeuvre led him to believe his enemy would attempt to turn away behind a screen of mines and missiles. There was only one possible area where they would be able to regroup, and he planned to follow closely enough to disrupt any redeployment.

A change in the attitudes of the three key ships he had marked as the leaders alerted him. "Flags, warn the Fleet. They're trying a battle turn. They'll launch mines and missiles to cover it. All ships, on my mark, execute a simultaneous turn to north ninety, then follow."

He watched the enemy ships for the first indication, and by instinct more than any visual indicator, he saw the beginnings of the evasion. "Now! Keep on top of them!"

As the enemy disengaged and turned through a full one hundred and eighty degrees to streak out of range and regroup, his own ships changed axis then flipped onto a parallel course to follow the fleeing enemy, the mines scattering into empty space.

Commander Nielsen picked himself up. Even inside the confinement lounge the blast made his ears ring, and the shockwave, transmitting through the walls, was powerful enough to knock everyone to the floor. He could see that the upper part of the dome had been stripped away. He gave silent thanks for the fact that all the cells and prisoner accommodations were on the lower levels, and the damaged portion was a simple shell designed to protect the occupants from the weather. Even so, some sections had fallen in on the far side, and the activity there suggested the collapsing section had damaged the guards' quarters.

A Consortium officer hurried toward him, on his way to the damaged area.

"Lieutenant," the Commander called. "Are my people in danger? You have a duty to protect us, you know. "

"Against your own bloody terrorists?" The Lieutenant's voice was sharp. "Commander, I'll see to your people as soon as I've got mine out of the wreckage. I don't know what they've used, but it's caused a hell of a lot of damage and casualties."

"Look, let me move the people on that side." The Commander thought briefly of the word Harry used in his note. "I'll give you our parole not to interfere with your people if you'll allow me to move them to a safer part of the dome."

The Lieutenant hesitated. "Okay, I'll do it. Move your people to the recreation and mess area—it's undamaged." He signalled a guard running past. "Let the Commander out and accompany him to release his people. Escort them to the Recreation Block, and stay with them."

The guard's anxiety made him jumpy and disrespectful to his charges. "Come on, damn you," he yelled, waving his weapons in the Commander's face. "Move it. My mates are under that."

"Take it easy, Private Yerevan." The Commander read the man's nametag. "I have given my word to the Lieutenant that we won't attempt to escape or interfere with you or your companions in any way. Now let's just take it calmly, and we'll all be fine."

"Look, sir." The man steadied. "Some of my mates are trapped on that side, and I want to go and help them. I don't need this detail."

"I know exactly how you feel. It's not easy being locked up in here and a target for both sides, you know." The Commander's refusal to get angry or give way steadied the man. "So let's get my people out and moved, and then let's see what we can do to help anyone who's been injured."

This seemed to work, and the prisoners were soon transferred to the mess hall, library and lounge area.

The Commander directed his attention to a medic. "Now that my people are safe, perhaps we can lend a hand, Captain."

Overhearing this, the Guard Commander replied, "Perhaps your people can help some of my men get our wounded out of the Barracks Block. It's collapsed, and we need some extra muscle." He frowned. "You'll have to give your—parole, was it?—not to attempt anything against my people, though."

The Commander saw the irony of the situation, but tactfully held his peace. After all, it seemed possible that he and his fellow officers would soon be dealing with whoever had caused the blast. If it was Harry and Ferghal, he hoped they had survived it.

"Certainly," he said, and called his fellow prisoners to where he stood.

Chapter 29

Harry's Gamble

Harry joined Ferghal, relieved to see his friend unharmed, albeit smoke blackened and spattered with dirt. "We have lost twenty at least in this, my friend. But I think the Marines will soon be upon us, and we can finish it. How did you fare when that explosion occurred? Have any of yours fallen?"

"Aye, two of mine were killed before the blast, and six more are injured now. What was it that exploded? I have never seen anything like it. It was like the stories told on *Bellerophon* of the destruction of the French flagship at Aboukir Bay in 1798."

"It would seem so." Harry frowned. "Though from memory I do not recall any telling of being thrown to the ground as far from the blast as I was." He checked the men gathering around him as the Coxswain limped up to them, his face cut and bloodied. "Mr. Winstanley, I am glad to see you—how many of our people have we lost?"

"I make the tally twenty-two, sir, with another thirty wounded. We were lucky when whatever it was exploded. It gave us the chance to get clean away while they tried to get themselves together." He gave Harry a crooked grin. "But I hope you don't intend to let off any more like that one, sir!"

"I think I would be cautious of doing so even if I knew what had caused it." Harry smiled, recognising the Coxswain's attempt to lighten the atmosphere, and he enjoyed seeing the grins on the faces around him when Errol Hill embraced Maddie Hodges as if he never wanted to let her go. "I am reasonably certain the Marines from other ships will be here soon. I observed some landing no more than five miles from us. I believe we should keep up the assault. Our enemy has withdrawn into the main part of the camp, and we may yet free our officers, but I think we must move with some caution. Cornered rats can give a fatal bite to the unwary." He glanced at Ferghal. "How is our store of munitions?"

"We have several grenades and shoulder rockets, but our mortar shells are all but expended—our aerial rockets too. I have sufficient charges and canisters for the guns, but there will be no cover for them once we approach the perimeter."

"Good. Sounds like we have enough to be a nuisance until the Marines arrive. And now for the good part—I propose a bluff."

Brigadier Newton read the handwritten note. She stared at it in some disbelief. Even more bizarre—the note had been delivered by a rocket fired into the guardhouse. When it failed to explode, someone plucked it out of the wall and realised that it was a hollow canister. She read the note again.

To the Officer Commanding,
Madam,
In the interest of avoiding further calamity, I propose that you surrender to me the remainder of your personnel and the Officers of the Fleet you hold here. Failure to do so will ensure the destruction of what remains of this camp and of that camp you call the Sinclair Garrison. If you do not surrender on the expiry of this ultimatum, I shall order the detonation of a further device and leave the rescue of any survivors to the Fleet Landing Force now on its way to join us. If you agree to my terms, you will display a single white flag at the gate of this enclosure and attend in

*person to surrender fifty yards before the gate. On
seeing you there unarmed, I will join you. If you
fail to respond in twenty minutes, I will give the
order to detonate our charges.*

I have the honour to be,

H Nelson-Heron

Sub-Lieutenant, NECS Daring

"Bloody cheek!" exploded the Colonel when she had managed
to decipher the beautiful copperplate handwriting. "He has to be
bluffing!"

"Maybe." The Brigadier stared at the delivery rocket. "And
maybe not. Bloody brilliant way to send a warning message, I hate
to admit. We don't know what the hell blew up out there—or what
caused it to. There's a hell of a lot we don't know about this man
and his people. They seem to have been able to come and go as
they please, blow up our outposts and vanish again without a
trace. Yes, I know they've had help from the Canids—but we
haven't managed too well against them either!"

"We've been doing everything we possibly can," the Colonel
protested.

Brigadier Newton made up her mind. "Signal the Landing
Force to land at Sinclair. That will give them time to assemble and
prepare to take on the Fleet's people. Take a small party with you,
and break out while I talk to this Sub Lieutenant. These savages
can't be watching the entire perimeter. If you use the armoured
personnel carriers and make a run from the garage, you'll be able
to get clear before they react."

The Colonel saluted and hurried away.

To her adjutant who was nursing a broken arm and numerous
cuts—the result of having been flung some distance from an
exposed position—Brigadier Newton said, "Order the troops to
hold their fire. I'm going out to parlay. Have the senior officer
from the prisoners brought here and a white flag shown at the
gate, please. I don't want to be shot by accident!"

The *Vanguard* lurched as she took a hit, but Admiral Heron
watched the battle display intently. So far he had managed to
frustrate every attempt that Admiral Enescu had made to extricate

her force, and the losses in ships damaged or disabled were mounting. He detected another change in manoeuvre. "Open the range again," he ordered. "They're trying to close for a missile strike."

"Should we request clearance for the primary, sir?"

The Admiral frowned as he considered this. The last occasion they had used what was referred to as the primary, it had resulted in a shockwave that rippled through hyperspace and caused enormous damage to everything it touched—not least the scanners and communications networks.

"Negative," he replied. "We know they haven't got it, and we can't risk blowing out our own systems in the backwash."

"They're attempting to retreat, sir," the Scan Officer interrupted.

"Maintain tracking and pursue. Message to the *Tromp*—she and Cruiser Squadron Forty-Two are to remain in system to mop up. Their cripples can still cause our forces a problem."

"Entering transit, sir. We have a tracking lock on their ships."

"Very well, message to all ships and to C-in-C—Intend to force an engagement or to push the enemy toward the main fleet."

This was going to be a long pursuit, but he had no intention of letting his opponent get away. To his Flag Lieutenant he said, "Let's see if we can provoke Admiral Enescu to make a mistake. She's inclined to respond badly when pushed too hard."

Brigadier Newton checked her uniform and deliberately unclipped her weapons belt. "Better avoid any misunderstanding." She grimaced. "I suspect this is the end of the road for me anyway, but here goes." She joined the waiting Commander. "Thanks for your efforts on behalf of my wounded," she said. "I understand your people have been helping to extricate them. Now, I'd appreciate your company to meet this Sub-Lieutenant of yours."

"Certainly, Brigadier. Offered to parlay, has he?"

"He's threatening to do to the rest of us what he's apparently already done to the operational side of the Base. He's offered me surrender terms, so I'm going out to talk. As you know him, perhaps you can assist me in negotiating."

"I'll do my best, Brigadier. Mr. Heron does have some interesting ideas and methods. I wouldn't put it past him to carry out his threat."

From beneath his Canid cloak, Harry saw the two figures step from the dome entrance and advance toward the gate. The rank markings at this distance were indistinguishable, but one of the figures was clearly a woman. The other was easily recognisable as *Daring*'s Executive Commander. A white banner had been erected a few minutes before attached to a pole raised from behind another smaller dome behind the gatehouse.

Harry nodded to Maddie Hodges. Both drew the Canid cloaks over their heads and vanished from sight. Harry stepped out of cover and walked quietly to meet the advancing officers, Maddie beside him.

Ferghal watched for any hint of treachery. He didn't have much ammunition left, but he fully intended to make sure any deception was repaid in a manner that would not be forgotten. He recognised the Commander and felt sure there would be no betrayal, but his confidence in the Consortium's behaving honourably was non-existent. Honour between enemies was something Harry could place his trust in. Ferghal had a much less noble view on the matter.

He checked his launchers were ready then concentrated on the waiting officers. He saw their start of surprise as Harry appeared in front of them, the cloak falling at his feet, and saluted Commander Nielsen.

The startled faces of the officers as he materialized in front of them made him struggle to suppress his urge to laugh. Instead, he said, "Brigadier Newton, I am Sub-Lieutenant Heron. Commander, I trust you are well, sir. Are our colleagues safe?" He received their acknowledgements and assurances. "Do you surrender, ma'am?"

The Brigadier had a sense of unreality as she stared at the wild-looking youth in front of her. His mop of hair styled to resemble the mane and ear tufts of a Canid, he looked like something from the very distant human past. How could this— this complete caveman, this boy—have destroyed all her efforts and run rings round her experienced troops?

"You are Heron?" she asked.

"I have that honour." Harry frowned. "The Commander will, I'm sure, confirm it."

"I see you have been making do, Harry." The Commander acknowledged him. "You seem to have made an impact here, all right. What the devil did you detonate just now? It almost blew us away."

"I shall have to refrain from revealing that at the moment, if you have no objection, sir. Suffice it to say we have another such device ready for firing." To Brigadier Newton, he said, "With respect, ma'am, do you surrender? If so, I will guarantee the safety and welfare of your people. The Canids are not savages and will provide the essential food and shelter until we may make more suitable arrangements."

The Brigadier stalled. "What if I refuse? I think you're bluffing, young man. I'll make a trade with you. I will release to you all the officers held here in exchange for safe conduct for all of my people to our second Base on this planet."

"Ma'am, I assure you that I make no bluff. The Fleet Landing Force is on its way to join us. I can present them with what remains of your Base now, or I can leave it as a crater and permit them to proceed against your other Base without pause. I have only to walk away from this meeting unaccompanied by either of you for my people to set in motion the final destruction of this Base."

She already knew the Fleet Landing Force was closing on their position, and a second force had already engaged the forces that Admiral Enescu had landed to support her. She studied the serious-faced young man before her. There was no trace of doubt or hesitation in his expression. He apparently meant every word he said.

"Very well," she replied. "I surrender my command to you, Lieutenant. I will order my people to stand down and to disarm and disengage the perimeter defences. Do I have your assurance that you will disarm whatever device you have planted?"

"I give you my word that the Base will not be destroyed, Brigadier, unless your people attempt some act of treachery against me or mine. Please give the order for your people to lay down their arms and form up in the open next to that dome."

Harry waited while the Brigadier used her comlink to give her orders. Troops began to emerge from their positions and collect in disgruntled groups. He turned slightly and said to an invisible companion, "Hodges, give the signal."

The sudden appearance of the ComOp surprised the Brigadier and the Commander. They watched as Maddie produced a pair of sticks with bright red and yellow flags attached to the ends. Turning away, she raised these and made a series of swift movements. "Acknowledged, sir."

Both officers exclaimed in surprise.

"So that's how you've been communicating your orders!" said Brigadier Newton. She thought of her officers' reports mentioning seeing someone waving colourful flags then vanishing. Why the hell had they never thought it was a means of communication?

"Indeed, ma'am." Harry realised that some explanation was called for. "It is an adaptation of the semaphore used to communicate overland between the Admiralty and Plymouth, Portsmouth and other ports. This system was in use when I first went to sea and continued for many decades thereafter. We have adapted it so a signaller may perform the motions."

The Brigadier shook her head in befuddled amazement.

The Commander chuckled. "You'll be telling us next that you took on the Brigadier's troops with cannon and swords. My God, Harry, you just don't think like one of us, do you?"

It was Harry's turn to look nonplussed. He was trying to think of a polite response to what he felt sure was a criticism when Maddie said, "But he did, sir—he and Mr. O'Connor and Mr. Rasmus dreamed up explosives and bombs—had us all making mortars, grenades and rockets."

"Thank you, Hodges, that will do," said Harry. "As a matter of fact, we have some cannon, and a few more missiles besides." He had been watching the assembly of troops behind the Brigadier, and now said to Maddie, "Signal Mr. Winstanley to take charge of the prisoners."

The Commander's head jerked up. "Did you say Mr. Winstanley? The Chief Master Warrant? He survived?"

Harry's eyes narrowed. "The same. He has been most helpful and a stalwart throughout our difficulties. Why do you ask, sir?"

"I was told he had died, that he was seen to be killed." The Commander's frown betrayed anger. "I'm going to have a very serious interview with someone. Now then, Lieutenant, what are your intentions?"

"With respect, sir, I will secure our prisoners. Hand over control of this Base to the landing parties when they arrive." Harry hesitated. "If those are your instructions as senior officer, sir."

It was the Brigadier's turn to chuckle as the Commander's face registered his surprise. "Oh? Yes, of course." The Commander recovered. "Since you've got us this far, Mr. Heron, what do you suggest?"

"May I suggest that you take charge here, sir." He paused as Maddie responded to a signal from somewhere out of the Brigadier's line of vision. He listened briefly to a whispered message then studied the expression on a senior Consortium officer's face. "It appears that some of your people failed to obey your order, ma'am," said Harry. "That is most unfortunate since it reflects upon your honour as their commander. Equally unfortunate for them, it appears they have encountered one of our minefields and a company of our forces at the same time. Their escape has been thwarted, and I have ordered them to be returned here." To the Commander, he said, "With your approval of course, sir." He gave a stiff bow to acknowledge the Commander's seniority.

The Brigadier shook her head. "It seems that you have managed to outwit us again, Lieutenant." She turned to the Commander. "I'll join my staff if you have no objection, Commander Nielsen." To Harry, she said, "I wish you every success, Mr. Heron. I am only sorry we have to be enemies. I could have wished you were on my staff."

Chapter 30

Subterfuge

Commander Nielsen watched the approach of the Fleet Landing Force with professional interest. They were taking no chances, and approached fully prepared for battle. Taking a leaf from Harry's book, he ordered, "Mr. Van der Pelt, you and I will go out to meet them."

The Lieutenant saluted. "Yes, sir."

"Make sure our people are clearly visible and identifiable as Fleet personnel. Keep our prisoners safe and quiet." He paused at the door. "Better bring a white flag. I don't want some trigger happy Marine burning me away at this point in the proceedings."

Stepping out of the damaged HQ dome, he walked to the gate, the Lieutenant joining him with a large white cloth tied to a long metal rod. "Best we could do, sir. Hope they saw the one the Brigadier put up."

"Looks like it." The Commander indicated a vehicle detaching from the main force and approaching. "That looks like an assault command vehicle." He stopped and waited as the unit halted, then several armoured troops deployed and an officer followed. Recognising the insignia of a Colonel, he saluted. "It's good to see you, Colonel. Commander Nielsen, Senior Officer, NECS *Daring.*

Brigadier Newton, her staff and the surviving members of her garrison are confined to the barrack dome and Officer's Mess."

Returning the salute, the Colonel offered his hand. "You were responsible for this?"

"Lord no. I am—was—the senior POW. This—" he indicated the damaged structures "—is the work of Sub-Lieutenant Heron and his men plus his, ah, allies, the Canids."

The Colonel frowned. "So who is in command here now?"

"I am, sir. Mr. Heron accepted the surrender and has gone ahead of you toward the second Base to the south. He left this for you." He handed over a carefully folded sheet of stiff paper. "It's a route map. Apparently, his people mined the normal route. This will enable you to avoid the traps and find the quickest way south." He watched the Colonel signal his own people forward. "I'll take you to Brigadier Newton and her staff as soon as you're ready, sir. They surrendered to Mr. Heron a half hour ago."

"That will be helpful." The Colonel grimaced and indicated the damage around them. "What the hell did they use against this place? It looks almost as if it got hit by a meteor strike on what must have been the landing and launch field." Handing the map to his adjutant, he followed Commander Nielsen.

"From what I've been able to piece together, ignorance on the part of the Consortium of a very old and rather simple explosive and a lucky hit by one of Mr. O'Connor's rather erratic rocket bombs did all this."

"Ignorance?"

"It seems they were stockpiling ammonium nitrate and a rather interesting perchlorate for shipping off-world, and when they needed space to store fuel cells—well, they put the two together. According to the scientist who's been working with Heron's people to make their explosives, a rocket must have ruptured a fuel cell and started a fire. The rest, as they say, is scattered all over the landscape."

"We saw it as we came down. Our scanners couldn't identify it either. So it was just an accident?"

Anders Nielsen grinned. "Yes, but young Heron had the balls to pull off the biggest bluff of all. He convinced the Brigadier he had another device in place and that he would blow us all away if she didn't surrender."

The Colonel laughed. "She won't have been happy when she discovered the bluff. I hope I'll get to meet this officer of yours—he sounds like a man who's not afraid to use his initiative. But how has he survived and kept his people alive this long? This place isn't exactly suited to humans, and from what my briefings say, there isn't a lot we can eat here either."

"I haven't got the full story yet," the Commander acknowledged. "From what I have learned from the men he left here as a garrison, they seem to have been living as the guests of the locals and some sort of alien life form. It provided everything they needed and sheltered them through the last two winters. Furthermore, it has infiltrated all the Base AIs and coms—so it knows everything on those systems, which means Heron and O'Connor know it too."

"How the hell?" The Colonel began shook his head in amazed disbelief. "Thanks for the warning. I'll keep my systems well isolated. Now, to business—the Fleet has taken off in pursuit of the enemy. We have a couple of cruisers and their escorts riding herd aloft, but essentially we're on our own until Admiral Heron returns. Are your people able to help the defence if we're attacked?"

Rear Admiral Heron studied his battle plot. "Admiral Enescu is trying to swing back toward Lycania. Set up a course prediction based on her evasions. I want to get ahead of her if we can."

"They've detached several ships, apparently to repair facilities or because they are unable to keep up, sir," reported the Tactical Officer. "Two of the cruisers detached are disabled and unable to transit. They've been left in stable orbits in the Tacitus system to wait for retrieval and repair. Three more have been damaged, with our frigate groups maintaining contact."

"Good, so we're eroding their strength." The Admiral scanned the plot display. "It looks as if they're planning to swing back along this track." He frowned. "Why? It makes no sense—unless they're setting up a trap. Where would be a good place to hide an ambush? It has to be someplace where our scanners will have difficulty identifying it."

"Here, sir," Captain Grenville interposed. "The radiation from the decay of the supernova and the shockwaves in the debris cloud in this region will set up background noise the scanners will take time to sift through and filter."

James Heron nodded. "Excellent. Contact the C-in-C and *Vengeance*. I think they may be planning a major engagement there. It has all the hallmarks of a trap. We'll have to make sure it isn't."

Harry led his group into the pass, alert to any possible enemy ambush. Just ahead, where it narrowed through a single defile, his people had set a trap for any vehicles moving through it.

"Signal from the scout party, sir. The trap caught a Con scouting formation. They abandoned their vehicles and retreated."

"Good. Where are the abandoned vehicles?"

"Just beyond the next bend, sir," a Corporal reported. "Our mines have made a mess of them. A couple are on their backs—the rest half buried or completely disabled. There don't seem to be any survivors, so perhaps they've taken them with them."

"Very well, we'll work our way past them and see how far they've gone. The weather looks set to change, and it would be unwise to remain in the open. We'll need shelter if it does." He wondered how many had been killed and how many injured in this trap, then put those thoughts aside as the Sergeant approached.

"We knocked out everything but two of their vehicles, sir. The survivors managed to get clear and work their way out to rescue some of the casualties. They got away on the remaining transports."

"Very good," acknowledged Harry. "Our own Landing Force will be coming this way, so we must ensure the Consortium forces cannot reciprocate against our people." He stopped as a voice called from the small ravine beside the road.

"Sir! There's a survivor here, an officer. He's trapped and injured," called a TechRate. "We'll need some grunt to get him free."

"On our way," Harry replied. "Sergeant, detail some men to assist, then take your people up the pass to ensure it remains clear—but beware, there is a storm in the making. I can feel it, and our host warns of it." Sliding down the slope, he ducked to peer into the interior of the vehicle. Hands joined his, and as the face turned toward him and became clear, recognition caused him to exclaim.

"You!"

His face bloodied and distorted by pain, Eon Barclay managed to gasp, "Bastard."

"Not according to convention. My parents were duly joined in matrimony at the time of my birth. Corporal, give me the medical pack. I'll try to deal with this man's injuries while you free him."

It took almost an hour to extricate Eon Barclay, secure his broken legs and get him up to the roadway. By now, the storm was almost on them, and they barely had time to reach shelter in a shallow cave before it burst over them in fury.

Leaving what had been the Consortium Brigadier's office, now used by Commander Nielsen and the Marine Colonel, Harry almost walked into Lieutenant Clarke. As the Lieutenant jumped back, Harry threw up a salute.

"Sir! My apologies, my mind was elsewhere."

Aral Clarke returned the salute, a sneer twisting his face. "Still playing the savage, I see. I hope you're satisfied. You almost killed us in your insane assault. What were you thinking of, setting off a bomb like that?"

"Winning an uneven fight," Harry snapped before he could control himself. Fighting down his temper, he added, "The Fleet Landing Force needed a distraction, and my intent was to obtain the liberty of all officers while preventing the Consortium strike craft from intervening against our landing force. Do you believe that we should have left your own safety to the mercy of an enhanced and prepared force?"

Outraged, Aral Clarke tried to assert his authority. "Show some damned respect! Your behaviour is totally unacceptable, and as for the outfit you persist in wearing—"

"Since I did not have the luxury of fresh clothing supplied at regular intervals, and still do not, I will, with Commander Nielsen's approval for myself and my people, continue to dress in this fashion, sir. It is functional, comfortable and at least free of any taint of collaboration with the enemy." Harry wrinkled his nose as if spurning a foul odour.

"How dare you!" Clarked spluttered.

"With every right, Mr. Clarke!"

"You could at least get a haircut, you filthy heathen. You're a disgrace to the Fleet."

Commander Nielsen stepped between them. "You have a task, Mr. Heron. Get on with it. I will talk to you about this later. Mr. Clarke, step into my office. I have some serious matters to discuss with you."

Harry, idle for the first time in the months he had been on this planet, had taken a shower and relished every minute of it. He had forgotten how restorative it felt to be truly clean. His confrontation with Lieutenant Clarke had upset him, and he'd been willing to admit his fault and accept the reprimand from the Commander. Word of the confrontation had got around due to its having been overheard by Maddie Hodges, who'd warned the Coxswain.

Still wearing the Canid outfit with his long, uncut hair styled to resemble the Canids' mane, he went in search of the Coxswain and Maddie to set about the task he'd been given. Like Harry, they were still wearing their Canid clothing as there was, at present, no capacity to provide uniforms for them.

The irony of the twist of fate that had seen him instrumental in rescuing Eon Barclay struck him. He realised he no longer despised Barclay, his old nemesis from Fleet College, but instead felt rather sorry for him. He understood some of the reasons that drove Barclay to such churlish bullying. It prompted him to wonder if the same things might have been the cause of the earlier Barclay's attitude on HMS *Spartan* all those centuries ago, most likely a distant ancestor of Eon's with the same questionable character traits.

Eon Barclay had been irritable but reluctantly grateful to his rescuers, and was now in a med-unit recovering from two broken legs and other injuries. Just before he was handed over to the MedTechs, he asked to speak to Harry privately and confided that his commanders were expecting a large force to come to their rescue.

"I shouldn't be telling you this—but I owe you for saving me, damn you," he told Harry. "Admiral Gratz has a scheme for exchanging his ships for others. That's why our transports haven't come to take us off. I think there's a plan to trap your ships somewhere and blow them to hell. So we'll probably be back in charge by the time I'm out of this med-unit."

"Thanks for the warning," Harry said, and conveyed the information to Commander Nielsen at the first opportunity.

"Better send that to Fleet, Harry. Immediately."

"Aye, aye, sir."

It felt very strange to no longer be in command, though he had new responsibilities that interested him. Harry was trying to discover what messages might be passing through the Consortium's signal emitter. He stiffened when he heard one in particular.

Why was a passenger liner requiring information on their ship movements? He tracked the signals through the network, and what he discovered electrified him and sent him hurrying to find the Commander.

"Sir," he said, having found Commander Nielsen just leaving his office. "I have been listening to our enemy's signal traffic, and I think they have launched a subterfuge to trap our ships."

"How—?" the Commander began then changed direction. He remembered that Harry and Ferghal were linked to something he and the Marine Colonel had only just begun to get to grips with. "What have you learned?"

"Sir, as I was listening to their signals, I realised the deployment and movement signals were sent from a passenger liner, not from their flagship. All the ships addressed are cargo liners or passenger vessels, but they request intelligence on the positions of our Fleet, and most peculiarly, the liner *Archimedes* asks for information from the Commander, who is now in the Sinclair Garrison on the minelayers and sweeper craft detached by Admiral Heron."

"The hell they are!" The Commander considered this. "Harry, transmit everything you've just given me to HQ. Repeat it to *Vanguard* and *Vengeance*."

"Aye, aye, sir." Harry paused. "Shall I add that the *Archimedes* and a large number of others are en route to a rendezvous with Admiral Enescu?"

"If you're certain of that, yes, tell them. Monitor everything and pass it on." He waited, but Harry had no reply, and stood very still with a blank expression on his face. "Is there anything else you need?" he prompted.

A smile flickered across Harry's face. "Nothing, sir. If you will pardon my silence for a few minutes, I can do it from here."

"Then go for it," the Commander ordered. "Let's hope we are in time."

Chapter 31

Clash of Titans

———————————————

Harry's signal was greeted with initial disbelief. A check confirmed enough to cause Admiral Hartmann to summon her staff. "We're going in. I want to hit any warships hard—but warn all Commanders there are freighters and cruise ships among them. I plan to disable them on a single pass and follow straight on to join up with Admiral Heron here." She touched the display map. "Once we've joined forces, we'll take on their combined fleet here." She stared at the display. "This time we'll make sure of it."

The Flag Lieutenant interrupted. "Admiral Heron online for you, Admiral."

"Morning, James," she greeted his hologram. "Gratz has managed to pull a switch on us. I'm going to cripple his dummies and take the shortest route to join you. Try to avoid being pulled into a major engagement until I can get there. They'll have an almost two-to-one superiority until then."

"As you say," James Heron responded. "Enescu's fleet has been growing slowly, and now that we've been given the tip, we realise that what we were reading as cargo haulers are actually cruisers and destroyers. I'm transmitting my assessment of where they plan to make a stand and draw us in."

"The area they are most likely heading for could be difficult."

"It's a bad spot for us if they can get there first, as they'll have time to tune out the background from their scanners, and we won't. So, I've sent a little trap of my own ahead of us and them. My minelayers will be there in a couple of hours to mine it. That will force their fleet to shift position, which will give us a small opening to exploit."

"Good. I'll be on my way to link up with you in an hour at most. The Third Cruiser Fleet can do the mop-up, and we should be with you in seventy-two hours. Try to keep them guessing until then."

"Admiral Gratz, good to see you. We will be at the rendezvous in four hours." Admiral Leandra Enescu's relief showed as she greeted the holographic image. "I've a signal from our Lycania Base confirming the arrival of Heron's minelayers and smaller escorts." She grimaced. "It's not going well there. We'll have to get a relieving force to them as soon as we can finish off Heron's fleet."

"Good. We'll be at our rendezvous about an hour behind you. Try to keep him guessing until we join you and can pull him into the trap."

Neither Admiral knew that their forces on Lycania had surrendered. The signal from the planet was from Harry. Nor could they know he was using their system to monitor their communications.

Listening to the latest exchange, Harry made some notes then composed a message to his guardian, Rear Admiral James Heron on the *Vanguard*. With that sent, he went to find Commander Nielsen.

James Heron studied the scan display from his scout drones scattered among the mines at the expected rendezvous point. It confirmed the information Harry transmitted to him.

"The intel from Lycania was spot on, sir," remarked his Flag Lieutenant. "Do you want the mines activated?"

"No. I want to make sure their main fleet is in the trap before we show our hand, and they haven't arrived yet." The Admiral paused. "As soon as we activate them, they'll show up on their scanners in spite of the background noise. Let them close in and deploy properly."

"But can we be sure they'll deploy where the mines have been laid, sir?"

"Admiral Enescu has a particular deployment she favours. If I've guessed correctly, the mines will even the score a bit for us and shake her up badly—and that's when she tends to make rash decisions."

The Flag Lieutenant grinned. His Admiral was a firm believer in the maxim 'Know your enemy.'

"And then it gets interesting," he said.

"Well, if we're lucky," said Admiral Heron, "it will be easier to out think her, and that is half the battle."

He looked up as the Coms Officer said, "Admiral Hartmann for you, sir."

"James," the Vice Admiral greeted him. "We'll be with you in an hour. What's the situation?"

"Enescu's fleet dropped out and is deploying as I expected." He smiled. "It helps that we had some inside information. They don't seem to realise their hypercom emitter and receiver is in our hands and capable of reading all their signal traffic. I expect Gratz to join her in about fifteen minutes. Then I have a little surprise for them."

"Great. If, as you intend, it disrupts their deployment and forces them out of their chosen ground, we have an edge they can't afford. I suggest we keep this link open so we can update the deployment data as we have it."

"I agree." Signalling his Coms Officer, who nodded acknowledgment, Admiral Heron continued. "I am keeping the mines inactive until we're ready. One of her ships is not where I thought it would be—but with luck, the mines will do quite a lot of the work for us."

Vanguard and her fleet dropped out surrounded by her escorting frigates and destroyers. On her flanks, the heavy cruiser and destroyer squadrons deployed on their prearranged formations and began the manoeuvre to draw the enemy into position. Admiral Heron watched as the holographic command display cleared to show the dispositions of the opposing fleet.

"Our scout drones are doing a great job," he commented. "The scan is clearer than I expected."

"We've been tweaking and tuning them since they went in, sir," the Commander responded. "But they may miss some of the smaller stuff because we're at maximum filter."

"A chance we'll have to take." The Admiral stiffened. "They've taken the bait. They're moving in to attack and don't seem to have spotted the mines—their scan filters must be at full power as well. Good." To his Weapons Team, he said, "Arm the mines on my command." He touched his comlink. "Richard, stand by, we're about to arm the mines. I'll want a turn away together just before I do, then a turn toward them as soon as their ships find the trap."

"I understand." The Captain's voice was calm. "Just give the word, sir."

The Admiral focused his attention on the scans, watching for his moment. "Now," he commanded. "Commence the turn away."

The Scan Officer tracked the markers on his scan and called, "They're swinging to intercept, sir. They've taken the bait."

The Admiral nodded. "Arm the mines."

The closing fleet adopted a tight formation, giving no sign of having detected the minefield. Successive massive bursts of energy clouded the scanners, blinding the automated targeting for a few seconds. This would have been a handicap, but *Vanguard* and her sisters had a visual targeting system as well—one developed from the crude system based on Harry and Ferghal's knowledge of seemingly 'ancient' technology when they first arrived so precipitately in this century.

"They've found the mines." The laconic comment from the Weapons Rate brought a sharp reprimand.

"Captain Grenville!" The Admiral kept his link open. "Target the lead ship." He nodded to his Flag Lieutenant. "Signal all ships: Engage your designated targets."

The *Vanguard*'s Captain watched as his ship swung toward the enemy formation. Several enemy ships were falling out of position, debris spreading out around them as they did so. He keyed his link. "Engage the lead ship. Target her weapons and drives." He hoped all the unexploded mines were able to read their 'friend' signals and would not react to their ships as they passed.

The great beams of ionized particles sliced into the leading ship. Still recovering from the explosion of several mines close to her and at least one against her hull, judging by the gaping hole in her side, the ship reeled. *Vanguard* staggered as several of the enemy ship's weapons found her and returned the damaging fire.

"The destroyers are launching missiles," his Plot Officer announced. "Enemy taking evasive action."

The angles changed on the leading ship, and her companions followed suit. The Captain opened his mouth to order a closing course when the second ship in the enemy line seemed to blossom fire and light. "She's found another mine," the Lieutenant in charge of the plot commented. "But a few of them are still in place."

"Which means we had better take care ourselves," snapped the Captain. "Hold our present heading. That mine disrupted their formation. Send in the strike fighters. See if we can blind the leader."

Admiral Heron watched the unfolding exchange then keyed his link. "First and second cruiser squadrons, engage their rear." To his team he said, "I want to nudge them a little further along the lateral plane. Admiral Hartmann is waiting for her moment, and we'll have them between us." He watched as the cruisers changed heading and swept toward the rearmost enemy ships, the swarm of interceptors showing as pinpricks of light as their drive pods lit up and powered them directly at the other side's response. The feint had the desired effect.

The smaller ships at the rear of the enemy line were all conversions, and shied away from the heavy cruisers. This exposed the flanks of the tail end of the enemy starships. A quick strike from the destroyer forces took the opportunity to launch another missile strike. A moment later, the entire enemy fleet turned away, one more of their ships apparently striking a mine in the process.

"Admiral Hartmann's fleet in dropout, sir," called a TechRate.

"Right on the button," breathed the Plot Officer even as the first bright streaks of plasma and particle beams lanced toward the enemy. "She's got them dead to rights!"

Aboard the *Vengeance*, Danny tracked the lead ship and carefully focused his weapons pods on her. An observer might have thought he was playing a keyboard as his fingers danced across the interface. "Concentrate on her secondary emplacements," he told his team. He noted the enemy changing angle in his targeting screen. "He's turning away. Shift target—his hangars are exposed as he swings. Target the landing bays."

His team adjusted their aim, and Danny pressed the firing switches. Plasma lanced from the turrets, and brilliant flashes lit the interior as they found their target. The angle changed again, and Danny gave fresh directions as he identified the other ship's scanner arrays. Concentrating on his task helped him forget the last time they had faced this fleet and his near miss with a damaged arm and the air escaping from the compartment.

This took his thoughts to Harry and Ferghal, and he missed them with a pang of longing. The three of them were like brothers now, and it had been too many months since he'd last seen them. At least he knew they were both alive.

He snapped out of his momentary reverie when he saw the angle of the other ship changing again, and once more, he had a shot at the hangar bays. This time their efforts were rewarded by a great flare from the forward facing launch bays on the leading edge of the fin. What he could not see was the passage of the same flare through the centre part of the ship, tearing out bulkheads and decks, and more crucially, severing communications with the fore part of the ship from the after end.

Admiral Heron saw the movement of the enemy cruisers and immediately gave orders to counter their threat. Frustrated in their manoeuvre, they fell back exposing the rear of the line of starships to a strike by his second battle group, and that provoked Admiral Enescu into turning two of her starships to concentrate the defence of her rear.

"Now we have them." Admiral Heron studied his battle plot. Spotting the deployment of smaller ships into the mines, he ordered, "Signal our ships: Close and engage."

The battle was brief but bloody. The concentrated fire of three starships, twelve heavy cruisers and the darting, stinging destroyers rapidly crippled three of the Consortium's starships and destroyed three of their cruisers before the remainder extricated themselves in confusion. Admiral Gratz was only partially successful. As his ships attempted their battle turn, they discovered that Admiral Hartmann had anticipated this move, and ran a gauntlet of intense fire. It rapidly became a case of every ship for itself, and those that were able to flashed into hyperspace on any bearing from which they could find an opening.

The CS *Khamenei*, Admiral Gratz's flagship, was the last to escape—damaged, barely under control, her Captain reliant on ComTechs in EVA suits to act as links between him, his engineers and his Admiral. As the *Khamenei* managed her escape, she left behind three starships in their death throes, one of them Admiral Enescu's flagship.

James Heron called up his senior. "Do you want me to pursue them?"

"No, James," Admiral Hartmann replied. "The C-in-C is in position to intercept them, and I have squadrons on their way to assist him. I plan to keep them running and scattered. Take your ships directly to Lycania and secure that planet." She paused. "And well done to your people. Your minefield was the crucial element. Your analysis of their inability to spot them in the background scatter was spot on."

"Yes," he responded. "Planting a few scan drones among them helped—it gave us the ability to come in shooting. And Leandra's tendency to react without analysing a situation also worked for us. The losses among their people must be horrendous." He paused as the plot screen showed a sudden bright star where his opponent's flagship had been slowly tearing itself to pieces. "I hope the survivors were clear of that..." he commented.

In his quarters deep inside their Canid host's structures, Harry paused in his preparations to move to the captured base on the surface. His mind wandered to the prospect of seeing Mary Hopkins again—if she'd not given him up for lost and taken up with someone else. He thought briefly of Maddie Hodges, and smiled. Several years older than he, she'd made a lively, sometimes cheeky, but always professional companion as his signaller. That she and one of the TechRates, Errol Hill, had formed a relationship made him envious. Pulling his thoughts back to Mary, he smiled. He had a package full of letters to send her, and hoped she'd be happy to receive them.

The signal traffic he had been half listening to, without consciously doing so, changed. A degree of desperation seemed to have entered all the enemy messages. He stopped to listen and realised that a huge battle was being fought somewhere in the stars.

Sinking to his knees, he offered a prayer, the ancient prayer he had heard on so many Sundays in freezing rain, wind or blazing sun aboard HMS *Spartan* all those years ago. So many dead, and so many injured in this conflict. He began his prayers with very mixed feelings.

"O Eternal Lord God, who alone spreadest out the heavens, and rulest the raging of the seas; who hast compassed the waters with bounds until day and night come to an end...."

His alien host, the Provider, watched and listened, thinking its own thoughts and, having learned this strange behaviour meant Harry wanted privacy, left him to his prayers.

The Provider was unaware that it was being watched, and through it, Harry was too.

Chapter 32

Prospects for Peace

_____

Niamh read the message from her brother with delight. At last, she had something to share with Mary Hopkins. She smiled at the thought. The young lady had contacted her at least daily asking for updates about Harry. Now she had something to tell her that wasn't already on the news channels. A news team had been aboard the *Vengeance*, and some of their recordings, taken from the ship's battle plot scans, had been playing almost non-stop. Already there was talk of the hope of peace.

That did finally seem possible, though Niamh and Mary were almost too afraid to believe it for fear of being disappointed. In the last hour, it was announced that a message was received from the Consortium Board and was 'being studied' by the President and the Confederation's allies. The only cloud on their horizon was no news from Harry or Ferghal. Both were still on the planet Lycania, but beyond that, they knew nothing.

Niamh looked up when her husband entered the room.

"Well, dearest?" she asked. "Is there going to be peace?"

"It certainly looks that way, though it isn't the outright surrender we wanted. They still have a few aces to play, and we will have to make some compromises—not that we didn't need to make some changes—but now it will be a part of the settlement, assuming we can get it through the Parliament."

Niamh frowned. "How can they hope to prevent the settlement? It seems to me that's the only reasonable course."

Theo smiled. "You won't find many among the representatives who disagree with that assessment. But, to more pleasant matters, what has James to say for his victory?"

"Oh, he's so reticent it drives me wild." She laughed. "He gives all the credit to his 'people' as he calls them. I've learned more watching the CBC and Interstellar News channels than he tells me." She looked serious again. "Do you think Harry and Ferghal will be sent home now? I shall be so disappointed if they are not. Surely they've earned some leave."

"If the intel reports I've seen over the last few days are anything to go by, they've more than earned it. Apparently, they've been very creative. They've certainly sown mayhem in their wake."

"Good for them. But now I see the League for the Protection of Sentient Life are making a noise about their contact with the Canids."

"My staff are dealing with a formal complaint from the League at present. They're claiming our boys used stolen alien technology to conduct their guerrilla campaign." Theo laughed. "I rather think the boot is on the other foot, but we will see."

"Harry." The Commander acknowledged his salute. "I'll be going aloft with the next shuttle. You're to remain here and act as liaison with the Canids until we sign the agreement with them. Admiral Hartmann will be coming down to deal with that, and once it's signed off, she'll give you your orders."

"Aye, aye, sir. Will they be sending representatives home with us?"

Noting the disappointed look on Harry's face, he replied, "Yes, they're discussing it now. I know you want to go aloft with Mr. O'Connor and the rest of your men. Admiral Heron is keen to have you aboard as well."

"As you say, sir."

"You led these men through some tough and difficult conditions. You pulled them together and kept them going, so that's a very natural wish, Lieutenant."

"I just did what seemed best in the circumstances, sir."

"More important at the moment, though, you made contact with and allied yourselves to the Canids. Protocol and diplomacy dictate that right now you should be here a little longer."

His eyes took in the thickening fluff of a beard, the wild mop of dark reddish-brown hair styled to resemble the Canids' mane, and the bulky Canid clothing. "You've made quite an impact on the Interstellar News Channel, and the Admiral feels you should be part of the treaty ceremony."

"Aye, aye, sir," Harry responded. It wasn't easy adjusting to once more being a very junior officer after eighteen months in command. He found taking orders on almost everything frustrating.

"It won't be long, and you'll be aboard." The Commander sympathised. He'd learned just how tough things had been at times, and this young Sub-Lieutenant—technically still below the age required for his rank—had managed to inspire his people to endure it. "The Marines will be remaining, so once this treaty is signed, you'll be shuttled up so you can get some well earned rest and relaxation. While I'm at it, I'd like to say that I'm really proud to have served with you on *Daring*, Harry. I know there were problems for you, and I think you have proved yourself more than capable of leading any men entrusted to you, and women. You've won the respect of the Rates and the Warrants, and that is saying something."

"Admiral." Harry saluted Karina Hartmann and the party who flanked her. "May I present the Canid Council?" He introduced each of the twenty Canid leaders by name, including their status and the role they'd played in the conflict. "They welcome you to their home planet, and look forward to hearing the proposals you bring."

"Lieutenant." The Admiral's salute was punctilious. "I thank them for their welcome and present to them the representatives of the World Treaty Organisation. Please assure them we look forward to welcoming them as partners in future." She looked startled when the device in Harry's hand growled and yipped the translation.

"I beg pardon, ma'am. It's a translation device. It has already conveyed your words into their language."

He stopped when the device broke into speech as one of the older Canids addressed the newcomers. "The young leader Harry Heron has shown us much and promised your friendship. We have learned that he honours his word. We look to you to do the same."

Harry almost laughed at the expression on several of the dignitaries' faces, but the Admiral responded with an assurance.

"Ma'am, there is another here, though we cannot see it. The Provider, the Canids' form of AI, is able to hear us and direct our allies through the medium of this translation device. You will need for the treaty signing." He handed over the compact device and stepped back as the delegates followed the Admiral into the dome for the formalities.

As he watched the ceremonial signing, he was conscious of the Provider listening to his thoughts, so he asked, *"When I leave this place, will our minds be separated?"*

"If you so wish. Now that we have learned from observing your use of the intelligences you call AI, we can find you if you wish us to."

"There will be those who are disturbed by that," Harry responded watching the expression of alarm on the face of the diplomat currently exchanging assurances of mutual respect with the head of the Canid Council. It put him in mind of two stiff legged dogs sizing each other up for combat—which it probably was, he reflected.

"My people are not used to having our communications and networks accessed by others. We are a very individual and private race."

"Then perhaps," said the Provider, *"if we understand this ceremony correctly, it will be best if we do not remain linked to you. But perhaps you will seek us out."*

"I can do so." Harry nodded, drawing the attention of the Flag Lieutenant. He had to signal that he was not trying to intervene in the ceremony before continuing his conversation. *"But I do not understand your desire to remain in contact with us."*

"You have been touched by the Siddhiche, as have we. That is enough to bind us to one another," came the reply, leaving Harry wondering once again about the mysterious Siddhiche.

The ceremony was nearing an end, so Harry made his apologies for an abrupt end to the conversation and turned his attention to the diplomatic exchange. Uncomfortably aware that he was the focus of several videographers, his Canid clothes making him conspicuous, he felt his cheeks flush. He was also very conscious that he looked like the 'noble savage' the news channels seemed to delight in calling him. Less complimentary networks, those funded by the Consortium (though they tried to keep this fact hidden), dubbed him the Savage Fugitive, but it didn't matter to him. He knew who he was, and his deeds were honourable. He inwardly challenged any of them to survive eighteen months on a planet in the back of beyond without a decent shower, shave or haircut.

The Admiral approached him, and Harry saluted.

"Mr. Heron, well done to you and your people. Your campaign here has been spectacular—far beyond anything we could have anticipated or expected."

"Thank you, ma'am."

"You've earned a spell of leave and your place aboard. My Barge will take you aloft to the *Vanguard*. You and your team will take passage on her back to Earth. There'll be a bit more for you to do there—a lot of people want to talk to you for one thing—but then I think you're due some Survivor's Leave and perhaps a spell in a less demanding post."

"Thank you, ma'am." Harry's delight was evident at being able to return to his friends and the comfort of quarters on a ship, especially the *Vanguard*. That ship had a special place in his heart because it was where he, Ferghal and Danny had first made their surprise appearance when they landed in this century. In his anticipation, it never occurred to him to wonder at his being sent aloft in the Admiral's personal barge. The prospect of a return to Earth, Mary Hopkins and the old house at Scrabo, his home and safe haven, filled his mind as he took his leave.

Chapter 33

Reasons to Celebrate

_____

The barge eased into the hangar deck on *Vanguard* and slid into a waiting bay. "There you go, Mr. Heron." The pilot signalled the hatch to be opened. "There seems to be a reception committee. They know the Admiral's not on board, so it must be for someone else." His crew grinned broadly as they tried to conceal their enjoyment from Harry.

Delighted to be home again, he missed the grins and the subtle hint. "Thank you for bringing me up, sir. I can't wait to get a proper shower and shave, and back into uniform."

"Better get going then." The Lieutenant was having trouble controlling his grin. It was true; this youngster really didn't appreciate just what he had pulled off. He couldn't wait to see Harry's reaction when he stepped out of the barge.

Picking up the small bag that contained his numerous letters to Mary and his family, he made for the hatch. There were dozens of sketches and written records of his eighteen months on Planet Lycania, observations and notes of his friends and the Canids, and many memorable events. It had been a life-changing unplanned deployment, but he wouldn't trade this experience or his memories for anything in the universe. He was an older, wiser man in many ways.

The Steward took the bag from him. "We'll see to that, sir. Your friends are waiting for you."

Surprised, Harry resisted. "I can manage, thank you, Steward. I've nought else to carry after all."

"Quite, sir, but an officer shouldn't carry his own bags from an Admiral's barge, sir."

"Touché, you are right." Laughing, he released it and moved to a door that slid open timed perfectly to his approach. As he stepped through it, he was deluged with flashback memories of his first reaction to such magical doors, and almost stumbled down the steps to the hangar deck when a Royal Marine band in parade dress struck up a rendition of "Hearts of Oak." A full side party of his original survivors waited under Ferghal's temporary command, with Rasmus at the end of the line stood at the foot of the steps. The rest of the men who had joined him were drawn up behind the ship's officers, with Captain Grenville ready to greet him.

Recovering quickly, he descended the landing steps and saluted. "Sub-Lieutenant Heron reporting aboard, sir," he stated, a fiery blush burning his cheeks.

The Captain maintained a straight face as he returned the salute then extended his hand with a big smile on his face. "Congratulations, Harry. Welcome home. A more comfortable arrival aboard than your first arrival in this hangar deck, I think. You've made a bit of a stir again. Not quite up to your attacking our Marines with a fire extinguisher, but possibly more effective. Come and greet your people, and then there is someone else wanting to see you."

With a feeling of unreality, Harry stepped forward to receive the welcome of 'his people' on board. He was very close to shedding tears of happiness and had to struggle to control his voice as he walked along the row of smiling men and women and said a few words of thanks to each. When he reached Maddie Hodges, he stopped.

"I've not had the chance to thank you properly for your work, Hodges—Maddie." He smiled and took her hand. "I could not have asked for a better or more willing signaller. You may not have realised it, but more than once you gave me the encouragement I needed. Thank you."

"It was an honour to serve with you, sir," she replied with a warm smile. "Any time, but let's hope for some peace and quiet for a bit."

He was quite choked with emotion, and merely smiled and nodded in response as he turned to address the group. He struggled to get the choke out of his voice as he spoke. "Thank you all for your support. I am all too aware of the sacrifices you made, especially those who are not here. I am aware I would not have survived had it not been for the help and support you gave me." He was unable to continue without betraying his emotions.

Chief Master Warrant Officer Abram Winstanley stepped forward. "Heron's Hellions, let's give it up for Mr. Heron. Hip-hip, hooray! Hip-hip, hooray! Hip-hip hooray!"

The cheers proved too much for Harry, and tears filled his eyes. Seeing this, Ferghal dismissed the parade and, signalling the Coxswain, managed to shield Harry and allow him a moment to recover.

Captain Grenville watched with interest and judged the moment exactly. "Mr. Heron, the Rear Admiral has suggested that you might like to take some time out to have a shower and change into the appropriate uniform. I'll leave Mr. O'Connor to show you to your quarters."

"Thank you, sir," Harry managed. "I am deeply conscious of the honour you pay me."

"Nonsense, it was no more than proper recognition of your achievement. Now get yourself comfortable and ready for the Admiral, after which my Executive Commander will find you plenty of work to do."

The ship greeted Harry like an old friend. *"Welcome aboard, Harry."*

"It is good to be back," Harry responded. The voice in his thoughts was exactly as he remembered it. *"I had begun to think it would never happen. Have you much damage?"*

A list of all the damage appeared in his mind's eye, and the ship said, *"As you see, the list is extensive, but nothing vital is damaged, and much of this will be repaired before we transit again."*

The door signal sounded and Harry said, "Come in."

The door slid back and Ferghal entered, a grin on his face stretching from ear to ear. "I thought I would bring you your post," he announced, waving a packet of letters. "Some of it has been waiting your return for some time, especially these from a certain Irish lass."

"You rogue," Harry exclaimed, snatching the package and hurriedly sorting the letters as he looked for the ones he had feared would never be sent to him. Harry found the missives he sought and ripped open the first.

"I have waited for these for so long, I can scarce bring myself to read her letters," he said.

"I'll leave you to it then." Ferghal smiled fondly. "But I should tell you the ship's barber is waiting for you and so is the Admiral. I'd advise you to get the haircut before you shower. Take your letters with you and read them as he shears you. You wouldn't believe the pile of matted ginger locks I left on the floor!" He chuckled at his joke and left Harry to his letters.

Nodding a reply, Harry sank into a comfortable chair and was lost to the world as he drank in Mary's words to him.

My dearest Harry,

I can't tell you how delighted I am to hear through your Aunt Niamh that you have survived and are thought to be hiding on a planet called Lycania — interesting name, and even more interesting inhabitants! Knowing your love of dogs, I hope with all my heart I can hear you tell me all about it soon when we can snuggle close together by the fire and enjoy the warmth of each other's arms again.

I don't know when, if ever, this will reach you, but it helps me to feel close to you just to write it. The news of the loss of your ship was devastating. I didn't know what to think or what to pray for. These past several months with no news have been the most painful I have ever experienced, and I can't wait until you are home to hold me in your arms again.

Joy filled his being as he scanned the neat handwriting that filled the pages with news of concerts and performances, walks by the sea near her home, and much more besides, finishing with a simple,

With all my love,
Mary ♡

Taking care to fold it neatly, he put the letter into its envelope and reluctantly put the rest aside to read that evening before bed. Then he went in search of the barber. Twenty minutes later, he was stepping into his shower. It didn't do to keep an Admiral waiting, even if he was a relative—perhaps especially because he was a relative.

Once ready, Harry presented himself in Admiral James Heron's outer office.

The Admiral's android service unit greeted him. "Go on in, sir," she said in a melodious voice, so close to being human that it always startled him when he heard it. "He's expecting you."

"Thank you." Harry admired the shapely titanium beauty afresh. "Good to see you again, Adriana. You're a welcome sight after these many long months." He flushed beet red and regretted this slip of the tongue as soon as it was out. *I've been away from polite society too long.* "I fear I was a little longer than expected in making myself presentable. My appearance needed more effort than I anticipated."

"Not at all, sir." Adriana opened the door for him. "Some of the Rates hoped it might catch on as a new look."

Harry laughed and entered the Admiral's quarters feeling somewhat flustered. He could've sworn he'd seen her wink at him.

"Well, young man." Admiral Heron rose to meet him. "Do you feel a bit better now?"

"Thank you, sir." Harry took the extended hand and, to his surprise, found himself being drawn into a hug.

"Harry, my boy." The Admiral released him but kept hold of his hand, guiding him to a seat. "I can't tell you how proud you've made me. Now I want to hear all about your escape from the *Daring*. I'm told you and your party had to use a launch on autopilot, and you not trained as a pilot—that's what we call flying be the seat of your pants! Well done. Ferghal's already told me how you rescued him from the Johnstone lab and of your campaign of disruption against the force on Lycania, but now I want to hear the rest from you."

The Admiral listened with focused attention as Harry recounted the *Daring*'s last moments as he and his people, as he still thought of them, had searched for a way to escape the dying ship. He told of his attempts to get the launch to help him fly it free of the wreck, and wryly admitted that the landing had left more than a little to be desired. His guardian listened as he told of his first encounter with the Canids, and then how Harry and his crew had discovered that the cities were a living entity, all part of a single sentient life form called the Provider.

When he had finished, the Admiral remained silent for a moment. "I know there will be a lot of people who will want to hear this and to ask you a lot of questions about it, but they can wait. Do you remember what day this is?"

"What day, sir?" Harry was surprised the Admiral would ask him this. "It is May twentieth, sir."

"And what is special about the twentieth of May, Lieutenant?"

Harry grinned. "It's my birthday, sir, but I don't see—"

"You will in a moment." The Admiral touched his comlink. "Are my visitors here, Adriana? Send them in please." To Harry he said, "I think a little family celebration is in order, don't you? After all, it's not every day you turn twenty-one."

Harry stood as the door opened and Danny rushed in just ahead of Ferghal and Rasmus. Behind them were Chief Master Warrant Winstanley, Maddie Hodges and the others from *Daring*.

"I thought a little celebration with your friends would be appropriate." The Admiral waved his guests through to the adjoining conference room laid out for a feast.

The party, slow at first because the Rates were a little overawed by the presence of their Admiral, soon relaxed. Once Commander Nielsen and the other officer survivors joined them—with one notable absentee whose name happened to be Clarke—the Admiral's ability to put men at their ease soon had the group relaxed and enjoying themselves.

It was a night that Harry would long remember.

Chapter 34

Truce

———————————————

"Sub-Lieutenant Heron." The voice heard through Harry's comlink was one that he didn't recognise. "Surgeon Commander Knighton. One of my patients is requesting a talk with you. He says you saved him from a wrecked transport."

"Barclay!" Harry exclaimed in surprise. "He's aboard the *Vanguard*?" His deeply ingrained sense of proper respect kicked in, and he added, "Sir."

"That's the one," said the Surgeon. "He's in a med-unit and repairing nicely, but he says he has some information which he'll tell you and no one else."

"Very well, sir, I'll come." It was a nuisance, to be sure, but he would do as requested. Barclay was hardly someone whose company he'd seek, and this was his off watch break, the first opportunity he'd had to enjoy some time alone in a quiet place—his favourite place, the Observatory Dome on the ship's uppermost fin. He had spent a leisurely hour sketching a few scenes from his memories of Planet Lycania.

He wanted time to simply be quiet and try to make sense of all that had happened while on that planet, and somehow make his peace with his God and those who had died under his command. But that would have to wait for another respite.

Gathering his sketchpad and paint-and-pencil kit, he made his way down to the Medical Centre, which had been turned over to the treatment of the prisoners evacuated from the planet.

The Surgeon Commander greeted him.

Harry saluted. "Sub-Lieutenant Heron, sir."

The Commander acknowledged the salute. "So you're the man that did all the damage these fellows are being treated for. What did you use? They have burns, ingrained foreign matter, puncture wounds and internal damage caused by concussive forces. We've had to reinvent surgical techniques we haven't used since med-units became available."

"I'm afraid we had little choice in the matter, sir, though I admit I did not anticipate our grenades and mortars would give them so much trouble."

"We've retrieved quite a collection of stones, bits of metal and other fragments," the Surgeon replied, "the removal of which has proved a bit of a challenge. It's made us go right back to basics." Showing a pass to the Marine guard, he ushered Harry through the door that opened in response to the guard's signal. "Security have cleared your visit with Mr. Barclay, and your conversations will be recorded, but don't allow the prisoner to know that, please. We have Mr. Barclay in isolation for now. Apparently he isn't very well liked among his people."

Harry refrained from answering, wondering if that explained how Barclay had come to be left trapped in his vehicle. He felt that recording the visit was an intrusion but knew that objecting would achieve nothing.

"I'll leave you to talk. Signal when you're done." The Surgeon Commander stepped back and shut the door.

"So you came." The surly voice that had taunted Harry in Fleet College had lost none of its aggression.

"Of course," Harry responded. "You asked to see me. I trust that you are healing well."

"As good as can be expected." Barclay grimaced. "I wanted to say thanks for pulling me out of that APC. I've a few scores to settle with the bastards who left me there." Barclay's anger and his bitterness turned the statement into something less than an expression of gratitude. Not for the first time Harry wondered what it was that seemed to run through the Barclay family that made them so aggressive toward anyone they perceived as being in competition with them, even though that usually was not the case.

Harry frowned as he sat perched on a stool nearby. "As the war seems to be coming to a close, and one of the clauses in the treaty requires the reduction of your forces, you will have little opportunity for that. Would it not be better to let such thoughts go? What is done is done. Perhaps they felt they had a score to settle, and all that has passed now. Surely this can only spiral to everyone's disadvantage, including yours."

Barclay was speechless as he gaped at Harry. "That might work for you. It all comes so easily to people like you, doesn't it?"

It was Harry's turn to be at a loss for words. *People like me?*

Barclay filled the gap. "Everybody likes you, you're good at navigation, and now you've proved you can get people to do what you want with almost no effort."

"Perhaps it is because I respect them and use persuasion instead of threats and contempt." Harry regretted his words as Barclay's face registered that the barb had struck home. He tried to soften his approach. "The people we lead have knowledge and skills we do not. Surely it is better to make them feel their contribution is important and valued, and to feel that we trust them to do the task without fear of reprisal if a mistake is made."

"That's not the way my family operate," Barclay growled. "We don't let sloppy work go without dealing with the idiot responsible."

"So that's it," Harry responded. "Your family will not be pleased with your having been captured. Are you worried they will punish you?"

Barclay laughed harshly. "No, but we will make sure that those who are responsible for the failure of our plans don't benefit from it." He hesitated then blurted, "I owe you this much, you're on my uncle's list of people he wants to make sure lose everything—and he has the power to do it."

"I thank you for the warning," Harry replied. "I shall, of course, have to consult the other members of my family on this, and that will mean revealing my source. If what you say of your family is true, that may have consequences for you if it were to become known."

Barclay stared at the ceiling. "Look, I face prosecution anyway for passing information to my contacts while I was in the Fleet."

He was silent for a moment. "And I've been told my uncle says I'm on my own. Damn him!"

Harry suddenly felt sorry for this twisted man and his family. On impulse he said, "You are only alone if you choose to be, you know. If that is indeed the case, why not offer to speak to our Security people? They may take a more lenient approach if you share this information with them."

"I might." Barclay studied him. "Thanks for coming. I wanted to warn you. My uncle is not a man to forgive or forget—just ask my father. You'll need a lot of luck from here on, or he'll wipe you out and leave you penniless and disgraced, and he'll pounce when you least expect it, just when you think everything's going great. That's the way he operates." He smirked. "I owe you that, but I haven't forgotten our first meeting either."

Neither had Harry, and he chuckled. "I'm afraid I responded without consideration on that occasion. I trust there was no permanent damage."

Barclay grinned. "Damn you, Heron. No, of course there wasn't." He shook his head. "How do you do it? I started out hating you because you're everything I'm not—and now I'm starting to wish we could have been friends. You'd better go before I lose it completely."

Chapter 35

Diplomatic Manoeuvres

The Fleet's arrival in Earth's orbital space was something to behold. Those watching the live telecasts saw the great flares at the transit gates as some of the smaller ships dropped out, but attention rapidly focused on the seven independent flares as *Vanguard* and her starship consorts appeared.

The ships' manoeuvring thrusters flared brilliantly as their command teams slowed them and brought them onto the proper bearing for their required orbits. In Navigation, Harry watched the flow of orders from inside the network, admiring the Navigation Commander's deft and sometimes very subtle adjustments to the ship's head as she slowed and gracefully assumed her allotted position. Stretching away on either beam, the other six starships and their individual escort groups of frigates came to rest, their formation faultless.

The Commander-in-Chief and his staff watched from their vantage point on the huge space station Orbit Three.

"They make a magnificent sight, Grand Admiral." The speaker was a smartly dressed woman, one of the senatorial representatives.

"They do, Senator."

"They are certainly impressive." She indicated the smaller ships assembling around the starships, frigates, destroyers, cruisers and the smaller minelayers and hunters. "Those ships look almost too small for interstellar travel."

The C-in-C nodded. "They don't have the accommodation the starships provide." He pointed to the minelayers. "Some of those set up the minefield that helped make the victory possible. Their contribution was vital."

Niamh L'Estrange joined the pair. "I couldn't help overhearing your conversation, Serazade. The crews put up with a great deal for our defence, I think."

"Hello, Niamh. Yes, I know all too well. My eldest son is serving on the *Ramillies*, and my youngest was killed at Regulus when his ship was lost." She paused. "I hope it was worth the sacrifice of the many lives lost."

Several more ministers joined them, and Niamh found her husband beside her. "Theo, they make such a fine sight, and yet they are so vulnerable. I'm glad they're home at last. Will we have the chance to visit James and the boys aboard their ship?"

"Perhaps sooner than you think, my dear." Theo smiled. "We are invited to a dinner aboard the *Vanguard* tonight. She is acting as Fleet flagship for the signing while the *Confederation* is repaired. The President is attending in person, though that is not yet public knowledge."

"Well, and so he should. Who else will be there?"

"The other ministers and their wives, Grand Admiral Cunningham, some representatives of the Consortium negotiating team, and, of course, the command staff and representatives of the ship's company." Theo grinned. "All the usual suspects, I'm afraid. I just hope we get interesting neighbours at the table."

"Coming from one, that is a canard." Niamh laughed. "You're right, it will be a relief to speak to people who aren't trying to read political motives into everything you say. I think I should call James and make sure he arranges the table so that we have some of his officers as companions."

Theo smiled. "Knowing his sense of humour he'd do the opposite—as would you, my dear. No, we'll have to trust him on this one." His personal comlink chirped. "Yes?" He listened to the response and nodded. "Very well, I'm on my way." To his wife he said, "I'm sorry, my dear, duty calls. I'll be as quick as I can be."

Rear-Admiral Heron looked at the table plan for the dinner. He knew most of the visitors by name, if not in person, and scanned the seating arrangements to check which of the ship's officers would be seated with the various ministers and their wives. On his own instructions, he had placed Richard Grenville next to Niamh, and Commander Petrocova, the ship's Executive Commander, next to Theo. Satisfied, he put the tablet aside and picked up the latest intel report.

The number of Consortium ships seemed to be shrinking. Some, of course, had been destroyed or damaged beyond repair, and others, converted freightliners, may well already be resuming their original role. But there was a worrying mismatch between known strength and the emerging deployment of enemy ships across known space. Added to this there were reports of survey ships of unknown type and origin mapping and exploring the very edges of humankind's explored zone.

The elusive ships were proving as difficult to identify or get a look at as the Siddhiche had been and still were. He had a feeling it was as well this war was coming to a conclusion; there was a lot still to discover in the universe. The latest contact with alien life on Planet Lycania demonstrated it might contain more surprises as they pushed the expansion of human settlement.

His link chirped. "Go ahead," he responded.

"The President's yacht is approaching, sir."

"I'm on my way." He stood up and settled his dress uniform properly, then left his office and, with his Flag Lieutenant, made his way down to the vast hangar bay in which the President and entourage would disembark. The Royal Marine band, the same one that had greeted Harry, was formed up in full parade dress; the ship's officers formed a solid block at one end of a representative formation of TechRates and Warrant Officers, their Lieutenants and Lieutenant Commanders in place to the front of each Division. The Admiral's own staff formed a smaller group alongside the ship's senior officers, and he made his way to stand alongside the Flag Captain, Richard Grenville.

"The Treaty isn't signed yet and they're celebrating already," Captain Grenville commented, saluting.

"Always the way. I've defensive patrols out and ready to respond, and all of the outlying ships are at Defence Stations—

just in case. I have no intention of being caught with my pants down, Richard." He smiled briefly for the news team and added sotto voce, "Out of sight of the media of course."

The blast door alarm sounded and a red light flashed as the huge pressure doors opened. Captain Grenville murmured, "Here we go." Behind him the band was being called to attention. The Executive Commander signaled, and the ship's Chief Master Warrant Officer drew a deep breath and bawled, "*Vanguard company—a-ten-shun!*" His voice reverberated throughout the hangar.

Harry suppressed a smile as he stiffened to attention. Ferghal, alongside him, remembering Harry's penchant for making amusing remarks while on parade, hoped he could keep a straight face if he did it this time. The luxury shuttle trundled through the now fully opened doors and rolled to a halt in front of the parade. The door opened and the landing ramp descended.

A figure appeared in the doorway, and the band immediately launched into the Confederation anthem, which Harry recognised as Bach's "Ein feste Burg."

At the foot of the boarding steps, the Admiral saluted as the President emerged from the barge, and on either side, the Marine Guard of Honour presented arms smartly. The President remained standing until the salute rolled to its climax, and then he descended to greet the Admiral. Behind him, other figures formed a large group at the foot of the ramp.

Several people detached themselves to join the President, and Harry used his cyberlink to say to Ferghal and the ship, "*Oh dear, now we're in the soup! Aunt Niamh is here with the Commander-in-Chief. I wonder if we can get a ship back to Lycania.*"

Ferghal's snort attracted a scowl from the Engineering Commander, and he had to struggle to suppress his amusement. It got worse when Harry relaxed his guard and the ship AI registered his interest in the group that had accompanied the President. Ferghal found himself linked and again had to suppress his amusement when he 'heard' Harry explain what was happening to the ship.

"*All the great and the good—and a few of the not so good, I dare say—come to tell us what a wonderful job we have done and then go back to pursuing their own interests and forget all about us until next time."* Identifying Theo and Niamh in the group, he amended his assessment. *"Except for my aunt and uncle, of course!"*

"Have a care, Harry," Ferghal begged. *"Be a little serious and have pity on your friends."* He had long since realised that Harry's tendency to become jokey on parade was a cover for his own nervousness.

Behind them, Danny Gunn stood with the Midshipmen. Like Harry, he was nervous for no reason other than that he might make a mistake and let the ship down. He wondered what the President could possibly find to say or whether he even listened to the answers.

The President, escorted by the Captain and the Admiral, walked slowly along the ranks, pausing to say a few words to each in turn. Harry studied the man out of the corner of his eye, seeing a spare man with leonine hair and a finely etched face. His artist's eye noted the delicate bone structure, the firm chin and mouth with smile lines etched at the corners, and laugh lines at the creases of the eyes. He noted too, the manner in which the man sought and held eye contact with each person he addressed and the fact that he appeared to listen to each one.

The President's dress was plain, a simple suit, not what Harry would have expected, being used to his King and court always being easily distinguished from those around them by their elaborate court uniforms. Yet, despite the lack of any badges of office or Orders of Chivalry, something about the President spoke of leadership.

Ferghal found the President in front of him and heard the deep, mellifluous voice saying, "I understand you are one of the officers who led the insurrection on Planet Lycania, Mr. O'Connor. A remarkable feat, one we are extremely grateful for."

Caught off guard and conscious of the array of high-ranking officers all focused on him, Ferghal slipped into his old accent and speech pattern. "Sure, and it needed doin', yer Honour. But 'twas Master Harry ... er, that is, Mister Heron that led us."

The President smiled and glanced at Harry standing rigid farther down the line. "So I am told. But you are the man behind the missiles and bombs. Well done—your combined efforts have been a large factor in bringing this war to an end. I have no doubt I will see and hear more of you." He turned to address the next officer as Ferghal stammered a response.

"Mr. Heron, I believe." The President smiled when he reached Harry.

"Sir." Harry's eyes locked over the President's right shoulder and found those of his Admiral and guardian. Confused, he averted them and found his gaze locked by the President's, in his view a serious breach of etiquette. He became aware of a hand being held out to him, and automatically accepted it, grateful for the opportunity to recover his wits and dignity.

"Congratulations, young man. I understand you led your people through extraordinarily difficult conditions. Your achievement is remarkable—all the more so because you lacked almost every essential."

"I had some of the best people around me, sir. They made it possible. I provided only the motivation and some of the ideas. Mr. Schülte-Lübeck, Mr. O'Connor, the Coxswain and my people turned it into reality."

"Indeed." The President smiled. His briefing had prepared him for Harry's response and reaction. "I am sure we will have an opportunity to hear more of it later." Imperceptibly he was already in front of the next officer and was soon among the Midshipmen approaching Danny.

Ferghal used the cyberlink to say, *"Phew, did I not make a fool o meself? I was not expecting him to know me!"*

"Or I!" Harry retorted. *"And I could not avoid his eye without being disrespectful to our Admirals or the Captain."*

"I don't think that rule applies anymore, Harry. And, even if it does, in these circumstances I think you'll be forgiven."

"Harry." Niamh finally managed to make it across the room to where Harry stood. "What a squeeze this is. I've been trying to work my way over here since we arrived. You look splendid—and we're all so proud of you." She waved a hand at the press of visitors and officers. "I'm so jealous of all these people who've had your attention until now."

Harry smiled. "Good evening, Aunt Niamh, I wanted to come over, but you were surrounded by such important people I decided to play safely away from where I could get into trouble."

"I noticed," she retorted with mock anger. "And Ferghal too by the look of him. Look at him over there—he looks guilty."

Harry laughed. "He probably is. We are under strict orders to mingle and not monopolise a single guest—and we both know that Ferghal is yet ill at ease in this sort of company. Perhaps we should rescue him. That guest has held his company for a while now."

"I recognise the man," Niamh replied. "He'll stick to you too if you go near him. Leave this to me—I'll rescue Ferghal."

Harry watched in admiration as Niamh sailed over to where Ferghal, his expression that of a trapped rabbit, listened in mute desperation as a large, florid-faced man held forth. Ferghal had several times attempted to excuse himself, thwarted on each occasion by his companion insisting on his explaining some new facet of his seemingly very important duties and activities.

Niamh swept between them blithely declaring, "So glad you've met my brother's ward, monsieur, but I must steal him away from you for a moment. I simply have to introduce him to our Cultural Secretary."

"Thanks, Aunt Niamh," Ferghal breathed as she steered him firmly toward the opposite side of the hangar bay. "Is he always like that?"

"Yes." She laughed. "Crashing bore. Now," she inserted herself into a smaller group and said, "Niall, I'd like to introduce you to my brother's ward. He's a fine musician, and you should see him dance. This is Ferghal O'Connor, everyone," she said, and in a conspiratorial tone she added, "and I've just rescued him from the clutches of Monsieur Le Roux."

The man guffawed and clapped Ferghal on the shoulder. "You're well rescued from that one then. I'm delighted to meet you at last. What is your preferred instrument?"

With Ferghal safely delivered, Niamh looked around for Harry and saw him engaging a smartly dressed woman in conversation, the wife of one of the senior ministers. With a glow of pride, she moved to join another party, as Harry was clearly adept at navigating these sorts of social occasions. His old-fashioned manners and courtesy served him well.

The dinner passed without interruption or incident, a fact that could be put down to the rigid application of long tradition and protocol. The President's speech was broadcast live, as were various responses, as well as the C-in-C's message to the Fleet, which in reality was a subtle message to the politicians listening to him.

Later, in James Heron's quarters, the Grand Admiral raised a glass of Irish whiskey with Theo, Niamh and his host. "Tomorrow we will see. The *Artemis* and her escort have been signalled and will arrive in lunar orbit at twelve hundred Earth Standard. Here's to a satisfactory conclusion."

"I'll drink to that!" The C-in-C drained his glass. "Time I hit the sack. All this diplomacy tries my patience no end. I take it everything is ready for the signing ceremonies tomorrow."

"It is. The signing will be staged in the hangar bay we've just dined in. I've also taken a few precautions. All ships, except this one, will be at action stations when the *Artemis* arrives—just in case. They will stand down as soon as the document is signed."

"I agree, no sense in not expecting the worst." The C-in-C stood up. "I've arranged for the President to return to this ship an hour before they arrive. I want him aboard something that can fight back if there is any treachery. He will arrive aboard an ordinary launch, and there should be a minimum of ceremony. The fewer that know he's aboard the better."

"Mr. Heron, Commander Petrocova wants you in her office pronto," said the Navigation Officer.

"Aye, aye, sir." Harry gathered his note pad and pens and stood up, wondering why the Executive Commander had not used her comlink to call him. He made his way to her office and met Ferghal hurrying in the same direction.

"What brings you here?" he asked. "I cannot think of any sin we may have committed at dinner last night that would occasion our summons."

"Nor I, but I think we shall soon hear of it. You go first, and I shall hide behind you if she is cleared for action."

Harry grinned as he keyed the door signal and stepped in when it slid open. "You sent for us, ma'am?"

The Commander waved them to seats. "I want you to shift to Dress Uniform and assist the President's staff in the signing ceremony. You'll have authority to provide anything they want at a moment's notice. I didn't call you on your links since those can be intercepted, and we don't want too many people to know that the President is coming aboard unannounced in an hour. You must be in the landing bay to meet him. The Admirals and the Captain will be there with a small guard. Make sure you are there early to offer any assistance needed."

Saluting, the pair hurried to their cabins and set about changing uniforms, arriving in the landing bay at the same time as the Captain and his party. A few minutes later, the Admirals joined them.

"The launch is leaving the yacht now," the C-in-C announced. "It will be here in a few minutes. We'll take him straight to the Battle Command Centre. He can watch the arrival of the *Artemis* from there."

Chapter 36

The Provider Speaks

The flurry of activity as the launch arrived and the VIP passengers disembarked kept Harry and Ferghal busy with the sometimes conflicting demands of the President's staff and their lack of familiarity with the ways of the Fleet and its structures.

"This is impossible," a petulant aide complained. "There are too few workstations for our needs."

"What is it you require, sir," Ferghal asked politely. He kept to himself the thought that if there were enough workstations for his Admiral to command a fleet from here, there were enough for this self-important popinjay.

"I need to have at least three workstations so that I can keep the news media briefed and ensure the presidential hotlines are open to Brussels, Strasbourg and the other Confederate capitals. And must we have this display on all the time?"

Ferghal checked his temper and said, "Step this way, sir. This console has four hundred comfeeds. If you would be so good as to inform ComOp Hodges what channels are essential to your needs, she will supply them for you."

Harry found himself fielding a barrage of similar complaints, most of them from an aggressive young woman.

"Haven't you people any consideration?" she demanded, launching into yet another tirade. "This display might make the President uncomfortable."

"I beg pardon." Harry's patience was wearing very thin. "How might it do that?"

"This sensation of being suspended in space," she snapped. "It's terribly uncomfortable—anyone who suffers from vertigo would be sent into a panic attack. Why can't it be turned off?"

"Does the President suffer from vertigo?" Harry asked politely. "If so, I'm sure we could make other arrangements, but then he will not be able to see everything or to communicate as readily as he can from here. If it were shut down, he would not be able to see the arrival, nor would the Admirals."

"Of course he doesn't." She hesitated, changing her approach. "But there aren't any seats near him, which means I can't sit down where I can be on hand if he wants me to advise him on something."

Harry saw the light. This young woman obviously felt overawed by the Command Centre and had to make her status clear. "I shall have a seat brought in for you immediately. Will you require anything else?"

A deep voice interrupted them. "Mr. Heron?"

Harry turned to face the President, surprised yet glad of the distraction.

"I believe you have a constant link with the AI that runs this ship. Is that how you sabotaged the Consortium's project on Lycania?"

"Yes, sir, it is." Harry kept his face neutral, not sure as to the motive behind the question.

"You're the man that broke the Alien-Human Relations Protocol?" the aide interrupted.

Harry frowned. "I beg your pardon? What protocol is this?"

She bristled visibly and opened her mouth to reply when the President cut her off. "That will do, Anita. Your concern for the Protocol does you credit, but, as I have told you before, it is an unrealistic ambition. Perhaps if you and your sponsors had some real experience of trying to survive in a hostile and alien environment, you would rethink some of your ideals." To Harry he said, "Is it possible for you to use your ability to show us some of what you learned of Planet Lycania?"

Harry thought for a moment. "Yes, sir, I can do that. Perhaps I can also, if it please you, prove that far from being a primitive yet pristine society that we have corrupted, the Canids and their Provider are a highly intelligent and advanced race who taught us much more than we taught them."

"Give us the information on the activities you sabotaged," the President replied. "Once we have that, anything you can give us on these Canids will be welcome."

"If you will permit me a moment with my Admiral, sir, I shall seek access to the information you require." Harry bowed in acknowledgement of the President's assent and moved to where James Heron was watching the scan displays. "Sir, I need your consent to comply with a request from the President."

The Rear Admiral studied Harry quizzically, "My consent to obey an order from the President? Why?"

"Sir, to comply I will need to speak to the Canid's AI known as the Provider, and I will need to use the hyperlinks to do so. That will give the Provider access to this ship's AI. I do not believe it will compromise our safety or the ship's security, but I believe I must seek your consent before doing so."

"You're absolutely correct on that!" The Admiral frowned. "How do you know this alien won't corrupt our systems or disable them? What if it has changed sides and is working for the Consortium now?"

"I don't know that, sir, but I am certain we may trust the Provider, and based on my experience with the Canids, I doubt they will ever ally themselves with the Consortium. I cannot explain the significance at this time, but it has something to do with the Siddhiche. I do not fully understand how they're involved, but it seems they caused the Provider and the Canids to develop as they have, and they had some hand in what happened to Ferghal and me. The Provider told me more than once that we were bound by their connection with the Siddhiche, a link, as it were."

The Admiral thought for a moment. "Very well, do what you need to do—but make sure you can shut down the hyperlink emitters if you have to."

"Thank you, sir. I shall need to use the ship status display screen to show the President the information he requests. There will be no other disruption."

"Do what you must," said the Admiral.

Harry linked to the ship's AI. *"Vanguard, open a hypercom link to the Provider on Lycania, if you please."*

There was a brief pause. *"Link established. What do you want from there, Harry?"*

"Let me speak directly to the Provider, please."

"You have sought us, Harry," said the Provider.

"Yes, I have need of your help to retrieve the record of what our enemy, the Consortium, was doing on your planet. As you know, the AI was not linked to the hypercom emitter after our interference, but now I need to speak to it."

"I can provide that link." There was a pause. *"You work through a new and interesting mind in orbit above a beautiful planet. Is this your home world?"*

"It is, but now I have my commanders and our President waiting for this information. Can we provide it? Then perhaps you can speak to them directly. There are those who think I have shown you things you should not have been shown."

"It is done. Show me where you want it." There was the briefest pause. *"I wish to address myself to the leader of your people. Tell me how this may be done."*

"Vanguard, show our friend how to display this information in BCC on Display ID Niner-niner-four-zero-four." Aloud he said to the President, "The information is now on the display to your left, sir. I am accessing all the data retrieved so that it may be recorded here. When you have finished, sir, the alien intelligence that provided us with all we needed during our campaign wishes to address you. He is simply referred to as the Provider."

The President and his staff clustered round the screen, astonishment, anger and then excitement evident in their expressions and exclamations. Eventually, the President withdrew from the group to speak to Harry.

"You said this Provider wishes to address me?"

"It does, sir. Do you wish to have it do so publicly? I am not sure what medium it may use to do this—with me it is always a voice that I hear in my thoughts." He smiled. "It is rather disconcerting at first, but efficient. I do not know if that may be possible for others such as yourself."

"Well." The President looked thoughtful. "Shall we see what it wants?"

"President." The deep voice of the Provider came from the ship's communications system, and Harry was aware of a frantic flurry of activity in the systems to isolate all but those in the Battle Command Centre. "Your people, the human race, have come to our world, some to take what they did not own and others to do your bidding. The Canid race is not as yours is, nor are you as we are. We did not travel among the stars because we did not need to. Now we have learned from our teachers, the Siddhiche, that we must do so, and we must seek your help in this. In return we will provide some of the knowledge you seek, and we ask only that we be respected as equals."

"I will need to consult my Ministers before we can expand on the agreement we have made." The President showed a remarkable degree of calm. "But I can assure you we are very willing to engage with you as allies in the future." He glanced at Harry. "Can you tell us why you assisted Mr. Heron and his people, yet you avoided revealing yourself to the Consortium and their representatives?"

"It is the command of the Siddhiche that we help all those whom they have touched. The one known as Harry and the other called Ferghal both have the touch of the Siddhiche."

"Did Mr. Heron and Mr. O'Connor—Harry and Ferghal—introduce you to things you had not previously known, such as how to build weapons?"

By now the whole BCC was silent, everyone listening. "No. We had knowledge of these things, but no need to use them. We have studied your race since you first ventured near enough for us to hear you, and we have been part of the AI networks that the people you call the Consortium built on our planet."

"So Mr. Heron and Mr. O'Connor *did* show you things you didn't know, specifically how to use those weapons," the President's aide interjected, glaring at Harry.

"That is true. They also gave us the ability to speak to you and to see everything your people have done and everywhere you have been." The Provider paused. "This contact has been to our advantage, not our detriment. Likewise, we have much to offer, just as you do, and much to gain, but this must be through mutual respect."

There was a long moment of silence when no one spoke.

"So you have monitored our newscasts," said the President. "Very well, we have other matters to settle among our own people, but we will return to this discussion at our earliest convenience."

"Sir." The Scan Officer broke the stillness that followed. "The *Artemis* and her escort are approaching dropout."

"Thank you."

To the ship's communication system, the President said, "How may we contact you again, Provider?"

"I will know when you seek me."

The President, his staff and the Admirals watched for the *Artemis* and her escort to appear. Harry could sense the Provider watching and studying everything. Ferghal nodded to Harry and used his private link to say, *"Here they come, and the Provider is watching too. I think we now have a new companion in everything."*

"Aye, my friend, I have pondered this for many months now."

When the first bright singularity appeared, Harry announced, "Envoy ship and escort in sight, sir, bearing fine on the starboard bow." He thought to correct himself when he realised that his audience did not grasp his directions. "I beg pardon, to your right looking ahead and about fifteen degrees above the horizontal, sir."

The starliner made an impressive sight as she dropped into normal space, flares showing as her braking thrusters fired. Leading her was a large starship, which Harry had no difficulty identifying as the Consortium flagship, her damage and repairs visible on the close-range scans. Behind the *Artemis*, another starship with eight heavy cruisers and a flock of smaller ships fanned out into a defensive screen.

All the ships had their beacons and identification lights active as they took up their agreed positions facing the Fleet ships clustered round the Presidential yacht. Involuntarily Harry checked the deployment of their own ships and saw with satisfaction that the six starships and their cruiser groups were exactly in formation around the flagship and in optimum positions should any treachery be planned.

"*Artemis* is hailing the President," the Coms Officer's voice broke the silence.

Harry caught the President's nod.

"The President would like it put through to his position."

"Mr. President." The measured tones of Chairman Bokelmann filled the Control Centre. "We have complied with the terms of the truce and await your invitation to meet. I trust we have your assurance of safe conduct still."

"Mr. Chairman, your safety is assured. Our meeting is to be held aboard the flagship *Vanguard*. I will join you there with my ministers and the representatives of the other states that are party to our treaty." The President looked at Harry and Ferghal. "I shall send two officers to conduct you to the flagship."

"Thank you, Mr. President. We await the escort."

Harry checked that the signal was terminated. "Shall I arrange with the Captain for the escort, sir?"

The President smiled. "No, I think I shall do that." He glanced at the C-in-C. "I believe you and Mr. O'Connor are attached to my staff. Take my personal barge and bring them directly here. It isn't often I am able to send the people our visitors would most like to meet to fetch them, but this is one such moment. Please make full use of the barge and make sure our guests have every courtesy paid them."

Chapter 37

The Face of the Enemy

The Presidential "barge," more a luxury yacht than a transport, boasted features no mere Fleet transport possessed. As Harry soon realised, the opulence concealed the fact that it had a full command suite as well as luxurious appointments. To Ferghal he said, "I had not thought to see such luxury in a service barge."

"Nor I." Ferghal grinned, taking a seat indicated by the human Steward. "Thank you," he added even as a slight tremor indicated they were about to depart. To Harry he said, "We had best make the most of this. I do not think we'll see the like again in our careers."

Harry nodded, his eyes on the display as the barge cleared the launch bay. "Is that not a breath-taking sight? I do not think I can ever tire of seeing it." His gesture took in the beauty of the Earth beneath them, the bright stars of the great docking stations and the lift platforms seemingly stationary in their orbits above the blue oceans, white swaths of cloud and multi-hued continents. The barge swung and the liner *Artemis* came into view, her escorts suspended in space around her. "I wonder what they will be like— the Consortium top brass? My flesh crawls at the thought of facing them. I confess I am not sure how I can respond civilly."

Ferghal nodded. "Nor I, but I do not think they will be too interested in the likes of us. After all, they are far wealthier and more powerful than a pair of mere Sub-Lieutenants sent to see to their comfort."

"True, my friend." Harry laughed. "We shall soon know. Look there, just ahead. We are already closing their docking bay."

The Chairman led the Board up the brow, ducking his head automatically as he stepped through the entry port. Behind him the thickset Mr. Barclay, Eon's uncle, elbowed his way ahead of the other Board members, his semi-permanent scowl and truculent boorishness drawing expressions of distaste from those he pushed aside.

Harry saluted as the Chairman straightened in the entry chamber. "Good afternoon, sir. The President's accommodation is at your disposal for the transfer." He indicated the forward passenger accommodation.

Meeting his gaze, the Chairman smiled. "The President has a sense of humour, I see, sending you two. Don't look so surprised. I know who you are, Sub-Lieutenant Heron." He held out his hand. "A pity we have had to be on opposite sides."

Harry hesitated a fraction of a second, struggling with the sense of being in the presence of a dangerous predator, then accepted the handshake. "I had not expected you to know me, sir, but I fear you have the advantage, for I know you only by your title."

The Chairman laughed. "Touché, Lieutenant. The title hides a great deal, the face and name seldom known except by the Board. I am Gerhard Bokelmann, and these are the members of the Board. My Director of Security, Mr. Barclay, I think you will know by reputation, and the others by name if not by sight." He noticed Harry's fleeting smile. "I am sure you have the list in the databank, is that correct?"

"Indeed we do, sir." Harry bowed his head slightly as each of the others filed past him and found seats under the guidance of the Stewards. "Though I confess it is the first time I find myself host to a group who not long since ordered my execution."

The Chairman acknowledged this. "I expect not. An apology is not really appropriate either. Sometimes one has to make such decisions, and you consider the greater good will be served—but sometimes we have become pawns to our own ambitions and ideologies." Indicating a seat beside his, he stared at the view. "When did you first have to take charge in a life-or-death situation, Mr. Heron?"

Harry thought for a moment, conscious of the feeling of being sized up as an adversary. "In 1802, sir, aboard a transport ship called the *Maid of Selsey*. We were attacked by Barbary corsairs, and I had charge of some of her guns." Harry had a faraway look as he recalled the terror of hand-to-hand engagement with the screaming corsairs as they boarded the becalmed transport and tried to seize the crew, the convicts and especially the younger members and "passengers" for their evil trade. He continued. "I had a swivel gun manned. We used it to clear the gangways, and I killed one of the corsairs with my dirk—the first man I killed in combat."

"Eighteen-o-two?" The Chairman looked at Harry as if the young Lieutenant had lost his mind. Then he remembered the origins of Harry's arrival in the twenty-third century. "Of course ... yes, I recall the story somewhat. How old were you then?"

"Not many weeks beyond my thirteenth birthday, sir."

Now the Chairman really was surprised. "Thirteen?" he asked incredulously.

Harry couldn't resist. "And a few weeks, sir. Eighteen months as a Midshipman then."

"So you were sent to sea in charge of grown men as a child? That might explain a great deal." He studied Harry for a moment. "Well, Mr. Heron, let's hope that we can draw this unpleasantness to a close—then perhaps all our talents and abilities can be used more productively."

Using a skill honed to perfection, the Chairman drew Harry out in an exchange that left both with a great deal to consider. From it, Harry learned a lot about commercial and political thought, not all of it revelatory or new. Locked in their discussion, they barely noticed the others, or the spectacle of the assembled fleet.

The barge was already entering the *Vanguard*'s vast landing bay when Harry took notice, and there was time for no further conversation. He had much to think about as he watched the disembarkation and reception and the subsequent signing ceremony.

Meeting Ferghal as he approached the Wardroom, Harry said, "The peace is signed. Do you think we will be beached on half pay?"

Ferghal grinned. "Likely, I suspect. Perhaps your new friend, the Great Chairman, can find us a ship. But I would not trust the man who leads their security team—the uncle of our old adversary Eon Barclay, no less."

"Nor I." Harry stopped as his link chirped. "Heron."

"Mr. Heron, report to the Commander-in-Chief." The voice was crisp, and Harry recognised it as that of his guardian's Flag Lieutenant.

"Aye, aye, sir." Harry grimaced. "I expect I shall now be advised that I have offended some matter of diplomacy in speaking to the Chairman." He got to his feet and headed for the door.

Ferghal smiled. "I shall prepare a wake for your return."

"Thanks, you're the best friend a man could ask for." Harry grinned. "Now, let me be off to the guillotine. Don't want to be late for the proceedings!"

Ferghal laughed. "It is certain to be no great matter. I'm sure you can handle it."

His guardian's Flag Lieutenant greeted him with a grin. "In you go. Enough gold braid and polished buttons in there to blind you." He winked. "They're waiting for you."

Alerted by the emphasis on the word *they're*, Harry entered the office. The Flag Lieutenant was right, and Harry had to suppress his urge to smile as he found himself confronting stiff, crisp senior officers all around, gold epaulets and buttons gleaming on their uniforms: Grand Admiral Cunningham, Admiral James Heron, Captain Grenville, two Commodores and Commander Nielsen. Snapping to attention, he saluted the Commander-in-Chief. "You sent for me, sir?"

The Grand Admiral returned the salute. "I did, Mr. Heron. I have accepted the recommendation of Commander Nielsen and others, and signed the commendation for the award of the Fleet's Distinguished Service Cross. We have also decided to promote you to full Lieutenant with seniority because of your extraordinary leadership on Lycania." He held out his hand.

"Congratulations, Mr. Heron. You do seem to be making a habit of this, but with the peace now signed, perhaps we can expect less dramatic times ahead."

"Congratulations, Harry." James Heron stepped forward. "You've certainly done us proud, but we mustn't rest on our laurels too long. Niamh demands your presence in Scrabo, and I think you've earned it too." He moved forward and unclipped Harry's rank markings then carefully replaced them with a new pair. Grasping his hand, he shook it. "Well done. The President was very complimentary, and so was the Chairman," he added with a chuckle.

"Thank you, sir." Harry was stunned by the award and the promotion. His mind in a whirl, he was temporarily at a loss for words. In his preoccupation he missed the difference in his guardian's own insignia. Pulling his thoughts together, he said, "But I must point to the efforts made by Ferghal ... I mean, Sub-Lieutenant O'Connor, and the others of my crew. I could not have achieved anything without them."

"True, and they will be rewarded as well," replied the C-in-C. "Your promotion is a recognition of your leadership, Mr. Heron. You took charge under circumstances most would find difficult. You escaped in a damaged launch and kept several others safe while doing so, then you organised and led your people under conditions no one would have considered viable." He held Harry's gaze. "I have no doubt we will see more of each other in future endeavours. Now, I believe you are due some leave and a new posting when that is over." He glanced at the newly promoted Vice Admiral Heron. "Your leave starts tomorrow with all the other survivors. Twelve weeks, James. Enjoy it, both of you. Well done, and well earned."

"Lieutenant Clarke." The small-framed Captain from the Advocate Admiral's Office glanced up and gestured toward a seat. "Sit down, please." He waited for the Lieutenant to seat himself. "The charges against you are serious: collaborating with the enemy, passing information, surrendering personnel to torture. A defence advocate has been assigned to you, but, of course, you are free to reject any officer so assigned and ask for another."

Aral Clarke shook his head. His career and his marriage were in ruins. What did it matter now? Delle had filed for a divorce, and his contacts and relatives in the Fleet Drafting Office were all "unavailable" to his calls. His anger gnawed at his stomach. Heron promoted and decorated, while he faced ruin. It was almost too much to bear.

"I'm sure that will be in order, sir," he said in a tight voice.

"You do understand that you will also be required to give evidence at the enquiry into the loss of the *Daring*."

Aral Clarke nodded. No doubt the bastards would also want to re-examine the testimony he'd given at the enquiry into the near loss of his previous ship, the *Arethusa*. He felt a chill as he thought of it. He'd had to be very creative to conceal the error he'd made there. Would they now expose it? He looked up. "Do you expect me to enter a plea now?"

"No. This is merely to apprise you of the charges. You should say nothing further until you are briefed by your defence counsel." The Captain stood up. "I will send her in now."

Harry made his way to the Wardroom and almost passed by the grinning group waiting outside the Executive Commander's office. "Mr. Winstanley! ComOp Hodges! Oh, famous!" he said with excitement when he saw their new rank markings. "Excellent! Congratulations, Mr. Winstanley. Commissioned Master I see, and you, Maddie—Coms Warrant Hodges!" His gaze took in the rest of the group. "All of you promoted. I could not be more delighted. You have all earned it several times over."

"Errol got his Master's badges, sir." Maddie's smile widened. "And I got this from him." She held out her left hand and showed off a dazzling diamond ring.

Errol stepped out of the Wardroom at that exact moment and caught the thread of conversation. "Yeah, and I spent the next three months' pay cheques on that rock," he quipped, grabbing Maddie around the waist for a quick hug and kiss.

Harry smiled. "I wish you both a very happy life together."

"We hope you'll come to the wedding," said Maddie.

"Of course! I should be delighted to attend. Just tell me where to be and when to be there, and—"

"In your smart new Lieutenant's dress uniform, no doubt!" Maddie said.

Harry beamed with pleasure.

Chapter 38

Together at Last

———————————————

Harry stood at the window and checked the roadway again. He was impatient; he had anticipated this moment for too long now, and it couldn't come quick enough. Why was the time dragging so?

Ferghal put aside the delicate piece he was carving, a part of the new model he had started to replace the one lost when the *Daring* was destroyed. "Patience, my friend, she'll be here in time—it wants another hour yet before she is due by my reckoning."

"I know it!" Harry snapped. "But she might yet be early." He flung himself down in a chair and grimaced. "I'm sorry. I cannot explain it, but I am filled with unease. What if she doesn't come? What should I do if she's unhappy with the room I've prepared for her?"

"She liked it the last time she stayed." Ferghal smiled. He was having difficulty understanding Harry's approach to the lady he was wooing. Ferghal had none of the genteel notions that were Harry's idea of proper behaviour, and he found it amusing. "And Aunt Niamh has ordered her favourite meals and arranged for you to entertain her with visits to all the places you felt might interest her. Be calm, my friend. What lady could resist your charms?"

"But what if she has changed her mind?" Harry bemoaned, leaping to his feet again to pace the room. "It has been almost two years since we were last together, and she may have met someone else. What if she is visiting me only to be kind?"

Ferghal gave a shout of laughter. "To be sure you are a complete innocent. After all the letters she sent you pouring out her undying love for you? How about those steamy holocalls before we lost all connection to the civilised world. Maybe you've forgotten, but I remember your flushed face and smug grin after those conversations. She would not be coming all this way to see you just for a pity visit."

The door opened and Niamh bustled in. "Why so on edge, Harry? Mary will wonder why you've worn out the carpet with your pacing. A cup of tea for you both?"

"He's afraid she's changed her mind and decided to take up with another," Ferghal teased, dodging a cushion Harry threw at his head.

Harry flung himself into the chair again, and managed a grin. "I can see there is no sympathy for my concern. Yes, please, Aunt Niamh, tea will help."

Exactly on time, a ground transport drew up outside the house. Harry had the door open and was at the transport's door before its occupant could operate the opening command. His delight at seeing the young woman who stepped out of the transport seemed to light his face as he almost swept her off her feet in an enthusiastic hug.

"You came!" He laughed. "How I've dreamed of seeing you again."

"I never would've guessed!" She gave him a teasing wink and grin, and allowed herself to be enfolded in his embrace before she planted a kiss on his lips.

Surprise and pleasure rendered Harry incoherent for a moment. "You tease me, but come, let us go indoors. Oh, wait—where are your bags?" He was a ball of nervous energy as he seized them from the luggage compartment and followed her through the open front door where Niamh greeted her with a warm hug.

"Welcome, my dear. Harry has been like a caged tiger waiting for you." She laughed. "But now you're here, you mustn't let him wear you out. Come and say hello to Ferghal. Danny is out with

Theo, but they'll be home this evening. You'll have time to settle and relax before you have to face all three of them." To the android butler, she said, "Take Mary's bags up to the room, Herbert. Help him, Harry. She's safe enough in my company for now."

Ferghal rose to greet Mary. "So glad you've come to rescue old Heron here, Mary. He is near enough impossible when he has to wait, especially for you." He grinned. "And it's a grand sight you make too—enough to make me sorry you're spoken for." He turned as Harry re-entered the room. "If we were not friends, I'd be after cutting you out of Mary's favours—but there it is." He sighed theatrically. "I shall have to enter a monastery and retire from all hope of winning someone so beautiful."

Mary burst into laughter. "Oh, Ferghal, you in a monastery? From what I've heard, half the Fleet and most of the women around here would go into mourning if you became a man of the cloth, and the Church probably wouldn't survive it."

"True!" said Ferghal, and his booming laugh nearly shook the walls. Harry guffawed too, quite unlike him, and he visibly relaxed for the first time that day.

The evening was filled with lively conversation and music as Danny, Ferghal and Mary performed an impromptu concert for the others. The whole house resonated to the wild tunes of Irish dances, and later to the subtle variations of calm and even melancholy tunes that flowed from their instruments. Niamh, Theo and Harry listened spellbound, sometimes adding to the chorus as well known and well-loved songs were sung, Ferghal's tenor complementing Mary's clear soprano, and Theo and Harry joining with a strong bass as Danny added the alto when his voice allowed.

It was the beginning of a crowded fortnight for Harry and Mary as he tried to share all the joy he felt in his homeland with her and the special places he had known and learned to love.

To Harry's dismay, she did not share his love of sailing.

"I am sorry, Harry. I know you love the sea and sailing, but I get seasick just watching you, and I really can't enjoy the water as you do."

"If you're sure." Harry hid his disappointment. "Then we can do something else. Would you care to visit the Giant's Causeway again? Or perhaps a walk on Slemish."

In the end, they settled for a walk on the mountain that had once seen Saint Patrick herding sheep as a slave. It was cold and threatening rain when they made their way down to the waiting transport.

"Thank you, Harry," Mary said as he helped her into it. "It's been a truly wonderful two weeks." She kissed him lightly on the cheek and snuggled under his arm for warmth as he settled into the seat beside her. "I've enjoyed every minute of it and having you to myself."

"And tomorrow you must return to your career," he said. He was still having trouble with the concept that a lady could have a career, never mind want one outside of a home and family.

Mary squeezed his hand and rested against his shoulder. "Yes, I must earn a living, and just as you enjoy your travelling through space and using your talents, I enjoy travelling the concert circuit to perform my music."

Harry listened, his feelings in something of a whirl. He didn't want her to go, and really wanted these weeks to continue. She made him feel complete somehow. Her presence in his life was something special he couldn't quite define.

"Do you really have to leave tomorrow?" he asked, holding her hand.

She'd been asking herself this question, but she knew the answer. "I'm afraid so, Harry. I've concerts to prepare for, and I've been skimping on my practice time."

He sighed. "I know, but ... well ... I suppose I'm just being selfish really. I dreamed about you a lot while on Lycania, and two weeks just seems such a short time ... not enough time."

She squeezed his hand and smiled into his eyes. "I dreamed of you too, often. It was terrible not knowing if you were alive or dead, and then when I knew you were alive, I didn't know whether you were safe, and then—"

He kissed her lips, gently. "And I was in a great fret that you might have found someone else."

She laughed and returned the kiss, pressing against him as much as the seat in the little personal vehicle allowed. "Really, Mr. Heron?" Her hand squeezed his. "Silly man, I was so afraid you'd never come back when your ship vanished—we all were." Her finger touched the end of his nose. "Promise me you won't do that again."

"I shall endeavour to keep that promise." Harry smiled, remembering the hardship of the months before the Canids took them in. "I have grown too soft-hearted for playing the part of a latter day Crusoe, I think." He hesitated. "Now, to complete this perfect day together, I've reserved the best table in the quietest corner of The Titanic Dock, so we may have our final evening with just our own company."

"That sounds divine, and I'm famished. All that trekking up and down the mountain really gives one a healthy appetite!" She smiled into his eyes and kissed him again. "Do stop worrying, and don't rush things, Harry. I love you and only you. There is no other man for me, not in this world or any other world out there. Dinner will be lovely—a special way to remember this holiday."

The dinner passed all too swiftly for Harry, who barely noticed what he was eating. Though the restaurant was crowded, it could have been empty of everyone but Mary as far as he was concerned.

"I can't believe how swiftly the last two weeks have passed," he said as he drained his coffee. "It seems only yesterday you arrived, and tomorrow I must see you back to Dublin and prepare to return to duty."

She reached across the table and took his hands. "My sweet Harry ... we've had a great two weeks, and I've really enjoyed being with you. It won't be so long before we can be together again. Come on now. Let's go home. I want to give you something."

When they returned home, the house was quiet, and everyone was asleep. They walked upstairs and stopped on the landing for one last kiss, and Mary hesitated to let go. Harry felt a fluster of nervousness, his old-fashioned gentlemanly manners telling him this was inappropriate, but Mary took his hands and invited him into her room. He had no choice but to follow, willingly.

"Harry," she said when he shut the door behind him. She smiled up into his eyes as she wound her arms around his neck and pressed her body against him. "I want to show you my thanks in a very special way." She kissed him slowly, longingly, and for a few moments, he struggled for control, but then he surrendered to the surge of desire, lost in the ecstasy of being entwined with her body. It was an unforgettable night for them both, and it sealed their love and commitment to each other.

Seated at the fireside the next evening, Harry stared into the coals and nursed his drink. Outside the darkened hillside settled under the frost as the unusually clear skies allowed the stars to light the great Lough below. He had earlier escorted Mary to Dublin to begin her next concert tour, and he missed her already.

She had taught him so much in one short night. More than ever he was determined she would be his wife, his constant companion, his friend and lover.

Ferghal had left almost as soon as he returned from Dublin to a new posting, and Danny had returned to Fleet College two days prior for his next course. Harry felt very alone.

Niamh watched him from the doorway to the study, her maternal instincts tugging at her heart, and her pride almost overwhelming her as she noted how young and vulnerable he looked. He glanced up and caught her eye, and his smile seemed to light up his face.

"Lost in your thoughts there, Harry?" She came into the room and placed a hand on his shoulder. "I hope they're all good ones, happy memories."

Harry placed his hand over hers and squeezed gently. "The best, Aunt Niamh, the best. I already miss Mary so much it hurts, and I confess I am saddened at being parted from Ferghal. It will be the first time we have been apart since the day he was told to mind me when we were but boys—and that was before I was first breeched. I hope he will be well looked after in his new ship."

"I think he'll be fine." Niamh settled into a comfortable wing chair. "And he said much the same about you and your new posting. He is concerned that you are going to the exploration ship the *Beagle*."

Harry smiled. "And he is to serve on the repair ship *Rotterdam*. I think he is facing the greater danger. Have you seen the fabrication units on those?" He laughed. "And they are giving him charge of one!"

Niamh studied him fondly. "He is concerned that you are going into uncharted space and may encounter some of the ships the Consortium seems to have mislaid. The news, you may have been too busy to notice, is there is a growing threat of what is thought to be piracy. He says the *Beagle* is all but defenceless."

"He is right, but I do not think the *Beagle* will be a target. She is too well known and in constant communication with Fleet HQ."

"As long as you remember to take care of yourself and come home eventually," Niamh leaned across and brushed his cheek with her fingers. "You mean a lot to all of us, you know." She straightened. "Care to take a walk up the hill with me? With such a clear night, the stars will be magnificent, and the air so fresh."

"Cold too," laughed Harry, rising to fetch his coat and hers. "Very well, Aunt, I am at your service."

Tomorrow would be time enough to prepare for his new appointment. Tonight he could take a walk in the frosty starlight on the hill above his home, something he had not done in a very long time.

A Note from the Author

If you enjoyed reading *Harry Heron: Savage Fugitive*, I would greatly appreciate a positive 4- or 5-star review on Amazon. Thank you so much for being a loyal reader. I couldn't make this journey to the stars without you.

Patrick G. Cox

Follow Harry on Facebook:

https://www.facebook.com/harrynelson.heron/

www.harryheron.com
www.patrickgcox.com

Printed in Great Britain
by Amazon